Antonia of Venice

Antonia of Venice

Ellyn Peirson

DEDICATION

And for my readers, "just the facts":
Antonio Vivaldi was one of the most prolific and significant composers of all time.

References to Vivaldi are found in Bach's interpretations of Vivaldi's *L'Estro Armonico*. However it was not until the nineteenth-century discoveries of his works in Dresden and twentieth-century discoveries in Piedmont that Vivaldi was wakened from his deep sleep. There are still great gaps in his biography. In terms of the period of his life described in *Antonia of Venice*, these are the known facts:

From 1703 to 1739, Vivaldi was Maestro di Violini at the Ospedale della Pieta in Venice and conductor of a renowned orchestra comprised of the female orphans who lived in the Pieta.

By 1732, Vivaldi had fallen from favour in Venice; by 1939, the Pieta purchased all of his compositions.

Anna Giraud, born in 1704, was discovered by Vivaldi in Mantua in 1718; he took her to Venice as his star pupil; she and her sister, Paolina, lived with him; Anna lived with Vivaldi until he died.

Vivaldi and Anna fled from Venice to Vienna by 1740; Vivaldi died there, a pauper, in 1741; Anna Giraud was with him. She died in 1750.

Several minor but telling details in the novel are matters of record, including the following:
Vivaldi's favourite exclamation was, "Domine!"
Bach "dabbled in glass-making" (Godel, Escher, Bach; Hofstadter).

Caffè Florian still exists, without having changed much, in Piazza San Marco.

Composition dates are as accurate as current research can establish.

The names and not the reputations of the Doges are accurate.

The Palio continues every July and August in Siena.

The rest is fiction.

Contents

I

"Pax Tibi Marce Evangelista Meus." So says the book the Winged Lion holds open for the Doge above the Palace Door. Two Venetian merchants stole San Marco's body from Alexandria in 828 and brought it to Venice. The relics were interred in the Doge's Chapel, and the Basilica was built as their final resting place. The Venetians claimed San Marco belonged to them because he evangelized Venice and prophesied the return of his bones to the city. The Alexandrians in Egypt claimed San Marco was theirs because he founded their church. Am I to believe that Truth can be manipulated? That Truth varies? That there is no Absolute? Ah, but I have seen the Winged Lion fly over the Bacino. And I have heard the Winged Lion sing as he stalks the brooding Night Waters. I know the truth of no absolutes. [Antonia, 1743]

From the beginning, she belonged nowhere. Placed on the third day of her life in the orphanage attached to Antonio Vivaldi's Venetian church, she was inducted into a proxy family of females and nurse-mothered by numerous women who assisted the orphanage. The only surrogate parents she ever knew were the Prioress of the orphanage and the celebrated Maestro Vivaldi. She accepted this separateness, this always being on the periphery of life, as an orphan's birthright. She never questioned it. Rather, she became skilled at slipping into backgrounds, shedding her uniqueness the way jasmine gives itself over to perfume. Almost ephemeral, she became one with the texture of her environment. Like the nun she eventually became, she learned early to glide into the diaphanous fabric of the spiritual and disappear from ordinary life. Or, prodigy that she was, she would become so much a part of her music that she was not the performer. This was her true habitation. The world of notes, captured only on paper. She was the instrument, the voice, the estuary for music itself. Her skills at invisibility were honed from her innate shyness and deep intellect. Very few people really knew her. This despite her eventual fame as La Stella di Venice. Antonio Vivaldi, violinist and composer, created her, making her his lifetime project. He raised her, trained her, shaped her, moulded her, bent her, broke her until she became his perfection. Until she became an extension of him, really. He took the young orphan and transformed her into Anna Giraud, his Magnum Opus. Anna Giraud, the centrepiece of all his compositions. His to shine from his private cosmos into the politics of Venice while he conducted from the podium. Orchestrating everything. Owning her—her music, her will, her soul.

Until she met Orlando of Siena.

He is the how and why of the intersection of my destiny with Anna's, whose true name was Antonia. It took years for me to meet her, of course. And then more years for my life and its loneliness to make sense.

When I came upon this woman, the very day my obsession with her began, I'd been struggling to believe, to find meaning. I didn't understand life. I didn't understand love. I'd chosen the cloistered life because it allowed my pain and embraced my quest for purpose. Ultimately, Antonia made sense of all this for me. In truth, her story had been woven into my family's story long before I discovered truth. My grandmother had spun the tale for me many times in my childhood. But until I finally spoke to her in her illness, I knew the Antonia of our family stories to be dead.

We didn't know each other very long. Not the way we in this world measure time, that is. But in the mystery of our ultimate, fateful attachment, our time was immense, and she entrusted me with her story and its relics—her music and the history she so painstakingly documented.

I saw her first in a hidden garden along the southern border of my convent. Tending to herbs and flowers. Singing quietly to herself and yet to someone else. At first, because it was holy music and she was an elder Sister, I thought she was using the music as prayer. But there was a more elemental quality to it. Dare I say passionate? Wistful, desirous, knowing. From outside the garden, I watched. From within the garden, she watched, too. And listened... to another world, a world invisible to most of us. I still shudder at the memory of sensing, knowing, she was "elsewhere."

I wanted to step into her world and join her. But I was an intruder. I knew I'd approached a forbidden place. Instantly. Who was this beautiful, frail creature who lifted her black skirt and bent to sift the dirt, to kiss the herbs, to look up into the hills? With whom was she communing? Or... was she waiting for someone? Whether she knelt to pull weeds or moved delicately through the basil and rosemary, she sang. Quietly and perfectly. Pure, clear, white contralto. As she became more immersed in gardening, she let go of her Latin words and sank beautifully into our mother tongue. I was privy to plaints, demands, desires. And I knew I shouldn't be there. And I knew I must be there... that I must know her.

It was late afternoon. Long shadows pressed against the warm soil, breathing life into it, urging new life to come forth. As polite and uninitiated as I was in those days, I couldn't leave the solitary singer. I felt I knew the innermost song of her heart. And yet, at the same time, I knew I was intruding into an intimacy that was not mine. It was no one's but hers. Hers and the one to whom she sang.

But I could not, would not, leave. I'd already disregarded orders to stay on the immediate grounds of the convent. My disobedience had brought me here. And so I continued to ignore my training as a well-mannered novice, and sat down on a tree stump near the purple clusters of wisteria. I determined not to leave until she left. I watched while she filled her hands with dirt and lifted them as if in prayer, her transgressions clasped in her palms. And then, shocked, I attended to the words, the words that were so at odds with her surroundings. For she sang of feeling her blood like ice coursing through her veins. And I watched and heard as she let the soil slip through her fingers to fall before her knees. Her voice modulated into a bowed violin until the last notes trailed off into the hills. And all was silent.

And then she sighed, raised her hands in an arc above her head and brought them down to her side again. She stood with some difficulty, as though her back hurt her. There were tears on her cheeks. And she was smiling. Brilliantly.

She turned toward the gate and bent to pluck a leaf of basil. She stared at it for a moment, crushed it, inhaled its fragrance and placed it in her skirt pocket. And she was gone from the garden.

I sat, my cheeks wet with tears—I had been that much a part of the interlude, that intensely connected to her—and let the coolness of the evening envelope me.

That night, I spoke to Mother Superior about what I'd witnessed in the garden. "Who is she, Reverend Mother? What happened to her?"

"That, my daughter Osanna, is for you to discover. You have stepped into your own story. Let it unfold for you."

From that day, the mystery of the woman in the garden took hold in my belly like the child I knew I would never conceive. Anna Giraud—though I was not to learn who she was for a few years—had implanted herself in me and began to occupy my thoughts daily.

All I knew that first night was this was a woman who had loved and who still loved. In a worldly way. And I must know her and her story. This woman had abandoned a lover for the cloistered life.

Or—had she been abandoned? And how had she, with such a vast love, reconciled with God?

You will ask what I, a nun, could possibly know about worldly love. And I will tell you I know of its pain and beauty, its consummation and destruction from this Antonia. For it is she who still haunts the dank halls of the Ospedale della Pieta in Venice. It is she who still runs freely through the lush Sienese hills. It is she who can still be seen and heard in the remote, shy garden of the convent between Siena and San Gimignano.

And it is she who still talks to me through her writings, her relics. For, like Saint Catherine of Siena, the saint she loved, she left a foot in Venice and her head in Siena. Unlike her saint, whose heart languishes in a sarcophagus in Rome, Antonia's heart rests here in her tomb, the undulating, richly carpeted Tuscan hillside.

And it is that heart's story I shall tell. For her sake. And for the sake of Orlando. This is my calling... to release their souls.

I found some old notes today. I'd written them years ago when I had returned from Siena the first time. Somehow they came here in a corner of an old trunk. For some reason, today was the day for me to find these pieces of myself. What am I to make of these remnants now? How can they possibly relate to Vienna? I'll copy what I can decipher into this book before all becomes dust... or ashes. And perhaps... perhaps... I'll write more and discover who I am. [Antonia, 1740]

UNO

VENICE TO MANTOVA

1704 – 1719

II

What I remember most vividly from my earliest years at the Pieta are the feel of water in the air, cloying, rancid, if water can indeed turn sour, and the sound of violins coming out of the walls and slithering under doors and through windows and out over the Bacino. And always, as continuo for this music of water and violins, was the taunting of the other orphans... cruel, biting, hideous. And I, as I am now, was alone.... [Antonia, 1739]

Another jab! Higher this time, on her shoulder. And it hurt!

Antonia waited until the harpsichord solo began before turning around to glare at the violinist behind her. There was Isabetta, smiling sweetly and innocently in the black and white garb of the Ospedale orphan, her left hand holding her violin upright in her lap, her right hand allowing the bow to hang down at her side. Only the slight movement of her bow hand gave her away.

Antonia glowered and whispered, "Stop! Stop now!" The ornate frescoes and statuary of the Church absorbed her soft voice. Buono! The Maestro hadn't heard her.

Isabetta merely smiled more innocently and looked up at the painted seraphim haloing the Madonna. As soon as Antonia turned around again, Isabetta poked the younger musician's back more forcefully, quickly re-assuming her angelic pose.

L'angelo di Satana, Antonia thought, as she dropped her bowing arm and thrust her bow backward.

"Ouch!" Isabetta cried out. "Ouch!"

With two quick claps of his hands, Antonio Vivaldi, his red hair fanning out wildly behind him, silenced his students. The young girls in his small, scrupulously chosen orchestra barely breathed as they waited for him to speak. "Domine! Who called out? Who?" Breathless and angry, he noticed all of the girls

7

had turned their heads toward Antonia and Isabetta. Again! Infuriating! What was the matter with his quiet, obedient Antonia? And there she was, her cheeks red and tears welling in her eyes again! What was this disobedience? And Isabetta again, looking hurt and upset! Domine! Unconscionable—and in the beautiful respite after the storm of violins! "Antonia, what have you done this time? Speak up!"

"Nothing!" The tears she so despised began to spill down her cheeks. She hated this public loss of face! "It was Isabetta... it's always her! She hit me with her bow!" Antonia felt powerless. She hated this ritual of manipulation and humiliation. Always, always, the intolerable frustration and then the loneliness. Loneliness because the Maestro never seemed to believe her. It wasn't worth trying to defend herself. Defending herself would serve only to force the Maestro away, to diminish his love. Oh, if only she could find a way to stamp her foot and change it all! Why do the others hate me so? Why? Why does Father Antonio not see what they are doing to me?

"Isabetta, what do you have to say for yourself?" Vivaldi turned to the older girl behind Antonia. "Speak up!"

Isabetta stiffened at the sharpness in the Maestro's voice. "Father Antonio, I did nothing. It was Antonia who hurt me," she turned toward the other girls in her row. All eyes focused on her. Oh yes, they will support me in blaming Antonia! They always do! Confident again, Isabetta looked demurely at the Maestro, "Ask any of the other girls, sir."

All eyes focused on the two contending violinists.

"I saw it all, Maestro," the quiet voice came from behind Isabetta.

As Antonia turned around to see who had spoken, she realized she had lost the battle again. Of course—it was Maria. The rest now was inevitable, as inevitable as the thunder that follows the lightning across the Adriatic and into the Bacino. Antonia knew she was already defeated. She had been deftly positioned by Isabetta and Maria. The following moves would see her effectively knocked down. How she hated all this! Sometimes she even hated the very musical talent that gave her Father Vivaldi's favour and the older orphans' resentment. Music was at once her refuge and her prison. Maria had spoken. And all was over. With Maria's words, music turned against Antonia. Maria was that powerful. She was leader of the orphans. She was the one most aggrieved by Antonia's preferential position with Father Antonio. Maria was on the prowl.

"And what did you see, Maria?" The Maestro's words commanded truth.

Maria looked down at her lap. Her resting violin mocked her, a reminder of her loss of position. From concert mistress to second violin! How humiliating! All because of that upstart, Antonia! That upstart who now acted as prima violino when the Maestro asked her! At eight years old! Five years younger and displacing me! She looked directly at the Maestro, "As soon as the harpsichord took over, Antonia used her bow to hit Isabetta, sir. I saw it all. And I was shocked! Isabetta was listening quietly to the harpsichord, and Antonia—looking straight ahead, Maestro—pushed her bow backward to stab Isabetta. Isabetta did nothing." Maria averted her eyes in obvious regret for having had to tell the truth.

"Antonia, what do you have to say for yourself?" Vivaldi's face was as red as his hair. Silent, none of the other girls dared enrage him further. They all turned toward the youngest orphan. Let her deal with the Maestro. And with Maria. Maria could be as intimidating as the Maestro. "Antonia, speak up—or leave this practice!"

Unable to speak, Antonia felt only fury and frustration. Her face flushed with a ruddiness similar to her conductor's. Glaring at him, the eight year old prodigy, her bow in her right hand and her violin in her left, stood, curtsied slightly and marched proudly out of the sanctuary of what had come to be known in Venice as "Vivaldi's church."

As she closed the door firmly and carefully, the tears gushed. They weren't tears of grief. Oh no, Antonia knew, with firm conviction, she was angry... as furious at her Maestro as she was at Isabetta and Maria. As the music resumed behind the door, Antonia stamped her foot. No! I'm angrier at him than I am at them! How could he... why does he... always take their side against me? Why?

Sobbing now, she ran down the hall. She needed the Prioress! Where... where would she be? Where? The question cleared Antonia's head. The garden! Yes! She would be in the garden! Antonia ran to the back of the austere building, flew down a flight of stairs and flung open the little door to the garden.

"Sister Paolina! Where are you?"

Now she could let her tears be whatever they needed to be. She was safe... safe in the garden of high walls, secrecy and wisteria.

* * *

Unadorned and imposing in its austerity, the Ospedale della Pieta rose out of the turquoise waters in the heart of the world's most preposterous city. Here, in the early eighteenth century, the Pieta flourished under the direction of the Maestro of music, Antonio Vivaldi. Due largely to his prodigy and extensive travels, Venetian politics, religion and music had become a trinity. It was an intriguing concoction that captivated people's imaginations in places as far away as Vienna and London. A short gondola ride away from the Pieta was Piazza San Marco, opulent in its Byzantine architecture and attitude. Directly in from the Bacino stood the Byzantine heart of

Venice, the Doge's pink Palace and his ornamented Basilica. Domes, angels, mosaics, stone walls, brickwork and above all, the Winged Lion of San Marco created an air of Eastern splendour and intrigue. On a murky day, the scene was jarring to the senses, like a bizarre dream. It was as though the Byzantine and Papal cultures had connived to form a third, fantastic religion, other-worldly, sinister.

The Doge, the head of the Republic of Venice, was in actuality a figurehead, manipulated by politicians and often controlled by his Envoy whose official role it was to advise and manage. Within the walls of the Doge's Palace, schemes were devised to expand the Republic's seafaring and civilizing supremacy. Within the Doge's private Basilica, attached to the Palace, prayers were uttered and often paid for to advance the reach and control of Procuratori, the governors of Venice. This immensely pleased the Doge and his Envoy who feasted on Venetian fame and the accumulated spoils of wars.

Emerging from the sea, Venice was the risen Atlantis, a multi-layered city supported by posts of wood under the waters and posts of fantasy deep within the contours of its collective psyche. This was a fabulous city, conceived by the elements of water and wind, a mythical city that could actually be inhabited. There was no pull within its heartbeat to the earth. Venice was not grounded. Nor were Venetians. In those who were powerful and talented, from politicians to artists, Venice bred grandeur and, more often than not, its delusions.

Academic and musical life flourished in the Pieta, so much so that it directed the ebb and flow of all creativity in Venice. If the Pieta were a midwife-priestess of sorts, the inhabitants, all females, were its Vestal Virgins. But this was not Rome in the height of her glory. No, this was La Serenissima, the Republic of Venice, the Byzantine jewel of the Roman Catholic world. This was the world of high Baroque life and art and politics, the world of a peculiar

Maryolatry and great variances in morality. Religion and politics, having travelled together along convoluted pathways from Rome and Constantinople, had found their home in the city. And Antonio Vivaldi had been born at precisely the right time for his destiny to be in alignment with his city's. The earthquake on the day of his birth had been no coincidence.

Now on the descent from its pinnacle, Venice looked for new ways to stun the world. And what better way to get the world's attention than through great music! More than the Ridotto, whose gaming tables, costumes and dalliances attracted the rich and powerful, the Pieta's fame fanned outward, taking music to key European cities and setting standards and styles for the affluent. And now the Maestro di Violino of Venice, one Antonio Vivaldi, had captured the cultured Venetian world by storm. Where once youth had been castrated to act as the virgins of music, now girls were singing and playing musical instruments. This Maestro had literally burst upon the musical scene, freeing the music women had, until now, hidden in their breasts. Perhaps, because of this Vivaldi, females would no longer have to sublimate their music in the cloistered life or in intimate lullabies to their children. Where in the eighteenth century's vast array of republics and dominions were females the cultural claim to fame? Where in the world was illegitimacy honoured? Only in the Republic of Venice! Only along the fluid streets that led to the Pieta.

When the plague had orphaned thousands in Italy in the seventeenth century, the Pieta became a warehouse for female orphans. The model took hold and continued, so that now, promiscuous noblemen brought their bastard daughters to be raised and schooled by the Priestess Mother Pieta. It was all eerily pious. The average population of the Pieta was one hundred girls.

Young, delicately handsome Antonio Vivaldi, almost-priest and brilliant violinist and composer, became the Maestro of the Ospedale della Pieta in 1704. He reigned as Maestro di Violino over a hand-picked company of twenty to twenty-five of the most musical orphans. Famous for a quick temper that could flare to match the fire of his hair, the Maestro was a perfectionist. Auditions were rigorous. Failing students were devastated. Chosen students were intimidated. Venice herself, the Serene Republic, having recovered from the shock of females performing musically, celebrated. Now, in her advancing profligacy, Venice was yet again unique and superior. After all, was it not wonderful to be the first in everything imaginable?

Within the walls of this most fortress-like of Venetian buildings, music was daily conceived, born and developed. The Maestro oversaw the birthing, and the Prioress performed the nursing. Both tended to the development, he to the entity of music itself, she to its vessels. The Pieta became more than music; it became a core component of the politics of the Republic. People flocked to hear the angelic music of Vivaldi as it was performed behind iron facades by the orphans. The most anyone ever experienced of these young girls was an ephemeral view of their habits and the intoxicating scent of the pomegranate blossoms they were allowed to wear in their hair. Adept at drawing sublime and intricate music out of his own soul, the Maestro was thus able to transplant it into the souls and instruments of the orphans. In this manner, he became capable of incrementally furthering his career through whichever Doge happened to be in power in Venice by stroking the egos of both the Doge and Venice herself.

Early in his career at the Pieta, Antonio Vivaldi became obsessed with the only orphan who matched the genius he had possessed as a child. In his understanding of the young Antonia, Vivaldi came face-to-face with the child he had been. Ah, but how much more prepared and able was he than his own parents and teachers had been to detect, mould and eventually utilize the gifts of a prodigy! For him, there would be no pitfalls of a family life and all of its trappings to draw time, attention and money away from what had been entrusted to him, namely the creation of the first-ever female star of Venice!

The Prioress, Paolina Giraud, while seeming to be deferential to the Maestro, in fact held great sway. Had she not been there as the calming, rational background presence, Antonio Vivaldi might not have been so prolific in his composing. Had she not been there as La Grande Madre of all the girls, he most certainly would not have been so successful in calling forth the immaculate beauty of the voices and the exact and passionate articulations of the instruments. Sister Paolina was indeed a peer of Vivaldi. What she lacked in musical prowess, she compensated for in structure, reason and maternal qualities. As tall as the Maestro, she was a strikingly beautiful woman with probing brown eyes, deep chestnut hair and a complexion worthy of Fra Lippi's brush-strokes. Giovanni Corner, the current Doge of the Republic, had been heard to utter, at a private violin recital composed and performed by Vivaldi, that the Pieta's Prioress had a "regal quality about her." He was quite unashamed of his fascination with the woman. Paolina, on the other hand, gave the Doge no recognition and let it be made known her attachment to the orphans was as a mother—una Madre Superiora.

While Sister Paolina embraced all the orphans in her maternal magnitude, she was especially protective of young Antonia, the most gifted of the orphans. With singular understanding, the Prioress provided the growing Antonia with meaning and comfort in her loneliness. Vivaldi had charged Sister Paolina with the full care of the prodigy. She was to watch the child's every move, from her singing to her sleeping, and keep her separate and safe. He needn't have bothered with the edict, however. The Prioress's attachment to the young orphan was anchored in devotion. Had anyone mentioned to the Prioress that she favoured Antonia, she might have denied it, saying all the girls were special to her. But in her heart of hearts, she knew she loved Antonia more than she had ever loved any child. It was simply that Antonia was so very special and possessed such a delicate loneliness. Regardless, Paolina set herself the complicated task of using fairness as her measuring rod in her care of all the orphans. Being fair was a difficult duty.

* * *

Older than most new residents, Antonia, at four, had been immediately placed to live and study with the Maestro and seemed unusually comfortable in the wingspan of his intimidating presence. Because of her genius, the Maestro had chosen to have Antonia and the Prioress live with him in his separate living quarters within the orphanage. He had never before made a choice like this. But then, neither had he ever had a student with talent of this magnitude. Had anybody questioned him—but no one dared—he would logically have pointed out that Antonia had begun singing as a natural consequence of her placement at the Pieta. He would further have pointed out that she had then moved effortlessly into resonance with the violin. Understanding this leap perfectly, Vivaldi would have explained that, with her perfect pitch and clear tone, Antonia's violin was no more and no less than an extension of her voice. How could anyone, Vivaldi often asked himself even though no one ever asked, not understand the need to protect and train such a talent?

He assigned to Prioress Paolina the role of substitute mother to this most gifted of his orphaned music students. Most of the other students held this exclusivity and separateness against Antonia. The few who perceived her pain and her rare and soulful beauty were, de facto, not allowed to form relationships with Antonia. Since no orphan had ever begun to study individually with the Maestro until she was eight years or older, Antonia was constantly ridiculed by the older students and ultimately resented for her failure to succumb to the ridicule.

In spite of Sister Paolina Giraud's intimate attachment to Vivaldi's protégée, the orphans understood their Prioress. Because of her generous nature, these girls knew they, too, were cared for as much for who they were as for what their gifts might be. Very few of these orphans faulted their Prioress for Antonia's special place in the Pieta. Young and abandoned, they chose instead to concentrate their feelings against Antonia, who thus found all relationships, aside from her relationship with her Prioress, painful. Never would they have dared criticize the Maestro!

Antonia was pure music. In order to keep this purity, she was sequestered, except for structured interactions with her peers during the schooling hours. In this separateness, Antonia shone. Hers was the gift that exceeded all others'. Hers was the gift that drove her to pursue music with a passion, often to the exclusion of all other activities. Hers was the gift that singled her out from the other pupils at the Pieta and brought her the strange, remarkable and sometimes questionable results that plague the prodigy.

Antonia's musical genius was stabilized by her greatest possession. Her highly evolved senses were rooted in an extraordinary spiritual intuition. This sixth sense allowed Antonia to be the most self-contained child the Pieta had ever raised. Her shyness, sensitivity and intuition allowed her to see deeply into the texture of the world. However, these qualities often caused her to be confused and hurt in verbal encounters with her sister residents and with the Maestro, whom she worshipped.

Whenever the Prioress found the young musician crying after a hurtful experience with another resident, she would comfort Antonia and force a resolution for the sake of both girls. When Antonia railed against the control and harsh criticism levelled by the Maestro, Sister Paolina meticulously dealt with every detail of the outburst so that Antonia would understand the Maestro's desire for the purity of her gift to shine forth. When Antonia cried bitterly over her failed attempts to have the Maestro banter with her, as he had done when she was younger, Sister Paolina pointed out the times when Father Antonio had boasted of Antonia's gifts.

"Pretty one," her surrogate mother would comfort her, "remember he is not only a man, he is a priest, even though he chooses music over the Church. He is so awkward when he steps aside from his music. He hasn't had life's ordinary experiences of fatherhood and routines to help him relate well to people. You are the only child with whom he feels some ease. Antonia, my dear, he is attached to you! You must understand this!"

"Why me?" Antonia would often protest. "I'm nothing to him! Why will he not find someone else with a special gift!"

"My sweet," Sister Paolina would cajole, "it's because you and your gifts are more than special to him. You may never understand how very special. And there is no one gifted as you are... no one."

Why then, the young Antonia would wonder, does such a gift hurt so much? Why does the Maestro not love me more than the others? Why is he so hard on me?

But the young Antonia would never utter these questions. No... to do so would be to question the time-span of love. She could never risk losing Father Antonio's love... ever... no matter what.

III

Ah, gardens! What would I have done without gardens in my life, without the lushness of green herbs and the purity of white flowers? And the warmth of the soil, from which Orlando came... the warm, orange Sienese soil. I came from water, murky water. He taught me much about the earth and how to move about freely without fear of drowning in the narrow alleys of my mind. Most importantly, he taught me how to root myself in love. Because of him, I shall be able to make my final peace with the soil, in a sense to be with him. I have already made my final peace with water. I need Venice no longer. He waits for me always, not in any waters, but in the soil of gardens, and I am comforted. The Prioress and I were odd Venetians. We loved gardens and tended lovingly to our tiny garden at the orphanage. I suspect she will be one of the first to greet me after my body gives itself over to the soil—when I make a final peace with it... and when I make my final peace with God for having given me this life to live. I look forward to that reunion, when time no longer matters. I look forward to that final peace. [Antonia, 1749]

Paolina dropped her old hoe and turned around. Had she heard Antonia cry? Making her way quickly from the back of the garden toward the Church, she heard the call again. The lonely olive tree could wait. What did it matter that it had difficulty growing behind the wall? So did her Antonia!

"Sister Paolina! Where are you?"

Yes, it was Antonia. Paolina moved quickly. "Here, my sweet—I'm coming! What is it? What happened?" She swooped down into Antonia's outstretched arms, lifting her, and carried her to the garden bench. Antonia could not have buried her pretty face more deeply into Paolina's neck! Well, let her stay there until she can talk. What harm do tears do to one's dress anyway? And look at those gleaming auburn curls. Lovable little one. "All right, little one, take your time; but you must tell me why you've become so upset." A torrent of tears and a great shaking of curls followed the simple directions.

When the sobbing subsided, Paolina ventured into the problem carefully. "Was it something the Maestro did?"

Antonia shook her head furiously.

"Something he said?" Paolina knew the path to take.

Antonia nodded her head and sniffled.

"Ah, then," Paolina's voice was low and comforting, "I would venture to think perhaps the other students were involved. Were they?"

"Oh yes, Sister Paolina!" Antonia's answer was punctuated with sniffles. "I hate them!" She jumped up, her fists clenched and her eyes glaring. Her face crumpled once again into tears. "I do! I hate them!"

Moved, Paolina reached into her pocket for her linen handkerchief. "I know how you feel, dear; but do remember what you've been taught about that word," she dabbed lightly at Antonia's eyes. "I understand how much they hurt you at times. But don't give in to them by falling prey to evil thoughts and nasty words. Now," she put the handkerchief over Antonia's nose, "take a deep breath and blow... good! Did Maria have anything to do with this incident?"

"Yes, she always, always does! I hate her! I wish she would die— or go to... to... Rome! And never come back! That's how much I hate her!" Antonia was fierce with an intensity she usually allowed only in her music.

Paolina sat Antonia beside her on the bench and put her arm around her shoulder, "Well! Antonia, my dear, your words again!" She gave the girl a strong hug, and Antonia sighed. "Ah... good, my dear. You're settling down now. And which student did Maria enlist this time?"

"Isabetta! Isabetta poked me with her bow... like this!" Antonia stood and mimicked the act theatrically. "Twice! It surprised me, so I jumped. And it hurt! I whispered to her to stop; but she did it again. So I jabbed her with my bow! And she shouted 'Ouch!' and the Maestro blamed me! It's so unfair! It is! And then, and then... Maria said she saw everything and I was the only one at fault. And then, Father Antonio said I should speak up or leave," Antonia stamped her foot. Tears trickled down her cheeks and dripped from her chin. "So I left! I did!"

Paolina pulled Antonia back to down to her side. If truth were to be told, she was quite proud of Antonia's audacity! "Well, I see... you were quite bold, weren't you? You should, perhaps, have submitted. But, my sweet, it will be all right. I'll talk to Father Antonio... as I always do. I'll make him understand... as he always does. Now come, our little olive tree needs a few words of cheer from you. You have the same way with the garden you have with music. It needs words from someone who is as brave and bright as you!" Planting a firm, quick kiss on Antonia's cheek, she held the child's hand and gestured toward the only area of full sun in the garden. "Your basil is growing wildly. Come."

The young musician tilted her head upward, shook her red curls and let the garden sing to her. And the anger was gone! "Thank you, Mother Paolina. I feel better now!"

* * *

As always when she had been ridiculed or manipulated by the older students, Antonia spent the evening in her room. More often than not, the evening would begin with a violin serenade to the waters gently coursing through Venice. She felt they were akin to her, like her own life-blood. And then the Magic would begin! She would conjure up another world where Love ruled and where she was Empress—Empress of Music and Magic, Empress of the Invisibles, her wonderful friends and subjects! Often, she knew, Sister Paolina and Father Antonio perceived her to be practising. In truth, she was creating her own music in her own world. Perhaps she should tell them. But, no! This was her world. This was her world of importance and life no one could share. In this world, people like Isabetta and Maria didn't exist. They were banished to an island far out in the Adriatic… as far away, even, as to the Land of Silkworms!

Tonight, as she looked from her balcony over the Bacino to the inhospitable form of San Giorgio Maggiore, Antonia wondered not only about water beyond Venice, but about "land." She had heard stories of places like Florence and Rome and Vienna. Where were they? Were they directly ahead? Or were they in that direction called "West"? Where did West go? Where did the world stop? Once, Sister Paolina had told her about a land under the waters, a lost land that had once had a great civilization. She had even told her about cities that were not built on water! How could that be?

Antonia took a deep breath and very quietly, for it was not a polite thing for a girl to do, she sang a little plaint she had composed… Oh, mio caro Dio, chi sono io? Dove sono le tue amorevoli braccia? Where indeed did she belong? Where indeed were God's arms?

Antonia, feeling her loneliness return, slipped back into her room. Loving Father, may I see… may I please see… someday… the rest of your world… Mary, please pray this prayer for me to God… Amen. The time had come for her to go to bed.

Once under the turquoise blanket Sister Paolina had made for her, Antonia felt little again. No longer was she The Empress Antonia. The cruelty of the day poured over her.

Ah… there was Paolina's tap on the door… love would now enter the room, and she would be tucked in for the night. "Come in, Sister Paolina."

Paolina closed the door gently and came over to Antonia's bed. "You sound sleepy, dear. Have you said your prayers?" She leaned down to kiss Antonia on the forehead. "Antonia, are you sad about what happened? I see tears in your eyes. Shall we talk about them before you sleep? That's always best, isn't it?"

Antonia nodded, "But we have talked about them, and now I feel sad again."

"Then, let me lie beside you until you fall asleep." Paolina adjusted the silken blanket so it covered her shoulders as well as Antonia's strong, slight body.

Antonia folded herself into the ample bosom of Paolina, and slept.

* * *

"La luna! Dove si trova!" Antonia shouted and sat up in her bed, gasping, frightened. She opened her eyes and looked wildly around her room to rid herself of the images in her head. The sadness lingered, a lament swirling inside her, mocking her. Shifting to the edge of her bed, she reached for her rosary and began praying, "Maria di madre, prega per me… Credo in Dio…" Her rich, burgundy curls cascaded over her busy fingers. Where did this fear and sadness come from at night? Why was she sometimes frightened by her dreams? Soothed by the ritual, she stretched and looked toward the balcony doors. She must go outside, pull herself out of the dream. The gentle lapping of the turquoise Bacino would calm her. Let the waters take her fears away! Out to the Adriatic, to those faraway countries she had dreamed about! Yet again, she had slept her way into the melancholy garden, the dwelling place of the strange beings and invisible forces. Yet again, the trailings of a violin concerto haunted her.

Antonia stood and walked over toward the balcony window. Her violin, its modulated colouring matching her hair, reflected itself in the mirror of her dresser and shone the image onto the window. It beckoned her outside. Was it to be trusted tonight, this instrument that sang meaning into her life? This violin that had become her voice? The full moon spilled through the narrow windows and cast its vaporous light over her curls. Shuddering, she pulled up the shoulders of her nightgown and buttoned the neck.

Antonia opened the doors and walked out onto the tiny balcony. The Venetian summer air, a heavy mask, stifled her breath. She bent down to pluck a leaf from her pot of basil. Crushing it and inhaling the aroma, she breathed easily again. The putrid breath of the Bacino drifted away—far and away across the lagoon to the unknown waters of other lands. Let the Atlantis of her imagination take care of the stench tonight. Let her be the Empress Antonia again, sending all ugliness away from her Empire. Let her Empire be the principality of music and painting and angels!

As her eyes adjusted to the haze and the low light of the moon, she could pick out the outline of San Giorgio. It seemed to flicker. The mistiness played an old game with her. And then a distinctive watery murmur... yes. Antonia looked down to the Bacino below her... there it was! A solitary gondola glided by and slipped into the mist past the Pieta, disappearing on its own sound. Would there ever be a gondolier to show her the world?

Now, it was only she and her moon, her Luna, in the hushed dimness. Luna understood her dreams. Luna understood her loneliness. Luna understood the music which connected her to her dreams and her God. She reached high, as if to touch her gossamer friend, as if to shine her soulful inquiry into the face of the moon. As in the dream, the moon spun dancing beams so that, as they touched the water, they whispered themselves into music.

Walking back into her room, the motherless Antonia covered herself in a blanket of music woven of the Bacino's waters. She slipped into bed and through the crack into the universe of her night-time habitation.

And the Republic of Venice, its soul prowling through the dank air and occasionally gliding along the canals, drew its watery curtains around the night.

IV

All I ever needed was Truth. Instead, I was given marvellous attention to a great gift... and lies. And so my gift tortured me. Inherent in it was a keen sensitivity to love. And a longing for love. After all, the gift was music. The torture was that love often came wrapped in lies... beautiful, musical lies. But, while my gift could torment me, it could also comfort me because I could intentionally use it as a delirious escape from this world. I had only to pick up my violin, stroke it with the bow, and I would have stroked my own soul. And then Inspiration would take over. That was truth for me—the delirium of being consumed. [Antonia, 1739]

Defiant, the eleven year old held her ground. She stood with her new violin, fashioned for her size by the younger Guarneri, in one hand and her bow in the other. Pointing the bow, she spoke up, "No! I will not do it that way! I want to do it the way I just played it for you. You must listen to my interpretation. I am the violinist. You are the conductor." Her eyes flashed.

Antonio Vivaldi was infuriated. "No one—do you hear me, child?—no one speaks to me like that! Ever! And no one—no one!—tells me what to do! I have never experienced such impertinence! Paolina! Paolina! Come in here!"

The Prioress was already on her way to settle the disturbance. She moved quickly down the hall, her footsteps echoing through the dank air as Venice moved from morning murk to clear sunshine. Why did these two not see how their differences were really their similarities? It wouldn't take her long to orient them and have them plunge back into the beautiful music they made together. They really should learn, each of them, to control their tempers. Antonia had become too like him at times. She supposed this temper and forcefulness were also Antonia's salvation from passivity. Not that Antonia could ever be passive! And when would Antonio learn to accept Antonia's suggestions and interpretations? Paolina opened the door of the music room and entered. The room pulsated with suppressed anger and notes left suspended in the sunshine spilling into the room from across the Bacino.

There they were, Maestro and student, as vibrant as the Venetian sun itself, glaring at each other, Antonia undaunted and Vivaldi wheezing with exasperation. It wasn't the weather that affected his breathing now. No—it was his personality—his anger—his always needing to be right! How foolish! This was a deadlock of Apollo and Diana.

"What is it this time?" Paolina, almost laughing at the scene, moved closer to the younger musician. She radiated a familiarity and calm into the crackling energy of the atmosphere. "Come now. What are you disagreeing about this time?"

Antonia turned quickly to the Prioress, shaking her wild auburn curls. "He won't listen to what I want so much to do in the D minor concerto. I want to make the Largo just a little more largo—that's all!"

The Maestro glowered, his face red, "I will not hear of it!" he fumed. "I write my music to be played the way I intend. And when I introduce this composition in concert next month, it will be the way I intend it to be. My word is final! No eleven year old is going to tell me how to conduct my music!"

Suddenly spent, he looked at his student and saw her fervour. His voice softened. The Prioress's presence always settled the Maestro. "Antonia, you are far beyond good talent. You bring more beauty to my work than do violinists who are twice your age. But next month's concert is supremely important. All of Venice, in particular the Doge, will be there to praise or criticize. The tendency is to criticize. My—and the Pieta's—future is dependent on the response to this concert. It's political, and you're too young to understand political workings."

Paolina saw the tears welling in the child's eyes, "And may she never have to understand politics, Father Antonio. Antonia, would it help if you could at least tell us why you interpreted the Largo that way? What were your thoughts?"

Soothed, the student spoke quietly, "I love this movement, even its sadness. I play it the way it talks to me. It does! It talks to me—to my loneliness. I know I can make it talk to the audience," Antonia's voice was husky. Her eyes glistened. "Father Vivaldi, the Largo speaks to my heart."

The composer leaned over and kissed the young girl on the forehead, the brightness of his unruly red hair harmonizing with the burgundy of hers. The Prioress touched Antonia's back and left the room.

"Come, my dear, play it your way for now and my way for the concert."

Maestro and student positioned their violins, looked into each other's eyes and gave in to the yearning of the dolorous music.

* * *

Antonia's challenge of the Maestro had not been fruitless. As their practices continued, Vivaldi, although he would not yield visibly, began to see his protégée as more than an extension of his own brilliance. In a guarded way, he admired Antonia for speaking up to him. Although, she must certainly not let this turn into precocity. Nor must it become habitual! Indeed, this novice had been specially endowed by God Himself. Not since his own childhood experience had he seen such natural and dazzling talent. And never had he encountered true genius like this in a female.

The reluctant priest thanked God that he had followed his heart in this matter, that he had, for his own reasons, cultivated young female musical talent, despite the resistance from Italy to England to women's involvement in music. News of this bold new trend, originating in the Pieta, had travelled far and wide, luring audiences of the musical and simply curious. People wanted to hear Vivaldi's music; but, more than that, they wanted to hear the orphan girls perform his music. The Maestro knew there was no musical presence that could match the excellence and uniqueness of his Chiesa's female orchestra!

Following their turbulent disagreement over the Largo of the Concerto he had chosen for her debut, Vivaldi surprised himself by considering Antonia's interpretation. Beauty and loneliness? Related? Joined? Co-existing? Hmmm... perhaps... but... Memories of his own childhood surfaced. His father's weary, stern face loomed in his imagination. Certainly, he didn't want to use his father's technique—motivation by fear. Nor did he wish her ever to feel as lonely and as driven as he had felt. And yet... and yet... if his father hadn't pushed him; if his father had given in to the death and mediocrity that had pervaded their family.... No, he, Antonio Vivaldi, the only gifted child of a barber, knew best about music. He would talk to Antonia and have her understand true inspiration. And he would—yes, he would—allow her, indeed encourage her, to proceed with her interpretation of the Largo. Yes, indeed, Antonia, the perfect child, the perfect young musician, needed that concession from him. Was it not his own father who had taught him to play the most exacting instrument on earth, who had nurtured and forced him onto the path that had been set for him before he had been born?

Was he not faced, here in the Pieta, with an extraordinary talent, much the way his own father had been?

This day had begun oddly, this day of the critical Dress Rehearsal. The Maestro found himself more highly tuned than usual. Whenever his thoughts wandered to his young star, a wave of something akin to pity splashed over him. It must have been the dream that had altered his mind and heart so....

* * *

Early that morning, he had wakened in the dream, lingering in it because of a strange desire to go further into the dream. And yet it had frightened him. He had been flying—soaring and diving—in the azure skies, with his violin propelling the journey while he played. Hearing another violin playing an obbligato to his melody, he took control, hovering and looking down to the earth. A lush garden began to take shape below him. Where was the music coming from? Locating it, he was able to drop down closer to the source. Domine! There was his beautiful Antonia, a few years older than in real life, floating on her back on a small indigo lake, her face looking toward the moon. She floated in midnight while he soared in brilliant noontime. As she played a melody he did not seem to know, she cried. And then he realized the indigo of her lake had been created by her tears. "Antonia! Antonia!" he called. But she could not hear him. Her world, wherever it was, was separate from his. Suddenly, he felt tremendously anxious. A force kept him in the air, in the sun, away from the girl of the lake. His heart pained him. This must be the pain of death, of permanent separation. "Antonia!" Her violin disappeared. She swam to the edge of the lake. The subdued colours of the garden became vibrant as the moon shone into her garden. Indigo became a brilliant purple. All grays turned to gleaming greens.

Antonia slipped out of her lake and followed an anemone and iris pathway into the garden. A weeping willow reached over to stroke her face and collect the last remaining teardrops in its leaves. A blue heron parted the wisteria for her. As she lay on a scarlet and yellow floral bed and slept, the hovering Maestro saw her as one with the garden. As much as any plant, Antonia belonged there. The heron laid a sprig of basil on her breast, and the arcane garden disappeared. The Maestro was left alone in the sun with his violin. Hit again by that same wave of pity or grief—which was it!—he tried to throw his violin away. But it stayed in his hands, playing furiously by itself—over and over again—until he awoke, crying out Antonia's name.

* * *

As early as it was, he had to rise. "I'll write—finish that aria. Yes! The dream is nothing!" He used the chamber pot, slipped on his robe and sat down to write, his red hair at times streaking through the fresh ink.

All day, he was haunted by his dream. It clung to him, affecting everything he did, making him moody. What did it mean? Why couldn't he forget it? Domine! This was not good for the Dress Rehearsal! He must shake it off. A dream was just that—a dream! No clinging memory would make it any more than what it was—a dream, a figment of his overworked imagination.

That evening, at the Dress Rehearsal, the haunting returned as Antonia stood to join him for the Concerto. Looking into each other's eyes, the Maestro and Antonia gave their bows the lead in the dark intensity of the opening D Minor Allegro. Back and forth, mimicking and echoing, beckoning and following, resting and running, joined in virtuosity, the girl and her Maestro were one. With the descent into fragmentation and its resolution executed, they released their bows, letting the heavy air absorb the music. The other members of the ensemble sat back, hushed.

The Maestro put his hands on his pupil's shoulders, ready to embrace her. Quickly correcting himself, he held her at arm's length and smiled. "Ah, Antonia, how marvellous, my dear! Beautiful work—and now the Largo. Antonia," the Maestro pointed his bow at the score on the music stand, "Antonia, I want you... I want you... to have the Largo your way... in concert. Would you please explain it to me?" He tapped his bow against the score.

Shocked, Antonia was momentarily speechless. She saw the sincerity in the Maestro's eyes. "Father Vivaldi, I... thank you. I am honoured." Her smile lightened the heavy air. Her spirits soared. Vivaldi, so often awkward in his communication, beamed back at his star pupil.

"May I then, Father Antonio, take the refrain here and extend it slightly? That is all I want... I want it to be played so that every soul is drawn in to the soul of the concerto. Like this," with the first four notes, Antonia called the soul out from the hidden centre of the composition. Vivaldi could see it—shy, amorphous, imploring— as she moved along through the first few bars of the refrain.

"Yes, Antonia, yes. This is the Largo. You have brought it fully into being. Again...," he raised his bow, assisting as Antonia's interpretation gently made its way into the world.

* * *

The promenade buzzed with vibrant energy. Frock-coated and gowned quartets of opinion had joined others until the din was almost musical. The audience had spilled out from the Chiesa onto the promenade and almost into the Bacino after a sensational concert.

No one was anxious to leave. Emotional comments here were offset by high criticisms there. "Spectacular!" "But did you miss the male voice? I mean, instruments are instruments; but a female voice?" "What did you think of the soloist? Was her voice not a little light?" "Ah, but she must be a lovely creature—very pure singing. It's a shame she'll end up in some convent. Definitely talented... with the violin, as well." "This is Vivaldi at his best!" "Yes, and always with something new up his sleeve! Shall we be off to the Ridotto now?" The performance had indeed been spectacular. Even Doge Giovanni Corner had joined in with the cheers and applause. A Doge was usually more restrained. God's representative did have to set standards.

The Maestro di Violino was once again forgiven his reluctance to embrace his priesthood. Stories of his decision against ordination were, as always following his successes, resurrected with as many embellishments as his solo voices and violins could offer in concert. The long-held belief was that he lived with a shameful secret only his music could assuage. Antonio knew their fascination and shrugged it off. His business was his business. And he'd had his reasons. He had had to be honest with himself. He could never have committed fully to priesthood. And—the priesthood would have shut down the life of his music.

But tonight!

Tonight he relished the audience's response! The holy praise offered up by his "Gloria" had been followed by his newest secular work, "L'Estro Armonico". The expert conductor could evoke deep responses from an audience in much the same way he could from musicians. It was all a matter of attention, genius and timing.

Tonight, as people straggled off to their gondolas or walked to the Piazza San Marco, he enjoyed leaving them in wonder—wonder over the lily-white solo soprano voice in the "Gloria" and wonder over the solo violin obbligato in the new work. The young girl, partially hidden in her black and white habit, would be his greatest star someday. Somehow, Antonia would come out of hiding and into the bright light of his world of music. Ah! If only she were male! Then he could take her to the dizzying heights of composition.

Enough! Her rare gifts and the fire of her beauty were enough. Antonio Vivaldi, amply satisfied with the success of the evening, was happy to see the last dignitary off into the sounds of the Bacino.

* * *

Antonia stirred to the light rapping on her door. "Antonia—are you awake?"

"Yes, Maestro; but I am almost asleep."

"Antonia, you were splendid tonight," the Maestro continued the conversation from outside the closed door. "Splendid! You brought the truth out of the music. And I... I want to thank you for your interpretation."

"Thank you, Maestro," she was accustomed to his awkwardness in personal dialogue. "I did it for you. And for God." Her response let them both slip away from the intimacy of thanks and recognition. Separated from music, neither was comfortable with the other.

"Go to sleep now, dear child."

"Yes, Father." Why could he not acknowledge that, at almost twelve years of age, she was no longer a child!

Antonia drifted back into her dream world, the world of spiritual beings and God and myths, the world of exploration and creativity. Now safe in her imagination, she squeezed her eyes shut, took a deep breath and imagined clapping her hands and stamping her feet.

Sparkling lights burst from her fingertips and toetips. "Come!" she shouted. The fragrant air began to buzz with vibrant energy. Hissing, gleeful, Antonia's Invisibles responded to her command. "Come to me!" she shouted again. And her rich lily-of-the-valley laughter bounced its way through the dense, winking energy.

Antonia, the lonely prodigy of Venice, was at home with her companions.

* * *

She awoke to voices, intense and suppressed, barely audible to her keen ear. It was the Prioress and Father Antonio. She heard her name! Slipping out of bed onto the cold floor, Antonia moved close to the door to hear more clearly. Ever so carefully, she opened it a crack, crouched down and put her ear to the opening.

"She will find out sometime, if you're not careful," Sister Paolina whispered harshly to the Maestro. "You must not hurt her, and you must not risk losing all that you have here." Antonia was astonished the Prioress had spoken so severely to the Maestro.

"The world is vaster than Venice, Paolina," came the reply. "If we move away from Venice for a time and develop a story of discovering her, we can bring her back to live with us publicly. As far as the orphan Antonia's story goes, she will have disappeared into celibacy and devotion. It is time, Paolina, because of her age and because of her great talent. We shall travel—with my music!— and bring back your young sister, Paolina. We can change her sufficiently so the few children who have seen her will never remember her."

"The plan is ingenious; but you fail to see she will not be accepted because she is female! You exasperate me!"

"You're wrong! I have achieved her acceptance already. This will simply be an extension of the Pieta. Tonight, your sister was born. It will be the gift that shines through, not the person."

The voices subsided. A fascinated and bewildered Antonia strained to hear more. They must speak up! She needed to hear. But she couldn't, and a short while later, rich laughter and familiar "Good-nights" ended the conversation.

Antonia returned to bed and stared numbly at the ceiling. The moon shone through her window and onto her bed. A plaintive, unfamiliar fugue began playing in her head. She felt dizzy, as though she were losing her grasp, her understanding, of the world.

Tonight your sister is born? Antonia pulled the sheets up tightly around her shoulders. Why did she feel so frightened?

V

It wasn't that the Maestro was always demanding and perfectionistic. I remember clearly the times when he would read to me or sit down to play backgammon with me. As fiercely competitive as he was, he was tremendously proud of me when I won. He would lean back in his chair, clap his hands and shout, "Domine, Antonia! You have beaten the Maestro! Soon you will be called the Maestra of backgammon. Perhaps one day Venetians will call you their Maestra of Music. Nothing would make me prouder!" And he would get up and come over to give me a big kiss on each cheek. "Paolina! Paolina! Bring us something chocolate!" And from the sitting room down the hall, the Prioress would laugh in her rich, contralto voice, and shout, "I'll be there in a moment!" How I wish I could bring her back for one of her moments. [Antonia, 1743]

Despite her constant demand for reasons, Antonia did not resist the announcement of the move to Mantova. The maestro and the prioress had no idea she had heard the plan two years earlier and that she'd been waiting for it to happen. Nor did they know of her secret fear of having to enter the convent life. Antonia could not tolerate the thought of being separated from her home. Sister Paolina, ready for protest, was shocked by the thirteen-year old's passive, indeed, almost eager, acceptance of the news. There was no need to tell her the Doge had ordered the move. For, indeed, he had. He was convinced the sojourn in Mantova would be good for Venice in two respects: the world outside of the Republic would further understand the Republic's supremacy in art and science, and Vivaldi would bring back a dash of the nether regions with which to enhance the flavour of his music. This was another way of pushing Venice's tactical borders and supremacy. Rather devious; but quite benign and very clever.

And, on a more personal note for both Vivaldi and the Doge—although it did benefit the Republic—this was the way to transform Vivaldi's best orphan into Venice's star! A beautiful woman as the darling of Venice would achieve wonders for the Republic. Powerful men in Venice would boast and foreigners would be fascinated.

And that, of course, fit precisely with what Vivaldi wanted—his own fame and a way to keep Antonia with him as his star pupil. He saw himself as a musical Ambassador. And indeed he was. An ambassador, like many ambassadors, with his own personal agenda. However, unlike other ambassadors, Vivaldi's personal agenda was as good for Venice as it was for himself. How wonderful he and the Doge were together on this!

The Prioress and Antonia had talked out the details of the move. Paolina remained unconvinced, "Antonia, I was certain you'd be upset at this information. We must leave soon. You understand that, don't you, my dear? You've seen the map. What more would you like to know about Mantova?" The Prioress turned and looked out over the turquoise waters of the Bacino. "Will you miss this music room and the Venetian waters? I shall."

"Yes; but truly, I'm not very curious. As long as I have you and the Maestro and my music, I'll be content. One place, I'm sure, is much the same as another. And I've never seen a city built on land!"

The Prioress did not know whether to be reassured or worried about the attitude that kept this child with only one foot in this world. Antonia continued her musing, "Father Antonio told me a story long ago of Claudio Monteverdi composing in the Mantovan court. He said he had always cherished the hope of composing in that court, too. I hope I can feel Monteverdi's music there—it must still be living in the walls and ceilings," Antonia's face brightened and she laughed, "dancing everywhere... little ghost notes bouncing and dancing and playing happily." She became serious again,

"Perhaps I'll also sense their Saint Osanna the way I sense Saint Catherine. But I rather doubt that. The other day, Father Antonio told me about Vienna and said that Vienna has an old connection with Mantova. He said Eleonora of Mantova introduced opera to Vienna's court when she married Emperor Ferdinand about a hundred years ago. He said I could be like that and introduce his operas to Mantova. I'm not quite sure of what he meant; but that's probably all I need to know, Sister Paolina."

And then Antonia flashed her most disarming smile and lifted her black skirt. Pointing her right foot, she curtsied to the Prioress and danced around the room, her curls, made tawny in the sunlit places, flying freely. Sister Paolina was quite taken aback at her abandon and beauty. "I'll love it there!" she sang out. "I'm very happy to be going! Do you know what else the Maestro said, Sister Paolina?"

The Prioress turned to follow Antonia's dancing. "I have no idea. But he seems to have convinced you that life away from Venice will be good!"

"He said that if Vienna has its young princess, Maria Theresia," Antonia was breathless, "then Venice has its young princess, Antonia of Music! Wouldn't it be wonderful to be a princess—a Princess of Music? I would send music flying into all the boring, sad, ugly places of my realm! I would go where I want when I want. I would stay up all night if I wanted. And—best of all—I would decree females could be composers of music and dreams!" Antonia whirled around and brought the Prioress into the reel with her.

Twirling and laughing together, they reached the doorway and stopped. They had come face-to-face with Father Antonio. The Prioress and Antonia stopped, breathless.

"Well... well, what is this? What has made you this happy and care-free?" Vivaldi couldn't conceal his enjoyment of the scene. "I must say, Paolina, I had no idea you could give in to such wantonness! Perhaps I should have given you music lessons!" Almost dancing, he stepped over to the balcony window. "You've learned much music through the years, Paolina; your dance steps were quite correct. What brought all this about?"

Antonia, still breathless, laughed and bowed, "Sir, I am Princess Antonia of Music! You gave me the position yourself!"

"Well now, Antonia, one must not spend too much time puffed up with oneself," he bowed grandly toward her and turned toward the Prioress. "And, you, Paolina, what delighted you so much?"

"The delight Antonia found in your discussions with her about Mantova," Paolina's smile looked more like a challenge than an affirmation. She offered the Maestro no further words.

Vivaldi became solemn, "Then you've explained to Antonia our plans for her in Mantova?"

Antonia interrupted, "Is something wrong? Have I done something wrong?" The swift change in tone and mood alarmed her. What was not being said here?

"No, no, Antonia; please, there's no need for fear." The Maestro put his arm around her gently. "Come and sit down, both of you. Since you've been discussing Mantova, we should talk further of our move now. Come over by the window. The light's better there."

But for Antonia, the light seemed to have disappeared.

Evening was approaching. The heat and humidity of the Venetian July blurred the boundaries between sky and water, light and dark, self and other. The Maestro's breathing was more difficult in this oppressive, sultry weather. A solitary gondola slipped in and out of their gaze, a muffled, bleary smudge. The stillness was hypnotic until the spell was broken by the almost imperceptible slice of the gondolier's oar.

Vivaldi steered the discussion to the move. "You will both experience the challenges and enjoyments of living in a new culture. I am used to these situations. Both of you are novices. I shall prepare you for social events," the Maestro stood and paced, his hands behind his back. "I have musical works that I must finish in Mantova. I want to put... to decorate!... my music with tinges of another culture. Not to inspire it... no, no... the inspiration for me will always be Venice."

"But surely... surely... there are other places that inspire music!" Antonia blurted her thoughts. "Surely other places are as inspiring and cultivated as Venice!"

Vivaldi stopped pacing and looked at his pupil. Antonia realized she had made the Maestro angry. Vivaldi sighed and sent Antonia's comments off into a corner with a flick of his hand. "My dear, learn from me. Indeed, there are a few paltry connections between Venice and Mantova. We have our Atlantis. They have their marshy lakes. Truly, the three of us will have more impact on the music of Mantova than Mantova will ever have on the music of Venice. Antonia, my intent is to introduce you gradually to the concert stage." He sat down beside her.

Antonia was unperturbed. "I'm used to concerts and performing, Father Antonio. Why should Mantova be any different for me?"

"Has the Prioress not explained your role in Mantova? I assumed..." He looked across the desk at Paolina who challenged his gaze.

"I left this part for you to explain. Antonia and I have talked about the move to her satisfaction. I, of course, have not talked to her about matters musical. That is your domain." Antonia was aware of an energy in the absence of words between the two. Her interest and her tension were piqued. She was about to learn something Sister Paolina found disturbing.

Vivaldi slapped his knees in frustration, stood and resumed his pacing in front of the window. Antonia looked to Sister Paolina for help.

Paolina relented, "Antonia, my dear, you are about to disappear. Forever." Quickly regretting her own manipulation, she added, "My dear, only in name and in your personal history. Father Antonio, you must give Antonia the remainder of the details."

Vivaldi sat down and took Antonia's hand. "Antonia, you know that the Prioress and I care for you greatly and know you to be of immense musical talent. You are also an intelligent and beautiful young woman now. We don't want to lose your talent," the Maestro caught Paolina's cautionary glance, "and we do not want to lose you. We are like a little family—a family founded on music and God's grace. We...."

"I'm not going to lose you, am I?" Antonia interrupted, frightened.

"Never! Never, my dear. But in another three years you should be leaving Venice, either to marry or to enter a convent. That is the way. And it must be followed. Your Prioress and I find that distressing. Your musical talent must not be thrown away. The cloistered life or marriage—are these choices you wish to make?"

"No! I don't want either terrible choice! I couldn't bear to lose you and my music!" Antonia stood and began to pace the path defined by her Maestro. "I never want to marry! Ever! The only man I have ever stood close to and talked to is you, Maestro. That's all I need!"

The Prioress approached Antonia and put her arm around her to calm her, "Antonia, give Father Vivaldi time to finish. It's all right, my dear; all will be well." She guided Antonia back to her chair. Antonia sat rigidly, her hands folded in her lap, her eyes fixed on her Maestro.

"My dear," the Maestro reached over to touch her hand, "my dear, we have set in motion a plan whereby we can remain together always." His gaze was intent. He must have her compliance in this venture. Compliance was mandatory. This young woman must be shaped. Yes, yes! Like a composition. As he would in practice, Vivaldi used his gaze and voice to direct. Unswerving unity was as important here. Antonia settled. "While we're in Mantova, you will remain at the court without being seen until we are ready to introduce people to the Prioress's younger sister. That, my dear, will be you!" Satisfied that his lines had been delivered perfectly, Vivaldi smiled at Paolina.

Antonia's anxiety, rekindled, was tangible in the space left empty by the Maestro. "But I'm not your sister," she looked anxiously at Paolina and then turned to her conductor. "I'm confused, Father Antonio."

Vivaldi put his hand on her shoulder, "My dear, my dear... you will have your debut in Mantova as Anna Giraud, the orphaned sister of Sister Paolina. That is all! We are playing with words here, inventing you as being an acceptable new... new... icon! Yes, icon... in Venice. The court already understands this. The Doge has helped set the path. In this way, we can return to Venice in two or three years, when everyone has forgotten about the star pupil of the Pieta, and introduce you to the concert scene as Anna Giraud of Mantova. Your immense talent deserves this, Antonia. You... you.... Yes! Yes—you owe this to yourself! And to your... your gift itself, Antonia... to your God-given gift! Do you understand?"

Antonia, her eyes brimming, shook her head. "No, Father Antonio, I do not understand. I do understand that no student at the Pieta can stay on as a musician, and I know that female artists are rarely accepted. You have explained all that. But I still cannot understand why I may not simply stay here with you. No one need know! And

I don't need to perform for anyone other than you. Why must we move to Mantova? Why?"

"My dear, my dear! You must understand this need. 'Performing,' the way you define it, is not 'performance.' Your gift must be made public. That is a fact, a clear and simple fact. The other clear and simple fact is that you must obey," the Maestro looked into her eyes and held her chin in his right hand. "Look at me, my dear... obedience now will produce fame and happiness in your future. Blind obedience—when one is in honourable and directing hands—is a worthy, musical discipline. Do you believe me and trust me as you would were I your father, Antonia?" Still maintaining his gaze, Vivaldi took his hand away from her chin.

Antonia smiled wanly, "I do, Father Antonio." She looked out over the Bacino. "I must."

The Maestro beamed. "No more facades for you, Antonia! No more hiding! No longer will you be an anonymous, invisible curiosity! Yes, you will be losing your name and your present identity. But, you will be public. Your voice and your violin will make us even more famous! Mantova will prepare you for Venice, my dear."

Antonia felt she would succumb to the sea of words. Her caretakers looked to the orphan for the way forward. How could she find her way to a new simplicity? How?

She broke the silence. "This is the only way I can stay with you?"

The Maestro of Venice and the Prioress nodded in unison.

"It is, my dear," Vivaldi turned to Paolina.

Paolina began to utter something and changed her mind. She looked down at her hands briefly, breathed deeply and looked up resolutely at Antonia. "It is. Antonia, I want to speak from my heart. For me, this has nothing to do with music. Yes, music is your life. But for me, you are my life. We have simply become too attached to you to let you go into the convent or into an unhappy marriage.

We—and I do speak for Father Antonio as well—are not prepared to let you slip away from us. That happened to my sister whom you are to replace. That Anna died without recognition in an orphanage outside of Mantova. We were orphaned when I was eighteen and Anna was not yet one. I was old enough to look after myself. I was not allowed to care for her." The mother of Venice's orphans stopped to regain her composure. "Anna was taken to the Mantovan orphanage. I never saw her again. She will now not have died in vain, Antonia."

"Then it shall be so." The orphan now understood many things. "However, I need to say I shall always in my heart be Antonia. I am Antonia, now and forever. But, I agree to be Anna. Perhaps I should say that I shall let Anna be who I am."

Antonia stood and walked to the door. "May I go to my room now, please? I need time alone."

"Yes, Antonia, you may," the Prioress struggled with her tears. The Maestro smiled weakly.

Antonia left the music room.

"She will be all right with this, will she not, Paolina?" Vivaldi did not know how to manage helplessness. "I truly do not want to hurt her. You know that."

Paolina wiped her tears and smiled, "Yes, Antonio, I know that. I know it well. We have no choice. Antonia will go to her balcony now. This is how she works things through. She will tend to her little herb garden, and then she'll pluck a leaf of basil and smell it. And then she will look out over the Bacino and let God work within her. That is her style. That is her spirit. And you and I? We shall hear no more of this from her."

The Prioress opened the balcony door and came back to her chair.

Above them, a plant pot scraped against Antonia's balcony floor. The fragrance of basil sank down into the music room on the heavy evening air.

VI

My time in Mantova was a strange time. I remember little of it in detail. There was always the sense of having to... having to perform, having to disappear, having to please—and having to practise! Practise, practise, practise... until I forgot what perfection was supposed to sound like... until I saw only the bar of music and forgot the composition... until I found I was the composition itself. And then, of course, there was the loneliness. I dressed like a nun. I acted like a nun. I managed to go out to pray. And I saw, for the first time in my life, or shall I say, I felt, for the first time in my life, the danger of physical attraction. My chief delight—because the Prioress was often called upon to assist in the court functions and many times could not be my companion—my chief delight was that I began to compose. The music came to me in visions, visions of colours... attracting, rebounding, playing, singing, swirling. That, and only that, was my salvation. And it was Jacopo who opened my eyes. [Antonia, 1741]

Once ensconced within the court at Mantova, the threesome had settled readily into life together. Maestro Antonio had become more overtly fatherly with Antonia, and Sister Paolina fussed over the two of them, making sure their practice sessions were balanced and that they were well-fed, well-read and well-rested.

In the first year, Antonia's voice developed in depth of tone and quality. Her interpretation skills sharpened, and her range increased. At the same time, she became more precise and bold with the violin. Her repertoire was rich and varied, a prodigy's repertoire. Sometimes the Maestro felt oddly deferential in the presence of the similarities of her two instruments, the violin and her voice, and by the impeccability of her approach and presentation. "She is other-worldly," he would tell Sister Paolina.

While Antonia understood that she must remain private until her debut, she hungered for spiritual connection. After much coaxing, balanced well with reason, her hunger was satisfied. The Maestro and Prioress agreed to allow their charge to have a spiritual time on her own away from the court. "You've proven yourself here over this past year, Antonia. You deserve this time. But you must be very careful and very discreet. Always walk quickly. Look down. Talk to no one. And be back before night falls."

From then on, every Sabbath evening, Antonia, dressed in nun's habit, walked to the tiny, circular Rotunda of San Lorenzo, tucked into the eastern corner of the Piazza delle Erbe. It was in this strange building, crackling with ancient presences, that Antonia prayed and listened. Often the sights and sounds of musical notes were so visually strong for her here that she was able to capture them in her mind's eye and later transcribe them to manuscript. She loved this form of daydreaming, this emptying in order to be filled. It occurred so easily. Its three requirements were simple—solitude, silence and prayer. Colours and sounds unfolded and revolved in her head. And then the melodies came. Was this the music of the spheres? Was this what it was to commune with God? Whatever it was, Antonia loved it. There was no loneliness in composition.

On a brilliant Sabbath day in her sixteenth year, Antonia composed the words and music of "Nulla in Mundo Pax Sincera." It was as though she were picking the notes out of the air as they approached her. She saw the layered world of her Saviour, the world Duccio and Giotto had painted. She heard the parallel world of music her Maestro continually created. The vocal ornamentations approached her as delicate beings of light, flitting in and out of Heaven. She must sing it this way. Yes, she would have to convince Father Antonio! She would do this when she finally dared to tell him she had been composing.

Antonia hurried home from the Rotunda and began to write her own motet at her desk by the window. Longing for the view and sound of her Venetian waters, she saw the motet as a love song to her home.

Father Antonio had knocked at her door; but she was oblivious to the sound. He watched her from the door, amazed at her concentration. After a number of light coughs from the Maestro, Antonia looked up.

"Father Antonio! I didn't know you were there!" She quickly put her pen down and moved the candle to the back of her desk. Smoothing her skirt, she stood.

"My dear, what are you doing? You seem so intent." He sensed her distress. "You were writing something, were you not? A poem? A letter? Why are you secretive?"

"Because I'm not ready to tell you what I've been doing. I'm not sure you will approve," Antonia desperately wanted to change topics. "Will you give me more time, please? Please wait until I'm ready."

The Maestro knew he should not intrude any further. "My dear Anna, you may wait until you are ready to tell me. I'll ask no further. Come now, shall we have one quick rehearsal of the 'Andante Molto' before you retire. It's late."

Antonia glanced back at her desk before she closed the door. Grateful for the Maestro's understanding, she set aside her compulsion to stay with her composition, to bring music into being.

Suddenly Antonia wondered if the Maestro would tell her composing was not suitable for a female. But, no! Surely, he, of all people, would never thwart true inspiration. Surely, he, of all people, would delight in his student's creations. She needed to believe this. And she needed to keep her passion hidden for a while yet.

VII

Inspiration has to do with love. Composition has to do with inspiration. And so, there must be love active somehow, somewhere, in composition. Love is not always happy. In fact, it may not often be happy. Love has the capacity to be painful, sad, very lonely and joyous. Therefore, composition must embrace all of love's capacities. Love herself attaches us passionately, deeply, painfully to another object. Whether that object is God or another human being does not really matter. Except, I suppose, that God is constant and does not die nor disappear. Composition replicates and unleashes the experience of love. Composition can tear the composer apart at times. [Antonia, 1745]

It was as though the music created itself. Once Antonia realized she was most creative after time at the Rotunda, she began to scheme a way to spend more time there. There was much activity in the Court that did not include her. In fact, she rarely attended functions. Life in Mantova was dreadfully lonelier than life in Venice. She knew no one, and, most probably, very few Mantovans knew she existed. In this longest, dreariest period of her life, Antonia longed for something to do and someone to talk to. Composing made loneliness vanish.

Sitting in the Rotunda one Sunday evening, she devised a plan. She would gradually extend her time at the Rotunda, starting with Sundays. She would do this for a month. That seemed reasonable. If there were no discovery, she would then dare to go on Wednesday afternoons. This was the perfect day! Court functions began every Wednesday morning and lasted until the early evening. Who, then could possibly notice she was missing? Servants came to clean the Maestro's quarters on Mondays and Thursdays. Again fortuitous!

There was no need to worry about people on Wednesdays. And Wednesdays cut through the tedium of the week.

* * *

Her experiment with Sunday evenings had gone smoothly. The path was clear now for Wednesday afternoon flights to the Rotunda. Antonia hadn't felt this excited since she had been allowed as a ten year old to go with the Maestro's manservant to San Marco to see an exhibition of Murano glass. Domenico had been so enthusiastic, explaining the glass-making process to her and showing her the beautiful flowered glass rods. The glass-blowers were magicians! Somehow they'd been able to blow clear glass around the rods to create multi-coloured patterns of flowers. Why, the reds and yellows and blues of the rods were like her musical visions! Patterns— patterns in music, patterns in glass, patterns in colours. The world was full of patterns.

She parted the heavy draperies and looked out the window and down to the grounds. Happy desertion!

Antonia sat on her bed. Oh, how much happier she would be in Venice – her Venice—her home of water and glass and patterns to be re-discovered and transformed into music. It had been so long since she had had any sense of time and place. She knew this time in Mantova was the only way to begin a new life together with the Maestro and the Prioress. But, she was weary. She was weary of captivity. That's what life was in Mantova.

Well, what good did it do to feel sorry for herself and be weary? It was time to test Wednesdays at the Rotunda! Antonia stood up, shook her skirt and threw her cloak around her shoulders. She slipped quietly down the stairs, walked outside and pulled up her hood.

Ah, the clear sun of the noontime—how liberating! Mantova was far more interesting in daylight than it was on Sunday evenings. Vendors rattled and talked their way through the streets, their carts and baskets almost empty, refuse falling here and there. Buying and selling were over. A few vendors hobbled toward home, almost desperate for the afternoon's sleep; but most gathered in groups to share stories. Dogs ran through the streets, barking and sniffing garbage. There was an order to life, even its rubbish. The aromas of cooking and baking—nutmeg and pork and garlic—wafted out from behind curtains and blended into a distinct neighbourhood aroma. Even the smell of sewage was strangely acceptable. These were living, working people. And because she had walked in Mantova so rarely, Antonia was still amazed the streets were stone and not water. Mantova was a city of thudding and clanking, rooted in the material world. Antonia, happy enough to be away from the Court, yearned for her world of water, which had no roots. Venice was simply heaven liquefied. There really was no heaven here in Mantova in the material world.

Her Wednesday pattern became established. She would leave the Court, with biscuits, a piece of cheese and some fruit in her pocket, before noon and proceed along the small alleys, rather than the busier streets—never looking at people. She would then cross the piazza and quickly slip in the side door of the Rotunda where she would stay for an hour... praying, thinking, dreaming. She would then return to the Court by a different route.

On her fifth Wednesday outing, Antonia hurried along her favourite alley. It was a busy, pleasantly noisy little alley... tidy shops, clean apartments, plants in many windows and always some windowsills draped with creamy bedding being aired. The roads and the small walkways were swept. The painted buildings were brighter than elsewhere. The sun was brilliant. The air was crisp and invigorating. Antonia wanted to throw off her hood and let the sun beam onto her face. She wanted to run, to laugh, to sing loudly and let her voice resonate around the tiny street. She had no idea of its name. In fact, she wanted to cast off her heavy cloak and dance. Instead, she hummed, picked up her speed a little and kept her eyes down.

"Signorina. Signorina." The voice was male, probably tenor, with the Mantovan dialect. Without thinking, Antonia looked up. The man, about forty years old, leaned against a doorway. He was striking, with very strong features, not fine-featured like the few men she knew. His face intrigued her. She found his smile engaging. Broad-shouldered and taller than the Maestro, he filled the doorway. His white shirt was open at the neck, revealing the dark hair of his chest, his sleeves were rolled up and there were colourful paint spatters on his shirt and his hands. His hair was wavy, thick, black and pulled back, but a lock had fallen over his forehead. He was powerfully built. But the most remarkable thing about him was his eyes. Standing about six feet away from him, Antonia was held by his eyes. They were green, like the olives she had seen for the first time last fall on the grounds of the court. The green was rimmed with black; the lashes were dark and thick. Antonia met his gaze. She knew she shouldn't, but she must. She pulled her hood forward. As much as she knew she must leave, she stayed. She stayed and looked at him.

He smiled. "Signorina, I see you come this way every Wednesday afternoon. And then I don't see you come back. I look for you, you see. So, I wonder—are you a Sister who travels in a circle that takes a week to complete?" He smiled again.

Antonia knew it was wrong to smile at a man she didn't know; but she couldn't seem to help herself. "Well, in a sense you're right.

Haven't you just defined life?" Antonia was shocked at her forwardness. "I must be off to the Rotunda." She looked down.

"Please, signorina, I don't mean to frighten you—nor anger you. Give me a few moments to explain myself." Antonia remained. "Simply put, I am a painter, and you are the most beautiful novice I have ever seen. Although I have a sense you're not a nun," he looked perplexed. "I have no idea who you are. But I want to paint you. My name is Jacopo Cardanno. I have a small following. I mean what I say. Would you consider this?"

Shocked, Antonia stared at the painter. He merely smiled at her, a kind, playful smile, and waited for her response. "I can't... I wouldn't be allowed, sir." She felt exposed, vulnerable.

"Wouldn't be allowed? By whom?" He smiled, "I'm right, am I not—you're not a nun, are you? Your walk, your beauty... no, you haven't been cloistered."

Antonia looked down at the road, "I must be off to the Rotunda. For my prayer time. And—I am and always have been cloistered." Putting each hand in the opposite sleeve cuff, safe in the attitude of piety, she began to walk away.

"No!" Jacopo held her arm, "Please hear me out. I must tell you. You needn't be concerned about me. I have a daughter your age. I wouldn't harm you, any more than I would harm my daughter. Trust me," he was irritated, searching for words. "I am compelled to paint you. You must understand that an artist must do what he must do." Antonia looked directly at him again. He dropped his grasp on her arm. "Will you let me?"

Antonia was at a loss for words. She had no repertoire for a conversation like this. She wanted to flee. And she wanted to stay. She found this invitation attractive. She wanted to accept. But she mustn't! What if she were caught? And she knew nothing of him. Was it a sin to be fascinated with something so worldly? "I'll... I'll talk to you next Wednesday. If you are here when I complete my circle again." As she began walking away, she looked back, "I do understand an artist must do what she must do."

Antonia turned and walked briskly toward the Rotunda. A short distance along the road, she turned and looked back. Jacopo was leaning against the doorpost, watching her. "My name is Antonia," her voice was clear and strong. She turned again toward her task, picked up her pace and rounded the corner.

"Come back next week, Antonia!" His voice carried around the corner.

Antonia ran to the Rotunda.

* * *

Jacopo was there the following Wednesday, standing in his doorway. Antonia had felt torn throughout the past week. What was right? What did she want? Did she hope he wouldn't be waiting? Of course, he wouldn't be waiting. He'd been playing with her on an afternoon when he hadn't felt like painting. That was all the exchange had been about... playing.

And here he was, as he'd said he would be. She realized she had wanted him to be there waiting.

"Antonia," it was as though he was confirming her identity... establishing that she was alive. "I'm happy to see you," he smiled broadly, and life didn't seem so mundane any longer. "What have you decided?"

Antonia's heart raced. She felt confused... excited... frightened. She took a deep breath, "I'd be willing to see what I think—for only a brief visit. You must have a studio you can show me. I can't decide today."

"Good!" He took her hand, "Come."

He led her in, up the stairs and along a hallway that led back to the front of the building, stopping at a dark blue door with a fascinating miniature painted on it—a Madonna as beautiful, she thought, as Bellini's in the Frari. A very human Madonna, with no halo and no heavenly look. No… an earthy Madonna, sensual and in love with her suckling bambino.

He noticed her interest. "The model was my wife," he opened the door. "Come in."

Antonia walked in and dropped the hood from her head. She was stunned by the space. Light flooded in through the windows and glinted off her hair. The walls were creamy yellow, the high ceilings azure, the same azure that framed the windows. Near the door was a stage-like structure with three chairs, a stool, a lounge and a table with numerous props on it—pitchers and bowls, spoiled fruit, fresh fruit, wilted flowers and vegetables. And everywhere there were paintings—some less than a metre square, some as big as three metres by four. "There must be fifty paintings here! And this space! A small ensemble could play in here." She clapped her hands. The sound was bright, lingering for a moment. "The acoustic is excellent!" She moved over to a painting of a woman hanging laundry out a window. There was movement evident in her arms and broad shoulders. There was a dream in her weary eyes and wistful face. Antonia turned toward Jacopo, "This could be Venice."

"It is."

"How do you know Venice?"

"How do you?" He laughed. "I was born in Venice. And I have a friend there. A painter. We travel back and forth each year, although I didn't see him last year. When he comes here this year, we'll go to Florence. All painters need to paint there." He walked to the large middle window and opened it.

55

The air drifting in seemed fresher than at the Court. Antonia took a deep breath and closed her eyes.

Jacopo had been watching her carefully. "Now you must tell me. Who are you? Besides a musician." Antonia looked surprised. "You gave yourself away when you tested the acoustic."

Antonia turned toward the door. Jacopo moved in front of her. "I don't mean to be bold. Please trust me." He put his hand on her arm. "I want to know who it is I desire to paint. That's all."

"I am a musician. And I'm from Venice." She walked over to the stage. "If you were to paint me, what would that entail?"

"Only that you be yourself."

"And?"

"That is all."

"Very well. I shall return next Wednesday and give you my answer. Buona sera, Signor Cardanno."

Antonia flitted out the door and down the stairs.

* * *

The following Wednesday, Jacopo Cardanno walked up the street to meet Antonia. As he turned the corner, she saw him and smiled freely.

"Ah, Antonia. I'm pleased to see you... and your smile."

He offered his arm. Antonia hesitated. This is no different from being with the Maestro, she thought and accepted the offer; why then does it feel so different?

They walked toward his building. "Have you made your decision?"

"I'm free only for an hour each Wednesday."

"I'm already aware of that," Jacopo was patient.

Antonia stopped and turned to her painter, her face questioning, innocent. "Signor Cardanno. Would it be proper for me to do this?"

Jacopo laughed. "My dear young woman—you must be a nun! For a face like yours not to be immortalized—that would be impropriety at its worst! Come," he held her hand, "we'll go to the studio and talk. Next Wednesday, I'll paint!"

Inside the studio, the painter placed a plain wooden chair to the right of a big window. He directed his subject to sit on it. "This is the place where I picture you. Sit there and tell me your story. I want to see you in that afternoon light. I want you to talk to me." He took another chair, turned the seat toward him and straddled it, pushing a straggling lock away from his eye. He leaned forward and rested his chin on his clasped hands, "Talk. Who are you?"

"I am no one," and Antonia told him her story.

As she began, he turned his chair around and picked up paper and charcoal. A few times he would tell her to turn a little, to drop her cape lower down from her shoulders, to smile, to look down. All the while, he sketched the face of the story.

When she finished and had told Jacopo about the identity that was being created for her in Mantova, he stood and walked over to her. He tilted her chin up, "Anna-Antonia, look at me. You're a beautiful, very young woman. Lose yourself in your talents. If you do, you'll live—and love." Releasing her chin, he brushed her hair back from her ears. "And now," he took her hand and pulled her up, "you must go. I can't have you caught in your tryst here."

Antonia threw her cape over her shoulders. "I'll be back next week." She pulled up the hood and walked out the door.

All the way back, she felt buoyant. She wanted next Wednesday to come soon!

* * *

For five Wednesdays, Antonia visited Jacopo Cardanno. For those five Wednesdays, Jacopo Cardanno painted Antonia. He did not paint Anna Giraud. The day he began sketching he knew that Antonia sat before him and that, should she be forced to remain always as Anna Giraud, her pain would be great. He loved this creature in her complex simplicity. As much as he hungered to hold her, to undress her, to enter her, to possess her, he could not. As much as his initial compulsion had always been to paint beauty and conquer it, to own it fully, he could not follow this pattern with her. Antonia was delicate and unskilled in the ways of the world. At the same time, she possessed tremendous resilience and insight. Her trust was not naïve. It was a powerful entity, demanding a powerful response. And he had promised. Were he to break that promise, Antonia would not recover. This was a difficult experience for Jacopo Cardanno. Self-examination was a rare process for him. Never before had his desires been secondary to any other person's.

There had been countless times when he had wanted to kiss her, to take her to his bed and teach her. So many times—when she touched him in trust, when she laughed freely at his stories, when she looked her loneliest—he'd known, with the skill of the expert lover, that he could have had her. And how often had he wished he'd never promised she could trust him? All it would have taken was a few words, a few touches, a few looks—and Antonia would have realized that she was opening up to love. It would have been so easy to convince her that she loved him.

Had Jacopo Cardanno admitted it, it would have been so easy for him to acknowledge he loved her.

On the sixth Wednesday, he and Antonia stood before the painting.

"Are you ready?" Jacopo stood ready to turn the painting toward her.

"I think so... yes, yes, please turn it around."

"Close your eyes." Jacopo turned the easel and canvas around and moved beside her. "Now... open them."

Antonia was astonished. She put her hand over her mouth and stared. Jacopo left her in her silence.

She felt dislocated. The young woman in the painting disturbed her. She sat, this beautiful woman, caught in the afternoon light, a faint shadow crossing her face, a look of longing and invitation captured in her eyes and mouth. Her eyes were questing, eager. Her lips, pink and glistening, were parted slightly... anticipating? What? Whom? Burgundy curls cascaded onto her shoulders, luminous against the black fabric. In her right hand, she held a gleaming gold scepter. In her left hand, she held up a clear glass orb that shone brightly, making the borders of the picture blurry. Black became grey, grey became blue, blue became purple until finally a blood-red haloed the painting. Was it a painting? Who was she?

Antonia moved nearer. What had she seen? Yes, at her neck—there was a crucifix! High at the throat, not dropping into the deep V of the purple garment covering her breasts. And, yes! In the glass orb was the faint reflection of a man's eyes and brow.

Stepping back, she demanded, "Jacopo, who am I? I see myself; but who am I?" She looked at the painting again. "Am I to be afraid of my life? Who is the man? Is it you?"

Jacopo put his arm around her shoulder. "Antonia, for me, I am the man... because I wish I could be he. But I am not. He is someone you are yet to meet.

"I don't want to meet anyone new. If I could, I would stay here. But I cannot. You know that." She began to pace. "Oh, Jacopo, how am I to understand this?" She turned toward the picture. "What sense am I to make of it? I'm confused. Confused!" Face-to-face with her painter, she glared at him, and then she walked over to the painting. "Who am I to you?"

"This painting, Antonia... this painting is the love I have for you. It is also about what your life holds in its wings. Your debut is about to happen. You will leave here and become famous. Perhaps someday I shall be famous as well. We'll never see each other again. I'll die long before you are old. I'll never forget you, Antonia of Venice."

The painter's voice became hard, his eyes distant. "And now you must leave. You must go. I must stay. You do not belong in Mantova, Antonia. You belong in Venice."

Antonia's eyes flashed. "I am angry!" She walked up to face Jacopo again, took his face in her hands and kissed him once, passionately.

Anna Giraud stormed out of the studio and ran back to the Court.

VIII

Perhaps for everyone, the first experience of Eros is bittersweet. For the Pieta orphan, though, there is the prior knowledge that the father who gave you life did not love you. You were his shame. I thought often about that while I was growing up. That essential abandonment, coupled with my adoration of Father Antonio, created a belief in me that love was based on exceeding the expectations of the one I loved. In addition to that, my cloistered upbringing gave me very few skills in relationships. And then I became the subject of a painting, the object of a painter's eye, the desire of his heart. [Antonia, 1741]

And so it was, in the lush spring of 1719, that Maestro Antonio knew, beyond any slight doubt he may have secretly entertained, that his senses had been correct. As he stood in the wings while the Mantovan ensemble began the final movement of his Concerto for Cello and Strings, he reviewed what lay ahead of him. The nascent fame of "Anna Giraud" lay in his hands as another composition. Very soon she would be presented to the Doge, his Envoy, Dante Tiepolo, and their specially chosen guests. All in Venice was ready. A myriad of planning letters had been exchanged. And, with the completion of this concert, now unfolding exactly as planned in the court, he and Anna would have generated more than enough excitement to find its way to Venice.

Yes! His protégée was indeed ready for her debut! Reports of Anna's "beauty and musicianship," would reach Venice and generate the perfect combination of rumour and curiosity. Certainly the Venetian trio had had their share of life in Mantova and were ready for the return to Venice. Antonia... Anna... had spoken up strongly last night about her homesickness for the gentle waters of the Bacino. One could almost sense she drew inspiration from their varying colours and moods. "Father Antonio," she had said, "when we return, I wish never to leave Venice again. I dream every night of her. And I miss—so very, very much—the lapping of the water outside my window. Oh, please, may we go as soon as possible? May we?" As always, his reassurances had settled her.

The Maestro relished these thoughts, as his keen ears picked up on the final bars being played in the court. With meticulous crafting and some consultation with the new Anna, Vivaldi had composed her programme to reflect the flawlessness of her vocal gifts. It would range from a "Tito Manlio" aria to the Maestro's "Beatus Vir". This was the debut of her voice, and Anna would shine like the most dazzling star in the Heavens.

Looking for her, Vivaldi took a deep breath and rubbed his hands briskly together. Ah! There she was! He beckoned her over, extending his hand. Anna took it and stood shyly before him in a simple black silk dress. Above the slightly dropped neckline, a gleaming strand of Paolina's pearls drew attention to Antonia's clear complexion, brown eyes and burgundy hair.

"My dear," he whispered in her ear, "you look truly beautiful. Now breathe deeply and let your shoulders drop. You're nervous. Understandable... but don't let the nervousness come between you and me. Think only that you are singing and playing to me and to the music itself. Let everything else fall away. This is the way of all great performers. And your smile?" Cupping her chin, he tilted her head so that she looked directly into his eyes. "Your smile, little one?" And he smiled broadly, his fine, handsome features softening as his eyes twinkled.

And with that, Antonia smiled and relaxed, "Oh, Father Antonio, I do hope the nervousness passes quickly!"

The music stopped, and the audience burst into enthusiastic applause. "They've given their own a standing ovation!" Vivaldi stretched, shrugged his shoulders a few times and put his ear to the door. "Well, is that not what I told you? The Mantovans are happy! Do you see how clever it is to give people their own musicians before you present the ultimate to them? The violinist did well in leading, did he not?" He opened the door slightly. "Ah, they have taken their seats. Come, my dear, your audience is waiting," he pulled the door open and took Antonia's hand, ushering her into the court. Before releasing her, he gave her hand a warm squeeze.

And then, with perfect timing that needed no prompting, Antonio Vivaldi, Maestro of Venice, swept into the room to the liberal applause of the Mantovan audience. The Maestro bowed grandly and reached for Anna's hand. Together, they bowed.

"Anna Giraud" lived! As all attention focused on her, the new performer—a young woman of all things!—released the composer's hand and moved to her place at his right. Vivaldi faced the orchestra, quickly scrutinized each section and raised his hands. Instruments snapped into position. Vivaldi looked to Anna, noted the slight nod of her head and raised his hands. And, in that moment of complete synchronicity, the genius of it all crackled with life.

As the disobedient daughter, refusing to deny her love for Lucio, Anna's voice lured the audience into the heaven and hell of adoration. "Show pity to your daughter." Her clear tones reached into the soul of the audience and plucked it. As she sang her duet with the oboe, she pleaded with her father's soul for freedom. Her pain, her passion became the listeners'. How had she become a woodwind? A pleading daughter? And as she transformed herself into the heavenly daughter of the "Beatus Vir," the audience modulated with her. This was the celibate's ecstasy. How had such purity of voice come from a female and not a young boy or a castrato? How? Barely a cough or a whisper was heard. The people of Mantova were privy to a bold new direction in music. At times finding her precision crushing, they were held hostage by the archaic tension between light and dark.

The programme complete, the audience was completely hushed. How, when to applaud? Who dares to be the first to break the spell? And then someone cheered "Bravo!" and the audience roared its delight in voice and applause. Anna Giraud curtsied. "Bravo! Bravo! Encore!" The thunderous applause poured forth until there was no denying what they demanded. She looked over at her Maestro. Vivaldi, beaming, nodded his head.

Anna walked over to the first violinist, who handed her his violin. Shushed here and there, the audience quieted itself into a questioning expectancy. What was she doing? Raising the violin to her left shoulder, Anna tipped her head closer to the instrument, drew the bow across the strings as she listened for the perfect A, audible only to her, and tuned. Anna, in a secret honour of the Antonia who had disappeared but would never cease to be, transformed the violin into the voice for the "Quoniam" of the Gloria. The pure white tones and embellishments drew the audience back and forth until doubt became the certainty… the understanding… the enlightenment… that her voice and violin were one and the same instrument.

The audience had given itself over completely to this Anna Giraud in a response that went beyond Vivaldi's always sizeable expectations. Anna's beauty and talent were affirmed. The audience let forth in a reckless abandon. And, in a reckless abandon of her own, Anna experienced what true passion was. For, unlike her usual nun-like self, Anna Giraud that night fell in love with and delighted in her lover, the audience.

* * *

On their last evening in Mantova in July, while Antonia was writing in her room, Vivaldi, violin bow in hand, paced around the music room. "Has she asked yet about her future in Venice, Paolina? She must be concerned. She must wonder!"

Antonia stopped writing and leaned back. What were they saying about her this time? Would they change their minds about the return to Venice? Oh, please God, no!

The sultry air clung to the Maestro's words, giving his question a heaviness and leaving it suspended between Antonia and the Prioress who wanted nothing more than to return to her "daughters" and move Antonia... Anna... back where she belonged. Antonia could barely tolerate the tension she felt.

"Nothing has changed. The Questioner has become the Nun, and I see no change. She is married, as you are, to music. It is her connection to the Divine. She has experienced enough of Mantova, and she has had enough exposure as soloist. Perhaps her old vitality will return when we are back home." The Prioress reassured the Maestro yet again.

And deep inside her heart, to the accompaniment of the well-known muffled voices of her Maestro and her Prioress, Antonia let herself feel her homesickness for Venice. She balanced that discomfort with the solace that would soon be hers. Soon—very soon!—she would be free to be openly with the two people she most loved in the world. Her return to Venice would give her the best of Mantova and Venice. Mantova had been a necessary preparation for living out her life in Venice. Without Mantova, Venice would have been lost. As such, the payment of her name seemed just.

"I shall be home and living publicly, naturally," she spoke aloud. "I am now Sister Paolina's sister!" Returning as Anna Giraud would protect the vanishing Antonia. She knew in her heart she would always be Antonia, even if everyone—including Father Antonio and

Sister Paolina—forgot there had once been an Antonia. Antonia, very much alive and aware, pledged she would never forget herself. God and Music knew Antonia. If she had nothing else, she had that knowledge.

In that moment, Antonia, ready to recede in identity like the spring waters of Venice, remembered the Pieta a stone's throw from the Doge's palace, the music drifting across the waters, her private garden and the smell of her basil.

"I am going home," she spoke aloud to the walls of her lonely Mantovan room. "And may I never have to hide again."

Her thoughts travelled further into Venice, her Venice as she had known it... La Serenissima's turquoise waters, the music of her Church, the muffled, mystical music of the very Bacino itself. And the call of her balcony, calling as it had until she had been compelled to walk out in the night and let her violin commune with the stars and her Luna. Longing... longing for the call of the seventh sonata, pulling, extending, reconfiguring her very soul... its minor key dancing with her lonely spirit until the hues of her dreams were called up... up to the balcony... up to the stars and the moon themselves... coloured notes now turning the lament into a bizarre Carnevale dance around gondolas and laundry billowing from windows... over to the Lagoon and out the Islands of San Michele and Cristofori... releasing the dead souls in the Lagoon to dance their way to the heavens. "Find the Heavens," the Island taunted its inhabitants, "find the Heavens or live forever in Hades." Remembering... remembering... and then... no! And then turning a corner in her mind onto the Piazza and into the control of the Doge over the Maestro's music, over the soul of Music herself. She quickly prayed for protection against the politics of Venice. She wouldn't do well in any worldly setting. "Dear God, please... may the Doge take no personal interest in me. Maria di Madre, please may I always stay with Father Antonio and Sister Paolina... always... Amen."

Anna Giraud of the Mantovan Court crossed herself and sighed. As Anna Giraud of Venice, she would need great faith. She might do well to send her foreboding away to the old kingdoms of her childhood. In the meantime, she must sleep. She had a colossal task ahead of her. Venice was about to receive Anna Giraud.

DUE

FLORENTINE, VENETIAN AND SIENESE STAGES

1724 – 1725

IX

Once I had seen beyond Venice, I yearned to see more. It wasn't that I wanted to return to Mantova. It was that the earthy places I'd heard of because of the Maestro's perpetual travel—Florence, Rome, Vienna—began to fascinate me. Why could I not go along with him, I wondered. And so I asked him. "My dear Anna," he said, "I know how shy you are. You would not want to meet so many people." [Antonia, 1741]

Nestled within the dense core of Florence across from the Orsanmichele, the Cristofori home was barely affected by the Tuscan winter wind that forced its way through the sleeping streets. Orlando Sagredo and Lorenzo Cristofori sat comfortably together before a mellow, gently crackling fire. The room, known and respected by family and friends as "Lorenzo's Library", saw very little company other than its master, his carefully chosen books and works of art and the oblation of Recioto. The rest of the household—Lorenzo's wife, his children and two servants—had retired for the night to the upper floor of the spacious, tastefully appointed residence. Lending its spicy bouquet to the air, the bottle of Recioto sat open on the fruitwood table between the men's roomy armchairs. The red of the fire flickered lightly against the soft yellow walls.

With his father's Sienese vineyards resting over the winter, Orlando was completing his annual January visit to Florence on behalf of the Sagredo Estate. The stay at the Cristofori home was now the highlight of his annual winter trek. He and Lorenzo had become friends through their business relationship. In fact, they had become close friends most probably through their individual relationships with their own fathers.

Taking membership in the Guild of Confectioners and Distillers very seriously, the Elder Sagredo held working relationships with major customers in high esteem. One of Orlando's winter responsibilities for his father was to maintain the commitment of merchants from Siena to Florence. Lorenzo Cristofori was one of those merchants. In 1720 Lorenzo had left his father's harpsichord business, opening an inn in the centre of Florence and acting as promoter for three artists whose work he believed in. Affronted initially, the Elder Cristofori had come to understand that his youngest son was simply not interested in the technical aspect of the harpsichord, much less in its possibilities of becoming more versatile in expression. No, Lorenzo had always been the dreamer and the one most interested in the artistic mind, not the technique. The father had reluctantly let go of his dream for his son.

"Tell me more about your frustrations with the Palio, Orlando. Surely you must be satisfied with the way you introduced changes last year." Lorenzo poured himself another inch of the Recioto.

"Yes," Orlando savoured the warmth from the fire and the liqueur, "but I found myself brooding about it one Sunday last month. Something was not right yet. It was a particularly dark day, so I'm sure my thoughts came in part from the darkness; but I think it was good that I pursued the thoughts. My desire for change hasn't been fully satisfied yet."

Lorenzo's interest was piqued. This was the quality of Orlando he most appreciated. Orlando was the consummate planner, particular in the minutest of details. He would have been well-suited to bringing about the modifications desired for the harpsichord. "What could be added to the festivity? The Palio has been an annual event forever for you Sienese. You've groomed and enhanced it exactly the way the horses and Siena move along in development. The people love it. What else could there be to add to it? You give yourself extraordinary tasks at times, my friend."

"Hear me out. A larger event could be planned. You mentioned the word 'festivity.' You're correct. We've made the transition from its military roots; but should there not by now be more substance to it?" Orlando sat forward on his chair now, energized, his glass almost disappearing inside his generous fist. "Yes, the event runs efficiently now; but it calls out for an infusion of something new, something that would sustain it. The race itself is long in preparation, but over in moments. The Palio needs something that would anchor the colour and competition and energy lavished on it by the townspeople... something that could start along with the early preparations in April."

Lorenzo was having difficulty visualizing what his friend could possibly add to the event. With his trip to the Palio as one of the major events of his year, he wanted to be able to join in Orlando's planning. "A larger event? A larger event would convulse Siena! You have no room for any additions!"

Orlando laughed and raised his glass to his friend. "Aha! But we do have room for something new! Tell me what you think of this. So far, I've kept my thoughts to myself. You see, on that Sunday, I found myself more taken by the music in the Duomo than by the word of God. At one point, there was a brief break in the clouds. I was drawn to the light streaming in through the stained glass. It lasted just long enough to remind me of the sun one early evening in Mantova. I attended an opera there with my parents when I was fifteen or sixteen. Father was tending to our estate's business and was teaching me as much as he could that year. Mother insisted I experience the culture as well. I was indifferent and went only to please Mother; but the experience took me by surprise. I was fascinated, particularly with the vocal performance. And so, the recollection last month led me to my idea—music! Do you see? The Palio could be broadened into a festival with music as a major theme. What

was that conductor's name in Mantova? An eccentric Venetian...
red hair flying wildly as he conducted... perhaps too dramatic at
times. You may have heard of him."

"And I thought you were going to try to introduce painting! We
all come from our own persuasions, my friend," Lorenzo laughed at
himself. "Orlando, I like the idea! The man you mention is Vivaldi—
Antonio Vivaldi—the pride of Venice. Venetian conceit personified! I
went to the performance of one of his operas two years ago in Rome.
The name eludes me... Hercules... Hercules and the... 'Hercules on
the River Termodonte'. There was a beautiful contralto aria that was
the centerpiece of the opera for me. But what are your thoughts?
Would you invite Vivaldi to Siena? He would probably entertain the
idea. He's creating quite a reputation as a traveller, more than any
other musician I've ever heard of."

"I've heard the same. I've investigated the idea through various
sources to come up with new life for the Palio," Orlando was at his
best in the realm of change, his eyes intent on the scenes in his
imagination. "I would invite Vivaldi and a small group of musicians
to come. From what I've learned, Siena would be wise to appeal to
Venetian arrogance in attempting to make this happen. Venetians
are amply endowed, but always crave more attention. Our Town
Fathers are quite enthused about the idea—their only stipulation is
that Sienese musicians augment the vocal and instrumental ensem-
bles Vivaldi would bring to the Palio. I see that as an excellent idea,
both aesthetically and politically. The expansion into a more formal
Festival would be tested for the first Palio of this summer, and, if it
goes favourably, it will be continued next year for both the July and
the August Palios. Of course, the next events would have different
musicians. I think this inaugural Festival would be all we would
need to advance the Palio to a new level. What do you think?"

Lorenzo lifted his glass, "Well done, Sagredo!" He poured more Recioto for Orlando. "Brilliant, my man! I could even see introducing painters at some date. Three or four well-chosen artists could be stationed strategically in the Piazza, near the Duomo," Lorenzo paused for thought, "and at the little church. Yes! I can see it now! This would add colour to the Festival and exposure—and perhaps income—for the artists. Have you approached Vivaldi?"

"No. As I said, you're the first person to hear about this... outside of the Sienese Council. I told them I'd be talking to you about the idea, and so they agreed with me to wait for some advice from you. You know Venice far better than we do. And I have no particular desire to know it," Orlando set his glass on the table and luxuriated in stretching back in his chair, his hands clasped behind his head and his feet pointed directly toward the congenial fire.

"Correct. You've been wise in waiting to see the best approach." Lorenzo wanted to grow roots on this winter idea. "You already understand the Venetian conceit, as you call it. I call it narcissism, blatant and adorned narcissism. Venice works this way musically—music is politics. The apparent political leader of the Republic of Venice is Doge Alvise Mocenigo. I say apparent because the actual leader is the Doge's Envoy, Tiepolo, a corrupt, power-hungry man. He controls the fop Mocenigo's every move and, therefore, Venice's every move. Vivaldi, in his naivety and musical enthusiasm, has fallen prey to the politics of Venice. Of course, he has no interest, anyway. He's thrilled as long as he can make music, foist it on his orphans and travel at will. So, what needs to be done, my friend, is political," Lorenzo was lost in the critical formulation. Orlando enjoyed watching his friend set the stage. "You must approach this politically, through the Doge and his Envoy."

Orlando saw his friend as the master of artistic promotion. It was time to be strategic. "When are you next going to Venice, Lorenzo?"

Lorenzo's laughter roared around the room. The surge of energy seemed to revive the dying fire, "I didn't see this coming, Sagredo! I walked right into it, didn't I? You're clever! And manipulative," he drank the last of his Recioto. "All right, I'll do the maneuvering for you. I'm scheduled to go to Venice at the end of the month. I have plans to bring their Giovanni Canal to Florence for a showing of his art, and I'll have to be three steps ahead of Mocenigo and Tiepolo in order to get them to see this as a profitable idea. So, I'll send a letter ahead to add the Palio to the agenda. It may help me with the Canal idea. Very sharp-witted you are, my friend. But, you knew I would relish this task."

"I knew I could count on you, Lorenzo," Orlando smiled broadly, leaned forward and reached out to shake his friend's hand.

Lorenzo clasped Orlando's hand firmly. He picked up another log for the fire. The dry wood sputtered until the bark burst into bright and fragrant flames, shooting light and shadow over the men's faces. He offered Orlando more Recioto. Orlando declined. "Well, here you are leaving tomorrow, and I've forgotten to ask a few personal details. How is your relationship with Alessandra progressing? Are you in love with her yet?"

Orlando shook his head. "We were far from suited." Lorenzo looked sternly at Orlando. "I know, I know! Yes, she's beautiful. But, no, we're simply not suited. I need more than physical attraction. Alessandra's interests don't fit with mine. She prefers the large group of friends, the more superficial approach to life. I could see very quickly we could never have a successful marriage. She would become unhappy; I would be intolerant. And then one day I saw how well-suited she would be to Enrico. Enrico enjoys life the same way, throwing himself into the moment, not scrutinizing affairs. I encouraged him to pursue her. They're to be married after the harvest."

Lorenzo laughed, "Ah, ever the perfect brother! And Helena?"

Orlando's mood darkened. "What good is it for me to continue that relationship, Lorenzo? She's a beautiful woman with great depth. But we flounder; we skulk. I hate that—intensely! Love turns sour and bitter on that diet. In fact, I see that happening to our relations now. I suppose I was initially flattered that an older woman was interested in me. We've been playing with fire, and, if we don't end our relationship now, great damage will be done. Her children are old enough to sense things. Actually, we ended our liaison before I came here. I'll miss her, but not enough to change my mind. Ah," he reached for the Recioto, "I shall have to take your lead and settle for an economic union. That is, if I actually do want to be married."

Lorenzo looked into his empty glass, "Well, it works for me, does it not?" He looked up at Orlando, "Sometimes marriage ruins love, Orlando. But—I tell you—I have seen more men fall in love at this point, the point where they make a decision not to be married. Perhaps you'll find a Roman woman on your trip there this year?"

Giotto's bell tower rang out the midnight hour in the heart of the Florentine winter.

"Well, my friend, I must sleep before I head back to Siena," Orlando stood and walked over to look out the window. Faint snowdrops drifted by only to disappear before they could touch the street, as fleeting as love itself. Winter affected him this way. He turned to Lorenzo, "And, the Venetian coup?"

Lorenzo rose and clapped his friend on the back. "Venice is accomplished! You can count on it. Tiepolo needs me for some of his contacts in this part of the world. He'll want to please me. It will happen, Orlando. Tell your Town Fathers to begin planning a more robust Palio. And I shall look forward to it! The guest room is ready for you, as usual. Go ahead. I'll do a little business before I head upstairs."

Orlando lit a candle, climbed the stairs and entered his usual Cristofori quarters. The white bed linens were turned crisply back. He placed a log on the faltering fire and extinguished the candle. The log caught fire and scattered blades of light around the room. And, in her eternal quest for the unanswerable, Reni's St. Cecilia, stationed on the wall above the bed, continued to look toward the sky in her world. In the time since his last visit to her bed, she had had no resolution. "Perhaps neither shall I," Orlando whispered to give her some semblance of companionship.

* * *

Within a moon cycle of Orlando's return, word had come from the Ducal Palace in Venice that Vivaldi and a troupe of select musicians would be pleased to provide "the musical substance" of the upcoming Palio. They would arrive in May to begin preparations and rehearsals on their own and with the Sienese. Vivaldi would accept the commissioning of a new motet.

And the Town Fathers of Siena exulted over their brilliance on behalf of their fortress town.

X

If I could paint, I would paint Siena! I would use only vibrant, brilliant, stunning colours. I would invent new colours... beyond orange... more pristine than blue... brighter than the most fiery yellow... holier than green. First I would spatter the canvas—a very large one—with yellow and orange. And then I would listen to the sounds of the colours and succumb to Inspiration, shaping saffron sunflowers and succulent grapes ready to burst into wine. The riotous flames of the sun would take over the centre of the canvas until the sun itself created Il Duce, clad in his armour and moving forward on his magnificent steed. And then I would open my arms wide to him... and step into the painting so that he could pick me up and we could finish our story together. [Antonia, 1750]

"Anna! Come here! Quickly! There is little time left. We must leave!"

It was time to go to Siena. The Maestro had accepted an invitation to write a Magnificat for performance at the Duomo in July. Antonia was excited. She, Anna Giraud, the persona of the Doge's conception, would travel along to sing in The Magnificat and to perform a recent violin concerto. Venice would be promoted. But for Antonia... she would travel again! Although she would have preferred Rome, she would be going to the birthplace of Saint Catherine. She had a strong affinity with the woman of visions and dialogues. Like Antonia, Catherine had left her cell to enter public life. The Saint had altered mediaeval Italian civil war. She had even convinced the Pope to reform the clergy! Perhaps, then, Antonia could persuade Father Antonio she needed nothing more than her private life in music. If she could travel with the Maestro occasionally, she would be content. She neither enjoyed nor wanted the Venetian attention any longer.

"Anna! Come! Now!"

From her balcony view over the misty, sepulchral waters, she recognized the self-focus in his call. The Maestro should know she would be organized and ready. He should also know she would saunter as soon as she heard him ordering her! A modest rebellion was better than none at all. Anna knew his minimal supply of patience was almost gone. She enjoyed this, playing with the edges, the way she would in a violin solo. But she would have to relent shortly. Just as in music, there was an art to this. Timing was key.

"Anna! Come, my dear!"

How could she tease him any further? He was so happy to be introducing her to the orange town and its Palio. She smiled as she remembered his description of the races and decorations and colours she would be a part of within a few months. She who knew gondolas and had never sat on a horse! She who was not in the least interested in horses or Palios. There was no music in such crude activity.

"Coming, Maestro!" And she flew down the stairs.

Full of spirit, Antonia flung the door open and walked out into the warm air of the Venetian prima vera. The promenade was busier than usual with people stopped to watch what was happening with the Doge's Bucintoro. There it was, flapping its red flags in regal impatience, rolling on the agitated water and waiting for its final passenger. Antonia's laughter joined the din of voices bouncing happily across the Bacino. Having dispersed the early morning fog, Apollo beamed down upon the departing troupe of Venetian musicians.

What more could she ask for than to live for a few months in the home of Cimabue and Duccio and their paintings of the Madonna and Maddalena? The home of Saint Catherine! The twenty-one year old musician was ready to lose herself to her two passions—God's love revealed in music and God's beauty revealed in painting.

She had no idea her God had other plans for her.

XI

In Siena's Duomo, there is a marble floor inlaid with a mosaic. One of the subjects is "the slaughter of the innocents." When I first saw it and walked across it, I was certain the little ones were reaching up to take hold of my ankles... to gain my attention... to plead with me to save them... to make this perpetual slaughter stop. I could hear them shrieking and see them bleeding. Were I to go back there now, it would be to look for one innocent, waiting for me to save her. I would pick her up in my arms and laugh and carry her out through the alleys into the fields and nurse her and play with her and teach her so many things. I would be Bellini's Madonna outside Siena. And she? Well, God would allow her to be His Holy Daughter. [Antonia, 1750]

On the gentle, fragrant fifteenth day of April, 1725, Orlando Sagredo, master planner of Siena's Palio, was on his way to the Piazza. Preparations for the Palio were underway. Having officially declared their entrance, competitors and neighbourhoods were busy making banners and flags and participating in intense training with their horses. As eldest son in the Sagredo family, Orlando was, for the third time, responsible for the Palio. Celebration, competition and safety in Siena monopolized his thoughts. With the arrival of the musicians from Venice, he had much to occupy his time.

Coming from the Via del Capitano, named in honour of the Palio, Orlando made his way into the Piazza del Campo. The view was spectacular here, with the Duomo rising, high and regal, to his left and orange rooftops spilling down into sepia at his right. Sun, cloud and sky enhanced the Duomo in its vast, dazzling glory. Everything shimmered.

Walking by the massive, layered facade, he was taken aback. Had he heard laughter or music? He stopped to listen. It was laughter, a woman's, swirling out of the open doors and tumbling down the steps. Musical laughter. Fascinated, he walked up the stairs and into the building.

"O, Maestro! Don't take me seriously! I was playing with the theme. You know I would never take that liberty in performance!" The clear voice matched the musical laughter he'd heard. Curious, Orlando wanted to see the woman. The acoustic and the shadowed interior confused the location of the conversation. He moved in quietly, finding a group of musicians in a shaft of sunlight. The stained glass windows filtered the light, breaking it into a pale spectrum. Five string players, a harpsichordist, a graying red-haired conductor and the most fascinating woman he had ever seen formed the small band.

The conductor clapped his hands—"Alma Oppressa, bar one! Now! This time—more of the soul in travail, reaching, reaching, seeking, singing to God!" As he raised his hands, the silence seemed alive.

The bows took aim and the woman, standing, arms at her sides, with violin in one hand and bow in the other, became centre to the fresco that had been created. Her burgundy hair was haloed by the sun; her stunning presence alert and ready to come alive in music.

All else faded. Eyes focused on the conductor. When all had become one, he led. Together the bows bit and moved back and forth across the strings, releasing a torrent of lustrous energy. The harpsichord multiplied the cascade. In the aftermath of the outpouring, Orlando heard a new violin take over the note of the resting violin—pure, white, straight, expanding. It came from the mouth of the young woman. Spellbound, he was taken onto the sound itself, developing into words with it. Time and thought stopped. He was consumed. He had experienced music this way only once before, a few years ago in Mantova.

Through the controlled soaring and plunging of the oppressed soul's voice, he was connected to the Divine. And, in the syncopation of that soul with the instruments, the connection was given and taken, given and taken. Orlando Sagredo, master of his own life, had fallen prey to the music of the spheres.

"Splendid! Enough!"

Orlando came to himself.

The conductor seemed delighted with the creation. "You all do my work credit. Thank you. Back to the G Minor Concerto, Anna."

"Oh, Maestro, may we have a time to ourselves? We've been practising for too long. Please?"

"A short walk, then. And—not off the property!" The puffing conductor stepped down from the podium. Antonia laughed again, and the other musicians straggled toward the door, lapsing into opinions on balance and interpretation.

And then the singer turned and looked directly at Orlando and smiled. Her beauty stunned him; but it was more than that. He felt he knew her.

Without thinking, Orlando spoke, "You are—your voice is beautiful. You are obviously the Venetians I've been waiting to greet. I am Orlando Sagredo."

"We are indeed the Venetians. I'm Anna Giraud. And, I must confess I have no idea what the Palio is, other than a celebration that involves horses. We are horse-less on our watery streets," her warmth reminded Orlando of the scent of the lilies outside the Duomo.

"Well, then, we're even. I had no idea about the effects of the singing female voice. Ours are silenced in Siena. I thank you for the introduction. I'd..."

"Anna! You asked for a rest!" The voice of the Maestro split the connection.

"I must go! The Maestro isn't pleased," Antonia's smile disappeared.

As she turned, Orlando put his hand on her arm. "Please, I must speak more with you!" He saw her fear. "I'll hear you again at practice. I won't say good-bye to you." Immediately, he walked over to speak to the Maestro.

"I'm at fault, sir. I was merely asking if you were the famous Antonio Vivaldi of whom I've heard much. My apologies for interrupting your practice. I'm Orlando Sagredo, Il Duce of the Palio. If there is anything I can do to assist you, I'm at your command. Your music this morning convinces me we couldn't have invited anyone more skilful. Thank you for beginning your preparations so quickly."

"Well, you are most welcome, young man, most welcome," Antonio blustered.

Antonia, enjoying the quick thinking of this man, found herself looking forward to future practices. And to the Palio.

XII

There came a time, while I was in Siena the first time, when I felt
Venice as a menacing shadow hovering over my life—Il Falcon,
ready to swoop. As life on land became more solid, Venice became
more amorphous. But the sense of Il Falcon's black, swooping
wings has never left me. Never. [Antonia, 1745]

Dante Tiepolo, a towering, brooding silhouette against the
streaked window, looked out over the Palazza Ducale courtyard.
In the heavy humidity of the late May morning, the lagoonal air
fell into the courtyard and clung to the forbidding privacy of the
Palace. He noticed three robed Procurators walk down the Giant's
Staircase and disappear into the gray Istrian stone. Purposefully, he
kept his back turned to Alvise Mocenigo, the Doge of his Republic.
Foolish, weak man! Easily led man. This is my Republic, not yours.

Elevated on his ornately carved chair in his private quarters high
and deep within the Palace, Mocenigo reached out to touch the
globes that gave him his sense of power. My Republic. My Most
Serene Republic. Tiepolo looks after You so very well. His robes
and headgear served only to make him appear smaller and more
delicate than he naturally looked. He looked over at his Envoy. The
breadth of the man's back took his breath away. He recognized in a
sudden conviction that all he wanted to do was to please this man,
this Tiepolo who had more power over him and who swayed his
emotions more than anyone else ever had in his rather ineffectual
life. He coughed to regain the Envoy's attention. "You will be leaving this afternoon, then?"

Tiepolo turned around to face his access to power. Buono!
Mocenigo, dizzy in the face of his dark magnetism, was transfixed.
"Yes, everything is ready. I intend to take my time on the journey
and stop on the way in Florence for a few days with friends there.

There's no reason to get to Siena quickly. I shall arrive in plenty of time to ensure our contingent of artists remains focused on their goodwill mission. Vivaldi is puffed so full with pride that we are assured of good relations with the orange town. Our use of the arts always serves us well, Alvise. Venice always comes out on top in comparison to other centres. Vivaldi and Giraud and the others from the Pieta will never be surpassed." As always, Tiepolo found himself intrigued with the transformation of the orphan Antonia into the musically powerful, beautiful Anna. But—this was unapproachable territory... for now. He could be disciplined when necessary, as disciplined as the musical nun herself. He regained his focus. Mocenigo had been left clinging to his words, taking everything in and trying desperately to make the ideas his. "Siena is only important in that it keeps our way clear and strong toward Rome. Lunatic town that it is. However, we need its friendship—and some of its art! We'll make them appear important with our music and have them eating out of our hands, like horses, for as long as we wish. I've already set up a meeting with the young man who is in charge of the Palio."

"How are you going to keep Vivaldi under control? You remember he now has an odd little following in Florence. The same could happen in Siena," the Doge looked even tinier in his foolish apprehension. "But, I don't take this Vivaldi fanaticism as personally as you do, Dante. Perhaps you could see him merely as the Republic's musical envoy while you are the political envoy?"

Dante Tiepolo's eyes flashed. His fury barely under control, he moved close to the Doge. Leaning onto the arms of the chair and coming to within a breath away from Mocenigo's petrified face, he hissed, "Never utter or even think words like that again, Alvise! Never doubt my power to be in charge of your power. Never doubt I am the one in authority in this place. You are nothing—nothing—

without me! We have talked of this before. I've asked you before if you doubt me! Do you doubt my power to make Venice the greatest force in the world? Do you?"

Speechless, the delicate Doge shook his head.

"Then never ask again," he allowed his final word on the subject to thunder forth, "Never!"

Dante Tiepolo stood tall and smiled, "Well, my good man. We are clear, are we not?" He reached over to clasp the Doge's arm firmly.

"Yes, we are," the Doge's gray face trembled. "I trust you. Implicitly. I always have." He must change the subject. "What else do you need for your journey? You are, in effect, Doge to the Venetians when you are in Siena," the words tumbled out of Mocenigo's mouth in a pathetic ploy to regain the Envoy's favour.

Tiepolo chortled, "I'm more than capable of being in charge of my own pleasure, Alvise, more than capable. You know that!"

"But what I mean is... is... you must keep your appetites under control in Siena. You know that," in his attempt to get the better of his Envoy, the Doge became more pathetic.

Looking the small ruler in the eye, Tiepolo laughed, "But Florence is another matter, is it not, Alvise? And that's where I'll stop for a few days to take care of my needs so that I can be your priestly envoy in Siena." He turned on his heel and walked out of the private apartment. "Go to your wife now," he roared and laughed his way down the hall.

Alvise III Mocenigo, the one hundredth and twelfth Doge of the Republic of Venice, tiny and alone in his massive chair, snuffled pitifully as the tears trickled down his face. The derisive laughter of his Envoy swirled in his head... mocking... mocking. How would he manage affairs while Tiepolo was absent? Never mind! He must simply remember his powerful Envoy would soon have the unruly

Vivaldi and his troupe under control. Siena was welcome to borrow them—once! But Giraud and Vivaldi were his—his!

XIII

Saint Catherine knew persecution. She knew austerities. She implored God to reform the clergy. I suppose it was God's direction to her to take her pleas to Pope Gregory in Avignon. She helped change the river of history. I feel I have known persecution and austerities, too. But, other than God, to whom was I to implore for help? And where have I changed anything? As much as it grieves me to do so, I question the spiritual life of penury and austerity. But I know no other. And as I write this, I ask for forgiveness. I must go to my garden... to the healing soil. [Antonia, 1745]

The early morning rehearsal over, Antonia made her way from the Duomo along the pilgrim-worn path of Via della Terme toward Saint Catherine's house. In this part of Siena, with its winding streets and hovering buildings, it was easy to feel unsettled. Windows became eyes, glinting, peering and then entering one's thoughts, prying them open, colouring them somehow with the distorted oranges of the rooftops and then filling them with umber shadows. Antonia had walked by the Saint's family home often in the past week, always captivated by God's early claim on Catherine's life. She had begun at age eight to receive her visions in this house. Anna felt a mysterious kinship. Sometimes it frightened her.

Shortly after her arrival in Siena, Antonia had heard of the annual April Festa della Saint Catherine. Eager to attend, she had asked the Maestro if practice could be suspended that day. Vivaldi had equivocated and allowed that practice would begin in the early morning and last for only two hours. "God would not have us abandon our practice even for one day, Anna. We shall please Him by placing our practice first amongst our responsibilities that day." Happy with the favour, she was eager to be an ordinary participant and not a musician. She looked forward to having no responsibility in this holy ceremony other than to wait upon God's Word and perhaps come closer to her saint.

This mid-morning of drizzling rain and gloomy skies was what she needed. She had had a difficult time falling asleep last night, thinking, thinking, thinking... about her attraction to Orlando... and about how disappointed Father Antonio would be were he to learn how preoccupied her thoughts were, how far away from music they had travelled... or was it... could it be... that this preoccupation was indeed close to music? The Maestro would tell her that her obsession should be solely music, that it was her area of Devotion and that she must be guided, of course, by the Holy Spirit. She had prayed for forgiveness last night and her answer had come in her sleep and her simple dream of the Maestro conducting an orchestral practice and frequently admonishing the players with a stern, "No!"

This, then, was the day God had given her, a dark day for introspection and holiness.

Antonia turned a corner into of a mass of people and noise. The townspeople—surely almost all of them—gathered around Saint Catherine's house! Laughter, shouting, music, colour—all seemed to come together in a unity against the dreariness of the day, dispelling it in a blast into the Heavens, forcing the Madonna of Mercy to fling wide her cape. Antonia's spirit soared. She lifted her skirt and ran toward Catherine's birthplace. Carried along with everyone in the passage through the alleys, she worked her way toward the leaders. Yes—there they were, just as she had been told. There was the Archbishop and his attendants, followed by the choristers—men and boys in their gowns with bright scarves in the colours of the seventeen Contrada. Yet again, the Sienese marriage of music and politics! What was it they were singing? This human deluge was noisier and more dangerous than the swells of the Adriatic! What music?

Yes! Simple plain chant! Why had it confused her so? Why had it seemed so distorted?

And here they were, crowding in upon the Piazza and coming face-to-face with San Domenico itself, rising up in its severity and daring the townspeople to face all aspects of Saint Catherine in its womb—pieces of her, Vanni's portrait... her perpetual offerings in the inhospitable atmosphere itself.

And then—dear God—they were in the cathedral. Surely this was not the sanctuary of her Vespers, her evening Solitude, her conversations with God! It had changed, become monstrous, terrifying, ugly.

The incense, the music, the pushing, the din of voices... it all seemed distorted, unbearable. Overwhelmed, Antonia felt as though she had no limits, no edges between herself and the hallowed inexplicable—was it Pagan?—conjured up by this building. She couldn't breathe... too hot, too noisy... too frightening... she pushed her way backward... against the crowd... let me... please let me past... I need to go outside... please, please! How had this become too much for her? Why had she come here? Why was she in this outlandish city of orange and sensuality? How had her God become hideous? This was Pagan, not Christian!

Suddenly she was free... a break in the crowd and she was released... falling on her hands and knees... looking up at... yes... at a candle... a candle flickering and Saint Catherine looking out... not at her... no... past her... to the Invisibles of the cathedral... angels and deceased but not departed souls, struggling still to take their leave of this world. Catherine herself had not departed. Her own people kept her imprisoned within the remaining artefacts of her once-body.

Antonia wept. There was no one to help her, no one to notice, no one to care. "Dear God... Mother Mary... help me."

A gentle hand took her elbow... the Mother took her elbow, guiding her to the pew in front of the candle, seating her gently in the precise place where Catherine had bled... bled... and the music poured over her, healing her. The music, the mass... ah, Palestrina... healing Palestrina. Antonia took a deep breath and let the Mass seep inside her. How had she let this place defeat her? Why?

Someone was near her. She could feel it. She turned round.

And there was Orlando. He smiled and put his finger to his lips, "Hush, you're safe now." His eyes danced. "You frightened yourself."

Antonia smiled weakly. "Was it you? Did you guide me here?" She felt sensitive, embarrassed that she had become so bewildered.

He nodded. "Crowds are frightening at times. Remember that the Sienese throw themselves into their rituals. Remember that when it comes time for the Palio."

"Saint Catherine has great significance in my life," Antonia's whisper was clear as she remembered her struggle for peace and purity last night. She must control herself, protect herself from her feelings, sanctify herself. She had received forgiveness for her thoughts of this man. She... her desire... must....

He smiled again and looked—was it in challenge? Was he daring her, daring her to react to the moment? "Then you must be happy with your accommodations so close to her and her church." His smile disappeared.

His gaze, though, did not waver. And Antonia, as much as she knew she should, could not, would not, look away.

Leaning slightly forward, he dared again, "You are very beautiful. The most beautiful woman I have ever met, Anna."

Antonia, more shaken, wanted... needed to run... desperately. Why did these words affect her so strangely? She must leave. She turned and stood, bowing her head toward the altar. Rallying, she spoke, "I do not know how to receive words such as yours. They seem unsuitable to the occasion." When Orlando continued to hold her in his gaze, she looked away... he disarmed her... she could not accept his bold words. More than that, she could not accept her feelings. "Thank you for your assistance." And she turned toward the aisle. Just as she entered the aisle, he held her wrist. She wanted to turn, to stay with him.

"Anna, I apologize for any discomfort I've caused. But I don't retract any of my words about your beauty and my fascination with you." She pulled away. "No—please—let me speak. I'll come frequently to your practices, and I won't disturb you. However, I will know you, Anna. I must." He released his grip.

All seemed timeless, as Antonia looked at Orlando. And then she turned up the aisle and rushed out of the cathedral. For a brief moment as she opened the massive door and exited, the now sunny skies shone into the building.

Orlando Sagredo sat back, captivated, and wanted nothing more than to know this woman better.

TRE

THE DUOMO TO THE SAGREDO ESTATE

1725

XIV

Was my flight to Jacopo in Mantova an omen, a preparation for Siena and him? If there was a Divine hand in our love, it was a fist. [Antonia, 1744]

Orlando had been true to his word. He had come back to sit in the Duomo almost daily during practices.

In spite of the enormous size of the Duomo, its many spaces and recesses, Antonia learned to anticipate his presence. She knew his footstep now. Her awareness heightened, and her pulse raced. Always, as he came to his place, where he could look directly at her, Antonia would fall more deeply in love with her music. Violin or voice would perform more exquisitely. No one had ever prepared her for this experience she both hungered after and feared. Except her painter. She had felt like this in Mantova. But this was more intense, more possible, more real. This would not develop into pleasant dreams, would it? Even the thought, away from the Duomo and especially in the evenings, of Orlando—his voice, his bearing and especially that certain look in his eyes that belonged to her—created confusion and desire. It was as though Orlando had become her music, her reason for waking... for living.

For two weeks, Orlando had not attempted to talk to Antonia. Rather, he would speak with Father Antonio. The two would talk intensely of music, and Orlando would finish by smiling at Antonia and taking on a task for the Maestro. Antonia found herself longing for the sensation of Orlando's hand on her arm. The imprint was still there. All she could do was return the smile. Confused and pained when her mind wandered into the future, she threw herself into her music and looked forward to her evening times on her own in the Basilica.

It was there one evening, as she sat quietly on her own, that she began to understand. Orlando was carrying out a plan. She had learned that it was he who had preserved the Palio by reviving Siena's life and pride in its history and rituals. He had not merely followed an ancient ceremony blindly. No, he had gone even so far as to bring this new musical element into the Palio's fibre. This was a man who knew how to get what he wanted, who knew how to plan. This was a man of vision and energy. That evening, Antonia made a decision to trust Orlando the way she trusted her music to support her. And so it did not surprise her that, following his gaining of the Maestro's trust, Orlando began to speak again— briefly, circumspectly—with her, always aware of Vivaldi's location. He moved from general and philosophical comments about music to declaring his particular opinions on her repertoire.

The prelude was over. Orlando spent more time talking with her about her love and conception of music. She dared to ask about his role in the Palio and about the Sagredo Estate. A new world of activity and harvest and freedom in travel opened itself to her. Orlando was the door to this new universe... the universe she had known as fable in her childhood imaginations of realms beyond Venice.

During recess in a June rehearsal, one in which the Maestro could not be satisfied, Orlando explained the appeal of "Dite, Oime".

67

"You're an extra string on the lute in that song. How can you express such beauty and grief, except that you've known it?"

"I felt it all when I was away from Venice. We were in Mantova. There was a grief within the Maestro that was kindred in me. I seemed to absorb it; I seemed to be part of it. Neither he nor Sister Paolina could enlighten me. He encouraged me to sing, quietly and alone, and let my soul speak through my voice."

"You wrote it, Anna?" Surprised, Orlando spoke softly. And yet, he was not surprised.

"Father Antonio and I wrote it. It is our secret. It will be part of an opera. You must tell no one, Orlando. It's improper for a woman to conceive music. I gave him the theme. He was proud of me. In fact, I was shocked to see he was near tears. 'Anna,' he said, 'you have drawn this out from my heart and yours.' We spent much time singing and writing, singing and writing. Finally, we shaped it, knowing it was a duet for voice and lute. He plays the lute as well as the violin."

Orlando's anger mounted against the composer who so fiercely controlled Anna. His attempts to understand the man left him no further ahead in his comprehension of the relationship Vivaldi dominated. Why would anyone so immensely talented want to bridle and absorb an identical talent? He wanted to take Anna in his arms. He wanted to protect her innocence and purity. He wanted to give her freedom. "You are indeed alike in many ways—the way you pace and create, violin in hand; your fieriness; your passion; your stubbornness. I suppose this comes from his being the only father you've known and your being the only daughter he's known. Anna, you could be free away from Venice!" He stopped speaking when he saw the alarm on her face.

"No! Think only of today, Orlando!" Antonia could not tolerate her panic. She must dispel it. "Today I could write a fantasia! I don't miss Venice. I love Siena. I love... I enjoy your company. And I'm here for another month."

"Anna!" The voice from another world brought her back.

Orlando, foiled, rose to depart. As he did so, he placed his hand on Antonia's knee. For a moment, Antonia couldn't breathe. The imprint of his hand lingered. She realized that she wanted more of Orlando—more from him—more, more. She wanted to follow him from the church and ask him what this meant. She wanted to touch him. What were these feelings she had? What was she to do with them? Should he have touched her? Should she feel as though she wanted more? And what was 'more'? Whatever the confusion, whatever the correctness, Antonia knew a deep well inside her had been released.

She was drawn to the orb of white light above the altar. It seemed that the light pulsated, luring her into extinction. Or was it offering existence? For the first time in her life, she contemplated life without the Maestro and Sister Paolina.

XV

I think I did not know how to laugh until I met him. Nor to play. He taught me to open up to joy and pleasure in the immediate moment—to touch, to feel, to listen, to see all that was happening in the world around me. I had no need to escape to my imagination when I was with Orlando. And so, I still touch and feel and hear and see him. He dwells in me. [Antonia, 1748]

"He is handsome, too, Paolina... well, perhaps slightly rugged. He wouldn't be the most comely of musicians! Well... perhaps a basso, although his voice has the texture of a tenor..." Antonia drifted. She had pulled a stool up to the table in the Maestro's kitchen to help the Prioress prepare supper. When had her hands ever trembled like this before? When had she ever had someone speak to her the way Orlando had so that she wanted nothing more than to see this person again, so that she saw him every time she closed her eyes. For a while, Jacopo had been like this for her. She was grateful for him. "I know you've often told me I would find a man appealing some day; but I truly, truly didn't believe you," Antonia trusted the Prioress's understanding. "And my feelings! What are these feelings? I feel more... turmoil... I cannot say what I feel... except that this is more than I feel before a performance. Paolina, how did you know this would ever happen to me?" Antonia dropped the parsley on the floor. As she jumped off the stool to retrieve it, she spilled the jug of water. The normally collected Antonia blushed the colour of her hair.

Paolina chuckled and threw Antonia a cloth, "Someone as passionate as you! Someone as beautiful as you! I knew it would happen. I've heard only good things about this Sagredo; but you must take your time and be sure he is trustworthy. Anna! Be careful with that knife, my dear!"

Antonia brought her attention back to her tasks. "I will be careful, Mother—if the Maestro ever lets me speak and act for myself!" Antonia scraped the vegetables into Paolina's bowl. The kitchen was fragrant with the savoury perfume of herbs. "Why is he so hard on me, Paolina? And don't tell me again that it's because he loves me!"

Chagrined, Paolina looked away. "Then I don't know what to say, Anna. Because that is the reason. He will not want to lose you to anyone else." She wiped her hands on her apron and went to the stove. "Perhaps you should keep your imagination within the realm of your music, my dear. I know how strong the Maestro can be, and I want to protect you from disappointment. Being in love isn't an easy matter. I'm afraid you will be hurt if you pursue this train of thought. Remember you're in Siena for such a short period of time and you have music to perform. Perhaps this isn't the best environment for love… infatuation…," Paolina felt relief…. Yes, this was how the feelings should be addressed! "This can only be infatuation, my dear. You haven't had time yet to know this young man. And you will not have time. There's too much for you to do," the Prioress, her eyes imploring, looked directly at Antonia. "Anna, my dear, don't let yourself be hurt—please!"

Antonia bounced off her chair and began pacing. "Hurt by whom? Orlando or the Maestro? I'm old enough to learn about love—and certainly old enough to understand my own feelings and take care of myself! Oh, Paolina! You need to see Orlando! And talk to him! He is clever and capable and so… so… very handsome. And tall! And his smile! I found myself almost staring at him… at his eyes… his fascinating eyes… Oh, Paolina!" Frustrated and at a loss for words, Antonia stamped her foot, "Are you saying Father Antonio would actively oppose my interest in Orlando?" How had this delightful conversation taken a twist into an avenue of shadows? "I cannot believe you are telling me to doubt my feelings and… and…

happiness!" Antonia was ready to give in to tears of frustration and pain.

Paolina continued to cook. She needed the comfort of the familiar. "Yes, Anna, I am telling you that your Maestro would oppose you," she sighed and looked at Antonia. It was time to be fully honest with her. And with that realization, Paolina knew where her loyalty must reside. "But I will tell you this, Anna, and this I promise. If, over our time here in Siena, you find your feelings for Orlando develop into love and not infatuation, I will champion your cause."

"Oh, dear Paolina, thank you! You are always so good to me; you're better than a mother. Here I am in Siena! Remember how I dismissed this city as too ordinary? And now, I'm completely turned in circles. I want to see Orlando again—and soon! He's in charge of this celebration, did you know?" Antonia gave Paolina no opportunity to respond. "And he was so clever—so perfectly clever—with the Maestro that the Maestro was smiling and happy with himself. He said he wants to talk more with me. How will he do that?" Antonia was pacing now. "Do you think there's a chance that he might change his mind, that he might not really care to know me? Oh—I need... I need... my violin!" Antonia kissed Paolina and ran out of the kitchen.

A few minutes later, Paolina heard "La Prima Vera" being played so spiritedly that it threatened to run off with Antonia herself. And she knew then that her Anna had found a new passion, a passion that was not going to move along an easy path. How angry she was at herself for all the time she had spent on conciliation. She should never have stepped on the beauty of Anna's joy. She should have told Anna she was happy for her!

* * *

Across and away from the orange town, high in the richness of the Sienese hills, Orlando Sagredo, master planner, lay in his garden, looking up at God's blue, blue apron… planning how he would bring the vibrant violinist into his life. There would be a way to begin seeing Anna outside the duomo. There would be a way of winning both her impresario's trust. Perhaps there would be a life together with Anna.

XVI

Why did the sun play a far more dominant role for me in Siena than it ever had in Venice? Was it love? The moon was my alchemist in Venice. And yet I hardly remember thinking about the moon during my two interludes in Siena. On my first two returns to Venice, I reconciled with La Luna, often taking my violin out on the balcony and playing to her. When I was most angry, I played the 'Adagio e spiccato' from the G Minor Concerto...pum-pum-pum-pum... 1-2-3-4... why-why-why-why... throwing my questions into the sky and letting them resolve into beseeching stars. At my angriest, I would launch into the 'Allegro,' my bowing furious... back and forth, back and forth, until I could contain it no longer. Until a neophyte melody emerged. This is how comets are born, the issue of creativity and anger.
[Antonia, 1749]

The eleventh day of June in the year of our Lord, 1725, was particularly glorious. The sky was as blue as the skirt of Bellini's Madonna and the vast clouds white as angels' wings. Orlando was in love with the world. Why? Well... because he was in love with this Anna Giraud... with her body and her mind, with her abilities and with her beauty and spirit. He hungered after every inch of her. And she was beginning to love him, as inexperienced as she was. The Nun of Music. Most importantly, she trusted him. And here he was sitting freely in the practice. Vivaldi would be a reasonable man. And no reasonable man would see the strength and reputation of the Sagredo family as being anything but advantageous for a young woman. Orlando Sagredo had found the woman he would marry.

The practice, underway as he sat in the pew, progressed perfectly. Anna's buoyant uptake of the arcane allegro created a platform upon which the second violin and the violoncello could perch. As irresistibly as she called the others into the dizzying convolutions of the allegro, she lured them into the moodiness of the adagio until they had no will but to follow her into the ultimate logic of the return to mystery.

Spent and radiant, the Maestro tapped his bow on the podium, "Perfect! We shall pick up on the largo later. I must be off now to meet with some of the local musicians. Go for a walk. Anna, you were brilliant, my dear; you may go back to the convent for your lunch and a rest. All of you—be back here at two bells for the rest of today's practice. I am very happy indeed!" The jaunty composer, violin bow in hand, went merrily on his way toward the massive exit.

"Maestro! Maestro! Your violin!" Antonia, knowing his need for props and performance, called to him, as she moved quickly down the aisle, violin and case in hand.

Exasperated, Vivaldi looked at the instrument in his hand. "Yes, yes, Anna. How foolish of me! What would I do with a bow and no violin at a council meeting? Domine!" He handed Anna the bow, watching as she secured his underpins in the case, and left, muttering, "What would I do without you, Antonia!" Only in the most private of moments did he use that name. How Antonia missed it, despite the pain it awakened. Who was Anna? There were times when Antonia did not know.

Orlando looked intently at Antonia and followed Vivaldi out of the elaborate building. The Maestro gave him a cursory nod as he turned toward the Piazza. Orlando crossed the street. When Vivaldi disappeared, Orlando turned back to the Duomo and went down to the side garden. He stood by the stone bench in the shade cast by the ancient oak tree. He knew that Anna had understood his glance and that she would come out from the side door of the Duomo.

And there she was! Beautiful Anna, always in black, her burgundy hair framing the exquisitely lovely face that proved the existence of God. "Anna! Come down here!" Her luminous smile melted Orlando's heart yet again. She hurried down the stairs. Orlando put his arm around her as they sat on the bench. "Anna, it is time to move into the sun. We must be done with hiding, acting as though we were too young, too inexperienced, to be together. I am used to taking charge of matters and dealing publicly with business and beauty." He lifted her chin so that her eyes could not avoid the truth, "I love you, Anna of Venice."

Ready to resist, Antonia looked into Orlando's eyes. In that moment, as the noon sun sought out the lovers, she recognized that she had no choice, that this was love and that love was an entity as powerful as music. Drawn to Orlando, she had no words. All she knew was that she wanted to become a part of him. She knew she was at long last discovered, known as she had never been. As they kissed, Antonia sensed their souls dissolving into one. The sun smiled brilliantly, blessing them.

Orlando framed her face with his hands, "I love you, Anna. I have since the moment I heard your laughter call me into the Duomo. I want you; I want you in my life—always."

"And I want you, Orlando. I could never have anticipated love like this before I met you. But this cannot be; you know that, Orlando. I belong in Venice. You belong here. I don't know what to do; but I cannot abandon the Maestro and Sister Paolina."

"Anna, listen to me," his words and voice were firm and commanding, "You wouldn't be abandoning them. They have each other. Venice is not an impossible distance from here. You belong here. They will want this for you."

"I wish this were true, Orlando. I wish they would give me permission to live outside of my relationship with them. And outside of my love for music," she leaned forward and kissed him, seeking, with a hunger that stunned her. As she began to pull away, Orlando held her shoulders and slipped her like a child into his embrace. Antonia had never felt safer. She began to cry. Surprised, she held Orlando tightly and sobbed.

"What is it, Anna?" Orlando stroked her hair and kissed her head. "Tell me, Anna. Why are you so sad?"

Antonia shook her head slightly, "I'm not sure, Orlando. Perhaps it's relief... relief to be known. Orlando," she looked up at this man who had taught her a new language, "Orlando, I'm not Anna. I am Antonia. I became Anna so that I could live permanently with the Maestro and Prioress." And, in telling the story, Antonia released her grief and an alien shame that she had long harboured.

"Antonia... Antonia... look at me," Orlando, moved by her story, needed her to see him, to hear him fully, "you are Antonia, and you will always be Antonia. I understand why this had to be done... at least, I believe I do. I don't condone it, though—there is a larger problem here. But that has to do with the Venetian politics that I'm becoming familiar with. I'm not impressed. As for us, though," he kissed her gently, "we are Antonia and Orlando. Always! You will never again hear of Anna from me.

Antonia, home at last, nestled into Orlando's arms. How could the voice, its cadence, the smell of one human being, the arms combine to take her to another world, to a place she had never so much as considered.

The bells tolled twice. She stood up quickly. "I must go," she touched his lips, "I must before I lose what little time I have with you. No!" As Orlando began to object; she pressed her finger more firmly against his lips, "Don't speak, Orlando. I'm expected back at practice."

As she withdrew her fingers from his lips and turned to retreat, Antonia transformed her intense desire into the duty that had long governed her life. Silenced, Orlando felt colossal anger toward the greatest obstacle he had ever encountered. And Antonia was gone, into the dappled shadows of lilies and oak leaves—into her world of familiarity and sacrifice.

* * *

Antonia awoke—was she awake?—in a familiar garden. She heard Luna's resonant contralto voice singing inside her head, "You have the key, dear one." In a sense, she was one with the garden—no more and no less than another plant or tree or flower. She knew everything by name. The air was fresh and fragrant with the mixture of garden scents. The cyclamen and bluebell joined hands to remind her of their power to celebrate and shelter. Jasmine Insights and Oleander Supplications wafted themselves her way to steady her. In the outpourings of the Trumpet Vine, she received a reassurance that the world was good. This was a garden of music. The plants were the instruments of the orchestra.

A booming basso profundo voice laughed her way, "For what reason have you summoned us?"

"For wisdom, old soul," Antonia felt frightened as she looked toward a massive, throbbing light.

The voice responded, "This is your time, dear one!" The Glee of her childhood Invisibles radiated in lightbursts that tumbled forward, creating a brilliantly white pathway. It seemed to be inviting her into a secret.

As Antonia stepped onto the pathway, her feet became white light. She tried to turn round; but her feet carried her forward. She had no will. She had no feeling but love and urgency. Carried along on the pathway until it stopped at an arbour of wisteria, she was assaulted by its hearty fragrance. How curious—the heavy clusters of purple flowers were rising and falling. Were they breathing? Yes! And the strange perfume, more herbal than floral, was their breath. The pathway of light vanished into darkness behind her. Now it seemed only the wisteria had meaning.

Parting the wines, she stepped out into the inky life of the night. She was drawn to the moon. It was full—perfect and luminous. Following its beams to its reflection on the black and silver of the lake, she slipped into the murky water.

"Follow me, Antonia. Follow me!"

And then, Orlando's face appeared in the indigo sky, his warm smile becoming laughter. He reached out for her.

As she joined in his delight and reached for his hand, she awoke. How had it all disappeared? Desolate, she wanted to return to the dream. Her barren room taunted her.

For the remainder of that day, Antonia could not shake her sense of foreboding. How would she ever be allowed to keep Orlando in her life? She must! As sure as she ever had been of anything, she knew she must never lose Orlando.

* * *

The lovers had found time together in the Duomo, away from the nave in the back seats of the chapel, while the Maestro catechized the instrumentalists repetitively over their ragged entries. Antonia and Orlando needed to make plans to see each other away from practices. They needed more than their hurried, whispered talks. The tension was relentless. When would the Maestro storm away from the instrumentalists and confront them?

Orlando saw Antonia's connection to Maestro Vivaldi as one of love and fear. "Who named you, Antonia? Why are you and the Maestro only a vowel apart?"

"I think—I believe the Prioress named me. I've never really thought about it. Perhaps the woman who gave birth to me named me. I must ask Sister Paolina. I found it extremely difficult to part with my name in Mantova. All we orphans ever had was our first names. But now you call me Antonia. I do love to hear that. When I changed in Mantova, I felt as though I no longer had an identity. I trained myself to become unemotional about it—until I told you! Now, you are the only one to call me Antonia. Although both Sister Paolina and Father Antonio let my name slip out occasionally when there's no one around to hear it. I miss that name; it's mine. 'Anna' is not my name. I cannot tell you how important it is to me that you call me Antonia."

Knowing only that her father had been a musical nobleman infatuated with a servant, Antonia had fastened her heart to the man who had spiritually fathered the music within her. The Maestro possessed and sheltered her. Until now, Antonia had accepted this because of her devotion to her music. Without the Prioress in her life, Antonia would have had no knowledge of the need for balance. At the same time as she loved and learned from her surrogate mother, Antonia was puzzled by Sister Paulina's dedication to the man of obsessions.

"I've been trained to take on Sister Paolina's history. I truly have no history prior to my move to Mantova. And so I tell myself my father was a wig-maker. A wig-maker, indeed! That's Sister Paolina's family, not mine! Is it any wonder she is musically illiterate? Father Antonio has assured me numerous times that my true father was gifted musically, though not having ample time for his gift. There are times when I've felt that I must be from another world. Outside of my faith and my music, I was without belonging until you walked into the Duomo. I feel a part of this world now. My senses are alive. How can this be wrong, Orlando?"

Orlando loved her quiet passion. "It's not wrong. Vivaldi is obsessed with you, and you have seen life only from his viewpoint. Surely with a little more time, he'll understand that we love each other and that I'm trustworthy. Let me talk to him, Antonia." Orlando was passionate now. "In all my business dealings with the Estate and with the Palio, I've never known anyone to compare with him. I don't like his world. It's devious. But there must be a man of love and compassion under all the control. There must be, if he can create music as he does. Let me talk to him, Antonia; let me persuade him."

"No, Orlando, he has told me yet again that you and I shouldn't talk so frequently. 'My dear Anna,' he says, 'you must not lose your senses to any man. Orlando is a fine gentleman; but he must never be led to think that you are freer for more than an occasional discussion. You are betrothed to music, Anna!' He says I am betrothed to music, as though I were a nun, and yet he could never yield to full priesthood! There are stories about 'Vivaldi's secret'; but no one knows what his truth is. And yet, I love him! I love him very much. How can I think of hurting him?"

"Antonia, there will be a way for us; there will. Give me some time, and I'll convince your Maestro to see our love," Orlando turned Antonia to face him. "And while I work on that, we must find a place and time that are ours without others nearby. How can we do that? I need more time with you, Antonia. Alone." Orlando craved time. Antonia would leave for Venice after the Palio, and he could not abide the thought of her departure from Siena. Tilting her chin upwards, he gripped her shoulders strongly, "Look at me, Antonia—

look at me! I pledge to you there will be a way. Either your Maestro will give you his blessing or I'll devise a plan for you to stay here."

Antonia winced with the firmness of Orlando's grasp. "The answer lies in this place, Orlando," she became her cryptic self. "There is a way for us to be together more often."

Still gripping her shoulders, Orlando raised his voice, "This is no time for veiled messages, Antonia. Speak quickly before you're called back into the practice. I don't want to wait until you practise again. I want to know now. I must, Antonia!" Orlando's impatience startled Antonia.

"I'm not being obscure," she twisted her way out of his grasp. Who was this Orlando? "I've given this much thought and prayer. I don't make this suggestion lightly. My eagerness to come to Siena had to do with Saint Catherine, even more than it did with music. From my childhood, I've been drawn to her and to her life here in Siena so long ago. In a greater sense than what I feel for Father Antonio, I feel akin to her. And so, since our arrival in Siena, I have gone into San Domenico every Monday and Thursday at evensong. I then stay to meditate and listen."

"Antonia, why didn't you tell me this?" Orlando's impatience, verging on anger, surfaced again. "We could have been together more often! Why didn't you tell me?" Slapping his fist into his hand, he paced in anger. Then, recognizing the futility of this questioning, Orlando leaned against a buttress and breathed deeply. He stared fiercely at Antonia.

"This is precisely what I meant about understanding and honouring my suggestion." It was Antonia's turn to be impatient. This willful side of Orlando was entirely too much like the Maestro. "And you speak of the Maestro's need for control, Orlando Sagredo. You are no different from him right now! Let me have a voice here!" She stared, unflinching, at her lover. "I've prayed to Saint Catherine and to God about this. I've agonized over my thoughts. I wondered, even, if they were evil. However, I'm beginning to understand this love, Orlando. No one prepared me for the force of what I feel for you. I believe in beauty. Our love is beautiful. And so, as Saint Catherine is my spiritual mother, I'm daring as I would never have thought possible. I'm prepared to share my private prayer time with you. And, as I say this," Antonia heaved a breath greater than her singing ever demanded, "I cannot believe I am saying it. I'm frightened—frightened. This goes against anything I've ever been taught!"

Appeased, Orlando reached for her hands. "I understand. And I honour your choice. And I apologize for my anger; it wasn't directed at you. It was directed at the possibility of losing you to… to foolishness. You shall never regret this, Antonia. The future is ours. I don't take my own covenants, nor will I ever take yours, lightly." Orlando was silent for a moment. His voice was now quieter, but more deliberate, "I will not—I absolutely will not—lose you nor let you go, Antonia."

His voice found its way into the barren corners that not even music had ever been able to reach within Antonia. "Come to the next evensong, and to every one until I return to Venice, Orlando. I love you." Antonia wanted nothing more than to have the courage to declare her love. What better place could there be to reveal the truth than here? What better time than now?

"Anna! You are required here! Now!" Vivaldi called sharply. The sharp rapping of his bow against the podium followed his words.

Antonia stood quickly, her face ashen. Her world had come into collision with Orlando's, and she wanted his. She wanted his. She stood and moved into the aisle to walk toward the conductor of her life, still sensing Orlando's hand on her back. How would she ever be able to convince her Maestro that loving Orlando this way did not mean that she loved him, or music, less?

XVII

The Prioress was my bridge to everything. Without her, I'd have become a recluse. She was a beautiful woman, powerful both physically and spiritually. She was my beacon. And she was the only person—the only person—who really understood Father Antonio. A touch here, a word there, and he was enabled to bring stunning, virtuosic music into the world. Sister Paolina was midwife to the music. [Antonia, 1742]

"I spoke with Tiepolo today, after the rehearsal," Vivaldi and the Prioress sat in the garden of their hosts. The evening breeze was balmy and fragrant, a soothing presence as they talked about their day. "In fact, he approached me to ask me if we were happy with our stay here."

Paolina was jolted out of her serenity. Even the simple mention of this man's name sent fear coursing through her veins. Her intuition was strong about Tiepolo. She had long ago assessed him as devious and grasping; but in Siena, her thoughts turned to Antonia's safety. Why was she so important to him? It made no sense, given his lack of musical understanding. Only Antonia's beauty made sense. What was he after? Antonio, on the other hand, could be prey to any devious man promising musical power. And Tiepolo was such a predator. He manipulated the Maestro with promises of musical glory. There was a way this all fit into a scheme, she felt, and yet she had no information. All three of them—the Doge, Tiepolo and the Maestro—saw fame for Venice when they looked at Antonia. But the Envoy had a personal interest. She sensed it, and she knew his reputation. "I dislike that man, Antonio. In the few times I've been in his company, I've sensed nothing good in him. He is a big man who uses his size and strength to intimidate and win. He sees everything as competition. Why would he, who controls the Doge, be in the least interested in our pleasure? He has no love for music. In fact, he has no conception of it. What did he want?"

"Paolina! I have never heard you make such a harsh judgment! He was most gracious. I told him we were quite satisfied and asked him to thank Mocenigo for supporting us to come here," the Maestro was personally affronted by Paolina's criticism.

"Oh, Antonio, you are either so gullible or so centred on your music that you fail to see the motivation of people's behaviour," Paolina didn't know whether to be angry or stupefied. "Tiepolo and Mocenigo are interested only in their aggrandizement. You and Anna are here to bring fame to their Republic. Through you, Mocenigo can have all the pompous celebrations he craves, and Tiepolo can gain access to the reins of power. Your role is to make them look exemplary."

Irritated by Paolina's judgments, Vivaldi stood and began to pace. The shadows of the wisteria threw a sibylline mask over the Maestro's countenance. His movements exuded indignation. "Paolina, you are presumptuous! Mocenigo does care for us and for my music."

"Then, tell me what else Tiepolo asked about," Paolina was surprised at the intensity of her reaction.

Vivaldi blustered, "He wanted to know how Anna feels as well. And you. Yes... he wanted to be sure you are not finding you have too much time on your hands... that you are enjoying Siena. And," regaining equilibrium, the Maestro took a deep breath, "he said he has been told Sagredo is bothering Anna. There! You see! He does care about Anna and not merely about her gifts. He asked if you and I feel capable of protecting her from the advances of a young man with no lasting honourable intentions!" Vivaldi, vindicated by his own words, looked intently at Paolina, whose eyes conveyed disbelief. "You are wrong, my dear woman, so wrong!"

"Oh, no, my dear man, I am so right! So right! What business is it of his how I am doing? What business is it of his—and of the Doge—that Anna has a friendship with Orlando? How dare he cast Orlando in such a light, this Envoy with the duplicitous nature and motivations! I cannot believe that you have fallen into the snare, Antonio," Paolina, standing now to face the Maestro, was passionate in her defence of Anna. "What else did he want to know?"

Vivaldi backed away, shocked that Paolina could feel so strongly about an inconsequential discussion between two men. He took Paolina's hand, "Paolina, my dear, you are not yourself at times lately. I know when you're not feeling well. Please, sit down." Paolina acquiesced. "Truly, Paolina, this was a straightforward chat we had. Tiepolo was sincere. He sensed I have concerns—and you, too, know I have—about Anna's enchantment with Sagredo. Mocenigo sent him here to oversee Venice's contributions to Siena's celebrations. That is all that this was, Paolina—a mere assessment. Why do you have such an intense dislike for the man?"

"I have seen him since he came to power, Antonio. I have watched him on many occasions."

The Maestro derided her, "My dear, he did not 'come to power'. The Doge did. And Mocenigo is certainly not a powerful man. I often feel he should be more confident and directive. There is no problem with power here!"

Paolina looked directly into Vivaldi's eyes, a look he knew as prelude to a directive. "Listen to me, Antonio. And believe me. I know whereof I speak. Dante Tiepolo is a dangerous, avaricious man. He has claimed the Doge as his gateway to power within the Republic. He will make the Republic his, if he can. He is already working on power within the Procuratori. And he will not stop there. I hear information from my sources, too. Do not trust him. He is the one who must be kept away from Anna. As for Sagredo, he is the perfect opposite of Tiepolo… and, by the way, Tiepolo would see Orlando as a competitor. Sagredo does have honourable intentions. The Envoy would quite simply enjoy the conquest of a beautiful young woman."

Vivaldi sat down beside the Prioress. "Paolina, we will talk no further about Tiepolo. Nor will we talk about the Doge."

The argument spent, the peculiar couple gazed over the garden.

Silence prevailed as the imperceptible breeze slipped through the wisteria. Paolina Giraud had trespassed into a political territory that had long forbidden her footprints. Now that she had attempted a few tentative steps, she knew she would only jeopardize Anna's situation by daring to return. She must support Anna in other ways.

* * *

Antonia, a shadow darting along the wall of the cloister, stopped and turned toward the grounds of San Domenico. She needed to be so careful in this second rendezvous with Orlando. Had she heard something? She was sure she had.

"Antonia! Antonia, come this way!"

Yes, Orlando was calling her, his voice barely above a whisper. Confused, she moved along the side of the cloister toward the voice. "Orlando, what are you doing?"

"Over here, Antonia… over here."

There he was, in the long evening shadows of the big tree near the well. "What are you doing, Orlando? You were to be waiting at the back door!" Afraid someone would somehow hear her, she was relieved to reach Orlando. "Why are you here?"

Orlando laughed and kissed her. "You're coming with me to the estate. My horse is waiting for us by the fence. Come," he reached for her hand and began leading her down the incline.

"Orlando, you're insane. We cannot do this!" Antonia wrenched her hand from Orlando's grasp and stood still. "What has possessed you?"

"You!" Again, Orlando laughed. "Antonia, you need to see more of the world. You need to see where I live. That's all. You'll be safe; I've planned this well. And I'll have you back here with no one knowing you've been gone."

Antonia stared at Orlando. This was recklessness. And yet, more than anything in the world, she wanted him. She wanted his passion, his strength, his touch. When she was in his presence, nothing mattered. But, after Siena, after the music here, there would be nothing. "Please—this frightens me!"

"Trust me. I would never let anything happen to you. I'd never jeopardize your safety. I'll have you to my property and back before dusk. Our estate isn't far out of the town walls."

Antonia's fear became anger. "You didn't ask me about this. You've given me no time to prepare. It wouldn't be right; I would have to lie. I'm already lying. What will happen if I am caught?"

"If I'd asked you, Antonia, you would have said no. And you would have retreated from me. I couldn't risk that. I saw this as the best way for you to understand me more... to understand life more. Come. I'm asking you to do something I know will be good for you. Come and see the olive trees. And the grape vines. Come into the countryside. My countryside."

As she looked into Orlando's eyes, she felt a new energy... and excitement. "Yes, I am coming with you! Orlando," her musical laughter tumbled into the evening air, "I want to!"

"Then, take my hand, and run with me, Antonia." The horse whinnied. There he was just down the hill tied to a tree.

Antonia grasped Orlando's hand and ran with him, down to the horse. "I've never ridden a horse. I've never dared to come this close to one." She stepped back.

Orlando steadied the animal and grasped Antonia's waist. "I'll lift you up... trust me, Antonia," he could feel the apprehension in her body. "Hold his neck and let your legs stay down at his side." Once Antonia was settled, he mounted the animal, "Lean back against me. Forget about the horse and trust me." He pulled his cloak around her. "No one will see you now, and you'll still catch glimpses of the countryside along the way. We'll be on my property before you have time to be frightened. All right? We're off!"

Orlando took the horse slowly down to the Porta Fontebranda. Once they were through the gate and outside the old wall, he commanded the horse into a gallop. And off they sped to the Sagredo estate and to the nascence of grapes and olives. Antonia, at last, would see into his world.

XVIII

*I remember Father Antonio telling me the story of Juditha when
I was twelve. He had just finished his opera about her. Giacomo
Cassetti wrote the libretto, as he had done before for the Maestro. I was surprised he had chosen a heroine to celebrate Venice's
victory at Corfu over the Ottoman Empire. "Anna," he said to
me, "Anna, you can grow up to be a significant musician. This is
not easy for a woman. But you can do it, my dear. You can—like
Juditha!" He was passionate about that. I knew he loved me and
wanted fame to prove my talent... and his, for having formed me.
My grief was that he did not see me as a separate human being.
He saw me as Juditha, as Anna and as extinguished Antonia.
[Antonia, 1743]*

"An excellent practice—worthy of a performance! Thank you."
The Maestro had just looked over his shoulder to be certain Sagredo
was leaving the Duomo. He'd go to wait for Anna in the garden.
Well, it would be a long wait today. Anna had been far too happy
and talkative lately after her vespers in the Basilica. "Anna, will you
stay for a moment, please?" The rest of the instrumentalists straggled into the nave.

Antonia felt irritated. She was impatient to meet Orlando on such
a beautiful day, with the practice over earlier than expected.

"Anna, come and sit down. I want to talk with you," the Maestro
looked ill-at-ease.

Antonia felt a resentment rise within her. No, it's anger! He
knows I want to see Orlando. And he dislikes that! Well, I dislike
being his eternal nine year old! She sat beside the composer.

"Anna, this is difficult; but it must be done," he looked earnestly
into her clear eyes and held her unyielding hand. He saw that he
would receive no emotional assistance from her. "My dear, you

know I have had concerns about your talking with the Sagredo fellow..."

"You mean Orlando," her three words cut through the chimera she was being offered.

"Well... yes... all right... Orlando. This young man... Orlando... is not good... is not...," Antonia refused still to offer any assistance to the Maestro's bumbling. "Anna, I shall just come out with it! He stands in the way of your music!"

Antonia was nonplussed, her eyes wide and disbelieving. She had not expected to hear something so ridiculous. Finding her voice, she stood up and spoke quietly but sharply, "Father Antonio, I have no idea what you mean! He 'stands in the way' of my music? Orlando is a champion of my music! He understands me and my music more than anyone has ever understood them." Antonia immediately realized she had committed the unpardonable sin; but she could not now undo it. She had placed another human being above the one who saw himself as ultimate in her life. Never mind! It was the truth!

Vivaldi, fuming, stood to face his protégée. They glared at each other.

Antonia broke the turbulent silence. "Why do you want to control me, Father? Why can you not be happy for me?"

Sensing the distress in her anger, Vivaldi softened. He reached again for her hand. She put it behind her back. "It is not only I, Anna, who am concerned. I have spoken to your Prioress about this. And the concern actually originates with the Doge's Envoy. He approached me a few days ago to say that you have been seen outside the Duomo—in the garden of all places!—sitting and talking with Sagredo. Anna—how could you! You are now seen as an embarrassment to Venice. And—there is a report that you and Sagredo kissed. But I know that is an evil rumour. I know you, Anna, and I know you would not stoop to such behaviour."

Antonia felt love lurch into a distortion of itself. What was so wrong? How could the beauty of her love be made ugly at worst, commonplace at best? No, she would not leave it this way. She would speak up for herself and for Orlando. "Father Antonio, will you please listen to me? Listen to me, and hear the truth. Yes, I have met Orlando in the garden. You know the garden is a sacred place for me. Yes, I do love Orlando, and yes, he loves me. You know I would not choose foolishly. You have raised me to be prudent... and loving. I have learned love from both you and Sister Paolina. Please trust me. Please let me love Orlando!"

"But, Anna, my dear, you know me, as well," Vivaldi now stood directly under the vaulted ceiling. The mid-day sun shimmered over the painted stars and down onto the marble floor. "Look, my Anna, look! This sphere of light is God's light shining on my music and on your part in it. Do not wander from this light!"

Antonia stood in the light, wanting to smash the constraints of piety and pride. "No, Father, you have the direction wrong! We must try to reach God's light. He does not shine his light on our prideful attempts to be Him. We make attempts to catch His Light. That is all—attempts!" Antonia was luminous, her hair on fire.

"But, Anna, you know you are where you are because of me. I have given you life! Your talents would have been lost, but for me. If it were not for me, you would be either married or in a convent. You would not know music as you do. Music is your soul, Anna. You must not abandon it!" The passion of the conversation was beginning to play havoc with the Maestro's breathing. He sat down, wheezing, his hands on his knees, his head slightly bent.

Antonia sat beside him and put her arm around him, her hand finding its familiar pathway to a gentle stroking of his back,

"Breathe slowly, Father. We have become too impassioned. Breathe slowly."

As it always had, Vivaldi's breath responded to Antonia's soothing words and touch. The Maestro sat back, "I do not like to have words with you, Anna. Anna, do you truly see me as prideful? I hope not, my dear; it is something I guard against."

Antonia felt the weighty weariness born of the numerous silences that had been placed upon her. How could she hurt this man, this man who had loved her more than many fathers love their own children? "No, Father Antonio. I only meant that you... and I... need to see God in more than music. I know you want only the best for me," she took her hand from the Maestro's back. "And I... I want... need you to see that Orlando is part of what is good for me."

"Anna, have I not known always what is best for you, often when you have felt otherwise?" And with that, Antonia knew she could go no further.

"We are done, then, Father?" Antonia stood to leave.

Vivaldi, surprised by her detachment from him, stood and took both of her hands lovingly, and looked down at the connection he could not bear to surrender. Pulling her hands to his chest, he looked into her eyes, "Anna, let Orlando go. Please, let him go."

An unbearable grief swelled from deep inside Antonia. As it broke through her chest, she sobbed and pulled her hands away. Her anger turned to ice.

"Anna," Vivaldi, tearful, reached out for her.

Antonia ran out to the garden where she and Orlando were to have met. Their time together had been stolen by the Maestro. Stolen! Orlando would be at his meeting. But he would understand. Wouldn't he? He would know the Maestro had upstaged them. Wouldn't he? Pacing around their bench, she stopped and looked up to the God she needed. "Please help me," she cried into the dazzling blue wall of separation.

* * *

"I find it unconscionable that anyone should have that much control over a young woman," Francesca Sagredo sat with her son in what Antonia had named the "Greening Place". The dancing of the bright sun and the leaves sent white and silver splashes over their faces.

A shaft of light cut through two thick branches and caught Orlando's eyes. He shaded his eyes and looked out over the valley. "This is what I want for her, Mother... this valley, this land and freedom. Antonia has never known real freedom. She was selected as uniquely talented in the orphanage. And that ultimately made her advanced over any other woman in Italy within the world of music. But that world is utterly sheltered for a female. She's purity and vulnerability, Mother, like a work of art herself. She doesn't know it; but under that applied veneer is tremendous strength. I want nothing more than to be with her for the rest of my life, to see her flourish, to..." Orlando looked over at his mother. "I know what you're thinking. I have changed, I agree!"

Francesca's gentle laughter merged with her son's, "You have! Where is the man who was beginning to talk of marriage as an economic union? Where is the man who was beginning to scoff at the 'notion' of love, as you called it?" She put her arm around her son and rested her head on his shoulder, "I'm so happy for you. You deserve this as much as she."

"But I find it so frustrating," Orlando stood. He picked up a stone and threw it into the valley. "I'm not a patient man. And Vivaldi is trying my patience. Antonia asks for understanding for him. I want to talk to him, frankly and honestly—brutally at times—and get this thing over and done with. I'm not used to dealing with people whose temperaments are so prized, in their own eyes, that they will not communicate directly. After all, music is a business for him. He should treat it that way." Orlando tossed another stone even further than the first. "I know he kept Antonia behind today to put me in my place. How pitiful that he hurts the one he professes to love in order to be more powerful than the one she loves. Pathetic!" Orlando turned to his mother. "I hate feeling this powerless. I've had to move into unknown terrain with Antonia. The politics of music! And the politics of Venice with its artifice. My God! Give me a good straightforward fight or race any day!"

"Come and sit down again, and we can think this through clearly together. You won't find any wisdom for yourself by throwing stones and being frustrated. Use your business mind. If this part is business, you cannot let your emotions rule," Orlando sat again and took in the vista. "You are clever in business; look at this as though it were business. Vivaldi is the volatile, temperamental wine-grower with the highest quality Barolo, and you want it. In this instance, you, Orlando Sagredo, would get it—with honour and integrity. Think. Be ten steps ahead of Vivaldi and the Venetian court. Your grandfather left Venice, routed by its pretenses and disguises. I know our name still has power within the Court of the Doge. Well, they are in our territory now, Orlando. You can be strategic here. What needs to be done?" Francesca's strength and determination were contagious. Orlando was intrigued, always, by this capacity of his mother. She was, indeed, a powerful partner for his father.

"Well, clearly, Antonia needs to stay in Siena. If she returns to Venice, she will be prevented from returning to me. This is not simply a fear; this is a fact. And obviously, Vivaldi and Venice want her in Venice. Antonia wants to be with me; but she is afraid to act against Vivaldi's wishes. Antonia loves me and is beginning to move out of Vivaldi's control. And, from what I hear, the Prioress is Antonia's advocate and protector," Orlando stood and looked at his mother. "Come, Mother, it's time to make plans for Antonia to stay here with me. So... what needs to be done? Antonia needs to stay with us, and she and I need to be together. It's as simple as that."

Francesca took her son's hand and stood, "And as complicated as that, my son!"

The mother and her tall, powerful first-born began walking back to the house.

"Would you feel all right supporting this, Mother? Antonia will have to live with us until plans for a wedding can be made."

Francesca put her arm through her son's arm and ambled with him across the estate. As their steps stirred up a bouquet of herbal fragrances, Orlando was reminded more acutely of Antonia. How she had loved it here—she belonged here! It was almost as if he could touch her in this moment, as if he could see again the tears glimmering on her face while he had led her—softly, tenderly, rhythmically—into consummation.

"You will love her, Mother," Orlando stirred from his reverie. "She has a lovely child-like quality; but she is very strong... and normally very quiet. Vivaldi controls—or tries to control—all of her strengths. But her greatest strength—music—has saved her, though, as well as placing her under his control. If she had not displayed such monumental talent, she would have been the perfect Novice by now, lost in some convent for eternity. I can see her loving this place, fitting in easily, enjoying all of us. I can even see Father becoming enchanted with her."

Francesca chuckled, "Then she must be enchanting! Your brother and Alessandra are still wondering if Alessandra will be fully accepted into the family. Orlando," Francesca stopped and turned toward her son, "Orlando, I know we shall all love Antonia. I'm beginning to feel already as if I know her. After four sons, two daughters—Antonia and Alessandra! Look, there's Carlo shouting at us. He probably needs you back for the Palio preparations."

Orlando embraced his mother, "Thank you, Mother. You are the best mother in the world—I've always said that!" And he picked Francesca up and spun her around.

As they laughed on their way back to the house, Orlando sensed the echo of Antonia's musical laughter join in with theirs. And he knew it would not be long for that laughter to take up residence in the Sagredo Estate. They were meant to be together—and they would be together. Nothing would stand in their way. He would see to that.

QUATTRO

THE PALIO TO VENICE

1725

XIX

*Had Siena not done away with its Pagan roots? Its celebration of
the Palio seemed so profane in some ways; not in the idea of the
races as such, but in all the other fuss and furor, as though the
horses allowed people to practise idolatry. I suppose it was more
the frenzy I found disturbing, much as I had experienced in the
Festa. And then one day, I began to laugh at myself. It was fear
that kept me bound this way, that made me frightened to open up
and celebrate with these people... fear that made me judge. I'd
had a sudden realization that the whole of Roman Christendom
had been built over—physically on top of—Roman idols! Saint
Catherine's sarcophagus in Saint Maria sopra Minerva in Roma,
I said to myself, is built upon the Pagan Temple of Minerva. I
laughed aloud when the realization came upon me—and I found
it very liberating. [Antonia, 1747]*

Lily-of-the-valley had given way to the Julian illusions of jasmine. Siena scintillated. Antonia was caught up in a dream as she
walked along with her Maestro. She felt detached from him and
from all the Venetian masquerades that directed their lives. Tomorrow she would see Orlando lead the competition.

Il Duce, they called him, their Captain. Orlando had been planning since last year's Palio and, now that the parades had begun, the
process assumed shape. Suddenly Antonia felt proud of him. This
was a monumental task, with a lengthy tradition. He had managed
to introduce fine music into the grand scheme. He had told her of
his close friend, Lorenzo, and their discussions about art and music. As she realized the extent of Orlando's work, Antonia saw that
Lorenzo had actually been instrumental in getting her to Siena. She
must meet him one day and thank him. And now, the final preparations had been carried out this morning with pomp and noisy

activity. What more could happen for excitement? For Antonia, the immediacy of the Palio preparations was a refreshing contrast to the secrecy and conceit of Venetian customs. For hundreds of years here in Siena, seventeen neighbourhoods, the Contrade, had met to compete against each other, form alliances and win. Competition was fierce. Ritual was paramount. Music, drums, shouting and cannon were mandatory components.

Initially, Antonia had found the atmosphere profane. In particular, the music was primitive, unsophisticated. The Piazza del Campo, the very Madonna's skirt, was festooned with the vibrant flags and emblems of the Contrade and inhabited by small musical groups, jesters, wandering families and magnificent horses and horsemen. The air was redolent with the sweet and the savoury and punctuated with the articulation of mandolins and flageolets. How far this all was from the honouring of the Madonna for which it had been created?

Or was it? Was it further from—or closer to—honouring her? Was it, perhaps... with its inclusive structure and its place for everyone... more reverent, even with its crudeness? Orlando had taken that crudeness and wedded it with culture. Skilful man. Antonia's thoughts of Orlando raised her anxiety again.

I cannot let myself be distracted from the excitement of this celebration by my fears, Antonia reassured herself. I must not think about losing Orlando. Saint Catherine, I implore you to give me a miracle. I did not know happiness until I loved him. Feeling disoriented, Antonia turned toward the Sagredo family's headquarters. Yes, Orlando and she would meet there. She must remind herself that Orlando was in charge—not the Maestro and certainly not the Doge's Envoy. She began to wonder what this Tiepolo looked like and where he might be at this moment. He was the unknown spectre. He was the one she was afraid of. Never mind, Orlando will always be close by.

Flaunting its adornments, a horse pranced by. Antonia was certain she felt the hot breath from its rude snorting! Fearful again, she looked for her Maestro. Although she still felt angry at him, she should never leave him alone in a crowd like this. But here he was, just behind her! "Father, do the horses frighten you?"

"No, my dear. Come over this way. You seem distracted today! You haven't heard what I've told you. I want you to understand this spectacle, albeit a rather uncivilized one. You will not likely ever experience it again. All of these flags represent neighbourhood areas of Siena. The horses are identified by the areas. Do you see the one over there... behind the table that is being set up? Look at its flag... it represents the Oyster! Look at all the work that has gone into the ornamentations. You sing music. They sew and paint it! Wonderful! Are you enjoying yourself, dear child?"

"Oh, yes, Father Antonio, I am!" Why had she worried about him? He was more comfortable in Siena than she! "I love it all! I'm even able to tolerate the music!" Antonia laughed. How could she be angry at this man who wanted the best for her? If only he could understand that Orlando was the best for her. But then, what did the wheezing priest know about passionate and pure love between a man and a woman? He who had known no woman.

Antonia stopped in her tracks. "Maestro, have you ever been in love?"

Vivaldi's face turned the colour of his red hair. "Anna! Domine!" the Maestro crossed himself. "How impertinent of you! What would ever make you ask me—me, of all people!—a question like that?" His breathing became shallower.

"Oh, Father, I am so sorry. I don't know what came over me; I truly do not. I should never have asked that question. Please forgive me. Come! Shall we go see the horses?"

Antonia had bewildered and shocked herself. Where had her audacity come from? She rushed the Maestro into the centre of Piazza del Campo. The great bell rang out the hour. Antonia looked up at the massive tower. Its imposing shadow seemed almost human to her. She realized she loved this orange town with its belief in wild festivity. "Eight bells, Father Antonio. Tomorrow at this time, we shall watch the Palio begin! Thank you for bringing me to this strange and wonderful place, thank you!"

She turned again to see the Sagredo building where Orlando and his brothers would stay tonight. Orlando had told her about the back entrance to the traditional Sagredo competition quarters. "I stay on the third floor in the room at the head of the rear staircase," he'd told her.

As Antonia and the Maestro began to wander through the Piazza toward the alleyway, Antonia thought of her time with Orlando last night.

She had learned so much from him, about what love really was meant to be. Yes, she knew she loved him. She had realized it when he had explained his love to her. It was as if he had been talking about his own significance in her heart. She felt one with him the way she felt one with music. She believed they shared the same soul.

"This is the beginning, not the end," Antonia whispered to herself.

* * *

They had ridden out again the previous evening to his property.

Antonia remembered the delicious perfume of grapes and herbs as it floated across the vineyards. This was freedom. This was abundance. "I love it here, Orlando! It's beautiful. And rich. I shall call it your greening place."

She knelt to smell some stray lavender. In that moment, Antonia knew her place in a world that had often felt so alien to her. Her place was with this man. Orlando would be her teacher, her lover, her partner. She and he were as fundamental to each other as the lavender was to the earth.

Orlando placed his hands on her shoulders, "Antonia, stay with me. Now. I can't abide even the thought of your returning to Venice. You must stay in Siena. I want you more than I've ever wanted anyone; I want you in my life—at my side, in my bed, joined with me—always. Now, Antonia."

Rising, Antonia took hold of the strong hands she loved and placed them on her breasts. Looking into Orlando's eyes, a subtle fugue born of a soft breeze, she moved first to his lips and then into his powerful embrace, fully trusting. Orlando, Antonia's Il Duce, undressed her. Slowly, tenderly, powerfully, revealing the mystery of their bond, he inhabited the beautiful woman who taken over his life.

* * *

"This way, Anna—be careful of the horses!" The Maestro seized her elbow. Her reverie, bent and snapped into time by her Maestro, disappeared with the pounding of the hooves that matched the thudding in her chest. The smell of horses colluded with the dissonance of the crowd, irritating Antonia.

"You really must pay more attention today, my dear. You will be injuring your wrist in a fall if you continue to be so inattentive.

There now, we are safe. Is it not truly exciting that we shall perform the 'Magnificat' tonight!"

Vivaldi looked directly at his protégée, "Domine! Anna, my dear child, you are crying! Did you hurt yourself—it's not your wrist, is it? My dear?"

"No, no, Maestro; something flew into my eye when I was looking at the horses. It's gone. Truly, I'm fine. Let us think about the rehearsal. You have only two hours to work our new Venetians in with the rest of us. I hope they aren't too tired after their journey. Some of the girls are so young. They were noisy at the convent in the evening. I'd like the 'Alma Oppressa' to come before the 'Magnificat'; I think it's more fitting there."

"Well, yes, Anna, you may be correct about that. You seem to have sharpened the dynamics over the past few days. Sheer perfection, my dear."

Each lost in separate considerations of music, Antonia and Vivaldi walked quietly from the Marketplace and up the street. Worlds apart in their conception of love and freedom, their love of music was all in this moment that they had together. Antonia realized, for the first time, the abyss that now existed between them.

As they approached practice, the massive shadow of the Duomo swallowed the two composers. And all that was left of Antonia's yearning to tell Father Antonio about her love... to have him understand and bless it... was silence.

XX

There's a madness inherent in invention. Great inventors use their madness to create something completely new. Father Antonio, the Red Priest, Maestro Vivaldi, was an inventor. He was not only a composer. He invented new music that took the violin to its furthest edges, that stretched the soul into the Heavens and taxed the voice. And when the Lustrous took over as in 'Alma Oppressa' or in the Concerto in A Minor, there was a danger the consummate performer might not be able to finish. Was his madness to see how far he could push the edges before God intervened? Was he attempting to meet God, to force His hand? Was the answer to his reluctant priesthood contained within that form of arrogance? Or did he know God could not be contained by or within anything... not even music? Did that, in a sense, drive him mad at times? [Antonia, 1744]

Antonio Vivaldi crumpled another sheet of manuscript and threw it on the floor. The flame of the candle flickered wildly in response to his irritated sigh. Yet again, he ran his fingers through his red hair and rocked back on the hind legs of his chair. "Domine! Why can I not get past this pattern?" He spoke to himself.

Leaning forward, he pulled another sheet toward him and dipped his pen in the ink. This time he would write the Introduzione to the second act over and over again, without stopping, until what appeared before him was exactly what he had heard in his head during practice this afternoon. He would force his mind to remember and engage in the feelings he had had. Wonderful, madding feelings. Conducting the Kyrie and hearing a new act pressing, pressing to be born.

But no! His mind refused... was scattered! What was he doing in this strange town, this once major enemy of Venice... and Florence?

And why had he ever thought this would be a good experience for Antonia? Even his music was rebelling against being here.

He stood and walked over to his window, pulling the curtain aside. Twilight. And all was still in the Piazza. Basilica San Domenico stared back at him, as unyielding as ever. And as dissimilar to the Duomo as sacred buildings could be. It was like comparing the Torcello and San Marco basilicas at home! From somewhere out to his left a man shouted and a door slammed shut. He dropped the curtain and walked back to his desk.

His room and its atmosphere certainly were more than pleasant, the art surrounding him of the finest Sienese order. No, he truly could not complain about how the Sienese were treating him. Indeed, everything was most conducive to composing.

Everything, of course, except the invasion by that scoundrel Sagredo. That was it! That was the block! And Anna believing she was in love with him!

Suddenly, he was overcome with grief. The pain was strong in his chest, this pain of Anna. Had anyone told him that this might happen, he would have laughed and blithely tossed the remark into the air. Not his Anna—never would she choose a man over music. Ah, dear God, there was so much ahead of her musically. And she was ready to abandon it all!

And here he was, Antonio Vivaldi who could command orchestras into unity, and he could achieve no harmony these days with Anna. He turned toward the mirror behind his desk. It would give him some semblance of the truth. Yes, here he was as crumpled as his manuscript, his shirt undone, his sleeves rolled up and his hair looking as though he had been blown in from some shipwreck.

Yes, that was what he felt like. A shipwreck. Anna would abandon him and so, apparently, would his music. Mutiny!

His music gone—evaporated... music lost in the air....

Music! Yes! His music! Yes! He had it now! Yes! Praise be!

The Maestro picked up another candlestick and held it to be lit from the other on his desk. Seated again, he picked up his pen. The Music, his new creation, was back! His brain resounded with it all! His hand flew across the lines. Notes poured out upon the page and upon each other. His hand and mind could barely keep up with what was being born. Black marks that carried the map to the Santo Grail of composition. Lines and notes, bars and dots, flourishes and rest marks took their places as Music herself commanded. Vivaldi could barely tolerate the sounds in his head, all of them demanding attention and perfect placement as they hung on the paper, waiting to breathe, wanting to reverberate in space the way they rang in his head.

Domine! Would his hand please keep up with his mind, this hand that sometimes ached! This hand that he needed for the violin... for conducting.... This opera must have all the space in eternity it now demanded. And how would the instruments be weighted properly to carry it forth on its journey?

Write, dip, write, dip... flick the hair out of the way... write, dip... blow the manuscript dry... write, compose, compose... would to God he could breathe it all out onto the paper! The ink found its way from the bottle to the pen to the paper and onto his face and hands the way the music found its way from his soul to his musicians to the public. And, above all, to God! Domine! To God!

And it was done!

Spent, the Maestro threw his arms down from the desk, pushed his feet forward under the desk and let his head fall backward. The papers were strewn about him... on the floor, on the desk... one in his lap.

Finally, a deep breath... ah... the aftermath. He was dizzy, excited, overwhelmed. How could he draw his energy back into himself and contain himself again? Where... where was she? Should he call her? Should... ah—yes... yes—there were the strong hands he knew so well, rubbing his shoulders and moving down his back.

"Ah, Paolina," he put his hand over hers on his shoulder, "how long have you been there?"

"Probably for an hour now," she began stroking his back. "I've been watching it happen... I knew you could do it, Antonio. It happens so rarely that I think it frightens you more than it would most composers when you become trapped. Your distress is gone... I'm glad."

"Yes. I was very worried this time. Until I realized that it was my sadness over Antonia. What time is it?"

Paolina laughed gently, "It is well past bed-time... almost midnight. That is why I came in. Look at the candles you have used. Come," she gave his neck one last kneading and put his jacket around his shoulders, "you must retire for the night."

Vivaldi stood up. "She must stop her interest in Sagredo, Paolina. She must! Will she listen to you?"

"Antonio, go to bed now. All the talk in the world will not change things. If we know anything, we know that by now." Clasping his lapels, she pulled his jacket more tightly around him and kissed him on the forehead, "Go off to sleep with this new music in your heart and be grateful. I must be off to bed myself."

The Maestro took both of her hands in his and scrutinized them, "You are right. The music is wonderful, you know! Act Two is finished. Yes—finished! One more act will do it," he kissed her hands and let her go. "Thank you, as ever, Paolina. Sleep well."

Watching her walk down the hall to her quarters, Vivaldi felt grateful for this woman of beauty and stability in his life. He closed the door and walked back to the desk. As he gathered the papers into neater order, they began to sing to him.

He sat down again. At the moment that he picked up his pen, the bell of San Domenico pealed twelve times. He dipped the pen in the ink. Just one or two little adjustments...

XXI

The longer I stayed in Siena, the more I craved land beneath my feet for the rest of my life. And the more I desired my Orlando in my bed for the rest of my life. [Antonia, 1749]

A hush spread through the prattling audience as Venice's star soloist walked onto the small stage erected in the Duomo. Antonia, her face a cameo in the black cape, turned and bowed. She sat as prima violinista and removed the cape, dropping it over the back of her chair. With her red hair, her beauty and composure, she was stunning. People whispered and then settled as Antonia began to tune the orchestra. Sitting in front row, centre, Orlando marvelled at the command Antonia's presence had over the audience. She had told him that the acoustic would be best mid-way in the Duomo; but he had preferred to choose his seat on the basis of vision and proximity. Certainly, he had seen her at practice often. And certainly, no one appreciated her beauty more than he. But he had not been prepared to see her in her own milieu before an audience. She was composed, secure and utterly beautiful. It would be very important for Antonia to maintain music in her life. He could see that at a much more essential level now.

The bell of Siena called into the Duomo eight times.

A deeper, more expectant hush fell over the audience as they waited for the Red Priest.

Vivaldi walked briskly onto the podium, bowed theatrically in acknowledgment of the applause and turned toward the small, hand-picked orchestra. Raising his hands and looking keenly into the eye of the orchestra, the Maestro de'Concerti brought the audience into the perfect hush of expectancy.

As soon as the voice of Antonia's violin took charge in the opening Allegro of "Le Quattro Stagioni", Orlando knew that he had lost

Antonia to the power of music. And he was lost... lost in her... lost in her tender awakening in Spring... in the wild tempest of her Summer... in her dance with the flying leaves of Autumn... and finally, ultimately, lost in her, lost with her, lost without her in her descent into the death of winter. No! She wouldn't stay there! Orlando could feel the arguments between Maestro and La Stella, as Antonia questioned, besought, ran from the conductor of her life. Surprised, he could hardly bear the tension. Had she won at the end? Yes! Yes—Antonia looked directly at him, as she dropped her violin and her bow to her side. As their eyes met briefly, he knew that she was telling him she was his.

The audience soared in a unified ovation, climaxing into a cascade of bravos as Antonia was directed to stand and bow. The Maestro wiped his brow. Always, in the final exhilaration of a concert, he experienced a divine forgiveness.

As the applause gave way, Antonia slipped into her black cloak and stood. The Pieta orphans filed onstage. They and the original orchestra were then augmented by Siena's best in castrati voices, countertenors and instrumentalists. The audience puffed with Sienese pride.

From the opening perfectly pitched surge of B falling to E and flowing from the woman's soul, the audience gave itself over to Vivaldi's creative genius and to God's most unrelenting manifestation. Oppressed souls were saved and magnified the Lord.

As Antonia, with two Sienese, a castrati and a countertenor, completed God's promise to all forefathers, she came to herself, feeling Orlando's eyes upon her. Feeling as though she were with him, she performed more strongly than she ever had. "Gloria Patri, gloria Filio, et Spiritui sancto" ascended and burst through the resplendence of the Duomo ceiling. "As it was in the beginning, is now, and ever shall be, love without end, Amen," the orphan heard herself sing. For she sang only to Orlando.

* * *

As Vivaldi and the rest of the musical troupe left the Duomo to be feted at the elaborate tables in the Campo, Antonia slipped out the side door. She was under instructions from the Maestro to return to the convent and rest. Instead, she and Orlando had seized upon this time as an opportunity to meet. Orlando would be a gracious presence in the Campo for a short time and then excuse himself. He also would need rest. After all, the Palio always began much earlier for him than for anyone else.

Antonia found her way cautiously in the shadows around the periphery of the Campo to the Sagredo building. Orlando would meet her here, near the back door. She pulled her cape more tightly around her and walked down the lane.

Had she heard something? She stopped and listened. It was her imagination. She began walking again.

A hand gripped her elbow. She stopped, terrified.

"My dear young woman! After a performance like that, how can you place your voice and your bowing arm in danger like this? All alone on the back streets of Siena." The voice was dark and sonorous.

Antonia could not see him well. She could make out the form of a tall man, hooded. She pulled her arm away. "Who are you—you have no right to touch me!"

"My dear, I have every right to touch you. And I must say it is a most pleasant right!" He laughed. "You may never have met me before; but you know me. I am Dante Tiepolo, your Envoy, your admirer, at your service."

"I need no service, sir." Antonia stepped further back, colliding with a wall. "Would you please leave me! Go!... or...."

"Or what, dear lady," the Envoy laughed loudly, "you will scream? No one will hear you over the noise from the Campo. You will tell your Maestro? I think not! You are going to tell him I accosted you on your way to the Sagredo quarters? Laughable!" He moved closer to Antonia and whispered into her ear. "Ah, bella donna, I have long wanted to be close to you like this. It would be so easy to have you now." He pinned her wrists to the wall.

Antonia turned her head and tried desperately to push him away. "Leave me alone!" She screamed, "Please leave me alone!"

Tiepolo turned her face toward him, holding her jaw and forcing her further against the wall, "You will listen to me now, Anna Giraud. Your every move is because I have brought it about for you. And you flaunt your powers in my face every time you see Sagredo, every time you undress for him. And, don't think about your Maestro. Should you tell him about our encounter—which I doubt you will—I shall deny it all. And he will believe me. As for me, I shall tell him nothing of this. To do so would be to sabotage my own plans. Do you understand me?"

Antonia nodded her head. As Tiepolo tried to kiss her again, she managed to push him away and kick him.

"Whore!" He clutched his knee and reached for her.

Antonia jumped back. "You are a vile man!"

Infuriated, Tiepolo limped toward her. "No one orders me to do or not to do anything!"

Knowing that she could out-distance him while his knee held him back, Antonia ran the length of the alley and to the back of the Sagredo building. She ran up to the door and banged against it with her fists.

"Antonia!"

His voice! She knew his footsteps approaching from the alley as he approached her. Antonia fell into Orlando's arms.

"Antonia, Antonia, what happened?" He held her tightly. "Everything is all right now. I'm here." He kissed the top of her head.

"Oh, Orlando, I was so frightened! Someone followed me from the performance." As Orlando moved to go to the alley, Antonia needed time to think. She held his wrist. I cannot tell him what happened... not yet... our plans are too important. "No, Orlando! There is no sense looking for him now. He will be back at the Campo. I think it was Dante Tiepolo," Antonia held onto Orlando desperately.

"Did he touch you... harm you, Antonia? If he did...."

"No, Orlando! No! I feel safe now. I am safe now. All I want is to be together with you, and that will happen tomorrow," she breathed deeply and looked up at Orlando. "Kiss me, Orlando, and everything will be all right."

Slipping her hood off and brushing her hair away from her face, Orlando kissed her on the forehead. "If anyone ever harms you... if that Tiepolo ever touches you, I will kill him, Antonia." He kissed her tenderly on the lips, "Come, Antonia. Up to my room."

Orlando slipped the latch and followed his lover up the narrow staircase. Never would she be without his protection again. He would rout the Venetians.

* * *

"Were you not so very proud of our Anna tonight, Paolina?" Antonia listened to the nighttime voices of her Pietan childhood. She had slipped into bed only moments before the Prioress and Vivaldi returned from the celebration. All she could think of was how comforted she felt now. Surely Father Antonio did not know the nature of the man who controlled Venice. Were he to learn of the incident tonight, he would cease any relationship with Tiepolo. Wouldn't he? "We must protect her."

"Antonio, you must know that she loves the eldest Sagredo. How can we, of all people, stand in the way of a love like theirs?"

"Because, Paolina, we are protecting a far greater beauty for the glory of God—for the glory of God, dear woman. I must be off to bed myself now. I shall sleep with the angels tonight. Anna seems to have a way of attracting them. Good night for now."

The Prioress was quiet for a moment. Antonia needed to hear her voice before she could settle. "Good night, Antonio. You have indeed made the stay in Siena worthwhile. However, you do need to understand what the greater glory of God is in terms of Anna's happiness. God does not abide only in music. Good night," her rich voice trailed off into the retreating footsteps of the Maestro of Venice who had taken his final bow in Siena.

God does not abide only in music.... Oh, Paolina, thank you for saying that. Surely God dwells in all that is good and beautiful. Surely He lives in my love for Orlando.... Why does the Maestro make this so hard for all of us? Why? Antonia turned over and looked at the strange painting on the wall. Now she knew where she had noticed the scene! It was the road to San Gimignano. Orlando had pointed it out to her when they rode out to the Sagredo Estate. How far away she was from the painting on her wall in Venice. Laundry blowing in the salty Venetian breeze. How far away she was from the waters that had spoken and sung to her all her life. But she could not have both the waters of Venice and the hillsides of Siena. No—she was now forced to make a choice. It should not come to a choice. It should have been inclusive.

Antonia cried herself to sleep. She would have to separate from the voices that had until now been the anchors of her life. Tonight everything had changed. Tomorrow, she would move into that change.

* * *

He knew he was dreaming, and yet he could not find his way out of the heaviness. The Venetian Maestro was captive to a music that enticed and frightened him. From his place in the core of an enormous light, he saw the air thicken and surge with a mighty energy until the light that sustained him was consumed by violet. Humming and buzzing, invisible beings produced torrents and echoes-upon-echoes of tiny words—"We are coming, we are coming, coming, coming, ing... ing..., dear Heart, coming." The words became music, rounded and running over itself.

Lightning split the lavender of the morning sky. A deep voice boomed out words in a language he could not understand. Never had he felt so alone. He called back at the voice of the invisible presence and heard only his own echo in response. Where was he?

Suddenly the lavender became a brilliant white cloud upon which he could fly. And then he looked down to see the luxuriant garden he knew. He stopped the cloud and concentrated. He needed to see into the garden. There! There was Antonia, resting on a bed of white and pink water lilies. Holding one lily at her breast, she opened her eyes and looked up into his eyes. Her plaintive smile of recognition broke his heart, and he called out her name. Antonia smiled sweetly again, closed her eyes and slipped below the surface of her indigo water. The lily remained resting on the still surface of the lake.

"Antonia! No!" Vivaldi woke with his arms outstretched. A gust of wind blew through the wisteria outside his bedroom window, calling him outside. Was it the voice of God or of the presences who had inhabited the dream? Pulling on his dressing gown, he went out into the limpid night air.

All was quiet. The full moon was silver against the indigo heavens. All was tranquil. Wispy clouds flanked the moon.

Antonio Vivaldi, composer and conductor, a man used to having his way, had never felt so alone. "Never will I lose Antonia. Never!"

XXII

*What marker have I left in Siena? Is there anything to prove that
I was reborn there? That I died there? That I was happiest there?
That, above all, he lived there and we loved there? Romulus, another orphan, left his Roman marker. His son, Senus, founded a
city—Siena! No one can find my marker. Ah... I speak as a Pagan
again! [Antonia, 1745]*

Antonia entered the Piazza at seven bells. The campo, glowing
in the rising sun, was packed with people. The energy was as wild.
Confident now, she knew she could embrace this magical town as
hers. Indeed, it almost was! In just a few hours, she would be with
Orlando for the rest of her life.

She scanned the Campo. In an odd way, she was seeing Siena for
the first time. There were the Sagredo accommodations. Over here,
the lean bell tower called out to the mother Duomo. Antonia looked
further up. Immovable, Siena's guardian angel gazed down over the
festivities. Here in the Campo, life surged in colourful excess. There
were the horses, magnificent in their decorations, prancing with
excitement, lined up with their riders. All seventeen were eager to
begin the races that would eliminate the weakest from the final race.
And off they all went, cheered by their Contrade, to be blessed. In
contrast to the Venetian Carnevale, the Sienese Palio was sponta-
neous and exhilarating. One did not have to hide and pretend.

Antonia thought about her choice to stay here. Truly, all that
mattered was that she would lose the two who had acted in the
best way possible as her parents. All the pomp and glory of Venice
did not matter. In fact, she would be relieved not to have to cope
with it any longer... out on its fringes... the fringes... where she
had been saved from her loneliness by music, the Prioress and the
Maestro. And, of course, God. Antonia was surprised that she had

almost forgotten to mention God. It was not that her devotion to
God had lessened. No, it was more that... it had enlarged.... become
unafraid. In being happy, she did not have to turn so frequently to
Him for deliverance from the pain that she had grown to accept
as part of her life. That place... below her heart... where it constantly perturbed her... that place was free! Oh, if only her Maestro and Prioress could see how very happy she was and be happy
for her! Although... Sister Paolina seemed to understand. Only this
morning, waking early, she had hugged Antonia and pronounced a
strange little blessing on her. What was it? Something about going
and returning....

A huge roar arose from the crowd. Antonia left her reverie and
allowed herself to be carried along by the throng. This must be the
parade to the tiny church where the participants would be blessed.
The crowd was like an artist's palette, brilliant, textured, colours
running into others and creating new colours. And leaders on stilts!
Antonia laughed, lifted up her skirt and ran along with the parade.

Once at the church, Antonia pushed her way inside and stood on
a pew at the back. She could barely see over the heads of the others
who crowded forward to see the Blessing.

"Vai e torna vincitore," the priest intoned. Antonia was shocked.
That was the blessing Paolina had uttered! That was the strange
blessing! How had Paolina known it? Why had she said it? She
stood on her tip-toes, willing herself higher with an impatient tap
of her foot, and saw four young men being blessed by the priest.

The four men—yes! The tallest one, the one in full body armour, was Orlando! She remembered that Il Duce wore body armour in honour of the military origins of the Palio. What a stunning sight! This was her lover! The others, then, must be his brothers. He had told her that he and his brothers would be the last to
be blessed. Surely they were the most handsome of all the horse-

men! The brothers were descendants of the Palio's founding family. From their estate, ex-contrade, they organized and financed all of the day's events. As the four Sagredos were the last to be blessed, the Palio track could now be approached.

The heavy incense and the whinnying of the horses made her dizzy. Like a single organism, the crowd veered and pressed back through the narrow streets, all the while cheering for the Contrada. Antonia was caught up in the blur of movements and sounds. She lost definition as she moved with the mass of voices, as though she were losing her mind. Why did she feel so unreal? It was so difficult to move to the outside of the track as Orlando had instructed. As she was finally able to slip out from the crowd, she faced the Palio War Chariot. The Madonna looked down on her. Frightened at her size and ornamentation, Antonia joined the crowd again. Another opportunity! She broke away successfully from the mass of people and found her way toward the starting line.

There he was! Orlando, magnificent in his gear, smiled at her and lifted his hand. He turned to give orders. The first race would start at nine bells. Pages held up the canapo, the starting rope. All eyes turned toward the bell tower.

At the first gong, the attendants dropped the canapo, and the race began. In moments, Antonia would enter her own race. Her finish line, however, would be on the Sagredo Estate. Antonia looked on, astonished. It was as though the Madonna of Provenzano had become Our Lady of Tumult! Everything was noise and blurred colours. Two horses were without riders, and then four – what did it matter when the horses were winners? Bareback riders were expendable. Was this the second lap? The second lap on this dangerous track? Never had Antonia felt a force like this!

The crowd emitted a unified cheer. The first race was over! Three laps that would be run again in August. Contrada cheered for Contrada. Competition was a strange thing here in the land of basil and wine. In the end, it was enjoyed for itself.

Antonia slipped into the shadows of the Sagredo building to wait for Orlando. She remembered last night's encounter with Tiepolo and shuddered. She focused on Orlando's plan. He would ride his horse here after the first race and take her away before anyone would notice her absence. His brother, Carlo, would run and monitor the minor races. Orlando would return for the final race of the day, and no one would have noticed or cared. Antonia was ready. She had consolation in the realization that, in the future, when Father Antonio had had time to adjust, he would be happy for her. She would take him gifts of olive oil and wine and a son who would one day continue the Maestro's musical work. Antonia smiled at what this joy would be for the ageing Maestro. It was all in the letter to Sister Paolina that she'd left with Sophia. The housekeeper would not present it to Paolina until the evening:

My dear spiritual Parents,

By the time you receive this note, I shall be gone from Siena and from your preparations to return to Venice. I have prayed and agonized over my love for Orlando Sagredo and realize that we are meant to be together. We have gone to a place where we can be married and shall return to his estate in two weeks. At that time, you and I can talk and discover how to move beyond your disappointment in me. Please find it in your hearts to love me for this. I love you truly and forever.

Your daughter in music and faith,
Anna

She startled at the firm grasp on her elbow. "Anna, you are to come with me." The voice was male, deep and dark. She could not see the face; but the man was huge. She couldn't see past him to the Piazza and the horses. She tried to flee; but his grip was too strong.

"Who are you?" She was terrified. And yet, she knew this was not Tiepolo. She knew that man only too well now!

"Sagredo has sent me to take you to his place. Come! Quickly!"

"But—he was going to meet me here. He promised. I need to wait for him," Antonia tried again to wrest her arm from the stranger's grasp.

"No! You are to do my bidding before anything goes wrong. Trust Orlando that he would not set you in harm's way," he steered her down the alleyway, away from the Piazza. "Step up in the carriage."

"This is wrong! Please let me wait for Orlando. Please!"

Antonia found herself on the carriage seat. The door closed soundly, and the carriage sped off. She couldn't open the door, nor could she see outside. The windows had been covered. She banged furiously on the door and shouted. "Stop," she commanded as she stamped her feet. "Now! Stop now!"

The carriage stopped. Antonia could breathe again. This was Orlando's planning! He must have had strong reasons. Perhaps he had discovered that they must leave earlier and in a different manner.

The door opened, but only briefly enough to send Paolina sprawling onto the seat beside Antonia. "Oh, my dearest child, I am so very sorry. I had so hoped that you would understand my message and run to Orlando before you were found. I am so very sorry! We're going back to Venice now!"

The two women fell into each other's arms.

"Go and return victorious, Anna. Go and return victorious," Paolina seemed unable to stop her dirge as she rocked the sobbing Antonia.

CINQUE

RESURRECTION IN VENICE

1725 – 1726

XXIII

Shadows... shadows... I've run from them and I've hidden in them. I've created them and I've neglected them. They are evidence both of Light and of Light being blocked... or stolen. Shadows cast by others may or may not be trustworthy. My shadow, though, is the shape of my invisible self. It proves I am more than my body or what can be seen. My shadow is my soul's impression... as light as a grace note. Taken over by the shadows of Darkness, my soul disappears. The soul is shy and beautiful and will not, cannot, dare not, fight the brutal powers of Darkness. That the person must do. I, I the person, have not been strong enough to step back into my own shadow. [Antonia, 1741]

October 20, 1725

Light of my Life,
At last I have found a way to reach you by writing! I think and dream of you always.

Antonia, I have had three letters returned to me from the Pieta. But I will not give up in my attempts to reach you. A week ago, I met one of our musicians who sang with you while you were here in July—was that a lifetime ago? How I burn to see you!

This man, who for now must remain nameless (there are strange political networks in Venice that can be dangerous), asked me if I had news of you. I was stunned! He said that he knew of our love and was grieved to learn that you had been forcibly returned to Venice. (I cannot tell you of the pain of that day for me; just as I know the agony you must have endured. That I could not protect you angers and disturbs me still.) He offered to set up a system by which we could communicate.

We are meant to be together, Antonia, and to that end, I pledge my whole strength. You taught me the power of passion and beauty and, above all, truth. No one can change the truth of our love—no one! And so we must begin planning to be together forever. On the whole, my family is pleased and optimistic. However, my father, as well-intentioned as he may be, seems to think that love can come in many "guises", as he terms it. I suppose his message, to "move on to new friends" comes from his concern; but he misses the mark seriously.

I shall move on—but only after you and I are reunited.

I am well, as I have learned you are. I have my sources, in the same way that your Maestro has his. It is difficult for me to understand the love you have for each other. If he indeed loves you as he claims, Antonia, why can he not let you follow your heart—your very beautiful, pure heart?

But I must not lose focus in directing you to begin your plans to leave (shall I say "escape"?) Venice. Sister Paolina will again be your greatest ally. I was saddened to learn that she has been ill. This must be very difficult for you. My new friend here says that Paolina wants nothing more than your happiness with me. Because of this, I know that she can and will be counted on to be your strong Venetian partner in your flight to Siena. I am consumed at times with the plans for bringing you here.

I want you here now! I want to look directly into your eyes and see your depth. I am driven to distraction and deep grief at times in sensing that I can almost see you and touch you and hear you. Harvest time was particularly difficult, as we had talked so much of how you would enjoy being with me at that time. On one particularly bright day, the sharpness of the basil and the sweetness of the grapes caused me to call out your name. (You live within my senses now, Antonia.) You felt so close and yet so far at the same time. My brothers understood.

In reaching me by letter, Antonia, trust everything to your Prioress.

I love you more each day, despite our physical separation.

Forever,
Orlando

* * *

"Her latest composition has some joy in it, Paolina," the man of obsessions wanted to give his ailing companion some joy in her life as well.

Paolina had fallen ill after spending the autumn aching like a mother in bereavement. Vivaldi worried about her; but knew that if she would stop grieving for Anna, both she and Anna would return to their pre-Siena state. Perhaps it had been a mistake to think that Siena was advantageous from a musical perspective. What did the little town know? It was certainly not a sophisticated community. Doubtless, they had forgotten the beauty of the musical profferings that had been presented to them. Both women now needed to rebound from Siena, realize the torment they had put him through and begin entering into the Advent season. He needed them—Venice needed them—to support and applaud him at this important time of year in the Republic. After all, the Republic itself was infirm, requiring better leadership and firmer principles. As Maestro de'Concerti, he could not do it alone. But he could inspire perhaps more than any other man in Venice! Yes! Definitely! The two women in his life had had enough time to recuperate from what he—and God— had been compelled to do in order to correct things in Siena. Anna would have given up her Divine Gift for the upstart whose family had long ago failed in Venice! By the end of this bleak and misty winter, the young woman would find Sagredo as amorphous as the shapes across the basin.

"Joy, Antonio? Truly? Oh, how happy that would make me! I cannot bear to see her suffer any longer. She has taken the delicacy of Juditha's 'Largo' beyond perfection. I can barely tolerate hearing her play it in her loneliness. She has worked it into the very fabric of this place so that her grief haunts the Pieta. Even our orphans, who used to delight in Anna, whisper in her presence. Are you certain that joy is returning to her soul?"

"Yes, it is joy, Paolina—a rather suppressed joy—but joy nonetheless. For some time now, I have been persuaded that she is composing. Since she has said nothing; I have said nothing. But now!— I have allowed her to rewrite the Andante for 'Salve Regina'. She asked! Imagine! Knowing that she was moving to the inspiration of the Holy Spirit, I was very encouraged. Rather oddly, she has scored it for a castrato. But—she will play the violin solo, Paolina! We must rejoice for that. I shall insist that she sing as the soprano for Easter; but for now, I am content to accommodate the Andante for Advent. It is appropriate enough for the beginning of Advent, is it not? 'Hail, Queen of Mercy, Life and Sweetness… our Hope.' How wonderful it will be to hear our Anna accompany those words, for is she not Life and Sweetness herself?"

Paolina was deeply touched to see tears well in Antonio's ageing, still penetrating eyes. She was consoled by her knowledge of his love for dear Anna.

The Maestro turned to leave the sickroom. "She will hear the essential word she has written into the score, Paolina—'hope'! Wonderful!" And off he bounded to the Pieta's musical chambers.

Paolina got up from her sickbed and walked over to the massive, ornate gilt mirror. The dreariness of the dark day framed her face. She was shocked at what she saw. "I am not well. Both my spirit and my body are broken. This cannot be; I cannot abandon Anna! What would she do without me? Paolina—get well! Dearest God, Mother Mary, heal my body and soul—for Anna's sake, heal me!"

She sat on a tiny chair, looked out over liquid Venice and wept.

XXIV

Plato wrote that if we turn toward the Light, our eyes will be "daz-zled." Job said God brings the "deep darkness into Light." When I turn toward the Light, I see the light of Siena. Orlando is Siena's light... still. [Antonia, 1741]

November 25, 1725

Dearest ever, Orlando,
How can I convey in words the joy your letter brought me? That joy, Orlando, has been turned into music. Because of your wonderful persistence, I have begun composing again.
I, too, dream of you, Orlando. The dreams are beautiful, and I awake into the continuing dream that I am actually with you. I sense your presence even at the time of awakening. When I come to my senses, the joy becomes bittersweet; but I would never want the experience to change, despite the pain of reality. I carry with me the memory of your beautiful hands. I truly have the sense of your hands... and your eyes almost, I would say, haunt me. Oh, how I wish it were more than a dream! I long to touch you.
I have taken your admonition regarding the politics of Venice se-riously. Despite my abiding love for Maestro Antonio, I know that he utilized those very systems to spirit me away from you and Siena. Sister Paolina and I are sharing our planning with no one here. (She seems to have improved somewhat since your letter arrived; but she has failed drastically, Orlando. It frightens me. I love her very much.)
Orlando, I was with you, in a spiritual way, for the harvest. I thought of your weather and what you would be doing, all the while grieving our loss. On the Friday of the second week of September, I felt intensely connected to you and actually called out your name in the late after-

noon. It was as if I briefly saw you at a distance. I wonder what day it was when you called out my name?

There is a greater force than our combined efforts in motion now, Orlando. By next summer, we shall be together forever. Once the Advent season is over, you and I, Paolina, our mutual friend and his friends will formulate a perfect plan.

I love you, Orlando, my most beautiful lover. I carry your soul forever within my music.

Passionately,
Antonia

XXV

Is life walked along a straight line? Or is there a descent that happens once childhood is over? Where does the innocence of trust go? Must it be lost? I suspect it must. I also suspect descent is inevitable. Hell does not like waiting in the wings. [Antonia, 1740]

Orlando Sagredo and Lorenzo Cristofori donned their cassock coats and walked out into the cold and windless Florentine January afternoon. There were few others out on the streets. As they walked briskly along the Via Rome, the porous bricks and stone radiated warmth from the brilliant sun. The hard edges of shadows created voids in the light of the late afternoon. The men made their way over to the Via Dei Calzaiuoli, away from the ubiquitous Duomo and south toward the Palazzo Vecchio.

Lorenzo put his hand on Orlando's shoulder, "Orlando, my man! We're moving as fast as your horses. Nothing on a quiet Sunday afternoon can be this urgent. Slow the pace!"

"Ah, I forget my surroundings at time these days! I'm perpetually impatient in planning to get Antonia away from Venice. I want to get to our plans, Lorenzo," Orlando slowed the pace a little. His face and body conveyed no patience.

"Yes, Orlando, I can imagine. You wrote before Christmas that you had at last received a letter from Antonia," Lorenzo was intrigued that his friend had not given up on his goal of returning Antonia to Siena. "So—do you still love each other? I've always maintained that absence is not good fuel for love."

"Well, in my case, you couldn't be more wrong. Antonia and I remain extremely strong in our love. In fact, our love has grown. I will not lose her again, Lorenzo. I will bring her back, and we'll never separate again. I'll never be careless again," Orlando was reminded of Siena as he and Lorenzo passed Orsanmichele. He stopped for a moment to look at the orange brick and the gray statues. The strange building was too organic for Florence. It would be more at home in Siena's marketplace where it would seem to have risen from the soil. Antonia would have seen the misplacement, the need for it to be secured within the orange city and flanked by the purple hills she loved so much. And, certainly, she would have sensed that Ghiberti's John the Baptist was uncomfortable in Florentine garb, away from his diet of locusts! Lorenzo had stopped ahead of him, disturbed at the moodiness and remoteness of his friend. Orlando looked up at Lorenzo and moved quickly along to resume his explanation. "The Prioress is part of our planning now. Even though she's ill, she will be a source of strength for Antonia. My chief concern is that Antonia feels it would be better if I stayed on the Estate and she came with another driver. She believes that, were I to leave to bring her here, my departure might be reported to the Doge. I think that this is being far too cautious. What do you think?"

Lorenzo became irritated with Orlando, "What do I think? I think I like this woman's thinking! Look, Orlando, you and I exchanged comments on this before Christmas. Why would you want to take a chance on this, even though it might be a remote possibility? Were you to leave Siena to head to Venice, Tiepolo's watchdogs could be in Venice as quickly as you, or even more quickly. Why in God's name would you want to take that chance? Why would you risk having harm come to either of you in Venice? Do as Antonia says!" Lorenzo's frustration was almost tangible. Orlando maintained a closed silence, his face expressionless. "She knows Venice better than you and I, Orlando. As much as you feel she is in her own world, that world is in the hub of Venetian intrigue. And Venice is separate from us. It fixates on the wonders of its republican identity. From what I had to deal with in getting Canal here for an exhibit of his art, I'd trust no one in Venice now... except your Antonia."

The men had passed through the Piazza Della Signoria now. The bell called out five times. "You're right, Lorenzo. As is Antonia. I accede... reluctantly."

Passing by the Uffizi, they reached the Arno. The few people who had come to the river were wrapped up in their own conversations. The friends leaned against the wall and looked into the forbidding waters.

Altering from yellows to burnished browns as it made its way into the evening, the Ponte Vecchio looked down on the friends. "You'll need a flawless departure from Venice on a well-lit night. A full moon would be best," Lorenzo was completely focused on the goal now, persuaded by Orlando's dedication to this woman. "And once the mainland has been reached, you'll need a driver who is strong, resourceful, adaptable and knows his way well, politically and geographically, from Venice to Siena. It will be best to have the boat and the carriage managed by the same person. You'll need a route planned out well, with safe places at which to stay. Antonia will need to bring very little with her. She will need—and has, according to your descriptions—the same qualities as her driver, albeit she's a novice and kind-hearted. There will be no room for kind hearts along the route. And I think it would be best to travel in the later afternoons into the dusk. What am I forgetting?"

"Not much," Orlando turned his back to the river and looked through the facade into the Uffizi's many eyes. "You and I are thinking along the same lines. Crespi, the castrato soloist from the concert at the Palio last July, has been a source of clever ideas and thoughts on where to stay. Sister Paolina befriended him; he has been pivotal in getting plans back and forth between Venice and Siena. He loves Antonia and despaired when she was taken from the Palio. Because of the demand for his singing, he has made friends in many places. With his contacts and those whom you and I can count on, there will be no shortage of safe stops along the route. However...," Orlando's voice trailed off and disappeared into approaching twilight.

"However? What do you mean, 'However'?" Lorenzo continued to look into the river. "Do you not think this plan will work? It will work. I've been involved in more treacherous escapades than this one. You might be shocked to learn how some works of art have arrived in Florence."

Orlando laughed, "And, this escapade involves the most precious work of art ever to be transported! No, my 'however' had to do with my desire to be with Antonia on this journey. I want to be her driver. I should be her driver, her liberator. It will be frightening for her. There could be danger. I should be with her!"

Lorenzo grasped Orlando's shoulder, "I've decided to be your driver. It would be folly to think of anyone else doing this! As second-best, there is none better than I. I shall take impeccable care of your Antonia."

Orlando looked directly at Lorenzo, "Thank you, my friend. I'll be able to tolerate this much more easily with you directing the plan. You're the only person to whom I can completely entrust this task. Antonia will be in good hands," he looked down at his own hands and thought about Antonia's love for hands and what they revealed to her about people. "She has a fascination with the legend of Juditha, Lorenzo. The female David. Slaying her giants. She has the strength of a Juditha... and she will need all of her strength— and yours—for the journey."

"Well, I must say that I am looking forward to finally meeting her," Lorenzo lightened the mood. "She must be quite unparalleled to have engendered so much loyalty in so many people. Come, we must return for dinner. I, it seems, will be the most fortunate of men to meet this woman who disappeared last year before I could meet her."

As the friends walked back past the Uffizi and into the Piazza, the wind picked up speed and swirled around the open spaces, blowing their coats out behind them. The men hurried their pace, ready for a good meal. "It looks as though a storm is moving in, Orlando. Shall we run?"

Gloomy clouds propelled their way over the fading Florentine pastels. The men rushed to the warmth of Lorenzo's home.

XXVI

I loved Orlando's light. And I loved receiving it. It harnessed mine. Together, we shone—we were composers of our own "Gloria." Our shadows were minimal when we were together... because we shared the same soul. [Antonia, 1741]

January 30, 1725

My dearest Antonia,

I have had a meeting with my close friend and business colleague. I have told you about him and how instrumental he was in assisting with your coming here initially. So...who better to consult with again than Lorenzo Cristofori! He left for Rome early this morning and will come back on his way home to Florence.

The plans are set for your return to Siena. During Lorenzo's visit, we worked out your itinerary. He and I have will have to be certain that the plan is fully implemented at least a month prior to your departure date. And there will be details that you and your Prioress will have to tend to in Venice. Nevertheless, I find it heartening to know already what to do.

We shall set the following details into motion:

DAY 1 - Night/Morning: Mira (W)

DAY 2 - Afternoon/Evening: Monselice (S); new team of horses

DAY 3 - Afternoon/Evening: Ferrara; new team, carriage

DAY 4 - Afternoon/Evening: Bologna; new team

DAY 5 – Afternoon/Evening: Imola; new team, carriage; west along Via Emilia

DAY 6 – Arrive Evening: Borgo San Lorenzo (S); new team, carriage

DAY 7 & 8—Florence; new team, carriage

DAY 9 - Afternoon/Evening: San Gimignano; new team
DAY 10 – Afternoon/Evening: Monteriggioni; new team, carriage
DAY 11 – Afternoon: Siena; HOME

In the places I've underlined, a horseman will be stationed to report your progress to me. As well, you will receive a trunk of new clothing in Florence. (Soon, you will have no further need for black in your wardrobe.) Both Florence and San Gimignano are chosen for you... you have wanted to see both.

And so you see, my dearest, that your desire for a pilgrimage will be satisfied on your way here. You could not have a better, nor more experienced, driver than Lorenzo. He deals in art, and he deals in life's complexities. There is very little that he cannot do in terms of information and safety. He also feels, as you do, that I should not be absent from our estate here while you are travelling.

More details will come as we work this plan into reality.

Antonia of Siena, I love you more than I had ever imagined loving anyone. You are my chief and only delight. You are my very heartbeat.

Come soon, my love. Come safely, my love. And you shall never leave my side. I touch you as I write.

Your Orlando

* * *

The unfolding of the Venetian primavera and the process of Lent paralleled each other to perfection in 1726. Antonia allowed herself to move from darkness to light, from separation to healing. Like Atlantis, she sank. Below the dank, inky waters of the Bacino. In her Lenten immersion, she, like Botticelli's Venus, would be born. Spring and Lent had conceived her. Never once did her spiritual gaze wander from her southerly love. There would be a way, a Via Jubilato, back to Siena. She would plan. And she would compose.

Beginning with a re-working of an old opera of Vivaldi, Antonia moved methodically and musically from fury and grief to peace and sacrament. Rather than banishing her dreams, she intentionally explored within their boundaries. Often her explorations would produce music and poetry. Never did they produce fear and dislocation, even when they were difficult. Orlando was alive and seeking her.

As Lent progressed, the Venetian Venus slowly emerged. Each morning, she would throw open her windows to the daybreak and look southward while the waters yawned and stretched with her. San Giorgio Maggiore gazed benignly back.

At its zenith, the shimmering full moon, the face of the Cosmos, called her out onto the small balcony. All was still and perfect. Time itself was carrying her to Siena. Surfeited, Antonia, cloaked in gossamer, returned to her bed, leaving her doors open so that Orlando would have no difficulty visiting in the night. The faintest breath of lily-of-the-valley drifted in the window.

XXVII

Siena "dazzles" like Plato's Light. I am greatly comforted dwelling in the gentle hills in the Sienese countryside. In turn, the shadows cast by the sun and the light of Siena in the distance shelter the hills. My shelter these days comes to me from the light Orlando left in Siena. And so, I can say he is still there. At times, I can believe it. [Antonia, 1749]

The Ides of March, 1726

My dearest Antonia,
Your ideas and the friends you've enlisted are excellent. You are clever in combining all of this with music and Easter! I respect your planning skills—I suppose this is much like composing for you.

It is all right to mention Lorenzo's name. Lorenzo is a different person from our friends. He holds power to the extent that the men who try to control your life would never harm him. He certainly is my most influential friend. Having him take care of your journey puts me at ease, as much as I can be, given that my desire is to be with you on the journey. Although, in a vicarious way, I shall be with you.

You wondered why I "crave" words. Antonia, they are all I have now. Indeed, a look into your eyes would tell me much more than words can. Your touch and how you respond to my touch would tell me much more. Your gestures would make many words unnecessary. But I do not have access to those parts of you now—that is why I crave words. That is all letters can handle. So I work hard with the only tool I possess. I look for clues in how you use words and in your choice of words (both used and not used). I wish I had the richer repertoire of input.

I find myself impatient. You know my impatience! I want you here with me now. I do not want to wait! But I shall, Antonia. I must. I know that with Paolina ill, it would not be right to urge you to come any sooner. And, with the spring come my Palio responsibilities of organization and preparation. Will I be able to lose myself in them or will they be a painful reminder of all that we had together last year? I would suspect that I shall experience both possibilities.

Writing this reminds me of your laughter, your music, your beauty and of the lily-of-the-valley outside the Duomo last April. I associate it with you, so much so that the thought of the fragrance heightens my senses in a difficult, poignant way.

Good night, sweet one.

Impatiently,
Orlando

* * *

"Anna, my dear! I have such exciting news for you! You are indeed the most fortunate young woman in the universe!"

In his limitless optimism, the wheezing Maestro was trying yet again to persuade Antonia to sing in the Easter services. Antonia knew that she would do so, and not merely to please her spiritual father. She was ready. She was bursting with the knowledge of seeing Orlando again. Her schemes to return to the Palio were becoming reality.

"Dear Maestro, you don't need to try so hard any longer to have me return to my singing. I've decided to sing at our Easter celebrations. I'm ready. And I am indeed happy again! I want to choose 'O Qui Coeli' if you would permit. Of all your motets, it best celebrates the Resurrection. Do you agree?"

"Yes! Wonderful, wonderful, dear child! Did I not know what was best for you last summer? I knew you would eventually understand!

The 'Qui Coeli' is the best choice of motet. But—I have even more exciting news for you than what you could ever have imagined!"

Antonia had never seen her Maestro this flustered. His hands shook. Never had this happened, even under the greatest of pressures. "Father, how can this be good, if you are so agitated? Whatever could it be?"

"Antonia, can you possibly imagine this? The Elder Bach is coming to Venice! Bach is coming here! To see me! To talk music! My music has reached that far. To Leipzig! We must tell no one yet. No one!" He threw his hands up, "Other than the Prioress, of course! He is coming for two reasons and does not want his presence to be known. He will arrive on Good Friday and will stay with us only briefly. I want him to hear your two voices. The 'Qui Coeli' will be perfect for you vocally. Perhaps the Concerto 11 in D minor for your violin? And, dear Anna, we shall tell him that you wrote the 'Rosa Quae Moritur'. He can share our secret! He will love the way that your interlude prepares the pathway for the 'Alleluia'! If he has sons who follow in his footsteps, I have you as a daughter who does the same!"

Antonia threw her arms around the befuddled composer, as much to orient him as to celebrate with him. She reached for his bow and placed it in his hand. The bow composed him. The delighted Maestro turned on his heel and left the music room. "My dear," he called back to Antonia, "Bach's second reason for coming is that he experiments with glass-making! Who would have ever thought that! The most exemplary musician dabbles in the ultimate in control! He will be visiting Murano as well. Johann Sebastian Bach, German glass-blower. Indeed! Domine!"

The Red Priest's sharp, rollicking laughter spun around the corner and out the windows to the Bacino.

Ellyn Peirson

* * *

The First Day of the Month of My Leaving, 1726

My Orlando,
Your impatience rang through in your letter, and I wanted you so much as I read about what you crave. May I touch you through this letter? And will you then put your hand on my knee? How much we could communicate last summer without anyone knowing! How I long for simply the smell of your presence! I lose my place in this world just thinking about you now.

My dear Orlando, you shall "have the richer repertoire"—your very rich repertoire will be richer and I shall be all the richer for being with you. I want to see your eyes. I want to feel your touch. I want to look at you and believe that you are real. When I tell you that I wrap you around me at night, I want it in person. Since your taking me to your estate, I have continued to sense you as a great cloak wrapped around me. You are like the Madonna's cape of your town's marketplace. Now, as I write and your presence becomes more intense for me, I see you dimly face to face. Face to face—oh, how I miss you and want you, Orlando!

I will also need something—I do not know what—to accommodate our actually being together again. There will be a rush (I cannot think of a better word) when I first see you—of happiness and of grief falling away. I feel it when I write of it.

Our friends here have set everything in order for my journey. I shall leave on the first full moon after Easter. Sister Paolina is writing to the observatory at Bologna to find the exact time of the month and the times of the rising and setting of the moon. I wish that the talk about building an Observatory here were more than talk—what more mystical place is there than Venice for viewing the messages of the heavens! But Padua will do. Pray for clear skies and good weather that night, my soul's completion. I am somewhat afraid; but the fear is far out-balanced by my goal.

Orlando, you are my goal, my essence and my very breath. Stay, my love, for I am coming!

It will be a circuitous and long journey. All is now in place. I shall become used to staying at different houses along the way. And I do understand the need to travel only from late afternoon into the late dusk. I shall arrive with none of my Venetian possessions. Everything is arranged. And the benevolence of the moon will never fail me. It will be hard to wait; but I shall leave immediately after the Elder Bach leaves on Easter Sunday. Imagine if I were to travel with him! I view his unprecedented visit as a sign for my journey. He is known for never straying far from Leipzig. How different he must be from Father Antonio!

I love you, Orlando. Be my cloak for the journey.

Forever,
Antonia

SEI

FLIGHT FROM VENICE

1726

XXVIII

Except for the sounds of music and teaching, the Pieta was silent.
We orphans may have been unique as females; but we were under
our own form of captivity. The Pieta was a museum in daytime
and a mausoleum at night. In the day, we were the artifacts of the
museum. At night we became the corpses of the mausoleum. And
the Lion of San Marco, guardian and director, oversaw it all—
from his position, high and disdainful over the Bacino. [Antonia,
1739]

Antonia stirred from her manuscript to the light rapping at her studio door.

Opening the door, she faced a tiny replica of her former self. "Yes?" She wondered at the loss of her own innocence and trust.

"The Prioress asks you to visit her, Maestra Anna," the girl smiled shyly as she used the familiar term the orphans had adopted for their music teacher.

"Thank you, Constanza. You need not return to Sister Paolina's room."

Antonia closed the door and returned to her desk. She tidied her papers, smoothed the skirt of her plain black dress and left her sanctuary. As she approached the door, she pinched her cheeks to give them a little colour. She could no longer be the cool, sculptured alabaster Antonia. Sister Paolina would be looking for proof that Antonia was healthier and happier.

She knocked on the Prioress's door, announced herself and walked in.

Would the shock never diminish? Daily, she found changes in the Prioress. Daily she saw Sister Paolina try valiantly to look well. Her eyes looked more sunken this evening.

"Anna! We have the times of the full moon! The Chief Astronomer from Bologna himself did our calculations. Let me read you his note:

Dear Prioress Giraud,

I am pleased to answer your query regarding the full moon in April. The full moon will rise at 7:30 on the evening of the nineteenth day of April and will set at 3:30 on the twentieth morning. It will rise to 17 degrees above the Venice horizon, after rising in the south-east. Also visible on that day will be the red planet Mars, which will be visible in the East until midnight.

From the central front room in the Pieta, as you described, the view will be splendid. I hope you enjoy the sight and manage to stay till midnight when the moon, barring heavy cloud cover, will fully light up your lagoons.

Yours very truly,
Dario Bassi, Chief Astronomer
Bologna Observatory

"Oh, Anna, we know you will have good light for your departure!"

Antonia guarded her reaction, "But, Paolina, the moon won't be full when I leave. We need the light."

"Yes, my dear; but if you leave earlier—on Easter Sunday, after the final evening with Bach—you will have good light," the Prioress delighted in the amazement dawning on her Anna's face. "And leaving that night will be a clever choice. Both Father Vivaldi and Bach will leave early the next morning on their various pursuits, the Maestro for Rome and Bach for Leipzig. So they will retire early. And you won't be expected for farewells on the Monday morning because of the early departure. Two weeks, Anna! God is smiling on you, my dear. He's giving you the good fortune of a waning full moon at the most opportune of times."

Antonia dropped onto the side of the sick bed and took Paolina's face in her hands. "The time is really here? I cannot believe it. Oh, Paolina, you are the sweetest mother to me. Don't cry—not even happy tears. I cannot bear it! What will you do without me? What will I do without you? Am I truly, truly going to be with Orlando again?" Her forehead against Paolina's, she wiped the sick woman's tears with her thumbs and, as mother would, soothed Paolina.

* * *

Blessed Seventh Day of April, 1726

My Orlando,

I shall begin my flight to you on the Easter Sunday, two weeks from today! I cannot dispel the sense that this is all a dream. But it is true, Orlando!

This now becomes the most difficult part of the whole plan. What can be harder than waiting when one can actually see the object of desire, just out of reach? What can be harder than waiting when one is alive again? I want to forget all caution and leave now, Orlando! I almost feel now, more than ever in this arduous process, that I will not last.

Thank you for the itinerary. I have memorized the details and will destroy the papers before I leave. I know that you have wanted me to burn your letters for safety's sake, Orlando; but I must keep them until it is time to go. They anchor my hope. They turn my night and day dreaming into reality. They make you real, Orlando. When I touch and smell them, they are you, Orlando. I have hidden everything very carefully and not even Sister Paolina knows that anything is left in my possession.

This will be my last writing. Think of me every moment on the departure night and until I find you again. Our plans will see us together at your estate ten days later. I will arrive with empty and open arms.

I love you more than Life itself,
Antonia of Siena

XXIX

I had simply never known a family until I met Lorenzo's family.
I had no idea of what it was like to talk in a group, to quarrel, to
laugh, to solve problems... and to love and hate. Were the other
orphans my sisters? No! Were the Prioress and the Maestro my
parents? No! My only family was made up of the Invisibles of
my childhood. I had to abandon them, of course. [Antonia, 1739]

Anna Giraud, Antonia of the waters of Venice, had brought about
the Holy Friday of her conception. With a formidable relentlessness,
she had petitioned the Almighty through Saint Catherine. And, in
return for her devotion, she had received strength and guidance. She
had turned the most profound of her religious observances into a
personal renaissance. Vivaldi had relented. The reluctant priest had
had no choice.

"If you'll allow me license for this one time, Maestro, I'll be ready
to return to singing on Resurrection Sunday. And I shall certainly be
ready to sing when the Elder Bach visits. I have prayed, and I know
this as surely as I know that you are the cleverest musician Venice
has ever produced! We shall keep this private; but this we must do in
order for my music to return completely." Antonia, shrugging off the
discomfort of dishonesty, had persuaded the somewhat confused
Maestro.

"I'll attend Mass as I would normally do. All I ask is that my own
ensemble be allowed to gather in our music room to perform your
work. You know how important Holy Friday is to me, Father! This
will be all I will need as readiness for Easter Sunday."

Antonia had explained yet one more time what she needed for
the day of Crucifixion. She urged Vivaldi to allow her a private time
during the afternoon at the moment of Extinction to conduct and
play his 'Stabat Mater'. Using her students, Antonia had created an

ensemble of four violins, two violas, a viola da gamba, a chittarone and a harpsichord. What gave the Maestro greatest difficulty was her insistence upon using the singer whose company she enjoyed in Siena. Vincenzo Crespi, the castrato, was coming to Venice. Paolina, who had also become close to him in Siena, had cavalierly invited him to be part of the Bach preparations. Antonia, upon hearing this, had begun begging to have him sing the Stabat Mater under her direction. Vivaldi was confused. How could two women be so interested in one castrato? Well—Domine!—Anna, the day-star of Venice was back and that was all that mattered! He decided that he would let the argument go shortly if Anna were truly inflexible.

"Anna, Anna! I have agreed that he can come early; but, my dear, how can you think of a male voice—a castrated male voice!—singing my work when it should be you? How?"

"Dear Maestro! I see it this way," Antonia balanced reason and passion. "What could be better than a neutered, pure voice for this work? I see this as the archangel himself singing to and for the Virgin Mother. I want to hear the Virgin Mother's experience as I envision it. Let me have my way this once—please!", Antonia's signature foot stamp underscored her passion.

Vivaldi, yielding to her fervour, smiled and shrugged. "Anna, I could not resist you when you were three years old and adamant. You are three years old again and adamant. Have your way, child, have your way. Your happiness is my incentive, as always."

Antonio's eyes twinkled with fatherly delight while Antonia's brimmed with anguish. How long he had known and taught her! And trusted her. The wheezing Maestro went back to his manuscript.

Antonia excused herself to visit the ailing Paolina. Her health would improve once she heard that their plan was underway.

* * *

Jesus was risen! Antonia was risen! Hallelujah!

Anna could not imagine herself happier. Resurrection music! The visit of the Elder Bach! And, above all, the plans of her and Paolina's conception! The Maestro being compelled by a great force, and he had no idea.

Orlando was more real and more present than at any other time in their absence from each other. She'd had a startling dream through the night, denser and more evocative than any she had ever dreamt.

She was in a strange garden filled with an array of the fragrances of basil and lavender. The atmosphere was one of enchantment, creamy air and harmonies and colours. Powerful and naked, she had soared in on the back of a glorious blue bird, landing behind Orlando, who was searching for something in a garden. As Orlando turned toward her, his clothing fell away and he drifted toward her, his hands held out to her. Antonia moved toward him as though joining with a part of her own body. She extended herself in an outpouring of melodic, vivid words. She could still see their notes and hues.

Orlando smiled, touched her lips and bent to kiss her breasts. Ecstatic, she touched his hair. "I am here forever, Antonia, forever," he lifted her as she kissed him and nestled into his neck. Purple spilled into shining lavender and all colour became light. They were in a floating world of soft, fragrant breezes. Whispers became music. Music became the substance of the garden.

"And, I am back, Orlando, fully back. I'm alive again. Happy. Without you, I lived without feeling. Instead, I became my music. Mathematical. Perfectly patterned. I found the key to heaven; but I couldn't enfold you into myself. Now time and distance are split."

Orange and red flames flared around them. "I come to you. Into the fire."

Orlando swept her up onto a horse and under his cloak. They were one.

XXX

The Tuscan hillside is often purple. I suppose the various greens and violets, the olives and the grapes, combine to produce the regal, deeply textured tapestry. And within that tapestry, in a small part of it, is my love story. Its sounds are muffled by the texture. That rich texture, created by the undulating breasts of Tuscany, keeps my story safe. [Antonia, 1750]

Orlando sat with Carlo, the second eldest of the four Sagredo sons, at the kitchen table. From the centre of the table, a pot of rosemary declared the arrival of spring after a tolerable winter. As the culinary and emotional heart of the Sagredo home, the kitchen was huge and well-equipped and guarded by pots and pans, hung high and shining down, ready for the service of family members. The gleaming white walls, green draperies, round oak table and massive work table and cutting boards absorbed the effort, laughter, tears and conversation of a family highly skilled in communication and social graces. This was a room where arguments had been settled, babies welcomed and suckled, children educated, and harvesters rewarded. A quiet, fresh herbal presence dwelt within the spaces. On this mid-afternoon, the brothers were sharing an almost silent communion. The sun was brilliant and spilled through the kitchen window to land in a pool on the yellow tablecloth. Partly consumed, Francesca's fresh bread and Gallo's favourite Chianti sat near the earthen pot of rosemary. Mother and Father were continually present in numerous manifestations, as human head and heart of the family hearth.

Carlo, almost as tall as his older brother, but finer-boned, sprawled out on his chair, letting his feet reach to the far side of the table. Orlando sat straighter in his chair, often tilting it back or forward to the ebb and flow of the mellow conversation. The brothers were very comfortable in each other's company.

"She will be ready to leave now, Carlo. Lorenzo and Pietro will be in the gondola on the backwaters. The carriage and horses will be waiting now at the Resmondo home. At midnight, Umberto will see that they are ready to depart. We've covered all details, have we not, Carlo?"

Seeing his brother vulnerable was a new experience for Carlo. Almost two years younger, he had always perceived Orlando as confident and extremely self-sufficient. Of course, he had never seen Orlando in love. "You've left nothing out, Orlando. Both you and Lorenzo have treated this like Generals. Now find a way to set it aside. The journey is a long one. And a safe one."

Orlando tore off a piece of the rosemary, crushed it with his fingers and inhaled the medicinal scent. He thought of Antonia in their greening place… Antonia with basil and lavender… Antonia at one with the garden. He walked over to the kitchen window. The breeze was refreshing.

"Ah, here come Mother and Father! You know it's spring when you see Francesca and Gallo Sagredo walk hand-in-hand through the field! They're a remarkable couple, you know, Carlo. Sometimes difficult. But remarkable." As they approached, Orlando could see they were laughing. Both were still handsome in countenance and stature. His mother, very tall for a woman, stood an inch or two taller than her husband. They were a gracious and striking couple. "Remarkable."

Carlo joined his brother at the window. "And complex, Orlando. I find Father frustrating at times. He made me angry last night. He can be opinionated to a fault. And Mother always defends him."

"No… almost always. But not always," Orlando dropped his hand from the curtain, and the brothers walked to the door. "I've seen

Mother defend you to Father. It depends on the importance she finds in the situation. And I agree—Father is rigid. You had cause to be angry with him over his comments about your visions for the Estate. They were good ideas. He'll come round."

Francesca and Gallo reached the doorway to the kitchen where their two older sons stood. Gallo removed his jacket, shook it and placed it on a hook. Always fastidious, he removed his boots and put on his "house shoes". The house shoes of each family member were kept in the entrance to the kitchen. Father had decreed. "I see you've been relaxing. Where are Enrico and Giuseppe?"

"Oh, Gallo, these two are not their brothers' keepers," Francesca had shaken her skirt and changed her shoes. As they walked to the kitchen table, Carlo took wine glasses and small plates from the cupboard for his parents.

"Bring some cheese and the roasted garlic, Carlo—and a knife," Francesca turned toward to her son. "The garlic is over by the oven. I roasted it last night for your father." As Carlo placed the cheese and garlic on the table, Francesca put her hand on his, "Thank you. Have some, you men! Orlando, how are you feeling? Are you anxious about Antonia's departure?"

"Carlo and I were just talking about it. I'm uneasy; but we agree that everything has been seen to." Orlando looked from his mother to his father, "I was also saying that you are remarkable parents. Not many parents have been called upon to support such an endeavour as this flight. I want you to know how much I appreciate you both."

Gallo Sagredo looked directly at his son, "Orlando, you're a creditable son, and you're a man in love. You've asked for my support in the most important relationship there is in life. I give you that support happily. I want your happiness, son. Now, shall we talk about how you—and we—are going to pass the time in relative ease while Antonia is on her way here?"

"Yes," Francesca spoke to her husband and her sons, "and let's remember, too, that we have each other. This is a solitary and frightening journey for Antonia. We must think of her and send our prayers her way. And we must do the same for Lorenzo. He is her only support. Thank Heaven he's such a strong, experienced man. This is a great love that brings Antonia your way, Orlando. She'll never be far from my thoughts."

The family conversation mellowed into the sound that is created of words and laughter blended with wine and herbs.

* * *

A fragrant zephyr drifted in through the Venetian window on the twentieth day of April, 1726. The Elder Bach stood and bowed toward the only female conductor he had experienced. Antonia smiled and bowed at the fascinating Lutheran.

Through the fusion of the language of music, semi-literacy in each other's tongues and the assistance of a translator, connection had abounded during the day, culminating in the familiarity they were now relishing. Bach's inclusion of Antonia in the afternoon's discussion and performance now assured her as she conducted the "Salve Regina". Crespi was the exquisite collective voice of beseeching souls.

Upon Bach's insistence for an encore, Antonia chose the violin, executing Juditha's "Largo" in perfect simplicity. The plaintively beautiful piece connected strongly with Bach, who sent his assistant to fetch a manuscript. In a matter of moments, the assistant returned. The Kapellmeister explained this new motet to his hosts.

Employing German, Italian and Latin, Bach asked Antonia to grace the new work with her voice. Hers was the voice that was "God-given" for "Ich Habe Genug". Antonia was intrigued by the unexpected charisma of this unassuming German. Initially, he had appeared austere, pedantic and lacklustre. However, within an hour of meeting yesterday, barriers collapsed. By the end of their first evening together, Bach had become almost fatherly toward Antonia and clearly interested in her talent.

"I would be honoured. Your request is a gift. Thank you," Antonia was able to speak this message in adequate German, pleasing Bach.

The Red Priest was greatly touched. "This affirms my intentions for Anna. I have been correct to keep her here in Venice," he told himself.

Bach turned to Vivaldi, "Your violin and my harpsichord will work well, I think, as accompaniment. Shall we simply let the music speak? I shall give you a little time to consult." He went to a desk and began transcribing a theme.

Vivaldi walked over to his violin. Anna moved beside him. While the Maestro tuned the instrument, both musicians began studying the manuscript. Gradually, the spoken word became sung and the sung word became bowed. "Ich Habe Genug" was responding to an unfamiliar breath of life.

As the clock chimed eight, the three musicians gathered around the harpsichord, Vivaldi to Bach's left and Anna to his right. Anna and Bach shared one manuscript; Vivaldi read from a manuscript poised on the harpsichord. Only Paolina and Crespi remained as audience.

The Elder Bach raised his index finger. On a unified in-breath, the three musicians melded and gave in to the music. Vivaldi supported the voice of the lover of Jesus. "Ich habe genug"—Antonia's voice soared in from the firmament as supplicant on the hovering wings of the Holy Ghost. In the union with her Saviour, she was at one again with Orlando. "So may I leave in joy; it is enough."

The final bars were of sheer divine intimacy and surcease. One voice, one violin, one harpsichord and one directing hand as Bach painted the last brush-stroke. The Venetians looked to the German for the way out of the music, the applause of Paolina and Crespi almost inaudible to them.

The Elder Bach reached into his pocket, pulling out a small object and offering it to Antonia. "My dear Anna, you possess musical prowess. I shall treasure this strangely beautiful time in this strangely beautiful city. Please accept this gift as our connection. I made this myself in Murano just before I came to stay here. Keep it to anchor your soul to your gifts and to all you love. And, my dear, be happy. Move to joy, and leave your pain behind. Ich habe genug."

As Anna looked down at the object in her hand, she felt dislocated. She was holding a sweet, naively made glass globe that had been blown around two glass stars and a glass moon. These were Contrade symbols from the Palio.

She spoke to the German. "Thank you for understanding me. I shall never forget our meeting." Her eyes brimming, she put her arms around the German interloper. "Thank you. I have no other words."

Anna Giraud of Venice, Antonia belonging to Siena, turned on her heel and walked briskly out of the music room.

* * *

Antonia stirred from her trance on the balcony. The midnight moon was perfect, round and serene in its occupation of the vast heavens.

She had come to the balcony after tucking Paolina in with song and word. As weak as the Prioress was, she had spoken clearly. "Antonia, you have always been Antonia to me. Go, dear one, and don't worry about me. Our souls are too close for us to lose touch with each other." She had raised Antonia's hand to her lips, "Continue with your music, and know that as the summer comes, my health will return."

She had been on her balcony for an hour now, whispering occasionally to be sure Pietro, Vincenzo's assistant and Crespi's friend, was in place in the shadows below. Pietro had whispered his coded reply, "Torna vincitore." Antonia had carefully passed him her violin in its case.

Now it was time. She whispered, "All is quiet, and the moon gives us the light we need. Midnight's here. Catch my cape."

"I have it. Be careful as you climb down."

Antonia re-entered her room for her final farewell. There truly was nothing she would miss. Her station for Saint Catherine would soon be replaced by closeness to the Saint's Duomo. It was easy to leave the modest altar behind. She turned to the painting a friend had given her of Rio dei Mendicanti. Touched by Antonia's care for the hidden poor, he had painted Venice's disgrace for her. "The clothing on the roof-tops is a reminder," she had told him in her gratitude for the gift. She had placed the painting on the wall across from the foot of her bed. Now she must leave it and let go of her grief in not having Father Antonio's blessing. She must also let go her need to understand his possessiveness.

She gathered Orlando's letters and maps from her desk. Finally, she was ready to part with them. She placed them in her small fireplace and lit them. Extinguishing her taper, she noticed a possession she could not bear to part with. Picking it up quickly, she placed the Elder Bach's paperweight deep into the pocket of her dress.

Antonia walked out to the balcony and looked over the railing. She pulled the back of her skirt forward between her legs and up through her belt. There was no need to look back again. Grasping the top of the railing, she pulled herself over, letting herself dangle. For a brief moment, she saw the humour in the new use for her violinist's arms. Her heart raced, "All right, Pietro!" Pietro reached up and took Antonia by the waist, breaking her fall. The loudest noise had been her whispered command. She landed lightly. Pietro motioned her to the waiting gondola.

The gondolier, his look intent on this utterly beautiful, agile woman who would be his charge for the journey, took Antonia's hand and assisted her into the vessel. How had the lantern lit up her face so? Her eyes were themselves like lanterns. No—hers were the eyes of a Maddalena, authoritative, fierce, demanding justice. This Antonia exuded strength. Dear God, Sagredo, I understand you now! "Antonia of Siena, I am Lorenzo Cristofori, your guide for the journey home to Orlando. Welcome to freedom."

Looking up at the broad silhouette, Antonia was speechless. All she could see were his eyes, boring into hers. While she realized she had been carefully scrutinized, she knew that she was safe in the presence of so commanding an authority. And this Lorenzo was Orlando's closest friend. With him by her side, she would be close to Orlando.

And then Lorenzo whispered, "We are off now, and we will be absolutely silent until we reach the mainland." The escape had been orchestrated flawlessly.

As the curious company of strangers headed away from San Marco and up the Rio della Pieta, the silver moon glinted over their obscure, watery path. They were on their way toward the backwaters, to Murano and then to the mainland.

Antonia, composed now in garb and being and as fearless as Juditha, never once thought to look back.

SETTE

FERRARA TO MONTERIGGIONI

1726

XXXI

In a rather morbid way, the Island of San Michele in the Lagoon always fascinated me. It seemed somehow sinister with its wall of cypress trees, and there were stories of trapped spirits haunting it and crying. The Francescan Convent there interested me as well. I imagined taking refuge there during my most difficult experiences growing up. No one would have thought to look for me there, desolate and off in the Lagoon as it was. Now I flee to another convent. [Antonia, 1741]

Awakening from a troubled sleep, Antonia at first could not orient herself. No matter how she tried to sort out the first twelve hours of her escape, she remained unclear. No image, other than clouds flitting over the moon like ravens, would come to her mind. No sound remained in her head, except the lapping of water.

The arduous flight to the mainland and to Mira by moonlight hovered like a strange dream, half-remembered, haunting. In spite of her preparation, she had been exhausted, as much mentally as physically. Lorenzo's skills and confidence had not been enough to dispel the fear that rose in her chest with every thud and clatter of the carriage and horses. The few hours of sleep in the back quarters of their hosts' home barely addressed her physical needs. But how was she to sleep well on such a journey and in places where hosts were strangers? And how was she to sleep at all, knowing this first crucial and dangerous day required that she must, no matter what the weather, reach Monselice? This was the day in which they must put ample territory behind them. They could not risk the faint possibility of being followed, and they needed to gain distance now in spite of the hills. If they could reach Monselice, they would have tempted the Euganean Hills and won. Rovigo and the flat expanse in the Po delta would be their reward. And their respite. For it would be further south that the hills and the weather might most truly conspire against them.

* * *

Antonia woke again. Where was she now? Monselice? She barely remembered the night she had spent there. Ah, yes… the San Giorgio of Monselice. Had she seen it? She couldn't remember. She reached out for another memory. But it was too elusive. She leaned over to pull a curtain back and looked out her bedroom window. This was not Monselice. A cart pounded over the cobblestone. That was it! Lorenzo had picked up a new team of horses and checked the axles of the carriage. He had said that the carriage would last well until Ferrara. And she had had no idea that horses could tire too much for further travel, nor that axles—what were they?—could break. The journeys to and from Mantova had been so leisurely and enjoyable. And in last year's journey to Siena with the Maestro and Sister Paolina, it had rained. And she had slept much of the time. Antonia shook her head and sighed.

And then it came to her – they had done it! Thanks to Lorenzo. Antonia felt more oriented and optimistic now. Here they were in Ferrara. She was safe now, and, at last, there was more time available. Relief became her elixir. The blur had evaporated. No longer was she in a dream. She was Antonia. Not Anna. And she would soon be with Orlando. She toyed for a moment with the relative nature of time. How very different one day could be from another. Hope, rest, fear, a goal… all played such a part in the perception of time. Here in Ferrara, she would concentrate on hope and her goal. She knew she needed spiritual refreshment. But she sensed that she would have to wait until further along in the journey.

As she leaned back against the pillow, a strange sense of uneasiness came over her. Despite the kindness and understanding of her hosts, Antonia did not like this town. She had felt the unease as they had entered Ferrara and it had pervaded the bedroom after she had looked outside. The D'Este family had left a dense pall, now two hundred years thick, over the town. She could feel it, evil and cloying. "It will never retreat on its own," she thought. There was no music for her here.

She climbed out of the bed, picking up her turquoise shawl and draping it around her shoulders. Sitting by the window, she looked into the face of the Castello's clock, staring back at her from across the moat. Her thoughts turned to Siena... its bell tower... the Campo....

A light rapping at her door interrupted her train of thought.

"Antonia, I have some food for you. May I come in?" Hearing her driver's voice, she felt even more secure. Lorenzo had changed his role from gondolier to driver when they had reached the carriage waiting at the Resmondo home. As soon as they were away from the waters, he had engaged Antonia in conversation about Orlando. Finally, she began again to believe she would be with Orlando soon. This was a man who knew Orlando well and who had the strength needed to keep her safe for the journey.

"Come in, Lorenzo," Antonia pulled the shawl closely around her. It dawned on her that Lorenzo had assumed Paolina's role in her life. She was becoming attached to this new man in her life. How quickly he had become her rock on this formidable journey. Robust, beneath a rather intimidating exterior, Lorenzo cheered Antonia. With his deep voice and intelligent, chiseled features, he would make an imposing basso in an opera. As unaccustomed as she was to the company of men, Antonia felt at ease with this man who was probably mid-way in age between Orlando and the Maestro. More than any other feature, his eyes revealed his generous nature. He reminded her of someone? Who?

Lorenzo closed the door quietly and put the food on the small table. "Ah, good, Antonia! You look well-rested."

"Please, Lorenzo, sit here," she motioned to the seat across the table.

Lorenzo sat with her, leaning back in his chair, enjoying her attentiveness to her breakfast.

Antonia, finished with the meat and bread, reached for the orange, breaking into the peel and inhaling its fragrance. She looked up at Lorenzo, "I hope you slept well. You look refreshed." It was good to see Lorenzo without his coat and hat and with his shirt sleeves rolled up to his elbows. "What are our plans for getting to Bologna today?"

"We'll leave in mid-afternoon and go directly to Bologna," once again Lorenzo was enchanted by the pure beauty of this young woman who was so unaware of her own charisma. She seemed so naïve—or was it that she seemed almost too serene? How had she come down to earth long enough to make Orlando the most fortunate of men? Lorenzo was taken aback at the rise of jealousy in his chest, "We are on the most difficult leg of this journey, Antonia. Orlando directed that we not stay on the roads long and that we be very careful about venturing from the homes we stay in. I've heard enough about Tiepolo to understand Orlando's caution."

Antonia laughed, "And so, I should not be lulled into thinking that this is a simple pilgrimage." Her smile disappeared, "I think often of Tiepolo, Lorenzo; he frightened me terribly last summer. I sometimes convince myself that I hear his voice."

"Once we get past Florence, you'll feel greatly relieved. As will I," Lorenzo's smile reassured her.

"Why is that—is Florence dangerous? Is it not just another city like Venice?"

"Florence is a city of many faces and moods, Antonia. As is Venice. But Venice is its own creature, and you have been protected by its insularity. Florence still relies on its reputation as one of the most powerful cities in Europe. And Florentines refuse to admit that the reputation is fading. So the faces and moods of Florence are changeable and deceiving, always transforming to please the most lucrative sources. Now that the Medicis are dying out, I fear that Florence could find it has no pulse-beat of its own left." Lorenzo's gaze was fixed on something out the south window.

"You're from Florence, are you not, Lorenzo? I can hear it in your voice." Antonia had heard the wistfulness and passion in his words.

"I am, Antonia. I am." Lorenzo broke his reverie, clapped his hands on his knees and stood. "And that's why you'll be staying in Florence in the safest place imaginable. You'll stay in my family home. And now—enjoy the next few hours. There will be bath water ready for you when you wish, and this home has an excellent library and garden. I'll come for you at three o'clock." How had he let himself become so drawn into conversation, even into personal remarks, when it had been his intention to be detached on this journey? He understood Orlando's needs even more now. He would maintain his detachment. After all, this was a business journey for him… that was how he must continue to see it.

As Lorenzo closed the door, Antonia found herself fascinated with the intriguing mixture her driver possessed—a mixture of Orlando's incisiveness and her Maestro's remoteness.

XXXII

The Maestro did have a very deep faith. It was carefully and exactly worked out in circularity to include his politics and music. He used politics to further music. And he used music to further his politics. His faith remained as the heart of it all for him. "People come to God through music, Anna," he told me in one of our invigorating discussions. I could not blindly accept his premise. "But what about painting? What about something like Bellini's Madonna or Titian's Assumption in the Frari?" I had been so affected by art after I'd met Jacopo. "No, no, my dear. Painting is static. It needs music to give it life!" He was so rational, so vocal. I was so reflective, so inward. I did not want to apply only my mind to my beliefs. They needed to be private and felt. The Maestro's feeling was quick and then acted upon. I wanted the slow unfolding mystery of the illogical, even peculiar. He was inspired by brilliant, hard-edged revelation, I by supple contemplation. In the end, I saw he was right. Music, more than painting, allows and encompasses all human differences and similarities within its wide-ranging borders. Perhaps, then, music, in its mathematical basis, is God, and other art forms are inspired by God. [Antonia, 1742]

"Sister Paolina, the Maestro is almost here. You wanted to know. Maria has spotted the gondola," Constanza closed the door behind her and moved to Paolina's bed to plump the pillows around the sick woman's back. The maid noted, as she brushed her stray hair back over her shoulders, how beautiful the older woman was, despite her illness. The richness of her thick hair was only enhanced by the streaks of gray. Her face was as beautifully chiseled as the sculpture of Saint Margherita. This dear woman, who loved the daughters of the Pieta, was not recovering from her illness. Oh, look how thin she has become! And still so sweet. And still so caring for the Maestra. She deserved greatness for all her loyalty and love, not the pain and diminishment of this prolonged illness.

"Are you ready for the wrath of the Maestro, Sister Paolina?" Constanza, despite her attempt at playfulness, knew that the truth was often couched in jest.

Paolina smiled knowingly at Constanza, "Please, my dear, don't worry about me! I know how to handle his ranting. What I pray is that he will understand how much Anna loves him and how hard this action has been for her. Please," she reached toward the bottom of her bed, "put my blanket around me." The mantle of silky aqua brought Antonia close. Paolina felt Antonia's arms enfold her.

Huffing and happy, Vivaldi bounded into the room. "My dear, Rome was a complete success! I wish you could have been there! How are you?" He looked around the room, "And, where is Anna? I thought she would have come to your room once she heard the commotion of my return. Paolina?" Vivaldi saw the distress Paolina was seeking so desperately to conceal, "What is it? Has she come to some harm?" He sat down beside the Prioress.

Seeing that the Prioress had not eaten her evening meal again, Constanza picked up the tray and left the room. She silently prayed that all would go well. The Prioress and the Maestra had suffered enough.

"No, Antonio. She is well. And she's happy. She has left Venice, Antonio. And us. We need to let her be. We need to let her be, and we need to carry on with our lives as though we had sent her on her way with our blessing." Paolina's voice was deliberate and soothing.

Vivaldi was thunderstruck. He shot up and spun around, grasping for the mistake in what he had heard Paolina say. "Domine! Domine! What in God's name do you mean, woman? Where is she? What did she tell you?" He pounded his fist against the bedpost and moved toward the window. Rubbing his knuckles, he came back to the sickbed, "Did she go to Siena? Paolina! Look at me, and answer me! Did she go to Siena?"

"Antonio, I do not know where she is. She is a twenty-two year old woman. She has made choices. We have to let her go. Let her go, Antonio, for the love of God, let her go," Paolina was suddenly exhausted and angry at this man who found it so difficult to exercise compassion and understanding. She began coughing. She felt so very infirm.

"I will not let her go! Never! Never will I let her abandon her God-given gift. She may be a woman; but she is an infant when it comes to men and love, Paolina, an infant," Vivaldi allowed himself a brief gaze over the waters. He turned from the window to Paolina, "I shall put a stop to her audacity now!"

Paolina, taking the deepest breath she could rally, pointed toward the man she knew more completely than he knew himself. Staring him down fiercely, she ordered, "Antonio Vivaldi, I demand you leave her alone. For the first time in her life, leave her alone. Now! I needed to give her life before I die. You have no right to possess her!"

For a moment, Paolina captured Vivaldi in her gaze. Would she be strong enough?

Throwing up his hands, Vivaldi broke the silence, "Domine! Paolina Giraud, you will not give me orders!" The Maestro of Venice turned on his heel and exited quickly, throwing the door shut behind him. Possessed by fear and anger, he moved more quickly than he had on his return just minutes earlier.

"Domenico, come back to the gondola! Take me to the Ducal Palace now!" As was his custom, the confused manservant did the unreasonable without question.

Travelling the short distance westward, Domenico interrupted the distracted Maestro as he slowly plunged the pole down into the waters, "Sir, do you have an appointment? You know that you cannot expect to see the Doge unless you have an appointment." Always, it was his role to steer all vessels of the Maestro's life. The Maestro expected this. "You are my map, my source of information about the details of my life, Domenico," he had once said.

"Thank you, Domenico," Vivaldi looked up at the oarsman, "you are correct. However, this matter is important enough that, if the Doge cannot see me, Tiepolo will."

"Might I suggest, then, sir, that you go straight to Tiepolo? I know where he is at this moment, which is more than can be said of the Doge. You know that he doesn't like to be bothered in the evening." Over the years, Domenico had become a master at shaping situations for Vivaldi.

"Very good, Domenico. I do need someone who will know exactly what to do. Besides, Mocenigo would hear me out and then say that he must consult with Tiepolo," Vivaldi's breathing became less laboured. "Where is he?"

"Without fail, sir, he's at Florian's every Monday evening. He and his cohorts meet on Mondays to talk over the business of the weekends. All the Gondoliers of Venice know this. This is how Tiepolo prepares for his Wednesday meetings at the Procuratie. I can guarantee that he will be there gathering information now. Here we are, sir. I'll let you out here and stay close by until you're ready to return home," Domenico assisted Vivaldi from the gondola and pointed toward the Piazza. His master's discomfort at such a worldly task tugged at the loyal servant's heartstrings. The man was so sheltered from the realities of life, so ill-at-ease in everyday life. "Keep going straight ahead, sir. And once you are almost at the end of the Ducal Palace, turn left. Florian's is a third of the way down the colonnade on your left! You will notice the smell of coffee."

Vivaldi did as he was told. The master of the Venetian stage felt at a loss as he put his hand on the door. Taking a deep breath, he opened the door and walked in. The acrid smell assaulted him. How in the world could anyone drink anything that smelled so dreadful! As his eyes became accustomed to the dim light, he attuned his ears. Within moments, he had heard and located Tiepolo's dark voice. He moved carefully by tables and into a back room where he found the Envoy. Only for Anna would he ever take on such a repugnant task as this.

From the centre of a group of men engaged in raucous conversation, Dante Tiepolo looked up at an incongruous. The Maestro of Venice stood there in all his vulnerability, striking in his red cape and open-necked white shirt. Framing his gently handsome features, Vivaldi's red hair revealed itself through the hurried powdering it had received. This was not a man inured to the ways of Venetian nightlife. "My God! Vivaldi! What in the name of God are you doing here of all places?" The Envoy stood up and motioned the Maestro to a seat. Tiepolo's companions, uncomfortable, stood and moved away from the table. The master politician of Venice motioned them out of the room. "Sit. Tell me what's happened," he poured the violinist a drink from the port decanter. "You've just returned from Rome, have you not?"

The Envoy exuded power. His penetrating black eyes flitted methodically in a continual assessment of the surroundings and customers. Seated across from the composer, he looked exactingly at him. The man was an irritant!

Vivaldi yielded to his control. "Yes, I came back an hour or two ago, and, of course, went directly to Paolina's bedside," the violinist's eyes made supplication for assistance in delivering his tale.

"Is it Paolina, then, Vivaldi? Come out with it, man. Tell me why you have come to me here, for God's sake! Is she dead?" Tiepolo's countenance darkened; his eyes burned holes into Vivaldi's brain.

"No, no; it is not that. Although Paolina is failing. No. Paolina informed me that Anna has left. She is absent from the Pieta," a wave of grief swept over him as he spoke the words. His eyes welled, and he reached for Tiepolo's arm. The Envoy drew back. "I know it is exactly what you and the Doge have warned me against. Oh, I pray that she is safe! I am at a loss as to what to do."

"Safe? Absent! What in the name of God do you mean, Vivaldi? Absent! Do you mean she has escaped Venice?" Tiepolo could barely keep his anger under control. No woman was going to play games with him! And this sniveling man in front of him! He grasped Vivaldi's bowing arm so roughly that Vivaldi winced. "This is mild treatment compared to what it will be if you don't get yourself under control now! Now!" He spoke in a rough whisper, "I will not tolerate this! Do you hear me? I have bigger matters of concern than your obsessions and stupid bumbling, Vivaldi. If it were up to me, I would not be bothered. Except that she makes me furious! But Mocenigo wants her will bent to Venice, as it used to be. The people want their shining star back." Letting go of the violinist's arm, he glared. "What exactly do you want, Vivaldi?"

Frightened, Vivaldi struggled for control and clarity, "Tiepolo, I want Anna back safely. And I am certain that the Doge's concerns would be the same as mine. And... and... Paolina is dying. She needs... wishes Anna to return home. Anna needs to know that. We... I want her back where she belongs. She will see that she belongs here and nowhere else." The Maestro's voice shook with emotion. He was on the edge of panic. What would he ever do without his star pupil? He crossed himself. God must help him here. Now!

Slapping money on the table in sheer aggravation, Tiepolo stood up and pulled on his black gloves. He looked down, coldly and disdainfully, into the Maestro's eyes. Vivaldi felt as though he were being consumed by the sheer force of the man. "I am vermin to him," he thought.

Tiepolo spoke. "Go back and search her room for information on her whereabouts. Obviously, she has gone to Siena. Try to find out how. Come to the Palace early tomorrow morning. I'll have explained the situation to the Doge by then." Tiepolo leaned toward the Maestro's ear and hissed, "I won't be embarrassed by an insignificant, rebellious woman, Vivaldi. Nor by you! Remember that!" He swept his cloak from a hook on the wall, threw it around his shoulders and left the room.

Antonio Vivaldi, knowing that Tiepolo would manage the situation perfectly, took a deep breath, let his fears for Antonia dissipate and thought how best he could leave this wretched place. As he looked around, he realized that the other patrons were busy with their own concerns. His panic began to subside. There had been enough noise to keep his and Tiepolo's talk private. Regaining his composure, he stood, straightened his shoulders, smoothed his hair and walked from the podium of Florian's stage into the fetid night air. "Domenico!" He called his manservant a few times as he turned the corner and headed toward the water.

Such a very difficult performance he had just given! But his Anna would be home safe and sound soon.

XXXIII

There is nothing so elegant as the arcane purple of wisteria blooms against a buttery rock wall. Wisteria understands and drops its petals on the Istrian stone in love for the beholder. I was Orlando's beholder. [Antonia, 1748]

It was the evening of the twenty-fifth day of April in the year 1726, the fourth evening of her flight to Siena. The shadows were long. The air was still and perfumed.

Antonia walked toward Bologna's San Petronio, Lorenzo's words of caution still in her mind. On their journey to the old town, she had related the story of the Elder Bach. "Bach told me about the effect San Petronio had on Martin Luther. I want to sit in that sanctuary and see if I can feel why it affected the man who so altered history. You see, ultimately Luther had such impact on music. Bach is tremendously influenced by Luther. And now I am influenced by Bach."

Lorenzo was puzzled by this woman, "Why? I understand the appreciation of his music. Although it is perhaps too Germanic, too thoroughly thought out. But why did Bach himself affect you?"

"He taught me what freedom is. He saw me as a separate individual." Antonia deftly moved the conversation back to music. "Luther is the German who most influenced Bach's creativity. Martin Luther himself prayed inside San Petronia, Lorenzo! German Luther in Italy... more to the point, German Luther being affected in an Italian church! Perhaps by sitting in the sanctuary for a while, I'll begin to understand Lutheranism. Perhaps there is freedom in it. I'm very curious."

Lorenzo had again reinforced the need to remain safe and anonymous. "Antonia, you push the edges of our plan too much at times. In so many ways, you know nothing of the dangers of this outside world. And you're entirely too trusting. This is not your safe quarters in Venice. This isn't the tiny, safe town that it appears to be."

Antonia had touched Lorenzo's arm, "My life experiences might surprise you. If I have been sheltered, and I have, that shelter has taken me inside myself. I do know how to become one with my surroundings. Someday, I must tell you about Mantova. I know how to blend into a town like this."

Now, with the hood of her black cape pulled up, the Venetian entered the church and proceeded in and out of the shadows of the flying buttresses and up to the altar. She knelt and let the feeling of the place engulf her. What was it that Luther had felt in this place? The profanity of Rome, of course. She had always sensed it, too. It was a holy profanity, if there were such a thing, a holy blending of Pagan faiths and Christianity. But she had learned as a young girl to slip beneath the surface, to touch truth. What did the exteriors of religion have to do with faith? Her faith was portable and palpable to all of her senses.

Antonia became aware of someone watching her. As she looked around, she saw a cloaked figure slip into a chapel. Icy fear swept over her. She thought she recognized the fiend who had snatched her and Paolina from Siena last summer. "Fear fuels the imagination, Antonia; return to beauty," a voice within stilled her.

Antonia returned to her prayers of gratitude and petition.

On her way down San Petronio's steps, Antonia again sensed danger. She looked over her shoulder. The same cloaked shape... was it the same? Who is he?... help me, dear God! The figure darted off to the south while Antonia fled into the openness of the Piazza to join Lorenzo. She ran up to him and took hold of his jacket.

"Lorenzo, I think I saw the man who took me from Siena last year. Twice! Inside San Petronio and just outside! Lorenzo, what shall we do?" Antonia held onto his jacket.

Lorenzo looked down at Antonia. He took her wrists gently in his hands, letting go reluctantly. He wanted nothing more at that moment than to hold her. "There's nothing we need to do. You're safe. It couldn't possibly be the same man. He was one of the others guarding us, stationed by Orlando. Talk to no one, Antonia, no one," Lorenzo reminded her. His confidence and authority settled her. "Orlando ordered this. Remember—do not engage in conversation with your hosts. Pleasantries only! We must leave no trail on the ground nor in anyone's mind. Your fears are just that—fears; but we'll be very vigilant here until we leave tomorrow afternoon. Even then, I'll watch more carefully than I usually do."

Lorenzo's countenance softened. Antonia brushed away a few tears. How very simple it would be to submit to his feelings. How very simple it would be to toss all responsibility aside and compete for this lovely creature. There was nothing left at home with Isolde but the comfort of familiarity and the need at times for pretense. Yes, how simple! He must remember his friendship with Orlando. "Come with me, child. There are only two more nights left before we reach our destination in Florence. As for tomorrow, I've promised to take you to the Observatory. You are safe with me, Antonia, safe."

Antonia clasped his hand. Her thoughts turned painfully to the other man who had once been as safe as a father to her. Lorenzo tried in vain to fix his thoughts on his family in Florence.

XXXIV

*Every year on Ascension Day, the Doge and a throng of noblemen
and musicians go out to sea so that Venice can marry the sea.
Once out in the Adriatic, the Doge throws a ring into the waters
and cries out, "We marry thee, O Sea, and this ring is the emblem
of our perpetual dominion over you!" Is that what marriage is to
Venetians? [Antonia, 1739]*

Tiepolo burst into the Doge's chambers just after daybreak.
Mocenigo bolted out of bed while his night-time companion merely
rolled over. Tiepolo threw Mocenigo's robe at him—"Put this on and
start thinking clearly!"

The Envoy wrenched the sheets away from the young man and
pulled him from the bed, "Get out! Now!" He threw the sheet around
the man and kicked him toward the door. Without looking back,
the Doge's erstwhile companion ran out and slammed the heavy
door behind him. Accustomed to night-life as he was, he knew better than to further inflame the Grand Master of Venice. Besides, he
would not want to fall from favour with Tiepolo.

Mocenigo scurried across the Turkish carpet to retrieve his belt.
Tiepolo shouted at him, "Your senseless plans to keep the Giraud
woman in Venice have failed! What a waste of time this stupid endeavour is! What a waste of time you are!"

"Tell me what has happened, Dante. You know that you're just as
married to this plan as I," Mocenigo, surprised at himself, spoke up
in his own defence. "You continue out of intrigue. I continue out of
pride." *And because it keeps me connected to you, Tiepolo....* Alvise
would not admit this aloud. Dante would find a way later to use it
against him. "What happened? Sit down."

Tiepolo sat across from the little ruler bundled in silk the colour
and texture of fine red wine. How he loathed him, and how he

needed him! "Vivaldi sought me out at Florian's last evening to tell me his 'little Anna' has escaped."

"Escaped? You mean 'fled', surely. She's never been a prisoner, has she? We've never imprisoned her." In customary fashion, Mocenigo went off tangentially.

"My God, man—think! She might as well have been locked up… with your rules and restrictions. You have your sources in the Pieta. Vivaldi and Giraud know that she is not to leave Venice. For God's sake—Venice knows! You have people watching her. You have Vivaldi eating out of your hand. What other word would you have me use? Giraud is gone, fled, escaped! She has mocked you, Alvise, mocked you—over pride and over an old family dispute that meant nothing to you when you first wanted Giraud as the jewel of Venice. The old Sagredo affair with your family meant nothing regarding her until you learned about Orlando himself. Use your brain!"

Mocenigo began pacing erratically. "I care for nothing more at this moment than her return to Venice. Forget Sagredo and his pathetic family—the Republic ousted them anyway! Giraud is mine! She is ours! She could not have escaped—with Vivaldi away, we increased our monitoring of the Pieta and the Bacino!" The Doge was stupefied. "There was no way that she could have escaped! She could never do that on her own!"

Tiepolo laughed in derision, "Well, she has done precisely that, Alvise—and under your very nose. Vivaldi's manservant brought me proof this morning. Vivaldi found remnants of letters in her fireplace. She has been in correspondence with Sagredo for months. It seems she slipped out during the night just before Vivaldi left for Rome and has four days' journey travelled already. If the Prioress weren't so ill, I would have this whole matter out with her. But Vivaldi protects her. He says she waited until he returned, that she didn't know whom to contact… that she was too ill to think this through. He might believe her; but I would never believe her. I should never have played into this idiocy of yours, this plan to make music central to Venice. Vivaldi himself should have been enough for the fame you hungered after... but, no! You insisted on a female counterpart!"

"Come now, Dante," it was the Doge's turn to laugh. "You loved the plan. It gave you greater excuse to travel. It gave you greater uniqueness and power. And Venice will always be known for the music of Vivaldi—more even than for its painters. Perhaps, but I hope not... more, perhaps... than for it naval prowess." The night with his young bed-mate had provided Mocenigo with a touch of power. "And—you still hunger after Giraud."

Tiepolo stood and began pacing. "All right—enough! But I have told you many times that I set my appetites aside when necessary for the greater good of Venice. Have I not? Now what shall we do? I favour letting her go. She isn't worth the trouble it would be to bring her back."

"No!" Mocenigo, eyes glaring, stood and shouted at his Envoy, his gesticulations making his Ducal ring flash on the walls. "I will give no Sagredo pleasure at my expense!"

"It is an old grievance, Alvise. Who would know or care anymore?" Tiepolo's voice was gentler and resigned.

"I would. And so would the old Sagredo," the Doge of the Most Serene Republic sat down and looked up at Tiepolo. "I will not be embarrassed. Bring her back. You decide how. Now, leave... please."

Tiepolo allowed himself a brief moment of sympathy. What good would any anger do directed at this pitiable character? He would focus his anger on the Venetian beauty. Bringing her back could be quite personally gratifying.

As he left the Doge's chambers, he snapped his fingers at the manservant waiting in the ante-room and pointed him in the direction of his master. "Look after him well. He needs it."

By the time he had reached the Giant's Staircase, Dante Tiepolo had hatched a plan.

XXXV

The Maestro was the most spectacular musician. In performing,
he and the violin became one. They soared... drifted... flew. They
spun and plunged, only to soar again. And they took the audience
with them... into the heavens—into the dark night of desolation
and into the face of the sun. There were times when I thought his
playing would consume him. I believe... I know... he touched
God. And then he would have to come back to earth. And to the
constraints of humanity. He found being human difficult. [Anto-
nia, 1741]

Lorenzo had been poetic in his descriptions of Florence. On the
journey from Imola, his words were paintings for Antonia as she
tried to get a sense of Florence. Now, as they made the breathtaking
descent from Fiesole into the basin of the Arno River, Antonia was
spellbound. How she wished Lorenzo would let her sit with him!
But he had refused. "No, Antonia. I will take no chances at this stage
of our journey. I want you to have time to experience the heart of
Florence, not feel that we have to slink around and leave early." She
had learned that Lorenzo's word was unequivocal.

Gripping the door handle, she stood as well as she could in the
carriage to see better. Long shadows competed with the height of
the trees, drawing the eye up and down and adding a chequered texture to the hillside. And there were the colours Lorenzo had spoken
of! Pastels—yellow, green, blue—modulating from tone to tone and
creating new colours. And wonderful estates whose gardens even
Antonia's huge imagination could never have pictured... ancient
walls overtaken by wisteria... the late afternoon sun releasing a
creeping sepia over the centre of Florence. She could feel and smell
the breath of this valley.

And there! There it was! Antonia gasped. The Duomo! Brunelleschi's dome! Unbelievable! She banged on the carriage door until Lorenzo heard her. He drew the horses to a stop.

"What is it, Antonia?" Lorenzo called out as he jumped down from his seat. He ran to the door just as Antonia opened it and stepped out. He reached up to help her down. "Are you all right?"

"Lorenzo, come over here!" She took his hand, almost pulling him to the side of the road that looked over the valley. "Lorenzo!"

How could he resist her disarming approach? In that moment, Lorenzo knew he would relent and say "yes" to her... always.

"You must tell me what I am looking at! You must!" Antonia's excitement was contagious.

Lorenzo's laughter boomed out over the valley. "I must?"

"You must!"

"Well, Antonia... I...," Lorenzo realized that he had very naturally put his arm around his charge, "do you see the Arno there and the Duomo?"

Antonia nodded, "Yes, I lost my breath at the sight of the Duomo."

"That area, then—around the Duomo—is the heart of Florence... her business and her arts and, above all, her politics. There's a legend that the Etruscans laughed down upon the Romans as they built in the valley. Do you see the river? It does flood at times. But the Romans prevailed, and the Etruscans disappeared. They probably saw the Arno as the Tiber. This side of the Arno is where you'll find most of the Piazzas I've told you about. And to the left of the Duomo... there... just a little further left...," he moved his hand gently to her shoulder to direct her eastward, "yes... that is the Basilica Santa Croce. It is home to the bones of Galileo and Michelangelo and to frescoes of San Francesco. And always, Dante's statue stands guard... rather ominously. And, across the Arno... across from the Uffizi, which you cannot quite see from here... I wish you could see it, Antonia, as that's where much of the plot to return you to Siena was hatched. So, then, across from the Uffizi, where Orlando and I talked, is Oltrarno, fascinating for its history as well. There's an old Roman aqueduct there and two old churches you would love to see... in particular, San Miniato. Yes... you would find the main fresco stunning with its Maddalena. And the view down from that building and over Florence is as beautiful as this view." Antonia scanned constantly, fascinated, while Lorenzo explained.

"Oh, Lorenzo, how can I see it all? If I had the luxury of time, I know I'd want to stay in Florence for a long visit. But, I must press on to Orlando—not even Florence must hold me back." Antonia became pensive. She turned her head to see Lorenzo as he looked at his city, and she understood. She understood this man's feeling for this place, his brooding spirit and his passion for art, as contrary as that sort of passion seemed against his forceful, burly appearance. Turning again to look over the hillside and into Florence, she pondered this new awareness of Lorenzo. The two travelling companions rested in the scene. "Lorenzo, I know you—as you said—'disappointed' your father by choosing art over the family business; but does your decision ever sadden you?"

Lorenzo was touched. Grateful for this time with her, it became bittersweet. Their loves of art and music had coincided. He saw Florence as new. He craved every aspect of this time, its peace, its perfection and, most of all, Antonia. "Not at all. My father is a gracious, perhaps even noble, man. He's grateful that all his children are happy."

"And you, Lorenzo, you are happy?" Antonia's voice was soft and direct.

He laughed quietly, "About my work, Antonia. I am passionate about my work." She knew. She had sensed him. On this trip of melodies and vistas, of pain and love, she knew his heart. And he did not have, and never would have, her heart.

Sensing Lorenzo's meaning, Antonia chose to leave the unsaid hidden. Instead, she pursued the answer he had given. "I see. What is it in your work that you love most? Is it the artists' lives? Their works? The process?"

"Ah—it's all of that and more. My passion derives from art itself, from how true art replicates the perfect form, from how it speaks of something much greater than the work of art itself, from how it draws people who know how to discern, from how it instructs... inspires... comments," Lorenzo realized that he had become, as Isolde would have been quick to point out, "carried away." Just as he was about to apologize, Antonia spoke.

"Yes, Lorenzo! If we simply look below us here—look again now at the Duomo—we see exactly what you have said about art in Brunelleschi's dome, in what no one else could conceive. Art does instruct and inspire," Antonia had stepped onto the path of her own passion. "The dome finishes all the works of art on the walls and ceilings and then finishes Florence herself as a work of art! Plato himself would have loved it. Amazing! Amazing because, like music, it glorifies the Creator."

"And what would that Creator have to say about Cosimo's part in the masterpiece?" Lorenzo wanted to test this woman's faith. Could she, as sheltered as she had always been, handle the tension all art produced?

Antonia's smiled, "What would God have to say about all the manipulations that went into producing your great Dome? I suspect, Lorenzo, that He places us all in struggle and perplexity, and often great pain, to see if we can make art out of our lives." She looked directly into his eyes again, "Lorenzo—look! Look again at what we have before us here. Look at how you've been able to teach me.

Look at how we can talk about all of this. We, Lorenzo—you and I—have made a work of art of this very journey. Have we not?" Antonia rested slightly into Lorenzo's arm, "Thank you for being my companion."

The Florentine strained against his feelings, "Perhaps we have… but you, Antonia, are the priceless work of art."

"No, Lorenzo, our story, the intersection of our souls… that is the work of art," Antonia's wistfulness re-emerged. "I'm a long way from Venice. In so many, many ways. Where is your home? Is it near the heart?"

Lorenzo returned to the reality of their circumstances and re-moved his arm from her waist. He took her elbow. He could not tolerate the agony of her closeness—and her distance—any longer. "Actually, my residence is not far from the Duomo. Come, we must move along."

Antonia turned back for a moment to absorb the vista. Reluc-tantly, she followed Lorenzo's direction. "I understand your love of Florence, Lorenzo. Now I shall be able to imagine you in your city. And I'll always remember this time we've had together, talking of art… and life. Always."

As they walked back in silence, Lorenzo tried to shake off the pain. Have I ever felt this way? Never! He assisted Antonia into the carriage and found that he could hardly bear the touch of her. As he closed the door, the taunting scent of wild roses drifted up from the roadside. This is what you cannot have, Cristofori…cannot have…cannot have. He climbed back into his seat. Where had these feelings come from? And why did they stay with him? It had been years since he had felt so drawn to a woman… to innocence, really. Had innocence not disappeared from the world long ago?

He jumped down from his seat and returned to the carriage door. Antonia leaned forward as he opened the door. Dear God, her presence! "We'll head into the heart of the city shortly, Antonia. I want you to pay attention to a few sights... the Duomo, of course, and the Baptistery. But, before that, see if you can pick out our San Marco and our Orphanage... Ospedale degli Innocenti... it was the first orphanage in Europe."

Antonia's face brightened, "Oh, Lorenzo, thank you! We were taught about your orphanage. I've often wondered about it. And I'd forgotten. Brunelleschi again, is it not?"

Again, she puzzled him with her innocence and her knowledge. "Indeed—and della Robbia. You'll appreciate the differences between our places and yours." He patted her hand... held it momentarily. Yes, the extra touch... the extra look... had been necessary. "We're off! Be discreet about showing your face through the window."

He closed the door—slowly, as Antonia smiled in her most captivating way—and within moments, the nondescript carriage with its curious cargo was off into the heart of his city.

* * *

Above the beauty and fabulous confusion of Florence, Antonia loved Lorenzo's family. His parents, his sister and brothers, his son and daughter and even the aloof Isolde warmed her orphaned heart.

Never having experienced family life, Antonia, on her first night in Florence, pushed past her sleepiness and stayed up late with Lorenzo and his sister, Maria, to discuss the life and art of Florence. How wonderful it was to be in the company of a brother and sister who knew and loved each other so much. Much to her own surprise, Antonia found reasons to join in the laughter and just as many reasons to inject a humorous viewpoint of her own. How had she been so deprived that she had never felt the full force of laughter?

Maria reminded her of Sister Paolina in much the same way that
Lorenzo did. Why? Antonia found herself as an observer at times,
a position she had grown accustomed to in life, and one that served
her well in analyzing situations. As she watched these siblings, she
began to understand that they, like Sister Paolina, were not afraid
to love and to speak the language of love to whomever they loved.
Often, Maria would reach over to Lorenzo and touch his shoulder
or arm. Lorenzo was equally affectionate with his beautiful, vital
sister. Antonia was intrigued. At one point, during a disagreement
about the merits of the new instrument that a relative had crafted
to replace the harpsichord, Lorenzo gave his adamant sister a kiss
on the cheek. Antonia was fascinated. And envious. I have heard
of envy; but never until now have I felt it! She quickly reassured
herself that music had been her sibling.

Lorenzo reached over to touch her on the shoulder, "Antonia,
you've gone away again! What do you think of this piano e forte
that we've been discussing? You must have some opinion about its
possibilities."

Antonia blushed. Lorenzo's hand had felt like Orlando's hand on
her shoulder. Like Orlando, Lorenzo had sensed early in their journey that she had a tendency to dwell within her mind. She appreciated his ability to bring her into the immediate moment. It was all
too easy for her to hide as the observer. "I'm fascinated. From the
way you describe it, it's completely different from the harpsichord.
My first reaction is to question its use for music that already exists
for the harpsichord. That's not to say that music cannot be written
for it. I would appreciate seeing it someday," Antonia began to miss
the music she had left behind, "Of course, I would have to play it and
have it played for me. I'd enjoy that... it could be played at a musical
evening with friends... however, many instruments come and go,
and only the pure prevail. I cannot imagine any instrument replac-

ing the harpsichord." And then in an after-thought that surprised her, she added, "Although I wish the harpsichord were better capable of handling feelings. Strings evoke more love than hammers. Nothing will ever surpass the depth and passion of the violin..." she stopped herself, "...for me."

Lorenzo loved her fervour. He poured more wine for each of them. "A toast, Antonia! To you! To you for being so brave as to run to the man you love. To you for not compromising love. To Orlando for his good fortune in being loved by one as lovely as you!" Maria looked quizzically at her brother. Antonia beamed. "Does Orlando Sagredo not produce the most sublime grapes, Antonia? This is his Malvasia. To Orlando! And Antonia!" Lorenzo's infectious laughter spilled over the room yet again. And once again, Maria marvelled at the return of her brother's gusto and at his enjoyment of Antonia's presence. This was the brother she knew, not the serious, sometimes silent, often absent, husband and father he had become.

The clinking of glasses and the rich accompanying laughter delighted Antonia. These Cristoforis inspired a new music within her heart, her heart that was once again peaceful and buoyant.

At midnight, Maria excused herself. Antonia stood to take her hand; but Maria embraced her warmly and left the room. Antonia turned to bid good-night to Lorenzo. Exhilarated from the fine wine and the company, Lorenzo followed his sister's example and embraced his guest. "Sleep well and hear music, young one." Framing her face with his broad hands, he leaned down toward her mouth, "You are beautiful, Antonia." As Antonia turned up toward him, Lorenzo felt the warmth of her breath. Only once—only once and he would let her go—only once did he need her heart beating with his. But her eyes did not reflect his intentions. Lorenzo corrected himself and kissed her forehead. Suddenly agitated, he stepped back.

He loved this woman who could never be his. He must rid himself of these feelings. Now!

Antonia picked up a candlestick and climbed the stairs to her room. Once into her nightgown, she ran her fingers through her rich auburn hair, shook her head and looked up into Reni's painting of St. Cecilia above the bed. She felt a warm connection to this pensive saint of music, so connected to her violin. Antonia bent down to blow out the candle on the night table, climbed into bed and drifted into sleep.

She dreamed that night of her sister orphans seated with her at an enormous harvest table. It was a noisy, happy dream, with wine, music and conversation mixing and flowing, creating watery colours and triumphant, sparkling music. Father Antonio and Sister Paolina were there, at the table, instigating the happiness. Antonia communicated with them through singing. They vocalized back to her in harmonies. She recognized the colours and the harmonies as being the components of pure love. Just as she was waking, Orlando walked into the dream, resplendent in a cape of verdant grape vines and extending his hands toward her until they blended into colours beyond the violet of rainbows. She awoke in bliss. A bliss that had been interrupted by Lorenzo's light rapping at the door.

* * *

Antonia had long harboured a desire to see Michelangelo's sculpture of David. It came from her fascination with Juditha. Often on this strange journey, the music of Juditha sang in her head. She took courage from Juditha's courage—"Wherever love of country lead me, And the sweet hope of freedom, thither, Guided by the light of heaven, May my steps go safely."

And her steps—and Lorenzo's—had brought to her the very place. Here she was, awestruck, on her own in the Piazza della Signoria on her second evening in Florence, gazing at the David. In spite of having studied Michelangelo in her later years of schooling, she was astonished at the size and the bold poise in the young man's countenance. So, this was the shepherd boy who had slain Goliath! Il Gigante, indeed! This, too, then, was Orlando who had taken her away from her own giant. Antonia approached the sculpture from another angle. Yes—Michelangelo had made a Goliath out of David! And Juditha, David's twin, his anima gemella, had given her the courage she needed for this journey. Unintentionally, Father Antonio had given her the heart of Juditha, and with this heart she could overcome any enemy on her return to Orlando.

Antonia looked around the Piazza. The evening was hot and misty, the city crowded with groups of people whose faces and voices coalesced with the darkening Florentine pastels. Antonia was spellbound by the ethereal quality of the air and the surroundings, lulled into memories of Orlando and bittersweet echoes of Venice. Venice, though gone now, would forever be a part of her.

Antonia realized that she had let her thoughts wander. It must be time now for Lorenzo and Maria to return from Oltrarno. She must watch for them. Before they had separated, Lorenzo had decided she would be safe for the short time it would take for them to visit a business acquaintance. With her black cape, she would be part of the crowd, indistinct. That was how she felt... indistinct... distorted. She walked over to Neptune's fountain.

Just as she reached the fountain, she heard the voice, dark, formidable. Somewhere in the dim perimeter... as though coming from the alley in Siena. Was it Tiepolo? One of his men? Her heart raced. Her breathing became shallow. She wanted to run. Where? Suddenly, everyone in the Piazza looked dangerous. The great bell tolled out eight times. As the rolling sound faded, it became a voice demanding, "You are to come with me!" Antonia ran back into the centre of the Piazza, falling over her skirt. Where had David gone? A hand reached out to her.

It was Lorenzo's. "Come, Antonia, you're safe," Lorenzo reassured her. He lifted her to her feet and steadied her. "Antonia, you've frightened yourself. Were you afraid of Tiepolo again?" As he put his hands on Antonia's shoulders, he realized he was losing his battle to keep her at an emotional distance. He felt her vulnerability in her shoulders. She had only to ask, and he would take this beautiful creature around the world safely and stay with her, wherever her heart might choose to rest, forever. Yes, he could abandon all else for her. He drew her into his embrace.

Safe now, Antonia settled. "I'm sure I saw him, Lorenzo. I'm so afraid I won't reach Siena and Orlando!" She drew away from his embrace.

I've lost again, he thought. Lorenzo reverted to his paternal role. "Antonia, you must put your full trust in me. I simply will not let anything happen to you. As for tonight, I guarantee you that Tiepolo isn't here. Come—you're here to enjoy yourself. We still have time to have a look at the spot where Orlando and I talked over our plans to get you away from Venice." Lorenzo offered her his arm, and they walked past the Uffizi and out to the Arno.

"I apologize for my foolishness. It's not—definitely not—that I lose trust in you. I lose trust in being with Orlando again. Thank you for taking care of me." Antonia was weary now. "I feel overwhelmed at times."

Lorenzo was silent for a moment, thinking of the January day he and Orlando had been together. "Our thoughts affect our life experiences, Antonia. Turn your thoughts to the life you know you will have with Orlando. You love each other in a way that's not often experienced. You're both very fortunate." Somehow the Arno was as cold and unfriendly now as it had been when he and Orlando made their plans in January.

"Orlando told me in a letter that you and he do business together and that he would trust you with his most valuable possession," Antonia's fears had completely disappeared.

"And that he has, Antonia. He has entrusted your safety to me. I had to convince him that he should not be the one to bring you back, that it would be much safer for you if you were delivered by an unknown like me. Come," Lorenzo took Antonia's arm again and navigated her back through the crowd. "You had that sense, too, did you not?"

Antonia remembered her last letter to Orlando. "I did. That was why I told Orlando I wanted this journey to be a pilgrimage for me. And it has been—a most unusual one." As they walked along together, she told him of her fears and of her great grief over her Maestro. "It's not that I am most afraid of being found, Lorenzo. It's that I am most afraid of a love that is possessive and suffocating. Father Antonio's violin arm has a long reach."

One by one, Lorenzo vanquished her fears. "You're the most disciplined woman I've ever known, Antonia. When I first saw you in the gondola, I was taken aback at your resemblance to a figure in one of my favourite paintings—Caravaggio's entombment of Christ. It is part of the altar in a Chiesa in Roma. For me, you are the strong Maddalena saying "no" and holding the heavens in place with your violinist's hands. I hope that you're able to see it one day."

Antonia smiled and sighed, "Oh, Lorenzo! My friend, Canal, explained Caravaggio's Juditha to me! He went so far as to sketch it for me. She's my guiding light," a wave of homesickness took hold of Antonia. "Father Antonio composed a wonderful opera of her...." Her voice trailed off into the walls of the Palazzo.

"I've seen that painting, too—again in Rome. It's equally powerful. However, the Maddalena stands back, reaches up and challenges—yes, challenges—God. And in doing so, with her arms upraised, she bravely takes death into its impending resurrection. As you have done, Antonia," Lorenzo moved her away from a group of mimes. "They're no more than beggars, this lot... not actors. You've conducted yourself as she would have. I will return you to Siena, to Orlando. I promise you. Ah, there's Maria... over there. She knew we'd come here. There's the Donatello."

Speechless, Antonia reached deeply into her pocket for the touch of glass. She walked up to the sculpture. Juditha, ready to cut off Holofernes' head, looked down at her prey. Antonia shuddered at the immediacy of the act. Such a beautiful face for such a hideous deed. Even the angels trembled and fled.

Suddenly, Venice and Siena collided. Antonia felt her great loss of the Maestro and their work together. Why were sacrifice and separation necessary? Why could love not have been enough for all?

And suddenly a sense of hope replaced the despair. She realized how preposterous her notions of imminent kidnap were. Such had been her fear that she would not reach Orlando. As Lorenzo had said, one's belief could bring things into being. She would not lose faith again.

Antonia turned to Lorenzo and Maria, "My fears are gone—I'm grateful to both of you for that—and to Juditha! I'm indebted to you for this time in Florence. Shall we return to your home?" Lorenzo and Maria, puzzled at her abrupt change, stepped in on either side of her. What had seeing Juditha done?

* * *

Later, Antonia sat reading a Cristofori journal by candlelight in her room. Lorenzo knocked on her door and entered to confirm the next day's departure plans. How beautifully right she seemed in this room. How familiar she seemed. This pain he felt, this loss of her, made him angry. He reminded himself that he would lose her soon to Siena. His duties would be over as he delivered Antonia to a life with his friend. "I'll tend to some work tomorrow morning, and we'll leave in the afternoon. Is there anything you need?"

Antonia smiled warmly, "Sit and talk with me for a while, Lorenzo. Your family chronicle has captivated me. Tell me more about yourself and your family."

"Not tonight, Antonia. It's best that you know no more about me. And best that I know no more about you. We have a dangerous journey to complete." He looked past her. His sternness had returned.

"Why? Why is that best?" Antonia was bewildered by the change in her companion. "Lorenzo, please explain what you mean."

"Memories are often best made from superficialities, Antonia. So that they can be lived with. Good night. Sleep well."

Antonia stared at the closing door, confused by Lorenzo's behaviour and remembering his earlier kind embrace... hurt by Lorenzo's sudden brusqueness... mystified at the complexity of her emotions.

And then she remembered Mantova and Jacopo. And she knew why Lorenzo often reminded her of someone else.

XXXVI

One of the Lagoon Islands succumbed to the waters ages ago...
when the Black Plague swept through Venice. San Marco in Boc-
calama. They buried La Piaga's victims there. By the boatload. I
suppose the island sank beneath the weight and the grief of it all.
The Lagoon can be like that... mysterious, secretive and deadly,
swallowing its victims. It's a doorway to Purgatory, I think. [An-
tonia, 1739]

Orlando lay back in the wild flowers and grasses. Somehow it now did not seem so long ago that they had become one last summer with the fading purple hills as backdrop. Antonia felt almost as near now. The late afternoon sun danced through the tender new leaves, casting mottled, undulating patterns over his face and arms. He could sense her near him. Was that her voice? No, her violin was singing, singing as he had heard it last May in the Duomo. Ah, her voice joined in. Antonia, singing on behalf of souls oppressed and struggling to awake. Alma Oppressa. Her violin calling out to those souls and singing as soul itself. Antonia convincing mere mortals of an invisible world just beyond the visible. He drifted with the clouds. Free. Joyful. As Antonia would be from now on. How she loved this place.

"Orlando," she seemed to call from over by a purple-flowered tree. "Orlando! Over here!" The hills rang with her laughter.

He stood and moved toward the voice. Where was she? He felt afraid. "Antonia! Where are you?"

Floating, she appeared before him. "I will not leave this time, Orlando. Look into my eyes. Hold me as you did in our Far Away Land, and let me lie against your chest. Come home, Orlando."

Turning from her, he became suddenly old. He withered emotionally, as though he had realized some alternate truth, as though a darker voice called. Yes—he could hear it! He felt compelled to leave her.

"No! Stay young, Orlando. Turn around!" Antonia's voice was more powerful than his fear, and he turned toward her. Her smile turned into sunlight.

"I've waited so long," he picked her up and carried her away into the fabric of the purple hills, "and we are both home now." He took her to a clearing and laid her down on the soft blanket of the greening place they knew so well.

As she rested against him, she found the tear she had laid on his chest so long ago. She touched it gently. Responding, the teardrop shone brilliantly and spun up into the sky where it stopped and shone upon them as a Day Star. Antonia reached up and pulled the Day Star into her hands. She clasped her hands around it. Its brilliance spilled out between her fingers.

Standing, Antonia smiled down upon Orlando and extended her hands toward him. In the utter beauty of conception, she opened her fingers. There within her palms was their child, smiling and reaching toward him. Orlando, jubilant and eager, reached for his child's hand, and the three of them wafted upward on a pure white cloud.

The sky was as blue as the Madonna's skirt.

XXXVII

Sometimes it amazes me that I can remember so vividly, given all the years that have passed. I am very grateful for this, in spite of the pain that can be part of it. I am certain Orlando and I visit in a way that will be understood once this life is over. There are times when I can run my fingers through his hair, when I can see his eyes and his slightly crooked smile, and when I can feel his breath until we are breathing together. And in my dreams, we come together and I am fulfilled. [Antonia, 1749]

The towers of San Gimignano behind them, Antonia and Lorenzo were on the final lap of their journey. Siena would be theirs after another night's rest. Antonia's original resolve and energy had returned. Until her stay in San Gimignano, she had sometimes had to fight the urge to give up, to yield to the pull of disbelief.

As the carriage now approached, Antonia could allow herself the luxury of feeling excited. Now she could stop worrying about Lorenzo's distant mood. He had his own reasons for withdrawing. But she missed him and felt hurt. She missed the life he brought to the journey.

As planned, Orlando had sent a friend to San Gimignano to be certain Antonia and Lorenzo were safe. The stay-over in Monteriggioni was a deviation so that Orlando's scouts could alert him if there were problems. While Antonia was safe in Monteriggioni, any of Tiepolo's men could be dealt with as they headed into Siena. Monteriggioni would never be thought as a stop on the way.

Antonia had been well protected in the town of invisible giants. The shadows of the towers and Orlando had done their duty. And she could claim citizenship in Siena.

* * *

Ellyn Peirson

The Night Before I Join You Forever

My dearest Orlando,

Here I sit in Monteriggioni, almost within your arms. You were wise in your choice of resting places and in keeping our time on the road as late and short as possible. The Sisters here have provided me with the means to write. I feel compelled to put some thoughts into words for you.

I know I am going to see you. I know it, and I believe it. And yet, this has been a journey of darkness for me. I say this as night falls.

The shadows of this journey have been long and severe. Minimal speech and lack of music have affected me profoundly. I suppose this has been my time in the wilderness. On this journey, I have sensed and understood the invisible line between life and death. It has many manifestations within both physical and spiritual domains. Wearing a myriad of Venetian disguises, it lurks in the shadows of our whole sojourn here on earth. But we neither apprehend it naturally nor through teaching. And when we are forced to confront it, we can, and often do, choose to shut it from our mind. The line still exists, though; nothing can prevent it from doing its work.

The choice is ours as to what this line means. It is either friend or foe. We choose which. If we choose to be with the line as friend, we become aware of life's wonders. With this awareness comes responsibility and immense complexity. Orlando, the reason for our brief lives here must be to re-create beauty for God! Together you and I have created a beautiful love, a love greater than we ever could have imagined.

This journey to Siena has indeed become a spiritual pilgrimage. I have felt kindred to St. Catherine. I now understand that there is no place for Pride within a properly perceived life. Orlando, I am so grateful that you are not a proud man. I love your sincerity, your strength, your compassion, and, Orlando, how I love your playfulness. You have taught me that life is to be lived, not observed!

The reason I write this is that I cannot banish my fears. Yes, I know I shall see you tomorrow. But I cannot dismiss or obliterate my fears that I will not have a long life with you.

And so, I want you to have my love in writing, Orlando. Whatever happens, I will never leave you spiritually; you are my heart and soul's delight—for eternity.

Orlando, if we are ever separated—by death or by ill intent—I shall belong to no one else, other than our Saviour. Should such tragedy befall us, the moon will be your constant reminder that neither death nor ill intent are powerful enough to separate us permanently. We share one soul, Orlando, for Eternity.

Forever,
Antonia of Siena

(Lorenzo has been a source of great strength and protection on this journey. You are fortunate to have a friend such as he. And he is now my friend. I have directed him to give you this letter only if some form of death separates us. May he never have to fulfill his promise.)
Amen.

* * *

Antonia sat back in her chair. The shadows and the falling night seemed somehow safer now. Orlando seemed closer. She was safe. And yet, something called her, nagging, melancholy, archaic.

Her thoughts drifted to the waters of Venice, the origin of her love and her fear. "I miss Father Antonio. That's what bothers me so. Why could it not have been different? Why could he not have blessed what I love even more than music? That would have been his greatest gift to me." She lit the lamp and dipped the quill into the ink, moving a new sheet of paper into place. "This is what I wish," she thought…

Near Siena, April 30, 1726

Dear, dear Maestro,

How I wish we could have parted in a loving way, with connection, joy and an acknowledged, natural sadness. These can be aspects of separation, dear Father. Instead, we parted in secrecy and dishonesty, features we had never needed in our relationship until I was ready for freedom and love.

I have reached the last night of my journey to Siena and life with Orlando. Only in your mind, where you live, does this new life exclude the possibility of our continuing relationship. How selfish of you to exert your will in this way. In making me choose between Orlando and you, you have broken my heart. For you have removed yourself from my life.

You have been my father, my mentor, my companion, my teacher and my inspiration. We have even become colleagues in music. How I treasure all of that! I know that deep within your heart in a place you do not know well, you have treasured these things, too. How can you, then, for the sake of pride and possession, reject your creation?

Until I reached San Gimignano, I missed you desperately on this journey. The carriage served as a nun's cell for me, providing me with time to pray and examine in private for hours. I touched what it could be to abide in an Eternity of incompletion. I was angry at you. I grieved. I was tormented by fears. Are these all aspects of abandonment? You, Father Antonio, have abandoned me as you abandoned your priesthood. You tried to capture God within your music. You bound me to it. But Music and God are about freedom, dear Maestro,

Freedom! Your unmusical utterances of "Domine" and your crossing
yourself distanced you from others and from God.
   I did not want to choose. You forced me to do so.
   During my stay in San Gimignano, I visited its ancient well and
suddenly understood all of this. In that moment, I took on the respon-
sibility for the wellspring within me. My soul was renewed in that
town of towers. With them, I reached for and touched Truth.
   I will love and miss you forever.

Always your daughter in music and faith,
Anna

Antonia looked down at the teardrops that had fallen on the letter. She smeared them into the ink, staining her palm. Murkiness
bleeding into truth… heartbeats on paper… smudged. She held a
candle to the letter and dropped the flaming paper into the ashbin.

Stamping her foot and giving a sharp clap with her hands, Antonia turned away from the flame. "Begone, Anna," she said, "you
were nothing but a dream."

Antonia of Siena placed Orlando's letter in an envelope for
Lorenzo and headed fully aware into a night of new dreams.

XXXVIII

*The Doge of Venice was a puppet. There were two puppeteers—
the Pope and the Envoy of the Procuratori. Many Doges fell out of
favour with their puppeteers, their only recourse being a retreat
into seclusion. Truly, they were set up to fail while making others successful. Venice, while contained in a serene body, has an
avaricious underbelly. The serenity channels itself through devotion to the Virgin Mary. The hunger channels itself through
the Lion of San Marco. It would seem to me, because the Virgin
Mother visited San Marco in a dream, that there is a Venetian
Trinity of the Madonna, San Marco and the Lion... Mother, Son
and Holy Ghost. Every night, the Lion descends his high post
near the Doge's Palace and skulks along the canals, taking care
of abominations. He sends the Refiner's Fire through the waters.
Hissing, the fiery waters expel Evil's debris into the Lagoon. The
Lagoon is exceedingly capable of extermination. [Antonia, 1739]*

"I have sent the Doge's envoy off, Paolina. He left yesterday." Antonio had come into Paolina's room to sit by her bedside. She raised
her hand. "No! Say nothing," Vivaldi put her hand back under the
sheet. "It is done! Here, have a little more to drink."

"Antonio, please listen to me! Send someone to bring him back.
Please! I don't want Antonia to come back for my sake. She and I
were able to say our farewells." Paolina, emaciated now, could no
longer sit up. Her voice was raspy; her eyes beseeching.

"I know you were, I know. I could not easily fall asleep last night,
and I woke very early this morning. Paolina, I must be honest. I was
in great personal unease. In my sleepless hours, I came to realize
that I did not selflessly make this move to return Anna. I saw my
selfishness late last night. I am a selfish man, Paolina. You know that
better than anyone. Paolina, you are dying, my love. The only way

I shall survive your loss is to have Anna with me." Antonio picked up her hand and began to weep.

Paolina pulled his hand up to her mouth, kissed it and stroked his fingers, finding the violinist's callouses she knew so well. His fingers became her rosary beads while her own tears spilled over onto their hands.

"Antonio, can you not give me this one gift... can you find it in your heart to release Antonia? Let her be free; please, let her be free. You can live without her."

The Maestro stiffened and looked directly into Paolina's dying eyes. "No, Paolina, I cannot. I am that selfish. I am so sorry. It is done. I will not undo it." He moved over to the window and looked out over the Venice that they knew so well. A dismal Venice looked back at him, accusingly. "I have been assured that everything will run smoothly and safely. It is done."

"Are you still angry with her?" Paolina spoke softly.

"No, Paolina, I am not. When I first returned home to find that she had been run away from us, I was crushed. Yes," he saw Paolina begin to form a question, "I was angry when I found her letters in the fireplace. No matter what you have said about the importance of the full moon to her, I have also realized that she chose a time when I would be away. I do not tolerate deceit and betrayal well. I suppose that I am still angry with you because of your part in the betrayal."

"Antonio, there was no possible way to be true to both of you in this. I chose to affirm youth and love. And, Antonio," Paolina struggled to speak, "please know that my dying is not a betrayal. If somehow I could stay to be with you only, I would. Whatever is eating me inside has won. And I suppose I've done my life's work. But it doesn't feel as though I have. More than anything, I wanted to age and die with you, Antonio. More than anything."

Antonio sat beside the bed again. "Rest now, Paolina. I am not angry with you—truly, I am not. Rest, sweet one. You and I and Anna are intertwined; we belong to the same vine. She will settle once again to her place in the world. All will be well. Rest." Paolina's pain succumbed to his sensitive hands. He began to hum. The familiar would soothe them both.

Dropping into the arms of sleep, she sighted Antonia's face. Her burgundy hair shone like a halo. "Antonia!" she called out sweetly as she moved into her dreams.

Antonio covered Paolina's thin hands and tucked her in as Anna would have done. He kissed her tenderly on her lips and forehead.

Closing her sickroom door quietly, he pulled his shoulders up, composed himself and prepared for a day of work. As he walked away from the odour of death, his customary jauntiness was gone from his step. Paolina would not die, of course… she would rally soon. Of course! Of course… all she needed was to see her Anna again. Yes… yes! He was doing this for Paolina… yes… not for himself… for Paolina… so she would not die….

OTTO

THE SIENESE HILLS TO THE SAGREDO ESTATE

1726

XXXIX

Il Croco, the flower, established San Gimignano's early strength.
Even though the trade for saffron died a while ago, there is still
evidence of the Crocus Sativus in the valley. The phantoms of the
lost trade are there in the reds and purples and in the texture
and breath of the valley. What stories that breath could tell if
we knew how to listen. It would tell us of the colours of love and
how love transmutes into gold. I often walk into the valley and
up the hill to the town. I visit the convent there. I pray. I wish
for the power of saffron to heal me. And him. I feel very close to
Orlando within the reach of the towers, as though he were one of
the towers. [Antonia, 1746]

"Orlando, settle yourself. Everything will work out well. Stop pacing! Find something to do. Something that takes concentration."

Carlo wanted to help his brother through this difficult last stage of Antonia's flight. Instead, he felt helpless. He, too, was anxious about the plans coming together today. There was no doubt that Antonia would arrive this afternoon. Their messenger had met up with Lorenzo in San Gimignano. All was well and on time.

"I cannot concentrate on anything other than her safe arrival. If I could, I would, Carlo. We know Florence and San Gimignano went well. And Lorenzo picked up the trunk of new clothing in Florence. Do you think I should have had Pietro stay longer with him before bringing us news?" The Master Planner was not doing well in an area where he now had no command. He moved yet again to the door to look out toward the road.

"You've asked me that already, Orlando. You did what was prudent and efficient—you always do."

"But this day is difficult, very difficult. She's so close now. What time is it?"

"Orlando, you asked me the time only a few minutes ago. Look at the shadows—noon is upon us. Come into the kitchen for some food." Carlo tried again to distract his brother.

"I won't be able to eat until I see her, Carlo. You go ahead. I'll go out and walk around."

"And wander around again in the places that they enjoyed," Carlo thought to himself, "just as I would if I were in his shoes."

Orlando walked into the field. They would be back here soon, to lavender and basil and lilies. A twig snapped behind him. He turned to look. And she was there, just as she was in the harvest. But, she would not disappear this time. He heard her musical laughter. He felt her warmth. He looked toward the road and knew she was coming.

"Carlo! She is on her way! I know it! I've seen her. It's time for me to go."

Carlo hurried out of the kitchen in time to see his eldest brother run into the stable for his horse. As Orlando urged the animal out and down the lane, Carlo shouted, "It's happening! I told you it would! Come back as soon as you can, Orlando—with your beautiful Antonia!"

After a few minutes, Orlando slowed his horse to a comfortable trot. "You and I won't lose her again," he patted the beast around its neck. With a quick slap to the horse's rump, Orlando Sagredo galloped off to the north to greet his Venetian love.

XL

When I was very young, I would beg the Maestro to tell me "the story of your earthquake...please, please!" He would banter with me and tell me that he was too busy. But always, he would make a grand drama of relenting and tell me... "Ah, la mia principessa, the fascinating story of my birth!" And he would laugh and set me on his knee. "Well, on that very day, at the very moment of my birth in Venice, there was an earthquake! It was so frightening that the mid-wife baptized me immediately, so sure was she that all of Venice would be killed!" And we would go on, I with my questions and he finally finishing with, "Because that earthquake was not the portent of a new plague, my mother knew I had been born for something very special." And then he would kiss me on the forehead and call for the Prioress. "Always remember, my Antonia, you have been born to fulfill a destiny, too. Music! You and I were born for music, Antonia!" I wish I could believe that now. I wish he were here to tell me. [Antonia, 1743]

Antonia was amazed at her sudden sense of exuberance. She snapped out of the monotony that had been created by the pounding hoofs and swaying carriage. Now she had no awareness of place and time. Her weariness, her sense of doom had vanished!

No longer would this carriage lull her. No longer would it be her balcony, her refuge! She could sense Orlando nearby. The hoofbeats of her horses were being augmented by Orlando's approach. She was certain. Energized, she held onto the carriage door and called out to Lorenzo.

"Stop, Lorenzo! Stop!" Would he never hear her? She picked a pebble off the carriage floor, leaned out the window and took aim, hitting Lorenzo soundly on his back. He turned around. "Stop, Lorenzo! Please!"

Lorenzo drew the carriage to a halt. He jumped down and came to the door. "What is it, Antonia?" He looked alarmed and then irritated. "Antonia! I thought there was something wrong with you. Now you're smiling!" He could not remain angry. He burst into laughter. "You have a deadly aim, young woman!"

Antonia jumped down from the carriage. "Orlando is on his way, Lorenzo. I need to sit up with you."

"Antonia, you know that is forbidden for the journey. Orlando himself gave the order. Get back in. We have less than an hour left." How could he resist her?

"No, Lorenzo, I am going to sit with you. I'll keep my hood up. Please—I must do this!"

Yes... the moment had come. "All right, Antonia, you win," Lorenzo smiled and shrugged. He took her arm and assisted her up to the driver's bench. Her hair brushed against his cheek. How was he to return to Florence and forget? How was he to turn the memories of this journey into nothing more than the delivery of a work of art? What was he to do with this anger he felt? Turn her over to Orlando, turn her over.... "I've said it before—Orlando is a fortunate man—if your persistence doesn't drive him to distraction!" Brooding, he urged the horses on. Never had his feelings taken over his mind like this.

"Ah, Lorenzo, I'm glad you are back. Your silence confused me. You're so important to me, and you became so distant in Florence. I wondered if I had offended you somehow," Antonia put her hand on his arm.

Lorenzo looked down at her hand and then glanced up at her face. Had she been looking at him, Antonia would have wondered at the cloud of pain that drifted over his austerely handsome face. Had she been able see within, Antonia would have been amazed at the fierce desire and anger that burned in his head as he vainly tried to make himself happy for her. "Be assured, Antonia, that I was never angry with you. I…," his response was cut short by Antonia's exclamation.

"Look—the top of the hill! Do you see something? Is it Orlando?" Antonia became silent.

"I believe so, Antonia." He looked at his precious passenger. She was absolutely still, her gaze unflinching. "Nothing will stop you when you love, will it, Antonia—ever," Lorenzo, pondering more than questioning, spoke into the wind.

* * *

Orlando propelled his horse toward the speck in the distance. No Palio could have ever been so important. "My God, I've missed her!" His heart was bursting with the feelings he had barely managed to keep under control for a year. Even the dust seemed part of the excitement. He spotted a little dot in the distance. Was it the carriage? It was! As it approached, Orlando noticed two drivers. His vision fastened onto the smaller person, shrouded in a cape. At that moment, the hood fell away, loosing an abundance of burgundy hair into the wind.

"Antonia!" They saw each other now. Orlando heard his name. Laughter followed. Was it his? The lily-of-the-valley laughter of the Duomo rang in his head. Where was he? He raced on.

The carriage slowed, and both Antonia and Lorenzo waved and shouted. Orlando steered his horse around the back of the carriage to come up to Antonia's side. Clinging to Lorenzo's arm as Orlando dropped pace, Antonia reached for him. And they touched. After all this, they were together. As the horses responded and stopped, Orlando slipped his arm around Antonia and pulled her onto his horse. Leaning into her ear, he kissed her, "Come with me, my love; you're home."

Antonia's took his hand and placed it over her breast. At long last, she was safe with her lover. Never would God allow them to be separated again.

* * *

At the gate to the Sagredo Estate, Antonia and Orlando led the horse toward Lorenzo. He had moved his animals slowly, giving the lovers a few moments together and himself time to let this strange journey conclude. As they approached him, Lorenzo looked directly into Antonia's eyes. Would there be anything there he could take home with him?

She smiled, "Please stay, Lorenzo. Please reconsider and stay with us until you're rested."

"I really must leave now. I can be back in Monteriggioni in time to rest and be ready for my return to Florence," Lorenzo was immovable. Unable to shake his pain, he wanted simply to remove himself from the source. He wanted to leave. He wanted to leave because he could not trust himself any longer. And he wanted to leave because it was over. His moment, if he had ever truly had one, was gone, as quickly as Antonia had gone from his side at the carriage. How he hated this feeling of powerlessness! And how, at this moment, he resented his loyalty to Orlando. He would return to his well-established patterns in Florence. He turned to the friend he might have betrayed. What good would it do to stay? "Shall we go to your house, Orlando? The two of us can carry Antonia's trunk to her quarters. Then I shall be off." He took Antonia's elbow while Orlando led his horse. He would have this one last memory of her.

The three friends, joined by separate, walked slowly toward the Sagredo house. "Oh, Orlando, I haven't seen your property in the daylight like this! How beautiful!" Antonia was enchanted. The mansion, imposing and elegant in its perfect lines rose up from the vineyards and gardens before them, declaring the Sagredo territory. "It's as though we can walk into the greenness and breathe it. And the fragrances!" She slipped her hand into Lorenzo's and clutched it, "You have been my protector and companion, Lorenzo. I wish you did not have to leave."

As they reached the house, Lorenzo wished he had been her lover.

"Lorenzo, lift the trunk with me to the door. That's all we need for now; Carlo and I can carry it in later," Orlando put his arm around his friend's shoulder as they walked to the back of the carriage.

With the task done, Lorenzo looked again at Antonia. Quite simply, she was radiant and not his. Yes, she belonged here. Or, more correctly, this place belonged to her. Her happiness was clearly evident. He smiled at her. Did his eyes express his secret?

"I'll miss you, Lorenzo. My words are inadequate; but I'll never forget your dedication to my safety and comfort. I'll never forget you. Give my love to Maria and the others." Antonia was reluctant to let the intense companionship of this special man disappear from her life. Truly, she would miss his strength and perfect attention. Surprised at the depth of her attachment, she felt her eyes fill with tears.

Lorenzo took her hand. He kissed it and, looking directly into her eyes, saw the tears, "Good-bye for now, Antonia. And I shall never forget you." Dear God, this was like some kind of punishment!

As Antonia moved to embrace him, Lorenzo turned toward Orlando, extending his hand. And the moment of recognition was gone. Had he let it happen, he could not have tolerated it.

Orlando embraced him warmly. "Your bond with us cannot be broken. This is inadequate compensation for all that you achieved. Thank you," Orlando placed a money purse in his hands.

Lorenzo climbed onto the carriage, snapped the reins and looked back only once as he and his horses galloped off to the north.

Orlando turned to Antonia. "Are you really here? I cannot yet believe it, Antonia. I thought today would never happen!" With Orlando leading the horse, they made their way, hand-in-hand, back to his house.

"Did you feel that way, too, Orlando? I was so afraid some harm would come that I imagined seeing Tiepolo in Bologna and in Florence." Antonia glanced toward the fields. "It's as though you've kept everything as it was last summer, as though time has stood still until we could be reunited. There's your greening place, Orlando."

"It's our greening place, waiting for you, my love. And this year, the house is yours as well. My brothers have left for now, and my parents have moved to the back wing of the house. Everyone is ready to celebrate our being together again. Enrico is married now, as I told you. Their happy news is that they are expecting a child." Orlando tied the horse outside the house and led Antonia toward the door. "Are you tired?"

"Pleasantly. And satisfied, Orlando—as though I have come home and can let go now." She looked into his eyes while he took her face into his hands, and kissed her. Antonia let her cape drop from her shoulders and stood strongly in the gaze of her lover. "I love you, Orlando Sagredo, now and forever. And that will never change." As she placed her arms about his neck, Orlando felt all of her being move into him.

"Come, I'll bathe you. You've had a long dark journey… a dark journey," Orlando picked her up and carried her upstairs. "The bath has been waiting for you, Antonia of Siena," he whispered in her ear. You are home now. And I'll never let you leave again."

His loss and fear over, Orlando felt his anger toward Vivaldi. Never again would this beautiful woman be harmed. Antonia of

Siena lived! Anna of Venice was dead now. Vivaldi and Tiepolo could perish in Hell!

NOVE

THE PALIO TO THE SIENESE HILLS

1726

XLI

Who created us? Was it Alaric the Goth? Was it Attila the Hun? Did we rise from the sea malformed? Surely it could not have been in God's plan to create us. Venetians are neither fish nor fowl, nor are we fully human. We have grown from marshes and water. We have driven posts into the lagoon bottom to give us legs. We have oars for gills, spires for feathers and Mother Mary for a soul. We cannot walk very far without having to cross the water and that water is full of salt, killing us if we drink it. Are we a joke, a Divine Comedy? Is a Venetian always a stranger in a strange land? If so, Moses, then, is my father. And like him, I am doomed never to see the Promised Land. [Antonia, 1739]

Antonia and Orlando lay in their greening place looking at the night sky. Thick indigo clouds fanned in and out and preened themselves in the face of the moon. Light and dark edges covered the lovers in the gentle aftermath of their love-making. In the crook of Orlando's arm, Antonia stretched sensuously and moved her leg over him. She whispered in his ear, "Stay joined to me forever, Orlando," and slid down to kiss his chest.

Orlando kissed her hair. He would protect this woman and the beauty of her vulnerability forever. No one and nothing would ever harm her again. Her hair had taken on the scent of lavender. He kissed her head again, resting there and vowing silently to his God that she would forever be with him. "Forever, Antonia," he pulled her close to his heart. She could feel it beating into her ear, bringing her heart into alignment with his. "A year ago, I was convinced that you would be able to stay here with me. I will not lose you ever again. So you won't go to the Palio until August this year," he kissed her head and lost himself again in fragrances of burgundy.

"Enough of this! You're safe, and we're here," Orlando shifted to look into Antonia's eyes.

Her yearning joined with his as she reached up to kiss him, lingering and kissing again and again. "I love you, Orlando. I want you again... forever." She had no sense of their separateness and wanted only to be consumed in his love once again.

With the gentleness of a mother, he lifted Antonia onto his body. As she molded to him, the ache and memory of their separation fell away. His beloved was here and would be joined with him forever. Her skin was warm and silky, her breath as sweet as the lily-of-the-valley that was part of his very fibre now.

Antonia traced the outline of his features with her fingers. He was the violin of her love, and she could seek the music in the same way that she brought it forth from her instrument. As he kissed the perfect sweetness of her breasts, Antonia was lifted again into the sublime. "Promise me that nothing will separate us, Orlando. I couldn't bear to lose you twice." A tear fell on Orlando's chest. He held Antonia tightly and pulled his cloak over and around them to wrap their oneness. They began again, slowly and rhythmically, to lose themselves in the power of the connection. Orlando's lips sought her spirit as her body began the adagio of this new music, this undoing of her self. Shade and sound blended. "Stay, stay, Orlando, stay," Antonia urged. As though warding off time and loss, the lovers clung to the ancient tempo of the universe.

* * *

"Everyone – a toast!" Gallo Sagredo clapped his hands to assure that his resonant bass had carried above the cheerful din of his family's customary Sunday meal together. Bianca had cleared the table. Francesca had excused her for the evening. Lemon and wine conspired now with the lingering aromas of garlic and basil, inducing the usual Sagredo discussions. As the voices subsided, he stood, proud patriarch with a glass of the Sagredo best raised in his hand. "My compliments to my beautiful Francesca on the excellence of the meal and on the timballo in particular. And on this beautiful May day with everyone here, we must salute two joyous family events, soon to be upon us!"

Everyone turned toward the Elder Sagredo. Francesca sat at the opposite end of the table from her husband. Enrico, Alessandra and Giuseppe sat across from Orlando, Antonia and Carlo. The lively air breathed with the flavours of the food and the conversations. Orlando grasped Antonia's hand. Antonia took it all in—the happiness, the family unity and Orlando's presence. This was an even bigger and happier family than Lorenzo's in Florence.

"Yes, Father! You're right!" Carlo was very happy for his oldest brother. They had always been the closest of companions.

"Here we are with two great events to celebrate! Stand up— Orlando and Antonia and Enrico and Alessandra." As the two young couples stood, the whole family stood and applauded. Gallo Sagredo continued, "Orlando and Antonia—Antonia... Francesca and I welcome you into our family with open arms. You love our son greatly. And Orlando," he turned to his eldest, "Orlando, you love Antonia greatly. May God bless you both. And may your wedding in September herald a great harvest for this family in produce and in love." Raising his glass again, the elder Sagredo opened the toast to the family, "To Orlando and Antonia – a long life!"

As the family joined in, Orlando took Antonia's face in his hands, looking into her eyes as though they were the only people in the room. "Antonia, you are already my wife. Now and forever, I cherish you."

Antonia responded softly, "And I you, my almost husband," Orlando kissed her to the cheers of the family.

Gallo turned to Enrico and Alessandra, "Alessandra, it is good to see you with your appetite and colour back. The early sickness was hard on you. Enrico, you can relax now, too," the family laughed. "We wish you, as you know, the same blessings as Francesca and I have enjoyed with our children. To the next generation of Sagredos, coming in the new year!"

"To our family!" As the family cheered and toasted again, Enrico and Alessandra beamed and kissed.

"Now, Francesca, il formaggio!" Gallo, in great satisfaction and pride, resumed his place at the head of the table.

Antonia and Alessandra slipped away with Francesca into the kitchen. Antonia looked back quickly to see Orlando and Carlo in earnest conversation again. She loved this easy exchange between the two brothers who could move seamlessly from political matters to matters of the estate, engrossed, serious or laughing as the topic and tone called for. Her own childhood had been so very lonely. Despite Sister Paolina's love, the resentment of the other orphans had left deep wounds. But now I am complete. I have brothers, parents, a sister-in-law. As she claimed these precious possessions, she felt her deep gratitude. I belong here.

Francesca embraced the two young women, "And I! I couldn't be happier to have you both in this family. I've been waiting for a long time for female company! Perhaps I shall even be blessed with a granddaughter!" She removed a covering from a large tray on the kitchen cutting block, "All we need now is the sweetened cream. Gallo will be surprised that we have this Pecorino," as Antonia placed the cream on the tray, Francesca stood back and surveyed, "Good health, indeed! Wonderful cheeses and fruits for the Sagredos!"

As they entered the dining room, Antonia touched Alessandra's arm, "Alessandra, I'm sorry you haven't been well. I didn't know. Are you all right now? Is the baby all right?"

Alessandra laughed and gave Antonia a warm embrace, "Oh, Antonia. There was nothing more than pregnancy wrong with me! Often, in the early days of pregnancy, the new mother is repulsed by food and smells and cannot eat. That's all! It passes. Mine has passed and now I often want to sleep. You'll find this all out one day, Antonia!"

"Truly, Alessandra? I had no idea. I know so little about things like this," Antonia looked embarrassed.

Alessandra gave her a quick hug, "You'll find out, Antonia. And don't feel shy. You have to learn somehow. No man is going to explain this to you!"

Alessandra's hearty laugh delighted Antonia. The two newest members of the Sagredo family returned to their places across from each other. Antonia smiled over at Alessandra who returned a knowing glance. And, quite surprisingly, Antonia laughed. When Alessandra joined in, the infectious nature of laughter took over until the two were wiping their eyes.

Somewhat embarrassed, but quite unable to stop, Antonia managed to whisper to the others, "She told me that pregnancy made her sick. Please excuse me; but I cannot seem to help laughing!" And she was off again, this time with Orlando joining in, enjoying more of Antonia's discovery of freedom. He called out, "Antonia has just learned all she ever needs to know about pregnancy!"

As the laughter rang its way around the table and out of the open window into the purple hills, Antonia believed that there could be no greater happiness than to belong to the Sagredo family.

* * *

"The basil and garlic are well-blended, Francesca. Do I add the pine nuts now?" Antonia had come to enjoy learning to cook with Orlando's mother. And she delighted in her company in the kitchen. There were times, however, when Francesca's gestures or glances were painfully evocative of Sister Paolina's presence.

"Good! Add the mix to the bowl – and perhaps some ground pepper – and use the pestle to blend it all, Antonia. Ah, the basil! I love that scent! You're beginning to feel comfortable in the kitchen, aren't you, my dear?"

"I love the kitchen! There's music in it. I'd never have known the kitchen in Venice… without you. I'd love to help make some of the food for the wedding! Or, would that be proper?" Antonia looked to the older woman for guidance.

"My dear, in matters of the heart, we mustn't always be guided by propriety," Francesca took the bread out of the oven. "I enjoy the way you let your heart guide you. Shall we follow your heart for the wedding? After all, there hasn't been a love story like yours in this family for generations—not since the Sagredos were routed from Venice by some other old family whose name we have forgotten. There! We can leave the rest of the cooking to Bianca."

"What is the story about the Sagredos and Venice? I know the old Sagredo palace."

"Well, that's part of Gallo's family. A few generations ago, the Sagredos and the other family disputed over property and some claim to headship of the Republic. In the end, though, Gallo's great-grandfather fled to Florence with the daughter of the other family… oh, what was their name? It began with 'M'… Monten… Mocenigo! That was it! You've probably never heard of that family."

Antonia laughed. "Oh, but I have! Some sort of equal justice must be running its course. It is our Doge Mocenigo who ultimately refused to let me stay in Siena! I wonder if this story has had any influence on him."

"I wouldn't be surprised, given the nature of men from wealthy families. Everything becomes a possession. But you'll never have experienced that outside of your Doge."

Antonia thought of her Maestro; but could not bring herself to speak ill of him. His possessiveness was because of his love of her.

"Come, Antonia, shall we go out to the garden? We can make some decisions about its use for the wedding."

The two women stopped and looked down over the vineyards and into the hills. Antonia savoured the freshness of the air. "I'm still amazed at your acceptance of me. It's difficult for me to believe this will last—being part of your family, marrying Orlando, laughing, dancing, planning." Antonia looked toward Siena. "After the Palio, the wedding!"

"Nothing has ever brought my controlled son to life the way his love for you has, my dear. His approach to life has always been from his intellect, although he wasn't that way as a child. The playful child became the calculating man," Francesca's description of her son took Antonia by surprise. Other than for his impatience, this was not her experience of Orlando. "I hope you have a daughter someday, Antonia. Sons distance themselves from their mothers once their education is done. My experience with my mother was that we became friends. I still miss her. Orlando is like his father—rational, reasonable, caring, but controlled. He and I became close again through this past year; he needed me for consultation and comfort. In that way, he's quite different from his father," Francesca's glance was not at her outer world. The texture of the afternoon Sienese hills was dense and mossy. Their shadows offered a blanket against the cooling air. The two women bonded. "As for me, in one year, I've gained two daughters!"

The moment evaporated. As the two women walked back into the house, Antonia's remembered the pull of Paolina's soothing whispers.

XLII

I think of Orlando in Rome often. And I wish I had visited the city. I wish I knew it. Would I find him viewing the structure of the Pantheon? Wandering through the art in San Pietro? Visiting someone near Santa Sabina on the Aventine? And would she be with him or waiting at home for him with their children? No! He has not married. For some reason, I cannot believe he is in Rome. He does not keep company with Hadrian and Vespasian. He is a Tuscan, not a Roman. I know this. I know this because I visit him at night in the purple fabric of dreams. [Antonia, 1744]

"You pledged you would bring her back safely!" Vivaldi and Tiepolo stood outside Florian's in the dense, sepulchral evening air. The conversational noises from inside drifted out and hung in the air. "I've completed the aria she had begun for 'Dorilla'. She must be here to sing it in the next performance. Domine, Tiepolo! You promised!"

Tiepolo's dark eyes blazed in the dull twilight, "Vivaldi, you would do well not to antagonize me further! She simply was not at the Palio. How many times do I have to tell you that? She stayed back at the Sagredo Estate. There was no way to abduct her from there."

"Then what do we do now? How do I get Anna back? You still haven't given me a new plan. Paolina is very ill, there is music to be made, and time is being squandered," the Maestro felt himself losing ground, succumbing to the Envoy's dark power. He needed this man he feared and was coming to despise. He needed to keep the man committed. He needed not to turn him into an adversary. "Mocenigo will want her back for the performance, too, Tiepolo."

"Quite simply, Vivaldi," the Envoy's voice was harsh and threatening as he moved closer to the composer and took hold of his collar, "you need to shut up and stay out of these plans completely now. I will bring your Anna back because I personally now need revenge – against her and Sagredo. She herself has made this personal. She will return in August… with me… by brute force, if necessary."

Vivaldi stopped breathing, his eyes wide open in fear. "No, Tiepolo, no! Please, please bring her back safely. Promise me. No one must be hurt."

Tiepolo let go of Vivaldi's collar and laughed in his face, "Then stay out of it, Vivaldi, and she will be back safely. One of my men was able to talk a young Sagredo servant into volunteering information at the Palio. Your Anna will be at the second Palio in August. And so will I. So will I," he clapped Vivaldi resoundingly on the back. Vivaldi gasped. "Go to your vessel and go home to your ailing Prioress. Leave me and my mission alone!" The Envoy opened the door to Florian's. "I leave in two weeks, and you shall see your Anna two weeks later. Now, go write an opera to that story!"

Tiepolo laughed and slammed the door behind him.

As the noise of Florian's surged out and was stifled again, terror took hold of Vivaldi's breath. He walked weakly to Domenico, "Help me in. We need to get back now. I need to tell Paolina Anna will be back soon."

Domenico settled the wheezing Maestro into the gondola. "Sir, these visits to Tiepolo are not good for you. You would do well not to see the man. There… now… be seated. And please, sir, put your mind on your music." The bell of San Marco cried eight times, adding to the heaviness of the evening air. "Someone is going to die in this undertaking," Domenico whispered under his breath, "and it may be the Maestro himself."

The faithful gondolier paced his vessel with the quiet slapping of the one that moved along the Bacino ahead of him. Now, if only the

Maestro would forget about the ungrateful Anna! She was not good for his health. She would be best forgotten.

XLIII

My friend, Antonio Canale, painted magnificent Venetian vistas. I would study them and wonder why he did not paint the true Venetians into his paintings. Why would he not paint Piazza San Marco with its hordes of noisy, untidy market vendors? Why would he not paint mess and bartering and poverty? "The wealthy, Anna, live in a city they have constructed in their minds. Venice is a myth. I am to paint their Venice. It's grand, immaculate, rational. That is why they created the Carnevale… so they can wear masks and once a year become myths themselves." [Antonia, 1739]

It had been a tedious day. On his way home from the August Palio preparations in Siena, Orlando re-lived last year's plans for the July Palio. His first thoughts were of the beauty which he had heard from within the Duomo. He remembered especially the bell-like laughter spilling out of the door; the laughter that had both tormented and sustained him throughout his separation from Antonia. He remembered the smell of lilies and basil and jasmine. And he remembered the sight of Antonia in command of both instruments, her voice and her violin, and the uncanny likeness of the two. "She must miss the constant presence of music, the constant creative atmosphere," Orlando yearned to hear her return to music.

He stopped as he led his horse toward the stable. He was surprised that he had actually conjured up the sound of her music. He could almost hear her violin coming from the vineyards. No! It was her violin. Quickly settling his horse, he ran toward the melancholy music.

The sight was dazzling. Antonia, her burgundy hair drifting out behind her in the gentle wind, was playing her own improvisation of "Dite, Oime…" "Tell me—must I live or die?" Orlando remembered her voice from their past life. He stood still, looking at the perfection of Antonia in unison with nature, the greens and purples splashed with the yellows of sunflowers. Antonia was the jasmine queen, white in cobalt, in the very atmosphere that supported and celebrated her in a more spiritual way than any duomo or edifice ever could. Orlando gave way to his senses as he had in the Duomo on that fateful April day last year. Eternal Antonia. Innocent, pure Antonia. The very hills were subject to her.

The music found its own resolution. Antonia stood for a moment, her violin held down by her side, her bow in her right hand balancing the picture. Closing her eyes, she tilted her chin upward and drank in the elixir she had created from music and nature. The Alchemist of Siena.

And then, clearly and perfectly, as though she were Bellini completing the Virgin, Antonia sang what she had just played.

Orlando waited until she moved.

"Antonia," he spoke softly.

Antonia turned toward him, "Orlando." She smiled, unable to pull herself back into time.

"Thank you, Antonia, for being here... for turning the hillside into music. Is this not a more magnificent cathedral than the Duomo?" Orlando looked over the vineyard into the hills. "I've been waiting for your return to music. You're still feeling your grief."

"Orlando, why could he not have accepted my love for you? I'm not sure that I've returned to my music. Nor am I sure that my music has returned to me. It all feels so very sad. I cannot feel my own creativity. My passion is dulled... blunted. Why?"

Orlando put his arm around her, while they gazed into the hills, "Grief will do that, I think, Antonia. Give it time. Let your passion grow out of our passion. Let go of Vivaldi's control," he turned her around, smiling, teasing her into lightheartedness. He knew she could not resist him. "Shall we go home and talk with the others in your realm?"

Antonia moved the bow into her left hand and held Orlando's hand. They looked into each other's eyes and laughed. In play, they ran toward the house.

Venice was now behind them and Anna's life was over. It had never been real.

* * *

Antonia and Orlando looked out over the Piazza del Campo from the upper window in the Sagredo accommodations. The orange town cast its glow into the window. "This will be your view the morning of the Palio," Orlando embraced Antonia, lifting her up and carrying her over to the bed. "You'll be safe here, Antonia. We'll be apart for only a few hours." Antonia luxuriated in the freshness of the room and the feel of the white bedclothes. A gentle breeze wafted in through the window. A plain white vase stood on the simple washstand. She would bring a small olive branch for it on the eve of the Palio! Orlando sat on the edge of the bed and placed his hands on either side of her head, locking her eyes with his.

The room and its ambiance seemed familiar to her. "I still have moments of disbelief, Orlando," she pulled his hands toward her so that she could examine them again. Now understanding the importance of hands to a violinist, Orlando accepted this ritual that Antonia often performed. She opened his hands and drew his palms to her mouth, kissing each one tenderly. And then she closed his hands and kissed them. Was she a priestess performing some kind of Eucharist... her own transubstantiation... matter into love?

"Lie with me, Orlando."

Orlando lay down and drew Antonia to his side. He wrapped himself around his soul-mate. They disappeared so easily into oneness. He wanted to stay here and love her. "I've never felt such anger and desperation as when you disappeared. I will never lose you again. We're prepared well this time for anything. I still would have preferred that you stay with my mother at home. But nothing will happen at the Palio. And you know that Carlo and Lorenzo will be with us for the races. Vincenzo is bringing your clothing from the convent." He kissed her on the forehead.

Antonia traced his profile with her fingers, letting her index finger dwell on his lips. "We have been careful, Orlando. You saw no signs of the Envoy or anyone associated with the Doge at the July Palio. No one asked for me. No one was suspicious. We must trust that," she kissed her lover's neck and folded herself deeper into his embrace. "I've never been so carefully looked after. I'm safer than I have ever been."

Orlando buried his face in Antonia's hair. It would be so easy to stay, to miss the meeting. The campanile tolled twelve. He brushed her hair from her face, "I must go. The Town Council meeting was to start at noon." Sitting up, he pulled his vest from the chair and slipped it on. He kissed her as he got up to leave. "I should be back in less than two hours."

The door closed and she heard his quick footsteps on the stairs. Still sensing Orlando's presence, Antonia rolled over into the comfort of the bed. Closing her eyes, she saw Orlando as she drifted into the realm of music. She remembered the Elder Bach in Venice and began to hear herself singing "Ich Habe Genug." Antonia moved easily along the road to her dreams.

Antiphonal singing surrounded her. She was unsure of her surroundings. People whom she had known through her years—the Maestro, Paolina, Constanza, Lorenzo, his sister and all the

Sagredos—and a beautiful woman of significant royalty beckoned her to follow them. She followed past olive trees and grapevines and onto a pathway strewn with flowers. A great chorus broke out above her in green and yellows. As the singing stopped, a huge golden cocoon was placed before her.

Antonia looked up for guidance. And from the green woods, Orlando, dressed in Palio finery, walked into the clearing. He held out his hands toward her. Taking his hands, Antonia kissed them. Her tears fell on his hands and became red and blue rings. His fingers shone. He moved back and knelt before the cocoon. A violin began to play a sweet obbligato.

Antonia looked across the clearing, and there was her Maestro, his red hair aflame. As he played, he moved in a contrapuntal dance toward the cocoon and knelt before it. She tried to reach across the woven golden orb to touch him. And in that instant, the cocoon split open and a miniature of herself stepped out, wearing a crown and a bright blue cloak.

"Hallelujah!" the choir sang.

"Antonia, Antonia," the voice came from another world, "you've been dreaming." Orlando kissed her forehead.

She reached up, "Orlando, such a wonderful dream. Come to me," she pulled Orlando to her and clung to him, kissing him passionately, passionately until she could find his skin and join with him.

* * *

The bell tower rang out five times. Orlando sat up. The August Palio depended on him to bring it to life within an hour.

"Antonia, wake up," he kissed her. The small, simply furnished room in the Sagredo building had been made theirs a week ago. The white bedclothes smelled of fresh air and herbs. The olive branch, with its tiny, black fruit, leaned toward them from the white vase. Antonia stretched and curled into him. "The bell tower just rang. I need to go. Remember—do not go to the little church. Come to the Piazza immediately before the races and stay in the shadows. And keep your hood up! Lorenzo will meet you outside the door. Vincenzo will maintain a station across from you until I am free to join you. And remember, Antonia – nothing untoward has been seen. You are free of Venice!"

Orlando donned his Palio clothing while Antonia watched. "I love you, Orlando. This time I shall be waiting for you at the end of the race." And, Orlando, we are three now! She was sure of the new life within her now. Francesca had been so helpful in confirming her symptoms. How she would delight in telling Orlando after the day's festivities were over. That would be the perfect time to give him the news!

Orlando moved to her. He put his hand under her neck and raised her to meet his lips. As he gently laid her down, he left a kiss on her breast. "I love you, Antonia."

Antonia's heart left with him as he closed the door.

She was filled with an urgency she could not understand. After trying to fall back into sleep, she got up to look out over the Piazza. The sun had already ignited Siena. The flames of Hell or the brilliance of Heaven? "You're to come with me." She heard the voice of last July. "No!" With her mightiest voice and her signature foot stamp, Antonia held out her palms toward the marketplace. "I declare you safe!"

With that declaration of power, something moved inside her. For the first time since her escape from Venice, her music returned. Her head became filled with chords and resolutions and melody, twirling, mutating. She lay back on her bed. "Speak to me," she spoke to the music while she committed it to memory. Healing and harmony.

"I shall write and teach here in Siena, and I cannot be stopped now!" Antonia bounded from the bed and began dressing. "All is well and all will be well! We are a trinity… Orlando, I and our new being," she sang, so great was her joy at the return of her creativity.

Anonymous in her black habit, Antonia made her way down the back stairs of the Sagredo building Orlando had introduced her to a year earlier. There was no one near the door. A wild, disorienting cacophony moved like a great parade of noise toward the Piazza del Campo. How well she remembered the hypnotic power of last year's crowd. She slipped carefully out and moved toward the front of the building. A priest moved directly toward her, startling her.

"Antonia, you were not to come down until the races started!" The chiding voice belonged to Lorenzo. "No, don't reach for me. You are a nun—remember! And I, my dear woman, am a priest," Lorenzo's laughter threatened to become louder. He coughed to end his playfulness. Antonia's smile lit up the space they shared. How he had yearned for this day to come. She was even more beautiful now in her habit, the severe frame around her face only enhancing her expressive eyes and full lips. "Do you see the priest across from us… just over there?" Without thinking, he put his hand on her shoulder to orient her. The recollections of the trip down from Fiesole flooded over him. He removed his hand. He removed it because he knew she would feel the fire burning through him. He removed it because he remembered Orlando.

"Dear Lorenzo, it is so good to see you again. Yes, I see him. Are you going to tell me that it is Vincenzo?"

"Yes. Even Pietro is here, circulating near us as one of the crowd. You're safe, Antonia. Now! The Palio is about to begin." Even this brief meeting would be enough for Lorenzo, enough to assuage, for a while, the void he felt in his life with Isolde. The void of the lone-liness of marriage. It was a void, though, that he would not trade for having had no knowledge of this woman who stood ahead of him now, her gaze seeking out her lover. Purposefully, he touched her arm gently, so that he could gather the visceral memory to take home with him, and moved behind her to watch over her. One de-liberate touch could be both so exquisite and so painful.

Antonia became aware again of the frenetic crowd. It was the same organism of last July—bordering on insanity and moving chaotically. She remembered the wash of fear when the hooded fig-ure had gripped her elbow. And then, recalling her declaration of safety to the day, she let herself go into enjoyment. The canape was dropped and the noise became wild. "Lorenzo, this is so exciting! I'm so happy to be back!"

Just as she turned to see why he did not reply, Lorenzo slumped to the ground in the arms of the man whose voice she could hear in her head. The man took his hand away from Lorenzo's mouth and threw an object into the shadows of the Sagredo building. The clank of metal.

"Dear God! Lorenzo!" Antonia ran toward Lorenzo. The blood! Someone pinioned her arms. She screamed and tried to locate Vin-cenzo. The crowd had taken over the spaces. There was no place left for the sights and sounds of her world that now catapulted into madness. "Orlando! Orlando!" She was struck across the face. It was Lorenzo's attacker. Sweet Jesus! Lorenzo was not moving. Lorenzo! Lorenzo! Move! Please move!

The dark voice of last year's encounters came from behind her. "You will be silent. This time, Anna, there are no rules. If you do not do as I say, Lorenzo will not be the only victim. I will kill Orlando, too; do you hear me? Do as I say! Now!"

Antonia tasted blood. Whose blood? Oh, Lorenzo, faithful friend. I have killed you. Your blood? My blood? Sweet Jesus. Help me. Fainting... fainting. Be strong, Antonia—stay alert. Alert... I must. Dear God...

The two men threw the nun over the horse and covered her with a heavy blanket. Antonia felt the suffocating weight pin her to the animal. I cannot... I must breathe... so sick, so sick... Orlando. The horse... so fast... so hot... my baby....

Antonia fainted.

* * *

Vincenzo pushed his way through the throng and across to the Sagredo building. It would be better in this mayhem for the three of them to stay together. Where were they?

"Father, Father!" It took Vincenzo a moment to recognize Pietro's voice and another moment to realize that he, in disguise, was being addressed. "Father, you're needed over here quickly!"

Vincenzo hurried to the side of the Sagredo building.

Pietro forcefully turned him around to face the Palio area. "Look across to the alleyway. The three horses. Look at the middle horse—there is no rider; but the saddle is too high. And the riders of the other two horses glance back every so often. And where are Antonia and Lorenzo?"

Vincenzo became alarmed. He turned to Pietro, "We must get over to Lorenzo. Come quickly!" His glance moved to the shadows at the side of the building. "Pietro—Good God! There's someone lying there. A priest's robe—is it Lorenzo? You go to Orlando. I'll check here and then come."

Pietro made his way rudely and desperately through the din until he reached Orlando. "Orlando," he heaved and pointed, "we think two men have Antonia! They went down the alley—three horses, two riders, Antonia under a blanket on the third horse—they'll be far ahead of you, Orlando; it took so much time to get through the crowd. Lorenzo may have been injured!"

"Carlo! Enrico! Over here!" Orlando's clear tenor voice cut through the din. He ordered the Palio victor to give him his horse. He was off in a split second with two of his brothers.

Reaching the place where Antonia was to be waiting, Orlando saw Vincenzo sitting against the side of the building, cradling a priest. The man's head had dropped back; his eyes stared blindly into the brilliant sun. Vincenzo's hands were bloody. Tears dripped from his chin. Knowing Lorenzo was dead, Orlando dismounted and ran to Vincenzo. Was this a dream? How had it happened? He knelt beside his friends, closing Lorenzo's eyes and making the sign of the Cross on his forehead. As he began to speak, Vincenzo shouted, "Go, Orlando! Go! Find them before they kill Antonia!"

Focused, Orlando ran to his horse and ordered his brothers to follow. His brain burning with rage, he was ready to kill. He must!

Giuseppe, seeing them fly into the alley, followed like the wind down the road and past the Duomo. His older brothers had succeeded in sending the crowds to the edges of the alleyway and into buildings. Many hung out the doors, watching Il Duce of the Palio, in full armour, tear through the town in a strange race of his own.

The brothers urged their horses northward out of Siena, down the commonly used road and up to its next northerly summit. Breathless, the horsemen stopped to orient themselves. Orlando's horse spun in circles, lusting after more activity. Orlando reined her in tightly and dismounted to throw off as much of the armour as he could. In his fierceness, even the air around him was charged with his energy.

"What if they thought to confuse us by heading south or east, Orlando?" Carlo knew the need to consider all possibilities. "They were carrying out a plan. Part of their plan would have been to confound us and send us off in the wrong direction."

Orlando, about to respond, caught sight of something. "Over there—look!—on the other side of the road... at the bottom of the hill. What do you see?"

"It looks like a group of people with horses. Come!" Enrico was off and down the hill ahead of the other three. Orlando followed swiftly.

The brothers slowed down near the group, dismounted and walked over to speak with the people who were discussing what to do with the three horses. "Is there something wrong here? We're looking for a carriage with two or three men and a woman." Orlando directed his questions to the man who appeared to be the leader. "This is extremely important."

"Well, the strangest thing has happened here, and we've been trying to decide what to do. We were walking into town from our farm over there," the man pointed to the north, "when we spotted three horses racing down the hill you just came down. There were two riders, each holding a rein from the horse in the middle. There was a carriage, with four horses, at the side of the road right here. The riders coming down the hill were going too fast for safety. We talked about it, did we not?" the man looked to his cohorts. They all began to talk together.

"Please! You must tell us what happened. Quickly!" Orlando could barely contain his impatience. "These are the people we are looking for. What happened?"

"Well, the rider-less horse got away on them and went headlong down the hill. And then—the strangest thing; but I tell you, we all saw it!—the saddle fell off and a person who had been under it—can you imagine that... a person actually under the saddle!—flew off. It was terrible! Terrible! We couldn't begin to imagine what was happening. We hurried down the hill; but the riders got to the person, and the carriage-driver went over, too. We hurried further down the hill; but we got close enough only to see that it was a young woman. And the blood! The blood! So much—all over her legs and feet," the spokesman turned to the older woman. "Mattia here unthinkingly shouted, 'She has lost a baby!' But it had to be from the fall; we could see no evidence here. Only blood! The men turned when they heard Mattia," the man was shaken at the devastation on Orlando's face. "I am sorry, sir; we couldn't do anything. They picked her up and put her in the carriage. But she looked dead to us, did she not?" The friends, wide-eyed, nodded in agreement. "She was dead, sir, I'm sorry to say. And off they went, leaving the horses behind. Two drivers, four fast horses and two passengers, one dead. What do you think we should do?"

Orlando mounted his horse and raced furiously into the north. "Antonia! Antonia!" The lament roared into the thickness of the hills. Hoarding the echo, the hills absorbed the pain and looked back blankly.

As alone and powerless, Il Duce seethed. He would find Antonia and exact his revenge upon Tiepolo, personally. And he would bring her body back home. Home to the hills and to his family. And he would still entertain a miracle, a miracle of Antonia surviving.

* * *

Orlando's brothers caught up with him. "Slow down, Orlando, slow down. We need to think this through." Carlo kept pace with his brother, gradually dropping in speed as Orlando's horse fell in step. Knowing their older brother's irritation with talk when he needed to think, no one spoke. Within minutes, Orlando directed his horse to the left. The brothers moved off into a clearing.

"We cannot afford to lose time, Carlo. We must head to San Gimignano at least and then decide what to do. We should be able to catch up with them; we're not hampered with a carriage."

Carlo wanted to agree that it could be so simple. He knew that his older brother needed to so this, that he would not tolerate the tension in wondering if he had missed the only opportunity to find Antonia. "And if we get there and haven't found the group, what will we do? They could just as easily have doubled back and gone off to Arezzo to head to the coast. I would have made a plan like that."

Orlando looked over at Enrico and Giuseppe. They nodded in agreement with Carlo. "I understand your reasoning. But if I let this go… if I use only my mind here… I either lose Antonia when there is no reason to be found anywhere or I lose the one chance I was given to find her quickly. So, I must act irrationally. I must." He turned toward the northern hills again. "And, regardless of anything else, I need to do something—I need to act!—or I'll not be able to withstand this powerlessness… this impotence."

"Come, Orlando, we need to go as far as San Gimignano," Enrico began to head north. He turned his head, "If we cannot find them there and if no one has seen them, we'll return home to get what we need to head to Venice."

"Good plan, Enrico," Giuseppe called out and headed off. Within moments the four horsemen were riding swiftly together toward the walled town of San Gimignano.

As it loomed before them, its sinister towers mighty sentinels, Orlando held out his hand to slow his brothers down. "If we cannot see them from any of those towers, that will be enough for now. We'll get a complete view from there in all directions. Running off without evidence will only serve to make us lose time. Come!" He was off with his brothers immediately behind.

As they rode through the portico into the market, Carlo called out to a group of women seated on a bench, "Has a group of strangers been through here? Strangers with horses and a carriage? And perhaps with a sick woman in the carriage?"

The women looked up in surprise and shook their heads. "No, sir, it has been a very quiet day here with no visitors in town. Most of our people are in your town to see the Palio." The Brothers' attire had not gone unnoticed.

The brothers called out their thanks and rode over to a tower. "Carlo, you and Enrico take the towers starting here. Giuseppe, you and I will head over there to start," Orlando led. "Call us if you see anything, Carlo."

Their tasks completed, the brothers met in disappointment. "This is no way to find them. There's no trace of them here," Orlando looked more angry and determined than desperate now. "They may indeed have gone over the Arezzo way. Or they may be in some farmhouse we passed on our way here."

Looking northward, Orlando spoke clearly, "I must go to Venice. On our ride here, I began planning. I began to feel we would not find them." Il Duce had returned. "I'll return home now for the essentials. Enrico and Giuseppe, you will stay in Siena. Enrico—you finish up the business with the Palio. Giuseppe—when we get back home, find Mother and Father, and tell them what has happened; they will be somewhere in Siena. Both of you do what needs to be done for Lorenzo and his family. Carlo, you will come with me to Venice. I will not return until I have Antonia with me." Sensing a plea in his brothers' eyes, Orlando became clearer, "Alive or dead. And I pray to Catherine that it be the former."

The four horsemen, with no need for further words, went their various ways, Enrico and Giuseppe more anxious than the older two. There could be no delay. Orlando had a great distance before him in the direction Antonia was never to have travelled again. If she had survived her injury, he would bring her back. If not, he would make new plans. In either case, he would have his revenge.

DIECI

THE PIETA TO SAN MARCO

1726

XLIV

Lorenzo's comment that I reminded him of Caravaggio's Mad-
dalena stunned me. He, like Jacopo, opened me up to who I was
outside of music. I had never thought of myself—ever—as sepa-
rate from music. Nor had I ever thought of Mary Magdalene as
separate from Jesus. [Antonia, 1744]

Vivaldi entered the sick room quietly and pulled a chair up to
Paolina's bedside. She turned toward him.

"Is she back, Antonio? I had a dream of her in green against
a beautiful blue sky. She was dressed in white, but she was surrounded in green... leaves, vines... it was a field or a garden. She
looked so beautiful, so...." As she smiled sweetly, her voice drifted
faintly into the air and disappeared.

Antonio lifted her head to give her some water. She could not
manage the task alone any longer and was always so parched. He
made a mental note to check the record book for the frequency of
visits from the students assigned to assist her.

"Paolina, there has been an accident." Ready for the immediate
alarm in her face, the Maestro consoled her, "Please let me finish.
Anna will be all right, Paolina." He realized he did not believe himself. "I have just received word that she is almost here and will need
medical attention when she arrives. I have arranged it. Here, have
a little more water, Paolina."

"What happened? Tell me now!" Paolina's voice had new
strength in it. "Now!"

"She apparently came willingly this time, once she heard you
wanted her to come."

Paolina interrupted. "What do you mean by that, Antonio?
Surely, the Envoy did not tell her that I was asking her to come

home!" Her cough prevented her from continuing and forced her to lie down again.

"Paolina, I did not tell him to say it. I told him two things—to convince, not force, her to come home where she belongs, and to be sure that she arrived home safely. What happened was an accident. The horse that she was riding from Siena into the countryside, where the carriage was waiting, went wild. Something must have scared the animal, because it broke loose from the group, galloped off and threw Anna."

"What did they do? How badly is she hurt? I haven't forgotten the Doge's Envoy. He's a very dangerous man, Antonio. He's a fighter. You wouldn't believe me last year, would you?" Paolina began to cry. She became agitated and wanted to sit up.

"Paolina, you must contain yourself and settle, for Anna's sake. She will need you." Vivaldi began to pace again. "Her room will be ready now. The Doge's physician has been sent for. Is there anything else I need to do? Domine! How did this happen? I hope her hands are all right!" He looked out across the basin, "I told him to keep her safe." The waters lapped dumbly, repetitively mocking him.

Paolina became still, drawing on an old strength. "Antonio, we need to be quiet and pray. Come and sit with me. Pray with me. All will be well."

Just as the agitated priest was about to turn from the window, he caught sight of the curtained gondola Lagunar, followed by the Doge's Bucintoro, standing out strikingly against the gondolas vying for space in the waters. Venetians would know that an important event was unfolding. The Doge visited the Pieta only for musical celebrations. Why, then, was the gondola Lagunar leading the way? Had the Maestro's strained breathing caught up with him? The surrealism of the brilliant red upon blue, blood upon spirit, threw Vivaldi into a panic. He crossed himself, desperate for for-giveness, desperate for Anna's wholeness, desperate to waken from his nightmare.

"She has arrived, Paolina. The wandering child has returned! All will indeed be well. It shall, Paolina." Leaving the sickroom door open, Vivaldi flew down the stairs with almost as much speed as Antonia herself had always been able to bring to the task.

He opened the door of the Pieta just as the gondolas were pulling up to the building and helped guide the first vessel in. A crowd was forming, as curiosity-seekers came from San Marco and Castello. After the gondoliers secured the boat, the first of the two strong, young men stepped onto the concourse. The Maestro made frivolous attempts at helping until he was guided away by Domenico. Once on the concourse, the men carried Antonia as gen-tly as possible into her Pieta and set the cot down carefully. The first gondolier pulled back the curtain.

"Domine! Oh, my little Anna, my little Anna," Vivaldi was over-whelmed by the brokenness that was lifted before him. Antonia was ashen, her face, though carefully tended to, cut and bruised. Her closed eyes were sunken, dark against the pallor of her skin. Her burgundy hair, haloing her face as always, was caked in blood. Her dress—no! Our Father, she is a nun!—was torn, the white around the neck bloody. Oh, my dear God—no, dear God—Domine! Her right arm was bandaged and secured against her side. Vivaldi dropped to the floor at her side. "Anna! Anna! Speak to me; please speak to me," he reached for her arm.

"Sir, don't touch her! You must let us carry her to her bed. Get up now and show us the way."

Vivaldi acquiesced, taking them to the room set aside for Antonia on the main level. The new Prioress and four senior students were waiting with everything set up as an Ospedale room. As the gondoliers lifted the broken body onto the bed, the attending women moved in to wash and settle their Maestra. "Be very careful with her arm and her back," the larger gondolier cautioned.

One of the students sobbed. "Constanza," the whisper came from Anna.

Vivaldi moved in to look at her. "Father Antonio," she smiled faintly. "Paolina?" The articulate Maestro was dispossessed of words. Never had he felt such powerful love and its attendant pain.

The physician, with his entourage, entered the room and clapped once, decisively. "Everyone out! Pieta women—stay! We have a life to put back together here!"

"Dear God," Vivaldi spoke quietly to himself, "what have I done?"

He climbed the stairs to Paolina's room, his heart broken, his spirit crushed.

* * *

"May I see her now?" Vivaldi stood in the hall outside Antonia's room; his eyes sought forgiveness in the physician's eyes.

"You may," the younger man was distant. "The students report that her night was relatively comfortable. Stay briefly and keep your conversation light. I have given my orders to Prioress Maria. She is very capable. It will take time for Anna's arm to heal; the fracture is below the elbow, not in the wrist. It is well stabilized. She has asked if she will play the violin again. I have been completely honest with her, as I find her very direct in spite of her pain. She may be able to play again; she may not. The worst is that her back is quite seriously injured. The wounds are dressed; but I cannot say how well she will recuperate from this injury. I suppose I can understand that a horse threw her; but who was responsible for getting her home? Why was she, a novice rider at best, allowed to be on a horse under such dangerous circumstances? And why was she not taken quickly for help in Florence? The ride home added further injuries." The physician looked accusingly at Vivaldi. "And who is this Orlando she keeps asking for? He needs to be brought here."

Vivaldi sank into shame and horrendous grief. "I cannot explain it all, sir, but I am assuming blame. For the rest of my life, I shall take care of her. I will never be able to make up for what has happened. I would rather die than have her lose her music." "She is extremely worried about Prioress Paolina," the physician gazed directly at the Maestro. "I think we must gather them together somehow. If I arranged with the Doge to have Anna lifted carefully to Sister Paolina's level, and if those men assisted her, could Sister Paolina muster enough strength to visit Anna? It would assist Anna's recovery. She won't be able to walk for a while, for quite a while. Nor should she move much."

Vivaldi spoke quietly, "Sister Paolina will do anything for Anna. She, too, needs to see Anna before it is too late."

"The Doge has given us very strict orders to give Anna the best of care and to keep everything private. He has established guards in the Pieta, including one at Anna's door, so that no one will come or go at will. There will be no visitors and, above all, no curiosity-seekers. I am to inform even you, sir, that you must be accountable to the guards. Anna's recovery is the most important matter in this place at the moment. You do understand, do you not?"

"Indeed, I do," Antonio noted mentally that the Doge's unsoiled reputation was even more important than Anna's recovery. "Please thank the Doge for his attention. We at the Pieta are grateful."

"There's one more matter that must be said, if Anna is to make a good recovery. Someone needs to know this. I believe that it should be the Prioress Paolina; but she is not well enough, nor will she be alive long enough, to handle this information."

"Domine! What more can Anna bear?" Fear took Vivaldi hostage, "Tell me! I shall deal with it!"

Speaking bluntly, the physician informed the musician, "Sir, this young woman lost a child. I was certain, and so I asked her. She was indeed in the early months. Whatever other grief was part of this horrendous accident, she will not recover from this loss. You sir, are party to the truth here, whatever that may be. You, sir, as the name she mentions as much as she mentions Prioress Paolina's, must take responsibility for Anna's care."

Leaving Vivaldi in a state of shock, the physician turned on his heel and left.

Vivaldi braced himself against the wall. His breathing laboured, he worked desperately to bring it under control. He pounded his fist against the wall. What has Sagredo done to her? What, in God's name have I done to her? The pain of his hand and the rise of anger brought some clarity into his devastation and remorse. My Anna needs me. He stood away from the wall, breathed deeply and brushed his clothing. Prioress Maria, standing in the doorway next to Antonia's room, watched with a perverted delight and relished her acquisition of yet another morsel to feed her friends.

Composing himself, Vivaldi entered Anna's room. The sight of Antonia at rest and cared for became almost more than he could bear. Sensing him nearby, she opened her eyes.

"Father Antonio, sit with me." As Vivaldi drew close to her left, she moved her hand out to hold his. "Why? Why, Father, why, if you love me, could you not let me go? Do you see me now?"

"Oh, Anna, I am tormented. I see you. I do see you. It breaks my heart, this thing I have done. I did it because I need you here and I love you as a daughter, Anna. How could anything go so wrong?" The priest kissed her hand, beseeching her for forgiveness.

"No, Maestro, you did not reclaim me because you love me. You did it because you love yourself and because you are not at peace with God, the God you taught me of, the God who inspires your music." Antonia's face was wet now.

"Anna, please forgive me. Please know that I did not give orders to have you taken by force. I could never conceive of injuring you. Never!" He wiped her face with the tenderest of gestures. "Instead of losing you to Siena, I might have lost you forever."

Antonia began to feel her love replace her anger. "But, you refused to believe both Paolina and me when we told you about the fierceness of the Envoy last year. Why would you not believe us? He is a frightening, evil man. And you sent him again for me, knowing full well that he is a fighter. He is trained to win wars, Father Antonio! He turned this into a war—because of the defeat he suffered when I returned to Siena. You inflicted an evil person on me. Why? How could you have?" Antonia's certitude gave force to her feeble voice.

"But the Doge offered this to me as the best plan, Anna. I trusted the Doge. And he has always cared for you."

"No!" Antonia's voice was strong now. "He has not cared for me. He has cared about the fascination I have added to Venice at times, the colour I have added to his precious Republic! Look at me now!"

"Anna, look at me—look into my eyes," Vivaldi spoke quietly and lovingly. "Trust me again, la mia principessa. This I pledge to you. When you are well, I shall give you my blessing on whatever you choose to do. I say this clearly and in absolute sincerity—I am devastated at my role in what has happened to you. I ask for and need your forgiveness. And I wait for it. You cannot give it to me now. In the meantime, your recovery is the most important matter in this place, your home."

Antonia saw the glistening eyes and heard the truth in his voice. She held his hand tightly. "Yes, Maestro, we shall wait and see how I recover." There was kindness in her eyes. "And, Sister Paolina? How is she?"

"She is not well, Anna. She needs to see you. Your room is on her floor. She will then be brought to your room." Antonia began to interrupt. Vivaldi silenced her, "Anna, there is no other way. You are simply not to move. Paolina will be carried to your room later this afternoon. Now, lie back and sleep."

For the first time ever, the Maestro discarded his discomfort with intimacy and stayed, holding her hand. As she let her thoughts drift, she realized he was humming "Ich Habe Genug." Involuntarily, the Maestro stroked the notes into her burgundy hair. It was an opus that conformed to an old manuscript of loss and attachment. And no words would ever be adequate to convey its message.

"Father Antonio, would you bring your violin and play for me—play 'Dite, Oime'?"

"Hush, child, sleep now; I shall play for you until you are well, and then forever."

XLV

What was it the Maestro wanted when he completed "Orlando Furioso"? Revenge? Forgiveness? Or was it, as he said, that he'd begun the opera years before and needed to finish it? Why, then, did he write completely new music? Who was Angelica? Who was Ranaldo? It was his most complex opera. And its name tormented me. [Antonia, 1740]

"Maestra, Sister Paolina is here now."

Antonia woke and tried to sit. A gentle hand on her shoulder reminded her of where and who she was now.

Paolina was brought in beside Antonia. "I have enough for comfort," she dismissed the students who were propping her with more pillows in her chair. "You may leave."

"Sister Paolina, we have been ordered to stay with you and the Maestra—in case you need anything," Constanza fussed with her again.

"Anna and I need to be alone," Paolina could not speak above a whisper now. Words came slowly and painfully. Antonia's heart ached as she perceived the extent of her Prioress's illness. She knew her spirit would depart soon. She was barely here now. "Go! Please, Constanza, we shall be all right. Stay over by the door—you only—I will let you know when we are finished talking."

Constanza sent the others away and sat by the door.

Antonia and Paolina looked steadfastly into each other's eyes. Their hands joined.

"Look at what we have been reduced to, dear one," Paolina's eyes brimmed. "Anna, you can overcome this. You must get well and return to your music and Orlando. You must. My strength is almost gone. That is all right, if I know that you are not broken by this."

Ellyn Peirson

"Mother, you are so tiny now. I want to look after you. What has happened to us?" Antonia wanted desperately to cradle the woman who had given her nothing but love. "I will get well, Paolina, and I will keep my music."

"I cannot stay much longer, Anna. I needed to see you. I needed to know that you would...," Paolina could not continue. "Oh, Anna, how can I let you go like this."

"Mother, I promise you I will recover. Please, you must not cry.... Constanza, call in the guard!"

The guard approached the bed, "We will take you to your room now; I'll get the others."

"No!" Antonia commanded now. "Paolina, you will lie with me. We will be together until you go. Move me a little this way, and lift her into bed beside me." The guard looked toward the door. "This is the way it will be. You will do this now. And then you will leave and inform the others."

Constanza and the guard settled the two women side-by-side and covered them with the blanket Paolina had made for Antonia so long ago. The guard left. Constanza, crying, moved back to her seat by the door.

"Are you all right, Mother? Are you comfortable enough?"

"Yes, dear one," Paolina held Antonia's hand and closed her eyes. "It is enough. You are my enough."

Antonia gazed from the ceiling to the end of the bed. For the first time, she recognized she was in her own room. Canaletto's painting was still there. The clothes were drying in the painting just as they had been when she had escaped with Pietro. Was God's love this constant? Was God's love present once innocence departed? "Ich habe genug, Mother, ich habe genug."

"You know, do you not, Anna?" Paolina whispered and clasped Antonia's hand more tightly.

"Yes, Mother, I know."

"How long have you known?"

Antonia breathed deeply. "I think I may have known forever. But I became aware and sure at the little church last year, before the Palio... when the priest spoke the same blessing that you had pronounced on me. 'Go and return victorious.' I knew that only a true mother could have carried out such an enormous commitment."

Paolina sighed, "Oh, my dear, why did you not tell me then? It had to be this way, so that I could be with you always. I placed you here and visited you every day. Father Antonio saw your talent very early and took pity on me. What would we ever have done without him, Anna?" Paolina was wracked with coughing. "Hush, my Mother. I have so many questions; but they can wait until we meet again. You need to rest. If all of this happened so that I would know from your lips without my asking, then I am blessed. I love you, Mother. You have no more strength for this world. But you have all the strength any soul could ever possibly need for the next." She lapsed into humming the "Largo" Paolina loved. The coughing stopped.

"Mother—may I ask you one more question?" Antonia had been silent for a few minutes, listening to her mother's laboured breathing. There was something she needed to know from her mother, and something her mother needed to know.

"Yes, Anna." There must be no secrets taken along into death.

"Was my father truly a musician? Was he a capable musician?" Antonia was child-like.

"Sweet Anna—he was. He was a most capable musician. I am very tired, Anna. And I am very happy to be with you," Paolina's voice was barely audible. "It won't be long now."

"I will stay with you, Mother, and walk you to the door," Antonia held Paolina's hand tightly, settled under the silk blanket of her mother's making and hummed very softly.

And Mother, Antonia spoke from inside her mind, Mother, will you tell my little one that I shall be along one day to meet her with open arms? And that I do not know how to live without her and without Orlando. Please, my mother?

"Yes, my Antonia," Paolina sighed, released Antonia's hand and slept.

* * *

"She called me just after midnight struck, Father Antonio. And she said a strange thing. She said very clearly, 'My mother has departed now. Please let the Maestro know.' " Constanza and Vivaldi were standing outside his bedroom door.

"Yes, Constanza. It was not a strange thing—the Prioress has been a mother to you all. Would you go to Prioress Maria and ask her to prepare the body? But I want to be with Anna for a while first. So the Prioress and her students must wait outside the door until I call them. And send someone for the physician." Vivaldi straightened his robe and smoothed his hair. He walked a long walk down the hall and entered Antonia's room.

The candle by the bed flicked the cameo in and out of existence. As before a canvas, Vivaldi stood by the door to take in the details of the painting. Paolina rested, a lamb within the crook of Antonia's arm. Antonia was quietly singing a new melody, a sweet lullaby, a lament, perfectly self-contained. Vivaldi feared to disturb the holy family.

He moved toward the bed. "Anna. I am here now."

Antonia stopped singing. She looked at her Maestro. "She left at midnight," her face was wet from the baptism. "My Mother left at midnight. As soon as I found her, she left me."

"Anna, Maria will take over now," he wiped her tears and whispered. "She was always your mother. Her spirit will stay with you, just as it did when you were away... in Siena. She loved you unselfishly... without wavering," Vivaldi leaned in and kissed Paolina's forehead. "Farewell, mio bell'un, go on your journey. Take your leave, Anna."

Antonia turned her head to bless Paolina's with a kiss. "Goodbye, mia Madre dolce, until we meet again." She kissed her mother and fell sobbing against her breast.

Vivaldi called in Maria and the guards, "Carry her carefully to her room and prepare her body. The Ducal Bucintoro will come within a few hours."

"Maria, wrap her in this blanket," Antonia offered her treasured blanket to Maria. "She made it for me when I was very young; but she let me choose the colours. I wanted them to match the waters. It will keep her safe and close to me on her journey." Maria sobbed and took the blanket.

Antonia turned toward the Maestro, "What are the plans?"

Vivaldi waited until the little group of weeping pallbearers left. He sat beside Antonia and held her hand. "The Doge wants her honoured privately. The Bucintoro will go just out to sea, and I shall conduct a small service. The senior chorus will sing. Paolina will then be lowered into the sea," the priest let go to his tears.

"Will you do one thing in my place for the service, Father?"

"Yes, if I am able, Anna."

"Play Juditha's 'Largo'."

Vivaldi looked into Antonia's eyes, "Yes, my little Anna. I shall play it as though I were you." He stood up and moved to the window, looking out over Antonia's balcony. "When did she tell you, Anna?"

"I knew. I asked her," Antonia spoke very softly, "I had known within my soul for a long time."

"How did she explain it to you?" The weary priest turned toward Antonia.

"She didn't have the strength left to tell me much. She said that she placed me here, and you took pity on her situation."

"It was not pity, Anna. I admired her from the beginning, from the beginning."

Vivaldi sat beside the bed and put his head down near Antonia's hand. Antonia put her hand on her Maestro's head.

I forgive you, Father Antonio."

* * *

"The body is in the Bucintoro, Father Antonio," Prioress Maria did not know how to talk to the usually distant, difficult man. She wondered if he would be able to carry on with the funeral. But really, Prioress Paolina had been ill for quite some time! He should be relieved that the struggle was over for him. And his protégée! How was she ever going to play her violin again? And the gossip! But she knew, and she had set the record straight with some people—it was indeed true that Anna Giraud had been pregnant at the time of the accident. Constanza, always so favoured, had also heard the physician give the Maestro this news. As pure as a nun—indeed! In the meantime, Anna's own students were being neglected. Truly— she would be glad when everything settled into routine again, and the Maestro started composing!

"Father Antonio?" He seemed frozen at the doorway. How could she get him out and into the boat? He wasn't the strong man she had thought him to be when she'd been a young student.

"Yes, Maria, yes." Vivaldi came to life. "Anna is settled. Constanza will stay with her until I return? You have made certain of that?"

Maria merely nodded her answer this time. He was really just talking to himself, anyway.

Vivaldi turned to the guard at the door. "If any gentlemen from Siena should call for me or for Anna, tell them to call again tomorrow afternoon." The Maestro had thought about the strong likelihood that Sagredo would be on his way to Venice. He would work out a plan whereby Anna would recuperate in Venice and then make a decision about life with Sagredo.

The guard nodded. He and Maria exchanged knowing glances. They knew the charade they were playing according to Tiepolo's script as clearly as they knew he would put an end to their relationship and their money if they disobeyed. Tiepolo's instructions had been clear from the moment of Paolina's death. It was Anna Giraud who was to be released into the waiting waters beyond the Bacino. This the public must hear and remember. Only the Doge, Tiepolo, Vivaldi and an exclusive few knew the truth. And it would remain safe with them.

Vivaldi opened the door. The bright August sun bounced and twirled over and off the gilt ornamentation of the Ducal vessel. The brilliant red curtains laughed in arrogant contrast to the black of the gondoliers' clothing. Slipping through the curtains, Vivaldi moved into the privacy of his parting from Paolina. He sat beside her body and put his hand on Antonia's blanket. "I am here, Paolina," he spoke gently, "Rest now." Never had he felt so alone. Desperate for the woman who had never left his side, he threw his arms around her body in a final embrace. The depth of his sobs opened his chest to the God with whom he had yet to make peace.

The gondola stopped at the Palace, to be joined by the Doge's Bucintoro.

Bewitching, the Lion of Saint Mark continued its refusal to reveal the secret of existence, while San Giorgio called the bones back to their watery origin.

XLVI

Less than fifty years before the Maestro was born, Venice was again visited by La Piaga. No marauder could torture and kill to the extent that the plague could. From 1630 to 1631, over 40,000 Venetians died... horribly, violently. An offspring of a wicked god, woven into the air, its spectre continues to haunt Venice. Venetians are prey to an offspring of that plague. It is an invisible plague, one of their own doing. It skulks around in the bowels of the city until it can attach itself to a grasping politician, a weak Doge, a power hungry Cardinal. People follow the politician, excuse the Doge and view the Cardinal as God's designate. They are then contaminated. My Maestro became contaminated. This plague destroyed Venetian music and broke Father Antonio's heart. [Antonia, 1741]

Having left their horses on the mainland, Orlando and Carlo made their way through the back waters of Venice. The closer they came to the Piazza, the more people they encountered walking away from it.

As they entered the Piazza, they were assaulted by sights and sounds and smells that billowed around them until they were not sure which was which. Shouting, music, spices, domes, heat, misty salt water... everything poured around them creating a bizarre theatre. Up, down and around... four bronze horsemen, a towering campanile, flags, market stalls, balconies, Byzantine ornamentation, the lion, boats, light, shadow, wealth, poverty... where were they to find a beginning for their search? Enveloped by the raucous noise and riotous colours, the brothers decided to find the group of people who seemed the most vocal and aware.

They spotted a cluster of people concentrating on a spectacular mother-ship, its red flag chattering in the breeze, its gold and red ornamentation animated by multitudinous oars. Beside it was its own amphibious off-spring, the precocious infant gondola.

Orlando approached the group. "Good afternoon, may we intrude for a moment? We have just arrived here on business from the south. Could you tell us what has been going on here today? Has something important happened?"

"A private funeral, sir. We cannot tell you much about it except that it is obvious that an important person died. The vessels belong to the Doge. And the Doge himself went to the funeral," the man, with his white wig and elaborate cape, was an oddity to Orlando.

"Well, we do know that the funeral must have been for an important person from the Pieta," a woman in the group spoke up. Made-up and adorned extravagantly, she seemed more fitting for the stage than for ordinary life. Orlando found her repulsive. How had the pure Antonia come from amongst people like this?

"How do you know that?" Orlando needed details. A dark fear flooded into his gut, murky, nauseating.

"Well, first of all," the woman replied, "Antonio Vivaldi accompanied the body. You have heard of him, have you not? A friend of ours saw him get on the Bucintoro. Then they went to the Doge's palace, and the Doge went along. Nothing can be very private in Venice!"

"Do you have any idea who might have died?" Carlo pushed the conversation further.

The woman enjoyed this. "There has been word out amongst Venetians that Vivaldi's star musician returned from the south and that she was thrown from a horse and seriously injured. She wasn't expected to live—or, at the least, that's what the talk has been. And so, the scandal continues—they say she died."

Orlando became stern, "There was an ailing Prioress, was there not? Could that have been who died?"

"Well, I suppose so," the woman obviously did not find this story as intriguing as her own, "but a Prioress would never have been given a funeral such as this one, with the Doge's vessels and with the Doge himself in attendance. But—Anna Giraud—now, she was a great favourite of the Doge. He would have ordered a funeral such as this for her!"

"The Pieta is down to our left, is it not?" Orlando's anger turned to contained rage.

The woman nodded her head. Disappointed that her audience would be lost, she tentatively held out her best morsel, "Of course, there was one piece of information that the public doesn't know."

Orlando became impatient, "Madam, I'm not being frivolous. I have business with Vivaldi. What is it that the public doesn't know?"

"Well, sir," the woman toyed with Orlando, "the new Prioress of the Pieta let it be made known that this Anna Giraud had been pregnant at the time of the accident." Orlando took a step toward the gloating Venetian, "Prioress Maria also told me that it was to be expected that the man who had led Giraud into sin and death might be found wandering our waterways." She smiled knowingly, relishing every word now, "You wouldn't by any chance be him, would you, sir?"

For a brief moment, Carlo was sure that his brother was going to lunge at the woman. "Orlando, come! Come!"

Orlando bolted, knocking over a cart to reach the nearest gondola. Carlo was on his heels. "Take us to the Pieta!" Orlando's fierce voice startled the gondolier.

"I doubt that you will be allowed in, sir," the gondolier cautioned.

"Take us anyway," Carlo ordered. "Orlando, sit!" He was afraid of Orlando's loss of control.

The gondolier obeyed, deftly moving the vessel down the short distance to the Pieta. "Go down that alley to the door that says Consultorio Pediatrico e Materno. I'll wait here, sir."

As they walked to the alley, a guard approached. "What is your business here, gentlemen? There is no one here to receive visitors. Everyone has been at a funeral."

"We know that. We have only one question for now, as we were on our way to meet with Vivaldi. And then we shall leave and come back later," Orlando measured every word in this insane fluid world. He brought his voice under control, "Would you tell us whose funeral it was?" It took all of Orlando's energy to maintain propriety and quell his urges. He needed his mind to be his ally. He must find out about Antonia, if only to have the details confirmed. And then he could formulate his plan with brutal reasoning.

"Where do you hail from?" The guard seemed not to want to divulge any information. "You say you are here on business?"

"Yes, Vivaldi is expecting us," Carlo spoke up. "He knows us from Siena."

The guard seemed to soften, "Yes, well, I did hear that someone might come to meet with Vivaldi. So, I can tell you that Anna Giraud died early this morning, sir. The body was taken out to sea at noon. Our Doge asked that we keep the information private. This Anna was the star of the Pieta and Antonio Vivaldi's favourite. A great loss, a great loss."

Carlo steered his brother back to the gondola and gave the order to return to the Piazza. It would be a long, sad journey home. And it would need to begin immediately. The Sagredo brothers had no bearings and no allies in this mad and separate world.

He sat across from his older brother. "Orlando, I am so sorry. She loved you very much," he placed his hand on his brother's arm.

"I killed her, Carlo. I killed both of them." Orlando sat erect, staring off toward the Piazza. His fixed gaze chilled Carlo. The older Sagredo, the master planner, seemed to have gone somewhere—to some impenetrable place in his mind.

"You have her letters. And you have her violin, Orlando," Carlo held his brother's arm more firmly. "And you have your family. We'll see you through this. Orlando," Carlo's words fell away, useless, swallowed up by the insatiable waters.

As the gondola glided past the Ducal Palace, the Lion of Saint Mark looked down on the two interlopers with disdain. An eerie silence had drifted in on the murky waters. And Carlo knew, beyond any shadow of doubt Venice could ever cast upon them, that his brother would never rest until he had avenged Antonia's death.

UNDICI

SAN GIMIGNANO TO THE NORTH

1727

XLVII

*Venetian politics has long been famous for its reverence of se-
crets and for its cruelty. I was subject to and the subject of both.
[Antonia, 1741]*

Her heart aching to be with Orlando for the harvest, Antonia sat
stiffly in a chair. She gazed southward from the balcony that had
once been her portal to freedom. Now she was imprisoned by it
and by her back. Numbness, physical and emotional, had replaced
passion in her life. Her only goal now was a return to the violin and
composition. She would be able to lose herself in both and assuage
the Maestro's profound grief at the same time. If only her arm would
cooperate, her violin would be her voice, her only voice.

Coming into her view, his gondola glided through the waters toward the Pieta. She would wait for him to come to her, and they
would talk of music and grief. And perhaps—just perhaps—this
time, the Doge would have relented, succumbed, to their pleas to
allow them to move quietly away to Siena where they would find
life and compose, bound by an oath never to perform again. Just
perhaps. Surely goodness and mercy would…

"Anna, my dear, you have not been too long in your chair, I trust?"

Turning slowly, she smiled in answer to this ritual of confession.
"What is your news this time, Father? Would the Doge listen to our
latest reasoning?" Antonia saw the answer in his eyes.

"Our meetings are over, Anna. He is unassailable. He will relent
on nothing." Vivaldi turned to look to the south. "I would never
have thought that I would resent these waters, Anna, that I would
become their prisoner. I feel them laugh at me at times. They have
taken Paolina from us, and now they take our freedom. Ah," he
slapped the railings with both hands, "I speak with no integrity.
Pardon me, Anna. I speak from powerlessness."

"Did he say your meetings are over permanently?" Antonia saw the defeat in Vivaldi's stooped shoulders. "Is there some way we can plan our leaving with help. My latest letter will get to Orlando. Bribery always works. Maria assured me. It should be there by now…"

Vivaldi turned to face her. "Anna, I must tell you this. I have pledged to be honest and use no deceit in our relationship; you know that. Maria cannot be trusted. She delivered your letter to Tiepolo," he retrieved the letter from his pocket and handed it to Antonia. The grief in her eyes crushed him. He reached out to touch her cheek, to prevent any tears from reminding him of his substantial sins, sins against the pure spirit of this broken child. "Yet again, your communication to Orlando—to anyone, my dear—is thwarted. And not only is the Doge unequivocal about our leaving, he has given orders about our communication through anyone to Orlando."

"But, if we are even more careful, very careful, who would know? I have lost Lorenzo." Would the pain ever stop? "But perhaps somehow I could get a message to Vincenzo or Pietro. I know I'll be able to gain strength. We must try, Father, we must." Antonia felt a desperation; it anchored itself in her heart as she looked at her Maestro's face. Their life had lurched onto a path of dissonance and distortion. Surely they were living in a dream that would soon end. The Maestro would have Paolina back to look after him, and she would wake up with Orlando. When would this dream end?

"This is what is so difficult to tell you, Anna. But I must. The Doge is tired of us. He has been "embarrassed" by us, he says. But I think we are no longer a novelty. He has no interest in music, really… it has always been his interest in what music could bring him in recognition and innovation. He is discarding us. Oh, we can go on composing, and we can have our little internal concerts with the students here. But, we shall never perform again in our home, except under very stringent circumstances. We are under arrest, my dear woman, under arrest!"

Shocked, Antonia searched for words. "Did he say that? Did he say exactly that?"

"He said that we are to consider ourselves under arrest. Those are his exact words—'Consider yourselves under arrest,' " the Maestro felt his anger rising. "That, Anna, is the measure of his gratitude for what I have done for Venice!"

"Then we shall escape this tyranny!" Anna's anger and colouring matched Vivaldi's. "We cannot give in to that kind of control!"

Vivaldi knelt so that he could look into Antonia's eyes. "Look at me and listen carefully, Anna. The Doge promised today—he called it a promise—to have Orlando killed if we make any plans to escape. He said, 'My Envoy would be only too happy to carry out the task.' "

Antonia turned to stone. She stared, unflinching, over and beyond the waters. Vivaldi, mortified, waited for some form of release. His guilt rose and faced him, challenging… taunting.

"Then what Constanza heard about Orlando will be true. He was here, and he was told that I had died."

The red priest cursed God for her pain. "I am afraid, my dear, that this is true, too. Tiepolo gave the orders to the guards."

Moving carefully, Antonia sat forward in her chair. "Well, then, that is good. Orlando has now had almost three moons to grieve my death. He is much further advanced than I. Soon he will be free to move on to love another. I'll go back to my bed now. Would you help me, please, and then fetch Constanza?" She accepted his assistance and moved without seeing.

As he guided Antonia inside, Vivaldi felt the crushing pain of multiple deaths. Where had his dreams gone? First Paolina and now Anna. And now—if truth be told—himself. Yes, Venice was killing him. All he had ever wanted was harmony and composition in the family he had gathered to himself. Music was fruit enough and now it was turning against him. Antonia would never be Anna again. Paolina would never be back. La Serenissima was becoming bored.

Dear God. Mea culpa. Forgive me, for I have sinned. And the wages of sin is death. And—Domine!—death has many faces.

XLVIII

Mothers threw their bastard newborns into the waters three hun-
dred years ago. Wrapped in seaweed, the little bodies were caught
with the fish. The Procuratori instituted a law against this and
founded the Orphanage, filled with suckling infants and wet-
nurses. And so I am alive because of the charity of the Procuratori.
And I am silenced because of their brutality. [Antonia, 1739]

Francesca knew she would find him here. "Orlando, are you going
to have some dinner tonight? We've had ours; but I kept some for
you." She stopped at the edge of her son's greening place, the private
place of his childhood imaginations.

"Mother, come over here." Francesca approached. "Sit with me for
a while," he patted the space beside him on the bench, as he continued to look ahead, always, always, searching. For what? Where was
God? There was only painful beauty left in this world of shades and
sounds, of fragrances and memories. And how was one to pay for
having led beauty itself into annihilation.

Waiting for her son to speak, Francesca looked out to the vineyards. Though he rarely spoke of it, her son's grief was palpable
to her. The long shadows assisted the sun to move on its nightly
journey below the velvet hills. Francesca longed for her son's healing. She knew her son longed for meaning, and without that, for
revenge.

"She's here, playing her violin; over there, picking the lavender;
down there, running up the hill," his gestures covered the view.
"She's in all of these places, Mother, and I cannot be with her. I cannot escape her here. I cannot escape her, and I cannot be with her."

Francesca touched her son's hand, "I understand, Orlando. I miss
her greatly as well. I always shall."

"Mother, I haven't been able to talk to you about this; but I must now. In fact, I haven't talked about it at all, not even with Carlo. Stepping into the pain of it would have been intolerable to me, and so I deliberately closed myself off from finding out the truth," he took a deep breath and looked into his mother's eyes. "But now I must do this. Now I must hear this. There is an inevitability to discovering what I already know in my heart. I know that I have kept family at a distance. I haven't wanted anyone to approach me about Antonia. There was a rumour in Venice that Antonia had been pregnant," Orlando's voice was almost inaudible. "If she talked with anyone, it would have been with you. She would have needed a mother first. Did she talk with you about this?"

For a moment, Francesca felt that the pain would consume her. "She did, Orlando."

"And she was?" It was her young boy who looked at her in trust, in the knowledge that she would always tell him the truth.

Dear God, take this task away from me. "She was, my son. Her plan was to tell you after the Palio was over. She was so very excited to tell you." Francesca looked down at the tears that had fallen on her son's beautiful hands. As she brought his hand to her mouth, her tears joined his. Her heart tore with his in the deep sob that came from his soul. Would that it were only her pain, that she could take it from him and that he could move on from here, healed.

Somehow there was consolation in the breath of the purple hills.

"And so, what have you decided, Orlando?" Francesca put her arm around her son's broad back, "You knew you would find your answer during the harvest. What is it that you must do?"

"I have decided to enter the priesthood, Mother. You know I have talked to the brothers in San Gimignano and in Florence. Florence would be too reminiscent of Lorenzo. And it didn't belong to Antonia. She awoke to freedom in San Gimignano, and it was there that

I knew I'd lost her to Tiepolo. So, it will be there that I go. In a sense that will allow me to continue to look for her."

"You are sure that Siena would not, in the end, be the best place, Orlando? Do you really want to be away from what you had with Antonia here?" Francesca's eyes filled at the thought of her loss. She could not tell Orlando that, in losing him to God, she would grieve her loss of Antonia even more. She could not cause incremental grief for her son.

"Mother, I am your eldest. With my birth, you learned what it is for a mother to worry about the loss of a child. We have always been together. Our memories will sustain us. One way or another, as you have sensed, I wouldn't choose to stay in Siena. Antonia's presence is too real in the ghosts of our Duomo. That will never change. I'll stay at home until the spring. That will give us all time to adjust to the change and to be sure that all of our family business is taken care of. How will Father feel about Siena?" Orlando fell into the well-worn pattern of channeling difficult messages through his mother.

"He senses that you will be leaving home. He has been talking about it and working toward an acceptance of losing you. He's still very angry over your loss of Antonia. He had become fond of her, Orlando. Well, my son, come with me for supper," Francesca stood, wishing she could console him and read to him as she had done in his childhood.

Orlando stood and looked down into his mother's brown eyes. He kissed her forehead. "I will require of my family one thing. And that is that I don't want anyone outside of our immediate family to know where and why I have gone. I will deal with my grief there and learn. The grieving is the first task. I need to form a new attachment to life somehow. There are many times when I desire death so that I might join Antonia."

Francesca tried to speak. "No, Mother, let me say that. Someone needs to hear it. Rest assured that I would not harm myself. That would injure Antonia's memory. I'm not as sure of spiritual complexities as she is... was.... Perhaps death brings a loss of earthly memories, and I'm not prepared to lose the precious little I have left."

"Then, why, Orlando, are you asking that we deny you?" Her son was demanding more than she could bear.

"Because, Mother, this is my way of joining her—marrying her, if you will. I've never been deeply religious. Antonia brought a passion into that area of my life, and I have a strange desire to follow in her direction. Perhaps in this way, I can find her path out of this world and join her on it. She believed in our reunion—you've seen the letter that was found with Lorenzo. I'm married to it." Orlando's face became stern and hard, closed to emotion. He looked past his mother.

Francesca understood. "Yes, Orlando. You require of me a monumental task. But another mother did it, and I shall follow her example. I shall spend much prayer time in the Duomo. That is how I shall stay close to you. And what, Orlando, are we to tell anyone who asks about you?"

"Tell them anything but the truth. I don't care what you say."

In a flash of anger, Francesca realized that in this very moment she had lost her son. This was the way it would be; this would be the way she would cope with her loss. As she closed down her feelings, she looked directly at the man she had helped create. "Well, then, Orlando, since I do not enjoy lying, my answer will be brief. I shall tell anyone who asks that you have gone south to work on your father's business there and to marry. This is your reaction to Antonia's death for the present."

"Thank you, Mother. Now, it's time to eat."

As they passed by the basil, Francesca felt drawn to it. She bent to pick a leaf. "This is for you from out there," she gestured to the purple, carpeted hills and the disappearing sun, "from Antonia."

Orlando took the gift, crushed it and inhaled the fragrance.

Briefly, he let the redolent breeze whisper to him. But Orlando had hardened his heart. He could allow no space for softness. Tenderness and a voracious hunger for revenge were irreconcilable.

XLIX

Venetians are obsessed with the construction and maintenance of two wooden instruments of travel. The gondola travels on water. The violin travels on air. Both transport people, and so people who live in luxury desire—demand—perfection. Woods, tone, colour, varnishes, quality—the making of both instruments follows careful rules and requires the ultimate in craftsmanship. But the Soul is the greatest instrument of travel, for it takes us into the mind of God. Venetians have no obsession for the maintenance of the Soul. [Antonia, 1740]

With the passing of winter, Vivaldi became imbued with hope. He was encouraged by Anna's ability to play the violin again, even if it did bring pain after an hour's work. She was regaining her former speed with the bow. It would not be long, with patience and persistence, before the bow hand would be able to match the now constrained ability of the left hand. He was relieved that Anna herself was able again to use Juditha's "Largo" to bring her solace. The reluctant priest noticed that he prayed more than he ever had in his daily routines. He had never understood prayer until now. It had become as much a requirement of his life as breathing itself.

He stopped for a moment outside her door to let his wheezing subside. The dampness of Venice's winter had been especially hard on his breathing this winter. Somehow even the constant worry over Anna and the loss of interest in his music seemed to affect his chest.

"Ah, she is playing well," he knocked and entered Antonia's room.

She was standing, pure beauty, on the balcony, oblivious to everything but her improvisations on the Tempest's Largo. The vibrant register transmuted into a mystical melancholy into which Anna seemed to be inserting questions and—yes—anger into her interpretation. She left a chord hanging, begging for resolution, devoid of any hope, and sat down. At that moment, she noticed her Maestro. Vivaldi was speechless.

"If I ever do manage to regain my performance abilities, I cannot see how my back will allow me to stand," her eyes glistened. "But I will not give up!" She stood again.

"Anna, my dear, sit. Put your instrument down. There is no rush. And, as for your hopes at performance—my dear, you can stand when you want and sit when you need to. That is the beauty of the violin," he extended his hand.

Antonia took his hand. Together, they walked into her room. She let the Maestro lead her to her chair. "Why did the Doge want to see you this morning?"

Vivaldi avoided her direct gaze, "To remind me of my place—yet again." He smiled weakly.

Antonia was not fooled, "There's more to this; I can tell. You know I can tell. What is it?"

Vivaldi sighed. He cleared his throat. "I was correct when I said that he reminded me of my place. And yours. First, Anna," he sought some look in her eyes to assuage his guilt, "he gave me these letters to Orlando and his mother that you got to Vincenzo's friend. And then he gave me the letter you sent to Lorenzo's sister." Vivaldi now knew what Hell's punishment was like. How could he find the strength to continue? But he must—he and Anna had a covenant. "My little Anna, everyone has either his price or his mouth that is his downfall. Please let these betrayals tell you more about the person's character than about what they have done to you. And, my dear, the Doge has had word of Orlando through Tiepolo," he saw the familiar veil cover her face. "So—the Doge wants you to know that he does not have to go after Orlando to silence him. His source in Siena, a friend of Enrico Sagredo, has informed him that Orlando recently left Siena and has gone south, likely to Rome, to work and to marry," he could not read her face. "Anna?"

"Yes," she turned her stony gaze out the window and toward the south. "It is what I would have wanted... had I died."

Vivaldi stared down at the floor. The intricate, dizzying patterning of Paolina's Oriental carpet seemed to come alive, swirling under his feet, disorienting him. Yet again, he felt that he could not bear it... the grief... the remorse... and the absolute culpability.

L

*It floated in through my window and under my door one night.
I had wakened from a dream of a garden outside of Siena with
an ancient, crumbling stone tower off to the side. It was a peaceful, still dream, all green except for the ripe red tomatoes growing
amongst the herbs. I might say the dream was fragrant, as odd as
that may seem. But, while it was peaceful, I was left with tremendous melancholy. And that was when I felt the music float into
my room... soothing, as quietly sad as my dream... played on a
lute. Was I still dreaming? No—it must be the Maestro! But so late
at night? I threw a blanket around my shoulders and went to the
music room. The door was open and a gust of Adriatic air sent the
music into my soul. I wanted to cry. And there he was—Father Antonio, leaning into his lute, his white and red hair falling over the
instrument, the offering exquisitely, painfully beautiful. "What
is it, Anna?" How had he known I was there? "This is not your
music, Father." On the end of an arpeggio, he spoke softly, "No,
it is a Passacaglia by a man named Biber. Stay if you wish." He
looked up briefly and I saw the tears in his eyes. "It brings Paolina
back to this room." I stayed, my chest crushed with the pressure
of a lost mother and lover, my Orlando. [Antonia, 1742]*

Orlando looked around at his room. "This is all I'll ever need,"
he spoke into an old, dusky mirror. He changed into the monk's
robe he had been given and put his worldly clothes into the bag.
He would burn them later. He slipped the cross over his head and
dropped his hood down over his back. "The world is gone," Orlando
turned away from the mirror and looked around at his new home,
"for now." Above the small bed, his broken Saviour bled and gazed
at his feet. Picking up the primitive desk, Orlando moved it in front

of the window. He would need the view for his writing. And the light. He pulled the old chair up to the desk.

Leaning over the desk, he took in the complete view from his position near the top of the old tower. The garden contained possibilities. Antonia would have seen them more clearly than he. He sensed her approach. "Save the olives and the grapevine, Orlando; free up what wants to live—touch, smell, taste. Give it life. Plant basil!" The echo of her laughter seared his brain.

What would it be like to be Brother Francesco. With an odd mixture of grief and relief, Orlando made the shift. "The world is gone for now," he reminded himself. "And that world I shall never miss."

He had been clear and honest with the Brotherhood about his intentions. As he had come to understand it, the remainder of his life would move into three intertwined spiritual areas—studying Saint Catherine's life, interpreting early paintings of her, and documenting and preserving artifacts related to her life and times in Siena. He would devote a life of celibacy, solitude and silence to this comprehensive plan. Saint Catherine and her followers would be his chief focus. His library would arrive within the month. He would be accountable to the Brotherhood through his weekly mentoring from Father Roberto. For the reflective substance of his project, Brother Francesco would pray for two hours every morning and evening, fast once a month and create a spiritual garden. No one would come to him. He would go out to no one other than to walk the few miles into town to the Brotherhood once a week. Father Roberto would gradually provide him with the Saint's artifacts that had been kept for years in the Duomo. He would return them to Brother Roberto with the documentation every few months.

Completing the removal of all earthly possessions, other than those intentionally chosen for their connection to God, Orlando tied the bag shut, according to his elder's instructions. He took the wrapping off the two possessions he had chosen to keep. Picking up the violin and bow tenderly, he placed them for the duration on his tiny dresser. And then he opened the drawer of his desk and placed the letter inside... "for Orlando Sagredo, in the event of my death". Burned into his mind, the words would never need to be read again. Daily his head taunted him with the litany: I cannot banish my fears... cannot... cannot. I want you to have my love in writing, Orlando. Whatever happens, I will never leave you spiritually; you are my heart and soul's delight—for eternity. If we are ever separated—by death or by ill intent—I shall belong to no one else. The moon will be your constant reminder that neither death nor ill intent are powerful enough to separate us permanently. We share one soul, Orlando, for Eternity. The paper, like the violin, breathed with the passion of Antonia. These relics would never part from his possession. These relics and his love would never die. Thus was he married to Antonia.

Picking up the bag of his old life, Orlando moved gracefully down the old staircase, despite its smallness. Outside, he tossed the bag beside the fire pit. He would burn it tomorrow. He brushed his hands together. "That is it!" he proclaimed to the dazzling blue sky, "It is finished!"

Thus it was that Brother Francesco took over the old tower on the outskirts of San Gimignano. Thus it was that Brother Francesco formalized his wedding vows. Nothing would destroy them. Indeed, what God had joined together, no man could put asunder. And the one who had tried would pay.

* * *

Brother Francesco made his way home along the road toward his living quarters. The towers of San Gimignano cast their protection over him and his developing spiritual acuity.

Father Roberto had been pleased to agree with the aloof Brother that the time had come for a period of fasting. "An odd man, this young Francesco," he had spoken aloud to himself after the departure of his student, "the kind of man who could divorce himself from the world and become so spiritually focused that he would need nothing, absolutely nothing in life—not even good food or music. He has that violin, though. But it's never used. He keeps it polished; but I doubt he knows much music. Well, he'll come out of the fasting a writer. Yes! That will be the result! Fascinating—and perhaps a touch intimidating." Father Roberto was satisfied with the analysis. "I could certainly never imagine being friends with the fellow. Too cold... too cryptic... hard to imagine how he ever came to be here. And from the very worldly Sagredo family!" He popped an olive into his mouth and followed it with a swig of his own wine. Ah, the muscat had been perfect last year!

* * *

Brother Francesco left the road and moved along the narrow lane that led to his tower. His anticipation heightened. Would everything work? The suspense accelerated his pace. Moving into a run, he reached the clearing. He whistled shrilly, the call of his boyhood. The door of the tower opened.

"Carlo!" the Brother raced toward Carlo and embraced him.

Carlo returned the embrace warmly and held Orlando at arm's length. "Orlando, it's so good to see you! I've missed you."

"How is everyone, Carlo? Is Mother happy?" The brothers entered the tower.

"We're all well. In some ways, Mother is the happiest, being a grandmother now. She has a joy to diminish her grief," Carlo followed the Brother up the tower stairs. "Orlando, Enrico and Alessandra have a daughter. They named her Antonia."

Orlando stopped momentarily on the stairs. Carlo waited. Would his brother respond? Resuming the climb, Orlando was silent. They entered his room, "It's good to know that everyone is well. Come; sit here, Carlo. Where did you leave your horse?"

"Exactly where you had described. I had no trouble finding the area. Vincenzo was very clear. He explained everything from the plan you gave him before you left home. Have you been able to set your plan in motion here?" Carlo wondered at Orlando's dispassion and distance from his family. He's like Father now, not at all like Mother, his thoughts wandered.

"Father Roberto understood the need for fasting to take precedence over our next weekly session. So, at the most, I have twelve days to do what I need to do and return. And the rest of my life to atone. I want to leave after we've had some food. Tell me exactly what you've learned." Orlando put a loaf of bread, tomatoes and olive oil on the table. "I have wine and water in those jugs beside the plates. Help yourself. And give me your information."

"Well, just as you'd heard, his full name is Dante Tiepolo. He has been the Doge's Envoy from the beginning five years ago and apparently functions as the Doge's brain," Carlo sat down with his food and a sharp knife. "Vincenzo explained that Mocenigo has fallen a perfect prey to the grasping Envoy. Incredibly, he's been given power over the Procuratori—the administrators of Venice's Sestieri. All nine of them answer to Tiepolo, and Tiepolo takes his version of the information to the Doge. He's a fighter and a thinker. He loves the best of everything and yet can live minimally when he wants to achieve something. He has many enemies and a few extremely influential friends. He's a man for all seasons. No one who knows him will cross him. He has made a career of winning. And that, Orlando, is your enemy."

Unwavering, Orlando gazed piercingly across the table at his brother. "He has much to lose, then, Carlo. I have nothing. What are his habits?"

"Well, he certainly had no need to be at this year's Palio," Carlo pulled a note from his pocket and referred to it. "He lives in the Ducal Palace. His days are spent acting as the Doge's private Secretary, planning and attending functions and meetings. Our most succulent piece of information is the key for you, Orlando. He has a great weakness for the Ridotto. He goes frequently and squanders his money on the gaming tables and women, obsessed with his drive to win. In fact, he's so obsessed that he will often slip out to attend the Ridotto at midnight. You may also find him at a place called Florian's—it's on your map, as well. Apparently, he and the Procuratori supported the opening of this shop to introduce some new kind of beverage. He goes there to preen when he feels the whim. And he plans some of his own private endeavours there as well. I think it might be a safe place in which to situate yourself so that you can become acquainted with the man and his cohorts."

Staring into his goblet, Orlando mulled over the information for a moment. And then, he looked directly into Carlo's eyes. "Perfect." He stood and moved to the window. "Everything's in the saddlebag, then? And where will I find the Ridotto?"

"It's behind the theatre; but the saddlebag has everything you need—directions, schedules, money. The gondoliers will also know everything, as you and I found out last year. It will be best for you to stay as close to the backwaters as you can and take a gondola to the Ridotto in the late evenings. I managed to get you permission to stay in a back room in the Palazzo Morosini," Carlo smiled wryly.

"They're no friends of the Doge and found our old family connection fascinating. They know simply that you are there on family business. Again, refer to your maps. There's plenty of money in the bag."

"Then it will be best for me to go to the Ridotto every night until he comes," Orlando sat down at the table again. "Now, tell me what he looks like."

"Vincenzo describes him as large and tall," Carlo referred again to his notes, "in excellent physical condition—like you, Vincenzo says, in physique... about forty years old. He's dark, clean shaven, and handsome in a penetrating, arrogant way, and he dresses simply and expensively. As you will remember from Antonia's experience," Carlo noted his brother's eyes momentarily lose focus, "his voice is deep and is used to impress or control... perhaps they are the same thing. And that's probably the most helpful characteristic for you—he takes over the spaces he moves in. You will notice him, Orlando, and you will know him."

Orlando stood. "Good work, Carlo. You and Vincenzo have done very well for me. Are the same innkeepers on the mainland secured to keep the horse until I return for him?"

"They are. And they know roughly when you'll arrive. They remember Antonia very fondly," again Carlo saw his brother brace himself against the words. There would be no talk of the love of Orlando's life. There could be no attempt to assail those walls.

"Well, then, Carlo—it's time for you to become a monk," Orlando removed his cross. He handed it to Carlo, who then began to disrobe as well. The brothers exchanged clothing. "And Mother believes you are away on business?"

Carlo looked in the dusky mirror and laughed heartily, "Am I not, Orlando? What better way to look for new grapes than to immerse oneself in the countryside! I'm frequently away since you left, anyway. Look at us! I'm a perfect Brother Francesco—except that I can laugh!" He gave his older brother a resounding clap on the back, "Go! Do what you must, Orlando, to free your soul. I'll find a way to be here."

"Thank you, Carlo. You're an exceptional brother—and friend. If Father Roberto should happen to come here, you simply keep your head down, don't look up and don't talk. He would only be making sure your retreat is silent. If I haven't returned in twelve days, go home. That will mean that I'm not returning at all." Orlando gave his brother a warm embrace and moved quickly down the stairs.

Carlo heard the door close and leaned across the desk to look out the window. Orlando disappeared into the woods. A few moments later, horse and rider sped past the tower and out of sight.

A shrill whistle drifted in the window. Carlo crossed himself—his brother would now be on the road to Venice. He turned around to identify a new sweet fragrance. All that he noticed was Antonia's violin looking back at him from across the room.

"Your murder will be avenged, Antonia. Orlando is off to Venice," he whispered to the violin. "Your lover will balance the scales… or die."

DODICI

THE RIDOTTO TO THE BACKWATERS

1727

LI

The Maestro and the Prioress kept me cloistered as a child. They were particularly concerned that I never trust anyone with a mask. "The tradition is evil, Anna," they would remind me. "It was once prohibited because of dreadful crimes committed by those concealed in masks. Even in convents! It's too terrible to tell you what happened. Now the mask is important again. Particularly when people go out to gamble in the night. Never go near anyone with a mask." How could this happen? As they would never let me out of the Pieta unless we went to the Basilica or the Scuola to perform, I could never understand this! And then one evening, when I was pulling weeds in the garden, I felt I must see beyond the doors on my own. I slipped out through the "Pediatrico e Materno" door, along the alley and into the concourse. It was dusk and a pungent, spicy aroma floated in from the Bacino. From the shadows, a sharp male voice called to me, "What are you doing, Novice? Come talk to me!" I looked up. He was approaching. I'll never forget my fear! Over his eyes was a ghostly white mask and from it dropped a veil of white, covering his mouth. The mask turned his eyes into black holes. On his head, he wore a three-cornered black hat. He extended his gloved hand, and I ran. He laughed and followed me. I fled back through the door and locked it. I can still hear his laugh and his strident knocking at the door. I never ventured out alone again. And I never told anyone. [Antonia, 1744]

In a fraction of the time that it had taken Antonia and Lorenzo to cover the distance, Orlando was in Venice and settled into his accommodation. One man, one horse and one deadly intent made for great speed and precision. And Carlo had been wise to secure the back waters of Venice for lodgings; it made movement natural.

Venice's size and magnetism allowed him to blend in as a visitor. He abhorred this absurd city and what it had done to Antonia. Except for the view southward and his connection to Antonia through it, he wanted the dank waters and sultry buildings, the pretentiousness and the deceit, to suffer more than Antonia had. Venice was his vision of Hell.

Having worked his way carefully across the Piazza to the Ducal Palace, Orlando, on his second full day in Venice, was seated in Florian's "Triumphant Venice". The apparent sophisticate, Orlando, food and coffee in hand, moved to a table beside a small group of finely dressed men and women. So this strange brown liquid was the ultimate in urbanity! Orlando marvelled at its new popularity. He would eat, read and listen. Hopefully, he would overhear some pertinent information today. Given yesterday's dearth of any worthwhile information, he could feel his old impatience. His days in the tower had eased him away from it.

The group of men and women left without having given Orlando a morsel of information. He wouldn't stay much longer. There must be a group of people talking of politics somewhere nearby in this city of people who had too much time on their hands and too few worthwhile thoughts in their minds. Unlike Venice, Siena....

Realizing his thoughts had drifted, Orlando became aware that two men had sat down at a table almost behind him, to his right. What was it that had alerted his consciousness? "Dante"? Had that been the word? Their conversation was animated.

"He should arrive back sometime this afternoon if all went well with the business Mocenigo assigned to him. If I know him, and I do, he'll be hungering for a visit to the Ridotto tonight," the voice was cultured, light and anxious.

"Have you ever known him not to make that his target for the first day back? His lust for domination cannot go long without needing satisfaction," the companion's voice was deeper, but equally affected.

Orlando wanted to see these men. He might need to identify them. He was torn between moving to see and staying unobtrusively seated to learn more and retain the voices. He chose the latter.

"He has said his chief complaint lately has been boredom. What do you expect it will be tonight, male or female?" the lighter voice rose in increased anxiety.

The darker voice laughed raucously, "We can only hope, Guido, and be there!" After their laughter subsided, the men fell into quieter talk.

Orlando closed his book, brushed off his clothing and left without looking back. He could afford no risk of being identified. He now knew his next move.

LII

My dream clings to me today. I am in a lush, green forest—
everything is completely safe, the air dense and crackling. I stand
before a river, a brilliant turquoise, gently undulating river. I am
alone, calm, at one with everything. I reach into the river and
pull out a beautiful feline animal, smaller than a lion. I hold it
lovingly and it looks up at me knowingly. I embrace the animal
in great love. Its hide is silver with large lavender spots. The water
has given it an incredible sleekness. I know I am in the presence
of supernatural beauty. I am comforted. And I do not know why.
I feel Orlando close, as close as he was when he pulled his cloak
around me and we rode off into the hills. I do not know why....
[Antonia, 1747]

"Once again, my dear, I have failed. The Doge will have nothing
to do with your coming to Florence for the performance. I even went
so far as to tell him that you have composed the new concerto. And
even that information did not sway him. In the past, that knowledge
would have had impact on him. But no longer! I know that Tiepolo
controls him; I know that is where his orders come from! Can you
imagine the impotence of the man! What could it possibly matter
anymore who knows you are alive!" Showing his colours, the Red
Priest looked across the music room at Antonia, seated at her desk.

"Did you explain that I can do nothing... that I know that Orlando has left? I cannot believe that he still refuses me life," Antonia
was still while the Maestro paced.

"Anna, I am delighted that your music has come back to you!
And, believe me, I was fervent in my advocacy for your right to
be in Florence. The Doge's biggest objection was his fear that you
might try to 'escape' to find Lorenzo's family. And he did use the

word 'escape', as though you are still under some kind of arrest." Frustration and anger colluded to fuel the Maestro's wheezing.

Antonia put her hand on Vivaldi's arm to calm him. "Well then, you have done all you can possibly do, Father. I was hoping that the political climate might have settled, given the Doge's precarious health; but I obviously still embarrass him. Now, if I were going along to be involved in 'Juditha', I could understand. But that he would be threatened by a little concerto...," Antonia laughed. "I shall stay here and write while you're away. Do you still plan on leaving tomorrow? Your trip will be shorter than it would have been with me."

"Only by a day or so, I am afraid—I was so hoping and so sure that you would be allowed to come along, Anna, that there is only one concert I have been able to cancel," the Maestro felt defeated. "I will miss you greatly, my dear. I would love to have seen the places you have told me of when... when... you were there with Lorenzo's family. And..."

"Yes, Father, I know. You would have helped me find Lorenzo's family. My nights would be less troubled if I could do that. Thank you for caring," Antonia moved over to the music stand. "I'll finish the flute concerto before you return. Go now, and see if Maria's preparations are in order. You know she always misses something."

Somehow vindicated—or had he been dismissed?—Vivaldi kissed Antonia on the forehead. Such was his relief that he gave her an awkward embrace, "I shall leave early tomorrow morning, Anna. It would make me very happy if you were still sleeping when I leave." He closed the door quietly behind him.

On the verge of giving in to her pain, Antonia, violin in hand, walked out to the balcony. The twilight of the sky matched her thoughts—part dream, part real; a blurring of the known and the unknown. The sounds and smells of the water and the beginning nightlife wafted up to the balcony. Antonia shivered. She looked up to her place in the sky. Where was her venerable friend? Where was Luna's blessing? The moon looked back, translucent, inscrutable. Had she lost all union with love? Had love lost its bond to her?

Remembering, questioning, she noticed the speed of a single gondola, gliding noiselessly over the Bacino. How strange, she thought, to see a gondolier dressed for the Ridotto. She watched it, spellbound, until it disappeared.

LIII

Plant jasmine when I die,
Against the towers in my dreams,
Climb to its deepest greens;
Upon the stones 'til blossoms cry.
Spin steps of perfumed sighs,
And in the billows where I rest;
I take you to my breast—
Soul-soaring One beyond the skies.
[Antonia, 1748]

Orlando, imposing in his green and black cape and white mask, walked confidently into the density of the Ridotto's developing nightlife. It was his intention to use his size and force to achieve his goal. Women turned to attract his attention, only to watch him as he continued on. He moved easily about the floor, appearing to determine how his gaming would progress. The place reeked with connivance, heavy perfume and debauchery. The most pitiable sight in Orlando's view was the robed members of the Procuratori sitting in charge of the gaming tables. How had Venice reduced its once-proud state to a mockery of its former self? The place, its noises and its smells nauseated him. He nursed his drink and placed a bet, all the while paying attention to the groupings of people and deciding where next to go. A woman moved in beside him.

"I can help you find your way about this place. There's very little I don't know about anyone here tonight... except you, sir," she smiled and moved her black velvet mask a little. Her voice was seductive, her manner engaging.

Orlando stopped himself from uttering an instinctive rebuff. This exchange could prove to be exactly what he needed. "And what

makes you think I might have any interest in anyone here tonight?"
He moved away from the table with the woman.

"Two things, my good sir. I'm an expert assessor of the life that
comes and goes in this place. And I have been watching you since
you came in. You're here for a purpose," the mask moved again, as
quickly as the beautiful smile flashed and disappeared.

"Well, then, my lady, I should think that you have just given me
enough information to cause me to find you highly untrustworthy."
Orlando's smile vanished as quickly as hers had. The two sets of imprisoned eyes locked. The next move was hers and would be critical.

"I'm bored, sir, incredibly and tediously bored. I find you intriguing. I find the rest of the people here, including my husband and my
lover, boring. Other than my own gratification for the night, I have
no motivation. Do I make my point?" Her gaze did not flinch.

Orlando was struck with the malignant, seductive energy of the
woman. He would use her. And entertain no guilt. She had presented herself as his emissary—his unwitting partner in crime. Perhaps there was just enough holy energy resting upon him to achieve
his purposes. Whatever the case, Orlando knew he had only one
mission at the moment.

"Yes, you make your point… an enticing point. Walk me about
the place and tell me of the people and their reasons for being
here. I'm most interested in a man by the name of Tiepolo—Dante
Tiepolo. Do you know him?"

The woman stopped and looked at Orlando. "Everyone knows
him, sir. He's the most well-known and despised man in Venice.
What is it that you have in common with him?"

"Nothing; I have nothing in common with the man. But I do have
a debt to settle, and he is my access to the debt. All I want to know
is if he's here tonight and then to be pointed toward him." Orlando
looked away, as though to move off into the crowd.

He felt a hand upon his arm. "He came in a few minutes ago. I can go so far as to introduce him to you. What is the nature of your debt? I must warn you that you are approaching the impossible. Dante is not a man to toy with. He is the power-monger of Venice and makes no enduring connections. I would advise you to find another way to settle your debt with him. Use an intermediary."

In union, the two resumed strolling about the Ridotto floor. Orlando wondered at the woman's understanding of the man. It was odd that she would be so knowing of Tiepolo's nature. Had she slipped in using his first name? "The nature of my debt, madam? Let us say merely that it is private and requires balance. What is your knowledge of the man?"

The woman stopped, moved her mask away from her face and looked directly into Orlando's eyes. Her beauty was stunning. "My knowledge, sir? Let us say that it is much the same as your debt," she moved the mask back. "Look over at that group by the door. There are three men together; do you see them?"

"I do. The man in the centre, the one without a mask—he's in control. The other men seem to be leaning on his every word. Is that Tiepolo?" The woman nodded. "The other two men may have been at Florian's today. From what I overheard there, it would seem Tiepolo has an insatiable appetite for both men and women. Would you know anything about that?"

The woman became calculating again, "Yes, I know a great deal about that. I can tell you more; but you must remember I require payment for the information I provide," the mask moved briefly away from her eyes again as she took in Orlando's acknowledgment. "His greatest compulsion is toward young girls, my friend. And my payment for making your debt easier to acquire? I require a night with you to wipe out your debt to me."

"I assumed that you would. I understand very clearly," Orlando smiled and bowed graciously. His plans had taken on a much sharper focus.

"I shall be looking forward to meeting you face-to-face, kind sir. Might I know the name of the one with whom I shall spend the night?" The dazzling smile flashed.

"Lorenzo, madam. And might I know your name in return before you introduce me?" Orlando felt an odd appreciation for the boldness of the woman who would do anything to alleviate her boredom.

"Sophia, Lorenzo. Sophia Tiepolo. Do come and meet my husband." Orlando was swept along in her force as they moved through the crowd toward the group of men.

"Dante. I've met someone who wishes to do business with you," Sophia moved fearlessly in to face her husband. As Tiepolo turned toward them, Orlando felt his rage explode in his chest and head. "This is Lorenzo, Dante. I shall leave the two of you alone for a while. I will see you later, Lorenzo."

Facing his nemesis, Orlando breathed deeply and steadied himself for the task ahead. The men's eyes met. Orlando despised the confidence in the man's darkness and carriage.

"You have business to do with me, sir? Do I know you from somewhere?" Tiepolo was callous, arrogant.

"We've never met; but we share acquaintances," Orlando began taking control. "The Gardella family in Florence suggested that I meet with you while I am here on—shall we say?—a trip of pleasures. They were very specific that my pleasures would fit with yours," the two men separated from the others. Orlando reached into his waistcoat pocket to retrieve a letter. "Here is a letter of introduction from Roberto Gardella. He knows you very well, he said.

He said you are particular to a fault in choosing your associates and that I would need his letter."

Tiepolo scrutinized the letter, "Indeed, we know one another well. Extremely well. He has never mentioned your name to me; but I see here that you are fairly recent friends. Tell me more."

"You have just returned from doing Mocenigo's business, have you not? You must be anxious to indulge," Orlando's continued to place his building blocks. "Roberto felt that my offering would be perfect for you." Il Diavolo was hooked.

"And for you, sir—what's in this for you? I've yet to meet anyone who doesn't give without great expectation," Tiepolo laughed darkly. "And, as I'm certain that you've heard from my Florentine friends, I have the greatest of expectations."

Orlando looked cautiously over his shoulder. "We need to go outside to talk further. Put your mask on." Tiepolo pulled his feline mask over his eyes. Orlando maneuvered his way to the door and out to the canal. The moon was full, casting a glow over the waters. Orlando was as cold and as impenetrable as ice.

Tiepolo picked up his step to match Orlando's. "Tell me then exactly what you have to offer me and what it is that you expect from me."

"I have a brother who needs to remove himself from Florence for a considerable piece of time," Orlando moved toward his gondola, "until the authorities find someone more appealing than he to go after. I would expect you to find him anonymity within your Republic's bureaucracy. He is with me back at my lodgings."

"And why, sir, would anything you have to offer make me at all interested in helping your poor brother! I cannot imagine what you could have that would interest me to that degree," the Envoy scoffed.

Orlando moved within inches of Tiepolo's mask and spoke incisively, "Because, sir, I have my connections—connections that take me into the one area that you have not been able to plunder. I have my connections with the Pieta, and, along with my brother, have a young musician at my lodgings who would do anything to get away from the orphanage and Vivaldi's control. She desperately needs help, and she needs it now."

Tiepolo froze. The stench of putrid water drifted around the corner from the Ridotto.

"Who gave you this information?"

"Only those who know. Your Florentine acquaintances are merely that, sir—acquaintances. They are no more your friends than you are friend to them. Now—there is an offer before you. Are you with me or not?"

"Who are you, Lorenzo? Never mind! Yes! I am with you. Shall we go? If what you have pleases me, I'll help your brother." Orlando stepped into the gondola. Tiepolo followed, "The gondola, I should imagine, is from your 'connection'? Your audacity is quite attractive!" He sat in the centre while Orlando took the oar. The moon glinted off the waters and through the palace filigree. The Ponte dei Sospiri would be next.

Orlando Sagredo was the new composer of Venice. This was his opera. And little did the Serene Republic suspect what was about to take place in the next act in its tainted, secretive waters.

LIV

*I pray for Lorenzo's soul every day. I loved him dearly. And he
loved me, I know. He laid down his life for me. The Romans gave
votive offerings to the gods three times for a departed soul. Is
praying for departed souls just as Pagan? I think not... if I remember it is for my need. [Antonia, 1744]*

Antonia awoke to her own cry. Sitting in her bed, she calmed her
breathing and put her hands to her sides to bring the pain under
control. How long would it govern her life?

Reoriented, she realized that the recurring dream had gone further tonight. She swung her legs over the side of the bed and stood
cautiously. The moonlight created a subdued laciness in the room.
The air was thick. She put her shawl over her shoulders and walked
out to the balcony. All was quiet. Why did she feel as though she
had been called? It must have been the dream.

In yet another of its relentless repetitions, the dream had taken
her running from a maniacal crowd into a field of basil. Her senses
came alive again. She smelled the heady aroma. She felt the assault
to her body in her fall and the appalling trip back to Venice, this
city she could no longer call home.

But there had been more to this dream. What was it? The vague
memory coursed through her blood, drawing her, drawing her. To
what? She looked down to the waters. The distorted reflection of
the moon mocked her.

Orlando! She had been with Orlando again! No! No! It could not
be. But yes! It had been so very real. Antonia was back in the dream
again. The horseman followed her into the field where she lay holding the medallion of glass. Looking down at her, Orlando smiled the
smile only she knew. She stood and brought her violin into her embrace from some peripheral world. Drifting away from Orlando, she

began to play and sing, "Tell me, must I live or die?" The country-side transmuted into a palette beyond the spectrum, bleeding and birthing itself over and over again until Antonia began to drift further into colours to become one with them. As she looked down, she saw Orlando reaching for her. She tried to pull him into her embrace; but her arms had become colours and her voice a zephyr. Unable to return, unable to call, she heard instead. He shouted her name, until she thought she would disintegrate into nothingness. "Antonia! Antonia!" Would the vowels never stop?

Antonia clutched herself and fell to her knees.

Out of sight, a solitary gondola slipped into the backwaters.

LV

July tears at my heart. Everything was planned around the July Palio that first summer of my life with Orlando. Would I were in our family, the way it all should have been. Instead, my family is memories of what almost was. I had simply never known a family until I met Lorenzo's family. I had no idea of what it was like to talk in a group, to quarrel, to laugh, to solve problems... and to love and hate. Were the other orphans my sisters? No! Were the Prioress and the Maestro my parents? No! My only family was made up of the Invisibles of my childhood. I had to abandon them, of course. [Antonia, 1739]

Despite his prey's vulnerable position, Orlando knew better than to act impulsively. He moved the vessel along to the della Misericordia. Passing by Palazzo Morosini and heading north by the Ca' d'Oro, Orlando took comfort in knowing that all traces of his having been at the Palazzo were gone. By the time he reached San Michele, all traces of Tiepolo would follow suit. A boat would be waiting for him in San Michele and his horse would be waiting for him on the mainland. When Tiepolo's body would finally wash up—if the lagoon did not send it out to the Adriatic—he would be long gone and never known. Long gone, along the route that Antonia and Lorenzo had taken so carefully, so meticulously, so that she could be free. He had failed her somehow—missed that chink in his mental armour that should have been in place—and Tiepolo would pay for the murders. And the old Orlando Sagredo would be gone, dead, paying too, with his soul imprisoned in the body of Brother Francesco. He savoured the thoughts, the sublime principles of it all—of his enemy's wife always recalling a man by the name of Lorenzo, a man who had agreed to spend a night with her, a man who had manipulated her into his murderous scheme. Divine justice on two counts—for both Antonia and Lorenzo.

"You're a Venetian in handling this vessel. You cannot have learned it and the navigation in one brief visit," the condemned man's last comments intruded into Orlando's thoughts.

"I was here briefly one other time. Purpose gives remarkable clarity and memory, Tiepolo. And I once had a Venetian friend," Orlando's curtness conveyed a message of its own.

"Who was that? I might know him. There are few people in Venice who aren't known to me in one way or another," the conceit of the man infuriated Orlando.

"You wouldn't have known the person; I can guarantee you that," Orlando's steering gained momentum. "We must be very quiet. There may be other boats near us, although I've chosen the right time to head into the lagoon. Once we get to San Michele, you may do all the talking you want. None of the Lagoon dead will hear us there."

As they moved along the della Misericordia, indigo clouds slipped themselves over the moon, diaphanous masking for Carnevale Sagredo. The playwright heard his star performer mutter about the darkness.

"Darkness for a dark man, Tiepolo," Orlando played with the script, knowing the words would whet his star's narcissism, "but I assure you I'm in control." He guided the gondola out of the della Misericordia toward San Michele. He steered silently and powerfully.

All was held together by the slip-drop of Orlando's rhythmic pole. Orlando, new maestro of the Bacino. Slip-drop... never had there been need for music such as this.

"We're almost there now," Orlando steered into the Lagoon. "Tell me, Tiepolo—do you know the famous composer at the Pieta?...

ah, his name escapes me. I mentioned him earlier to you. He travels incessantly. Antonio...?"

"Ah, Vivaldi! Of course! I know him better than he knows himself! Stupid man, really. He can be led to do anything if it relates to his music. Venice has become disenchanted with him. Why would you ask about him? You don't strike me as an artistic man."

Just as the full moon shook off its covering, Orlando dropped his mask in the murky waters. Floating, it looked back blankly at him. "When I was here last year, I wanted to meet the man. But he was at a funeral. There were guards at the door of the Pieta. When I asked them about the great commotion, they told me one of Vivaldi's stars had died. Was that correct?" The gondola struck the wall as Orlando maneuvered the vessel into the shallow waters of Michele Island, "Ah, we are here." Dropping the oar, he reached below his knee and moved deftly in behind Antonia's murderer.

Tiepolo turned round, "What are we doing here? We cannot... My God! Sagredo...!" His words were throttled by his own shock and Orlando's grip around his neck. Battling with his full strength, he could not break Orlando's hold. His arms and legs flailed. His strangled cries were absorbed by the petty breeze. His eyes bulged. Playwright and director, Orlando balanced the props and movements, soulless, responding to a vengeance greater than any force he had ever known.

His voice was cold and forceful as it penetrated the nether regions of Tiepolo's brain, "You killed her, Tiepolo. As surely as you plunged the knife into Lorenzo, you killed Antonia," as the Envoy tried in vain to shake his head, Orlando tightened his grip on his neck. "You killed the most exquisite creature Venice has ever produced," his prey could not budge the lethal arms, "and for that—and for Lorenzo Cristofori—you die now."

Orlando plunged the heavy knife upward into Tiepolo's side. Twisting and withdrawing the weapon, he whispered into dying ears, "May God have mercy on your soul, as Lorenzo's is now freed." He let Tiepolo fall into the boat. His eyes pleading, his voice gurgling, the Envoy looked up at the Palio master. Orlando knelt and put the knife blade at his victim's throat. The Envoy's face was a map of perfect terror. Here at his mouth a little rivulet of bubbling blood. There at the eyes a cemetery. "Dante Tiepolo, I send you to Hell for the death of Antonia of Siena. And for the child whose life you took. Only God could have mercy on your soul." Press... Slide... Like the oar of a gondola. Wretched, pleading eyes gave up the spirit; blood poured around the onyx head.

Orlando stepped out of the boat and into the shallow water. With a massive wrench and thrust, he turned the gondola over on its side. The fetid waters poured in to complete the task. Dante Tiepolo's body slid out into the eternal mouth, and a great sound came forth from the trapped souls of the deeps. Ravenous as always, the Lagoon consumed its newest resident.

Orlando roared, "Let the dead welcome the dead—forever!"

The only audience was an ecstatic host welcoming home one of his own.

Brother Francesco, his hands summarily washed in the waters, made his way onto the island to reach the other boat in hiding for him. Once he reached the mainland, his trusted animal would be waiting to take him back where he belonged for the remainder of his earthly days.

Orlando Sagredo no longer lived on this earth.

LVI

Come with me, my love,
And I shall fly you to the land of basil and glass
That you may walk the old walk with me
Of watery stones and mysterious melodies....
[Antonia, 1750]

Antonia slipped her dress over her head, shaking it into place as it fell about her. A green dress today, rather than the usual black. Today, Ascension Day, was the annual Festa della Sensa. And her mother had loved this day. She had made this dress for Antonia, three years ago in Siena. "I love to see you in green, my sweet; it makes your curls gleam. And the Maestro is quite pleased for you to wear this as his first violinist in tonight's concert. Shall we call it an 'in between' dress? 'In between' an orchestral member and a soprano soloist." And they had both laughed. And Antonia had said, "In between Father Vivaldi and Orlando!" And they had both being lighthearted, conspiratorial, seeing no shadow of evil. How she missed her Prioress, her laughter, her love and her strength.

Antonia flipped her hair out from the neck of the dress and tied the rich green and gold embroidered sash around her waist. Too many memories.... She sat down in front of her mirror, picking up her hairbrush. The rhythm – smooth, brush, smooth... tame the curls – soothed her, taking her deep into her memories. She felt the Prioress near her. How many opportunities had they lost as mother and daughter? Or had they truly been lost? As she thought back, Antonia could see there had been many, many times when they had indeed been mother and daughter. She put the brush down, holding her hair back in her left hand and picking up a ribbon. Still that movement to the back of her neck was so painful and restricted. Never mind—this also reminded her of Paolina.

Life was so lonely now. That was the problem. No matter how much she felt she had let go of her grief over Orlando and the Prioress, she was simply so very lonely. So very lonely. The physical pain did not matter. The loneliness did.

A loud cheer flooded in through the balcony door. She let her hair fall about her shoulders and went quickly out onto the balcony. The hordes of Ascension Day pilgrims on their way to the Holy Land would now have poured out of the Basilica. They would celebrate Ascension Day with the Venetians and tomorrow board Venetian vessels bound for their pilgrimage to the far-off Holy places.

There was the Bucintoro, gently rocking as it rested in the Bacino by the Doge's Palace, tinier vessels fluttering and fussing in its wake. It was such a strange embodiment of Venice herself—eccentric, flamboyant in its red and gold ostentation, batting its eyelids and flashing its dazzling, if affected, smile. There would be ninety guests on board, the oarsmen in the dark, forgotten floor below them. Toiling in the darkness so the wealthy could sit in the light.

Startled by an explosive fanfare coming from the Piazza, Antonia realized the Doge would soon approach the Bucintoro. She strained forward. Yes! The processional was coming. Brilliant—the Maestro had chosen Monteverdi first. And here she was, back on her balcony, joined again to Mantova, Monteverdi's home. Dear God, how had so much happened to her? How had she lost so much? How had she travelled so far away from the innocence of the faith and love of her Mantovan years... and so far from the purity of Orlando's love?

The Doge and his wife were in the Bucintoro now. His personal attendants and the Envoy would follow and then the Doge's vessel would lead the entourage of other highly decorated boats out past the Lido to face the Adriatic. And no one would know or care that their own Envoy had killed a man and a baby. And just as she had done every year for a thousand years, Venice would wed the sea. And this greatest of Venetian Feasts would be marked by the Doge casting a wedding ring into the sea.

Mother! Antonia sensed Paolina's presence and realized Paolina's burial at sea had been her own Ascension Day. After all her stories of Atlantis, she had married the sea.

And if the Doge sealed Venice's wedding with today's toss of a ring, so would she, Antonia, seal and celebrate her mother's wedding. She would mark her mother's union with the sea.

Antonia hurried from the balcony and returned to her bureau. She opened a small carved box and plucked out a ring. After turning it around in her hand a few times, she closed her fingers around it. Orlando had sent it, a simple band with a single sapphire, in one of his letters. She had worn the ring until learning she had lost him to Rome. She had had to put the ring away... away in the box. She hadn't touched it since. She opened her fingers, kissed the ring and placed it on the middle finger of her left hand. Back where it belonged.

"For you, Mother, and for you, Orlando, I do this for you both. And may we all be set free by God."

Antonia walked downstairs and back to the large kitchen. The whole building felt empty. "Domenico! Domenico!" She opened the back door and called again.

Vivaldi's manservant came round the corner. "What is it, Maestra?" He walked toward her.

"Domenico, I wish to go... I must go out to the sea. Would you take me... please?"

"But, Maestra, is that not too dangerous for you?" Despite his early resentment of her, Domenico had come to respect this sister of the Prioress. But this was not like her. It was foolish... rash! Far be it from him to be part of any further damage.

Antonia was even more determined, "I shall be very careful, Domenico. But I must do this for Sister Paolina. And then her soul will rest. Please take me."

Domenico was silent for a few moments. And then he took Antonia's arm. "All right. Come, then. But not too far, Maestra. You aren't as strong as you once were. And there are many vessels churning up the waters today." Domenico stepped down the stairs first and offered Antonia his hand. After assisting her into the gondola, he stepped in and thrust the boat away with his oar. "Shall we follow the route of the Bucintoro, Maestra? They'll stop soon at San Nicola."

"Yes, but I don't want to join them." Antonia stared ahead.

She is like a statue these days, Domenico thought, the Athena of the Orphanage. How sad everything had become since the Prioress's death. Try as he might, he could cajole neither the Maestra nor the Maestro himself now. He steered nimbly through the Canale della Grazie. The Lido lay before them, glittering in the noonday sun.

"Were you there when she was lowered?"

"Maestra?" Her voice had startled him.

"Were you there when the Prioress was lowered into the sea?" Antonia continued to stare ahead. "Do you know where it was?"

"Yes, Maestra, I followed the Bucintoro to be sure the Maestro was all right. I was very worried about him that day. He was so very troubled about you... and so sad...." The gondolier leaned toward her and pointed to the northeast. "They went straight to the east of the Lido, not to San Nicola."

Antonia turned slightly toward Domenico. "Then, that is where we shall go." Antonia turned back to stare ahead again.

"Yes, Maestra," Domenico felt her determination. This was not the time for words. "I'll stop at the place—as close to it as my memory and this vessel will allow." The Maestra's green dress enhanced her rich mahogany hair blowing back from her face. Domenico was captivated—the red and green against the azure blue of the sea. Rarely was the Maestra seen without a covering for her head. She was far lovelier than her severe clothing ever revealed. Against the glassy waters, she was ethereal.

"We're here," Domenico steadied the boat in the placid waters. "The Bucintoro stopped just out there. The Mass was completed and the Maestro played his violin as the body was lowered into the sea." He whispered out of respect, but also because he sensed that he and the Maestra were engaged in the mystical.

Antonia stood and looked at the ring on her left hand. Fascinated, Domenico watched as she eased the ring from her finger and began to recite the words of Ascension Day.

"Desponsamus te mare, in signum veri perpetuique dominii." She closed her eyes as if in prayer.

And then the Maestra repeated the phrase.

But—what was that? In this second recitation, she had used the Prioress's name and changed a word at the end. She had said, "Paolina Giraud marries you, oh sea, as a symbol of perpetual devotion." Why would she have said that? How long would she stand there? She seemed to be in a trance.

And then the Maestra, despite her pain, threw the ring in a large arc into the Adriatic. The ring was quickly consumed. Pain was alleviated. Reconciliation was achieved. And the sea settled, its Atlantians satiated. The Maestra stood still, statuesque.

Domenico was stunned. What had he been privy to? The Maestra had observed her own sacrament. Like some priestess! Yes, that was it! Like a priestess, her rich voice giving more meaning to the phrase that might at this very moment be offered in recitation by the Doge. But, "perpetual dominion" had become "perpetual devotion." Why would she alter the words that had stood for a thousand years? Why would the Prioress marry anyone, let alone the sea itself?

But, oh my… the Maestra was crying. Perhaps he should have remained firm that she not undertake this venture. How could it have been good for her to come out here and feed pain to an unresponsive sea? "Maestra," he put his arm on her back, gently. "Sit down, sit down, and I'll take you back now."

Antonia obeyed.

And they began their way back to the Orphanage.

"I saw a strange ceremony once in Siena, Domenico. The Feast of Saint Catherine. I had no idea why it frightened me so. Until today. We must not cling to the souls of the dead. Did you know that, Domenico? The Sienese keep Saint Catherine's head and finger in their Basilica. And the Romans keep the rest of her body in a church in Rome where she died. We Venetians have her foot. I don't think her soul has left yet because of that. There are three souls I hope I freed today. But I cannot free my own."

Domenico felt tears come to his eyes. What had music done to this woman people gossiped about? "She was pregnant, you know." "The Maestro would not let her stay with the man she loved; he forced her back." "Well, does the Maestro love her?" "It was Tiepolo who killed a man in Siena. He had his eyes on that woman, you know." Ah, yes, yes… an incredible story about that evil man… this morning. Perhaps the Maestra would appreciate the diversion.

They entered the Canale della Grazie again. Shadows encased them. It was cool now.

"There was an interesting happening last night at the Ridotto, Maestra. Everyone was talking about it today." Domenico spoke softly so that the Maestra could decide whether she wanted to hear more.

"Are there not always stories from the Ridotto? There is much corruption that comes out of that place."

"True, Maestra; but this had to do with the Envoy Tiepolo."

Antonia's shoulders stiffened, "Tell me."

They were approaching the Bacino.

"Well, Maestra, he has disappeared. Apparently, he went off with a stranger at the Ridotto very late last night, and he hasn't been seen since. They say his wife is angry. Not sad, not worried... angry. I don't know much more than that; but you can imagine there are many people intrigued with this story. Tiepolo has many enemies." *Domenico cut the oar more quickly through the fetid waters.*

"And I one of his chief enemies," Antonia's shoulders drooped slightly and she took a deep breath as they entered the full sun of the Bacino.

And no one heard the story shared between a servant and a musician on the only gondola in the Bacino at three bells on Ascension Day, 1727. Nor did Antonia tell Domenico about her sighting last night of the single gondolier dressed for the Ridotto. Whoever he was, she would never forget having seen him.

IL EPILOGUE, PARTE TREDICI

VIENNA TO SILENCE

1741 – 1750

LVII

The Viennese, for all their sobriety, have a parallel life to Venetians... music, Pagan Roman roots, Holy Roman roots. They tell the story of Pope Silvester who drove the demons out of Austria in the fourth century. Constantine named Silvester Pope. I dislike history establishing Constantine as the bridge. The bridge between Pagan and Holy Rome was his mother, Saint Helena. Like the Venetians I know, Constantine was driven by power and control. It was Theodosius who truly made The Roman Empire Christian. There are many stories of misplaced credit becoming history. [Antonia, 1740]

IN THE YEAR OF OUR LORD, 1741

Anna Giraud closed the heavy door behind her, shutting out the driving rain. She shook her skirt and ran her fingers through her hair. Except for the small curls framing her face, the dampness had turned her hair to polished mahogany. At the foot of the steep stairway, she mustered her resolve, feeling the need for more endurance than usual today. How much longer could she lay hopeful messages at the feet of her ailing Maestro? How many more potential benefactors could there possibly be in Vienna? She was so very weary from her daily treks around the Ringstrasse to beg entrance to the doors of the influential. No one, from Rome to Germany, was interested in the Maestro and his music now. There was nowhere else to go. And the Pieta now owned most of his works. Venice had purchased and banned his soul. His routing from the Pieta in the autumn of 1739 had effectively terminated Antonio Vivaldi as priest, composer, violinist and conductor. How could the Cardinal possibly have construed that she and the Maestro had an illicit relationship? Why? Why had he set this course of pain in motion? Why had it been only Vienna wanting Vivaldi's music? Why had Vienna lost interest so quickly? Why had God allowed all this torture and stagnation? Why? She was so tired of these questions and God's silence. Grieved, she made immediate petition to the Almighty for forgiveness for her unholy thoughts... weary thoughts... wearing thoughts.

How she loathed this northern, deformed Venice! The meagre Danube and the elongated architecture of intellectualism paled in comparison to the wild opulence of her home. And how could a July day turn so cold? No wonder the Roman Empire had abandoned Vienna as its capital. There was no heart, no passion here. Her thoughts moved southward. The rolling gentleness of Siena, the enfolding gentleness of Sienese hills, the fragrant gentleness of basil and wine, the greenness of grapevines, the greening place of Orlando, the tenderness of him, the abandon with him, the anguish of what should have been, the loss, the loss. Antonia breathed deeply and squared her shoulders. "You are Anna Giraud," she spoke her tattered litany aloud, "now and for the remainder. Anna Giraud. The Maestro needs you."

Ah! The stairs! Yet again the stairway of false tidings. Yet again the need to climb to contrived optimism in the face of poverty and illness. Antonia gave her hair one last shake, pinched her cheeks, assumed a smile and climbed the stairs. Her back ached from the coldness of Vienna and the winter in her heart. Cold upon cold; ice begetting ice.

As she entered the apartment, Antonia sensed the familiarity of death, quiet, musty, pervasive. This, always now, in spite of the cleanliness of the tiny, Spartan living quarters. Only one crumpled manuscript lay on the desk today. As always, Father Antonio was seated at the window, looking out over the grounds of the Orphan Asylum and toward the forbidding Danube, willing this Godforsaken location into being his Pieta. As always, she wanted to lay her head in his lap and be young and start all over again.

Could we begin again in truth, please? Would you weave an aqua tapestry of music and truth and bundle me in it, and let it be my safety in the face of chimera after chimera? Would you be my Truth and feed me the truth? And when I find my soul-mate again, would you celebrate and bless me? Would you release me, Father, release me, for I have died and loved you all these many years? Would you? Father?

"Father," she spoke firmly as she closed the door and placed her cape on the hook. "Father Antonio, I'm back. I left your letter and manuscript with Lotharingen's manservant. I've finally come so close to the Archduchess, Father! Isn't that wonderful? A clever young violinist from Salzburg introduced me personally. He was most impressed with your work." Antonia was so tired, so very tired.

Vivaldi turned slowly toward her, smiling the same brave smile she sent to him. The man who had composed Venice for so many years was now a prisoner of the illness that held his breath and heartbeat as ransom. "My dear," he tried to stand and fell back in the chair coughing. Coughing, retching, gasping, his gaunt face pleading for breath or release, until Antonia felt more desperate than she had with the previous episode during the night. Oh dear God—the blood! She moved quickly to him.

"Breathe with me, Father. Steadily," Antonia spoke with soft reassurance. When would this end? Her thoughts returned to her long lost mother. These parents of her sojourn here would be together soon. And she would be alone. "Breathe, Father. Slowly. Deeply. Match my breathing. Good." She could breathe again as well. As the spasms yielded to her control, an ethereal composition took shape. The twinned instruments tuned to each other. Anna the concert mistress. Anna with her bowing hand on the composer's chest. She began humming and letting the words form themselves, "Resplende, bella, divina stella." "Dear God, we are driven into a thousand agonies; my soul is fainting." How could he have written this music so that it now haunts and torments us both?

Antonia put her hand on the Maestro's forehead. So hot. I bless you in the name of the Father and the Son and the Holy… oh, my sweet father. What will I do without you after all these years? But I know. We must talk. We must speak to each other before it is too late. "You're so hot, dear Father. A cold cloth. Yes, let me get you a cold cloth. I put a wet cloth by the window this morning. I will…"

"Anna, Anna, no. No, we cannot do anything now," Vivaldi's voice, though frail, commanded, slipping onto a well-worn pathway. His eyes, ever perceptive, joined with hers. "Please, my dear, help me to my bed. Let me lie down and listen to you talk. And sing to me, Anna. It will not be long now. I know that. You know that. Let my music go, Anna. Let your music go for now, Anna," he reached for her as she slipped under his arm and lifted him to his feet.

There was not much left of him, truly; he had been evaporating so gradually. Antonia supported him the short distance to his bed. The coughing started again. Dear God, his chest will burst. Is there no one who can be with me? "Let me sit you here first, and then I'll lay you back in the pillows," she pulled his legs up. "There, dear Father, I'm so sorry if it hurts." The dying Maestro smiled sweetly at her. She drew the blanket up and gently pulled his arms—those arms which had embraced and excluded her, composed and destroyed, conducted and severed—over the blanket and into a resting position within her hands. His hands, his sweet and frightening hands, clasped hers firmly. She looked at him, this man she loved and feared, this man she wanted never to die.

"You have been a good daughter, Anna," the words were barely audible. "You know that, do you not? Why can we never speak of things until it is too late, Anna? Why, my dear?" Tears found their way down from the corners of his eyes into rivulets worn from a lifetime of control, love and laughter. His chest rattled.

"It is never too late, unless the words are never uttered, Father. I understand. I have always understood." Antonia moved his wasted hand gently to her lips. "Now, be my father until you die. Oh, please don't die, please! I cannot live if you, too, die!" Her tears spilled onto the hands that had brought the music and the pain out from her soul. She kissed each thin finger, composing a living, dying rosary. The waters of the Bacino lapped in her head, the continuo of a labouring requiem. And the violins began—she and the Maestro playing in foil to each other, propelling, spinning until the music soared out of the leaking Viennese roof and into the vaulted heavens. Angels sang. Notes and colours blended in the patterns of a composition.

Antonia let her head droop onto the bed beside her father's hand, his perishing breath her only consolation. The breath of her father... her breath... her father.

* * *

Antonia awoke to the cold night. The Maestro... her father... was he still breathing? Yes... his breath rattled continuously now. Throwing her shawl over her shoulders, she moved stiffly to fuel the dying fire. The night was so damp and chilly. She knelt to blow the embers into life.

He had been breathing, had he not? Antonia looked over toward the bed. The wood flared and crackled. He was too quiet. Too still! She stood quickly, starting to return to his bed.

"Anna—Antonia."

Where?

"Antonia," the resonant contralto voice sang inside her head. Where was she?

"Yes, Mother," Antonia pulled the shawl tightly across her cold breasts. She moved closer to the fire and closed her eyes.

"My little one, it is over. Rest now, my child. Your father is in the first portal and will soon be here. Rest in love now, my child. And then do what you know you must do."

Antonia opened her eyes. Nothing and everything had changed. She was warmer... less lost. Her father had joined her mother. They were reunited now, and she would see them again, when it was her turn.

It was now her time to carry out her plans. When she had realized that her Maestro would die soon, she had begun to plan what she would do with the rest of her life. She must look after the body, set the spirit free, and she must look after herself. She must return home.

As she came to the bed, she smiled at her father's remarkable face. There was his legacy—the face that gave evidence of a life lived daringly. She understood it all now... the possessiveness, the prodigy, the love, the control. If only....

"Father?" She put her ear to Vivaldi's chest. "Oh, my father, you have gone so easily." Antonia spoke with the sweetness and trust of her childhood. She walked to the pitcher of water on the nightstand.

She poured some water into a small bowl and returned to her father's bedside. Dipping a cloth in the water, Anna Giraud of Venice, the tender secret of the Red Priest, washed the blood from the sides of her Maestro's mouth. She anointed his forehead with a few drops of water, making the sign of the cross with her middle finger. "Through this holy unction and with His own most tender mercy, may the Lord pardon thee whatever sins or faults thou hast committed by sight, hearing, smell, taste, touch, walking and carnal delectation. As witness to your confession of who I am, your daughter, I send your soul on your journey home, blessed and forgiven. Farewell, Christian soul, go on your journey." As his soul departed, music inhabited the spaces left in its wake. Antonia blessed the body with a kiss. Thrice orphaned, she moved to the other side of the bed, slipped off her shoes and climbed in beside her father's body, sharing his blanket. She had come home.

Like tiny birds fluttering in her head and chest, chords and whispers ushered Antonia into sleep. She wanted to hear more. Why couldn't she see? Wings of lost songs—that was the fluttering... lost songs fluttering and then flapping... hammering... too much... too hard to hear anything but noise.... And then a song sang itself to her, quietly, almost silently. "Non timebo mortis horrores, tam cara face gaudendo in pace si contemplabor vos." I shall not fear death's horrors; I shall rejoice in peace when I look at the light that is sent out from you.

It was over. He was gone. For the first time in her life, Antonia would not have the Maestro in her life. He would not come home, as from a trip to Rome. Nor would he send someone for her. There would be no more danger. There would be no more music.

* * *

Antonia awoke. The sun's rays beamed through the bedroom window. The room was warm. And she remembered. Yes, her Maestro was there. And gone. She held his cold hand for a moment. Rising like a surging wave in her belly, her desolation dared her to give in to panic. No! She got up slowly. There was business to be tended to. Bathing and eating could come later. She pulled the threadbare sheet up tidily over her father's shoulders and folded it over the old heavy blanket they had just shared. His hands must stay covered. They were so cold. Combing her father's hair with her fingers, she kissed his forehead.

How could she leave him for even a moment? Yes, yes—he was gone! But how could he be, this man who had never been gone from her life? She touched his hand and left the bedroom.

Pulling her cape from the door, she flung it on as she hurried down the stairs and outside. She would simply retrace her steps from yesterday. The world had changed. Did anyone know? She must set her plan in motion. Turning the corner by the Palace onto Wahringer Gasse, Antonia felt a tremendous release. Her steps were light and young again. Father Matthaus would now be able to help her with what needed to be done. They had planned together. The funeral would be tonight. If only the Archduchess would decide about the manuscripts. Father Matthaus had told her yesterday that Maria Theresia would discuss the music again with the violinist from Salzburg. And he had seemed interested...

Antonia crossed the Drilling Grounds into the Inner City. This city had not been unkind to her. No indeed, Venice had been unkind to her. But she could not feel at home here in Vienna, living in poverty and the sharp edges of opinions on music and art. As she passed by the Arsenal, she thought of Venice's Arsenal and the shared history of these two cities. Try as she had to make this place a home, she felt no affinity with the people, the climate, the outward expressions of life and faith. They were from two different worlds. And she needed to—she must!—return to hers.

As she turned toward St. Stephen's, she hungered for her Basilica's roundness and Byzantine embellishments. Her longing for Sienese art and architecture flooded over her. She tuned herself to her task again. There was no time for longing, no time for the bitter sweetness of re-living lost love. But urges and desires sink below the surface when death is a long, long process. And when it's over...

when it is over.... She felt all those urges and desires rush back in, with the force of water through a ruptured wall. She entered the cathedral. Moving toward the altar, her footsteps resounded in the thick acoustic. She lit a candle and sat near the altar. Waiting for Father Matthaus, Antonia prayed.

She startled to a hand on her shoulder. "Anna, you're back so soon?" The priest's blue eyes reached in and probed. "Your Maestro?"

"Yes...yes... early this morning." And the weight of Antonia's long held grief took over, tearing through her breast. How could his powerful presence be gone? Gone! A thousand furores screamed inside her head. Dear God, where are you! Where is music now? Antonia did not know any longer what was inside and what was audible. Was that her voice? Her sobbing?

"Anna," the hand once again brought her back. "Anna, it has been a long journey. His journey is over now. What do you need?"

The hand... the voice... the witness... these were all she needed. The storm subsided. She put her hand over his hand on her shoulder, "I need to move ahead."

"The Archduchess will leave for Rome on Sunday, Anna, and you'll be with her," he felt her shoulder relax. "She said last night that, in exchange for the manuscripts, you may travel with them to Siena. She'll take care of all of your needs on the journey. Shall we get your preparations underway? I'll send Jerome with you to help. I think it would be best for Jerome to let your friends know of Father Antonio's death and ask them to come to Cathedral tonight. Do you agree?"

"Yes, Father. It's all right. We did talk about the paupers' yard. We agreed that nothing—except music—is of any consequence. When only music remains, God is satisfied."

"Come, then, Anna. It is over," the priest ushered her away from the dark altar. "I've already spoken to the priest at St. Charles' Cathedral; they will bury Father Antonio there. The funeral service will be there, as well. Shall Jerome tell your friends to attend the service at evensong?"

"Yes... I've made all the preparations. I don't need much. Once I get to Tuscany, my needs will be taken care of." Home... where her heart belonged.... "I truly don't need much, Father." It had been a very long time since she had been where she belonged.

"Come, then. We'll find Jerome," Father Matthaus guided her through the sanctuary. "His first task will be to take you to the Archduchess."

He closed the heavy, ancient door. It was time for another home-coming.

Ellyn Peirson

LVIII

Suppose I were to return to Venice to find Saint Catherine's foot. Suppose I were to wander into the city—leave the turquoise Bacino, cross canals, fly over domes, swim under bridges, gasp in the putrefaction where sea water is trapped and sinks into torpidity, where no fish can live, where the Goliath is fed human creatures— would I find that foot? If I found it floating in the Lagoon, would it take me south by water? If I found it in a maze of bridges, would it take me to its body in Rome? If I found it in the Basilica, would it take me out of this world? Or would it have washed out to sea—finding its own salvation and uncaring for mine? Ah, but if I found it in the herb garden, would it take me to its head in Siena? Her feet took her to and from Siena and Rome and Venice. And mine cannot take me south—to her home... and mine. Only will they do it, if he is not there but gone. [Antonia, 1742]

In the warmth of the green Sienese countryside—within the gaze of the towers of San Gimignano—Brother Francesco had finished his morning tasks. His early morning prayers had been followed by reading, cleaning, breaking his fast, making soup and setting bread to rise in the warmth of the sun by a small window in the tower. He had then walked through his garden to pick a few tomatoes, harvest more basil and simply get down on his knees to sift and loosen up the earth where it was needed. In his fourth decade, Brother Francesco was physically vigorous and intensely intellectual. Certainly, he was still the most ardent of loners. He needed no one. He craved instead the feel of the soil and its evocative, musky odour, replete with beginnings and endings, solitude and the numinous music that often wafted his way from the violin in his tower.

He moved to the old oak bench, took a deep breath of the sultry Julian air and sat down for his morning meditation. Ritualistically, he looked up at the purple wisteria that had wound its beautifully persistent way through the arbour over and over again over mul-titudinous years. The abundant flowers hung heavily, like clusters of grapes ripe for transformation. As always at this time of year, he was acutely attuned to the aromas he had just aroused in his morning gardening. It would be good to have a rain soon. July—the Palio over, his family busy and thriving in their summer life without him, the estate, the Duomo, separated from Siena, Antonia gone, her Maestro alive and no longer able to control her. An unforgivable sin avenged. A life of mastering atonement. Such were the great costs of transgression.

The basil and wisteria made this time of year acutely alive. Brother Francesco had learned to let the memories happen. The manifold methods of resisting them—cursing, denying, writing—had only heightened the pain in the first few years here in his un-earthly home on earth. And so, he had found intentionally letting the memories have their way brought more relief than the attempts at suppression did. The best time to do this was immediately be-fore his morning meditation. This way, he could purge his soul and empty his mind and then move into his daily writing. His latest as-signment from Father Roberto was far more personally engrossing than the prior one had been, and for this, Brother Francesco was grateful.

There were still times when she seemed to be near, when, if he only knew how to do it, he could reach out and join her. This morn-ing, her presence was particularly painful. How strange that one could hate the pain and love it at the same time. She was not dead to him. No, she laughed and sang in his head every day. And every day, as he moved to the old bench, she was over there on the hillside playing "Dite, Oime." And the tall, severe priest would tell her, the elegant musician from the other world, that she must live. And he could touch her and taste her beauty. Ah, if only he could love this meagre garden into the lavish gardens that she loved. Green, lush, lovely—like Antonia herself.

And then the dying face of Tiepolo flashed into the vision, stealing the beauty. And the old, deep, powerful anger arose within Brother Francesco, until he wanted to kill the man again. And the archaic tension between love and hate flapped like a caged raven in his head. The music of Antonia herself was again contaminated, eradicated in this unending repetition that was his life. That, he supposed, was his penance.

Brother Francesco shut down his emotions, as he did daily. And, priest that he was, he moved into prayer for things that were not, and never would be, his.

Once again, the wisteria, priest-like itself, absorbed his confession.

LIX

*San Paolo said we see through "a glass darkly." He was talking
about spiritual things. In that, I agree with him. In the matter of
my love, though, I see all too clearly... through an open window
on a sunny day. And I am a prisoner—behind glass. [Antonia,
1740]*

The gondola swayed gently against the Piazza landing. In the vessel, the two women sat in silence. Antonia seemed to be listening
intently to an invisible world, beyond the life that pulsated around
them. Maria Theresia, elegant in rather ordinary Viennese clothing,
sensed that there was a great turbulence going on within her friend.
She would wait until Anna spoke.

Severe and beautiful in black, Antonia looked across the Bacino.
"I no longer belong here. What was mine is gone. Or perhaps it
never was mine. It is all the same and all different. No one now
would have any idea who I am. Nor would they care—not even
enough to force me to leave again. Life is a fickle illusion, Maria."

"Is this too painful for you, Anna? We don't have to stay."

"No, I love it here. And this is good for me. I needed to do this,
and I sensed it would be safe. It is. So many things in my life have
been incomplete. This visit—and I know it is a visit—is a completion.
Venice is over for me; it has been for many, many years now. But
this ride allows me to say good-bye. Being able to make the choice
to say farewell is so important, is it not? I wasn't allowed to come
here, to the Piazza, except for musical performances. I truly spent
most of my time in Venice in the Pieta, dreaming up what Venice
must have been like. Although I did see Canaletto's paintings of
the light and dark of Venice," Antonia looked at the teeming life
of San Marco. "I left the painting he gave me behind. I think of it
often. I wonder if it's still in my room in the Pieta. What are all these

souls searching for on the Piazza, I wonder?" Antonia's bowing arm swept the noises and smells of the Piazza into the gondola.

"What are souls anywhere searching for, Anna?" The Archduchess found the Byzantine sight fascinating, like a dream gone wild. Onion domes, countless gondolas, winged lions, gold leaf and mosaics, sumptuous patterning, people everywhere, some in fine linen, others in what looked like sackcloth. "Venice or Vienna—it matters not, I think, where we are. The questions are the same, and the answers are as difficult to find. Although I doubt that most souls are listened to by the personalities they inhabit. And that may be a strange blessing!"

The gentle laughter of the two friends broke the sombre train of thought. "Ah! Look at the little group of musicians over there, Maria! Just past the market stalls." Antonia came to life, almost standing in the gondola. The gondolier balanced the craft. "They are like a modern group of troubadours. Now that warms my heart! Venice is still in God's hands if music occurs spontaneously."

The Archduchess was delighted to see Anna vivacious. She reached over to hold her hand.

Antonia looked up at the gondolier, "Take us past the Pieta, please... and go slowly past the Doge's Palace."

As they glided past the magnificent Palace, Maria Theresia was spellbound by the pastel colours it threw into the Canal. The filigree cast its patterns onto the women's faces. "Look Maria—we're wearing masks for the Ridotto!" In that moment, Antonia remembered her last connection to the Ridotto and the perplexing image of the solitary gondolier, dressed for a night there. How desperate she had felt at that moment... news of Orlando having gone... to Rome, to another life... she, a prisoner to her broken body and the evil of Rome's politics.

"Anna?" Maria Theresia, noticing Antonia's meditation, squeezed her hand, "Are you all right?"

"I am," Antonia smiled. "Look, there is the Pieta!"

"Stop here, Jerome." Jerome spoke to the gondolier, who pulled the gondola to rest across from the Pieta. The Archduchess became as fascinated with Anna's face now as she was with their surroundings. Anna had become young—beautifully and radiantly young—her face glowing with anticipation. Maria Theresia was amazed that so severe a building could generate such life in Anna. The Pieta, grey and cold, stared down at them with contempt. Somehow she had expected beauty and warmth of the building that had housed so much music and imagination.

And then Antonia gasped.

"What is it, Anna? Is something wrong?"

"My balcony! My balcony is gone, Maria! It is as though it never existed! Why? I've been erased from Venice," her shock was palpable. "And my mother and father with me. And it all seems so small and forbidding now."

"Which was your room, Anna?" Maria Theresia wanted fervently to understand this strange story.

"Antonia pointed to the window on the second floor, "The furthest window on our left—the one with the little railing around it now. Do you see which one I mean?"

"I do." It all looked so innocuous to the Archduchess. "Do you suppose that this was changed as a reminder to the orphans—to keep them in their place... because of you? Tell me what it was like for you," Maria Theresia found the building itself hostile. And yet it had housed a great love and an unparalleled stage for women. "How odd this city is, Anna. It's as though it is no steadier than its waters, as though great moments come and go at the whim of some Water

God. And yet this city gave birth to great music that will last. And it has given birth to great loves."

Antonia became the storyteller, weaving her mythology of the Pieta in green and lavender and silver for her friend—the tales of her life with the Maestro and the Prioress; the music room; the balcony where she communed with the moon and where her little garden wafted its fragrances into her soul; the doorway that she entered, broken, before her final rest with Paolina and from which she left finally and forever. The Archduchess looked at this complex, serene creature, already a nun, perhaps always a nun, and wished for her the birth of all her dreams. And she knew this was not to be. "Tell me more about your balcony and the moon, Anna. Do you still commune, as you call it, with the moon?"

Antonia looked directly into Maria Theresia's eyes, "I receive great consolation from the moon. I'm still drawn to find her at night. I used to lie on my balcony and talk to her... or think to her... or pray in her presence. I have always loved the way the moon beams upon us. She does not get much in return from us. I can feel her. And I sometimes sense that she sings... in a rich contralto voice. My connection with the moon has been one of the greatest blessings of my life. My perspective changes when we have been together."

"Jerome, we need to go now," Maria Theresia lay back in her seat and smiled. "You have given me Venice, Anna. Thank you. It doesn't feel like such an odd place to me now. Perhaps here in this watery habitation, you have been closer to the origin of life. Perhaps. Have you thought about your Orlando while we've been here?" The Archduchess, choosing the time carefully, believed the question needed to be presented to complete the moment.

The shadow of old pain passed across Antonia's face. And then she smiled, "Oh yes, Maria. Orlando is always alive to me."

"Do you think you will ever see him again, Anna?" Maria Theresia's face held the expectation of a 'yes'. She herself needed a 'yes'.

"Not in this lifetime," Antonia looked at the plea in her friend's eyes, "but, don't feel sad for me, Maria. I cannot explain this well; but I believe I shall see Orlando again after this lifetime. I've come to believe we come from somewhere and we leave this world to return. The sense of homesickness that plagues us at times in this life is our dim memory of our real home. I am married to Orlando's soul."

The gondola had arrived again at the Piazza. It was time for a return to the orange and sepia town and the velvet hills that had been calling Antonia for so long now. She was going to the land of Orlando. And from there, eventually, she would leave this dimness for her ancient home of light.

Such was Antonia's consolation.

LX

I have sudden bursts of understanding my life. They disappear just as suddenly, but leave remnants of meaning. I gather the remnants. I spin them into yarn. I use that yarn as ink for my writing. [Antonia, 1746]

The entourage drew to a halt outside the Duomo. "Are you certain you are all right to remain here alone, Anna, absolutely certain?"

"Yes, I know Siena well; it's very safe... now. The Duomo is like a home to me. And the family I shall stay with will have been watching for me at the Duomo daily for three or four evenings now. I'll go in and wait. I love the sanctuary. I performed here long ago," Antonia took Jerome's hand and stepped lightly out of the carriage. He returned to his seat. And she thought of Lorenzo.

The Archduchess reached out to embrace her. "Thank you, Anna, for the interesting stories and our discussions. I wish you God's blessing in all you do." She released her friend. "Go back to composing, Anna. Send me your manuscripts," Maria Theresia's eyes glistened.

"We shall see if my music comes back in a new way," Antonia smiled and picked up her bag, all that was left of her physical life. "God speed, meine liebe Freundin. And thank you. I won't forget your kindnesses," Antonia closed the carriage door, knocked on it to signal Jerome, and watched as the Archduchess left her life.

Looking up at the vast facade and blue sky that had inhabited her dreams, Antonia breathed deeply and walked into the Duomo. There they were! Everyone! Her Maestro. The members of the ensemble. Orlando. Orlando—ready to come into her life, ready to be her life. "Bar one! Alma Oppressa!" Antonia's voice involuntarily intoned the perfect A of her violin—the A of her soul, as though God Himself were drawing the bow. The note drew her toward the altar;

she genuflected before it. Slipping into the front pew, Antonia put her bag down on the seat and knelt to pray. "I thank you, Almighty Father, that I am home." She moved into the sheer silence of prayer. Transported, Antonia remained in prayer for the remainder of the afternoon.

The bell tower called out six bells. Antonia moved from the pain of kneeling prayer and sat in the pew, allowing her memories to take over. The night of the reckless abandon of fleeing to the Sagredo Estate... the performance here with Orlando looking into her soul... the Palio... the preparations for their wedding... the power of her father's conducting... the power of Orlando's planning... the power of Tiepolo, evil Tiepolo... the retrieval and death of her mother... and then her knowledge of her father... the pain... the loss... the love... the love... the constant reminder of it all in her back. Juditha bowing her plaintive Largo back and forth over and under the echoes in the recesses of her mind... back and forth, back and forth... like gondola resting in the Bacino... resting... swaying... gently....

"Sister Catherine?" A voice intruded. "Sister Catherine?"

Antonia turned to see an old nun, her strong face etched by multitudinous prayers, her eyes commanding discipline, her voice rich and low.

"Madre Superiora?" Antonia smiled.

"Yes. Come along; the carriage is waiting."

Antonia picked up her bag, and left the Duomo for the last time.

The two women stepped up into the carriage. The old nun sat across from Antonia and reached over to close the door. "There is room for your bag on the seat beside you. I shall have to examine it while we're on our way to the convent, and we'll talk to be sure you are prepared. After that, as you have covenanted, your days will be spent principally in silence and in writing."

"I understand, Mother, and I am ready. My bag contains only my cape, a change of wardrobe and the one possession I have chosen to keep, a small glass globe from Murano. I received it a very long time ago to remind me to celebrate," Antonia rested against the seat. "Ah," she took a deep breath, "the Italian weather is much more beautiful than what I was used to in Austria. It is good to be home."

"Good. I am glad you feel you've come home, my dear. The trip to San Gimignano is not long. You must be tired. Now tell me what your intent is as you begin convent life. I've been looking forward to this conversation. Your letters have been most interesting."

With the sound of the horses' hooves, Antonia Giraud of Venice and Siena took her leave of this earth.

LXI

I had a dream last night... a different kind of dream, far more symbolic than detailed... moody... ethereal, if one word must be chosen. I stood on a tiny Venetian bridge. An indigo fog drifted around me and the small group of people talking at the end of the bridge. It was dark, and a gondola, with an eerie light in its prow, passed under the bridge. He was the gondolier. He looked at me, so I ran to the other side of the bridge to see him again. It seemed to take so long for him to come out from under the bridge. When he did, he would not look at me. I was bereft. And then I noticed I had on a creamy, elaborate ball gown. And on my eyes was a mask with cat's eyes. Is life my Carnevale? [Antonia, 1739]

The young man awoke within the dream.

The floral burgundy of her hair covered his face. Confused, he brushed it aside and struggled against sleep's seductive clutches. He wanted to go back into the recklessness of deep dreaming. He felt drugged and wanted deeper intoxication.

Why was it so hard to surface?

She murmured and wrapped herself around him. The scent of lilies made him heady.

A violin played somewhere—in a minor key that insinuated its way around the silver moon and into the room. The notes fell and clung to him. The fragrance... where was he?

The room was small and simply furnished. The white bedclothes smelled of fresh air and herbs.

He kissed her breast and moved upward to whisper in her ear. "Wake up! We've fallen asleep. You must awake!" He wanted to lose himself in her. "The Palio waits. We cannot risk discovery! I must go! You must!"

In a moment of utter connection, her eyes opened and looked into his soul. Teardrops pooled as she took his face in her hands and kissed him. Letting go, she left her longing in his upturned hands.

"No!" he cried, as she drifted upward and out of the window. Her forlornness mutated into the rare beauty of devotion as she smiled his way and dropped something into his hands.

"Antonia! Come back! Antonia!"

The young man ran down the narrow stairway and into an alleyway. The silver moon had given way to an orange sunrise over a marketplace buzzing with activity and multitudinous, jarring noises. The dread of the dream consumed him. Where was she?

He saw her running into the orange crowd. He wanted to run to her. He felt a need to save her from darkness.

Someone called him from behind. "Orlando! Hurry! Where were you? Get up!" And in the dream's energy, he was swept up onto a magnificent horse.

Frenzied contests and riotous colours clawed at him as he tried to break loose to find her. Finally in control of his horse, he saw a wild band of townspeople, like some organism gone berserk, screaming its way down the alleyway toward the cathedral. He sensed they were after her.

Shouting for her, he urged his horse around and past the clamouring insanity until he flew out into a glorious green clearing where complete tranquillity abounded. Where was he?

Even in his dream, the man knew this place as sacred. Where was she?

"Antonia! Antonia!"

He could not bear the emptiness inside him, the separation from the only being he had ever truly loved. Like a father seeking the vanished child, he knew he now also was abandoned.

He dismounted his horse and began to wander, his vision blurred and burning.

Calling, calling, beseeching, commanding, he wandered until he stumbled into the whiteness of pomegranate blossoms and lilies. She lay in her delicate brokenness, the purity of white disrupted only by her black habit and the burgundy of her hair and blood.

The dreaming man's cry of profound lament joined the awakening priest's cry of fear and grief.

"No!" he shouted back at the universe, "I have disciplined myself against this! Leave me alone; I have no memory."

As if needing the reinforcement of reality, the priest turned to the mirror. Instead, ageing, mournful eyes looked back into his soul.

He fell on his bed, lost and overcome, while the gentle breeze drifted in through the open window.

And he remembered.

LXII

After I returned to these hills, I began to dream the same dream frequently. In the dream, I jump from my balcony at the Orphanage and run to the water. Lorenzo is there waiting for me in a gondola. He assists me into the vessel, and we leave for the mainland by the light of the full moon. As we come near the shore, I step out of the gondola and scoop seaweed into my arms. Lorenzo shouts, "No, Antonia. Leave it alone. Put it back where it belongs." I look down at myself and see that my dress has turned into murky turquoise seaweed with flashes of silver in it. I drop the seaweed from my arms… and wake up, wondering, confused. Until last night. In last night's dream, I disregard Lorenzo's fear. I sit down in the water in my dress of seaweed and gently open the seaweed in my arms. A beautiful infant looks up at me and smiles. And I understand the dream. And Orlando is with me. [Antonia, 1750]

IN THE YEAR OF OUR LORD, 1750

I knocked on the door and slipped quietly into Sister Catherine's room.

She was not improving. Mother Superior told me she had gone further down the path of separation and illness that had gradually become hers over the years. She said, "This time she will not find her way back, Sister Osanna. She has never been well since she arrived here nine years ago. She had always suffered from severe back pain, and, in the past year, her breathing has often become laboured." With this new siege of fevers and poor appetite, Sister Catherine could not seem to regain her strength and banish her cough.

As a senior Novice, I had become inexplicably drawn to the Silent Sister and to her singing, an apparent contradiction to her vow of silence. Mother Superior had chuckled over my questions regarding

Holy Silence, explaining that Sister Catherine had worked out a brilliant defense of her music. According to Sister Catherine, music was a form of Silence. Wonderful! I loved the merriness of this interpretation and sensed the inordinate understanding of the heavens that seemed to be forever calling to the Silent One. So often through the past few years since my coming here, I've watched Sister Catherine write notes and words, notes and words, until she herself could hear their breath whisper through the sanctuary and into the air that gives life to this Convent. And, true to our persuasion as the Sisters of San Francesco, the Silent Nun gardened. In the early evening, she could be found moving through the vegetables and flowers that give sustenance, flavour and fragrance to our modest Convent.

And each time in the garden, she would pluck a leaf of basil, crush it into her palms and inhale its pungent aroma. "A strange stigmata," I found myself saying one sultry evening when the basil seemed to have induced a holy trance in the serene nun. I was somehow drawn to look southward with Sister Catherine toward my own family home on the outskirts of Siena.

Sister Catherine that night noticed me watching her. I felt ashamed, but she had smiled at me and beckoned me over to sit with her on the old wooden bench under the wisteria. Long, soft Sienese shadows rested on our shoulders that evening, that evening when I felt closer to God than I had ever thought possible and in a more gentle way than I could ever have imagined. "What is it that you wish to ask me?" the Silent Nun had asked—spoken!—as though she could see into me. "Don't be afraid," she put her hand on my hand. "I am taking the liberty of breaking my silence—not my vow—for a time of words with you, Sister Osanna. I believe it to be of significance."

"It... I find... words are difficult, Sister Catherine," I was enchanted with the musical, rich quality of the Silent One's voice, "but could you tell me how you have achieved such communion with the spiritual? I have seen you write as though you hear things others do not. And I have seen you smile as though you were in private communion with God. And I want to know about that and find it myself! Please tell me how I can have the beautiful life you have! There are rumours here that you will disappear if you become any more spiritual!" I stopped in embarrassment, "Oh, please pardon me, Sister Catherine; I have overstepped my bounds. I am impertinent. I am sorry!"

But Sister Catherine took my hand and smiled in a way that made me feel wonderfully known. And we talked of God and music, as though God and Music were One, until the shadows blended with the dusky sky and until the hills of Siena disappeared, allowing the full silver moon to reign over the night. Never had I felt my own soul more active, more attuned to another's. Never had I felt less attached to the world.

All I ever received from the Silent Sister from that time forward over the next few years was the occasional brief and knowing smile. And the acknowledgment sufficed, beyond words. The Holy Inexplicable could be known!

And so it was that I at last dared to ask Mother Superior if I could be Sister Catherine's caregiver in this wracking illness, this illness that had not fully silenced the elder sister's voice, the clear voice with the purity of a violin. Quite simply, I felt compelled by—almost obsessed with—a need to assuage my own grief, a grief I had not discovered until then. It had lain dormant in me from early childhood, calling me to spiritual life. Sister Catherine had somehow re-created or re-awakened the grief. Oh, if only Sister Catherine would speak to me again before she died. How I longed to know her earthly story. I knew we were kindred souls. The connection was that powerful and that wordless.

On my second evening of tending to her, I began to prepare Sister Catherine's ablutions.

"Sister Osanna." Had it been a cough? "Sister Osanna?" I moved over to her bedside.

Sister Catherine smiled at me. I marvelled at the beauty of this dying woman with the short burgundy and silver hair and the alabaster skin. Even in her gauntness, there was a powerful beauty. Did I dare speak to the Silent One again?

"Sister Osanna, sit with me. I wish to talk with you before I go." I sent a silent prayer of thanks, drew a chair to the bedside and sat down in my disbelief. "Thank you, my dear. You need to know that Mother Superior knows about my intent to speak with you. All of what I am about to tell you I have told Mother. Would you prop me up a little, please?" I rearranged the pillows, lifted the dying nun and opened the curtains. Sister Catherine looked out over the grounds of the Convent and into the hills, "How I would love to run through the hillside one last time, Osanna! Do you miss the hillsides of your home, my dear? These are your hillsides, are they not?"

I was so taken aback, I gasped. Sister Catherine reached for my hand. "My dear, from the time you arrived here, I've had a sense of who you are and where you are from. I've watched you grow here. You are a beautiful, devoted young woman. Why did you enter the convent?" Her smile and the warmth of her gaze somehow steadied me. Once again, I felt known.

"My earliest memories are of a sense of being drawn to God—or by God," I began to settle. The warm comfort of our time together a few years earlier returned. "For as long as I can remember, I have desired the spiritual life."

"And your spiritual name, my dear? Why did you choose Osanna?" A prescience emanated from her eyes. I could see it. I could feel it.

"Well," I faltered, "because of Saint Osanna of Mantova, of course! I've been drawn to her for as long as I can remember... and to her story."

Sister Catherine managed to squeeze my hand, "Ah, how well I remember Mantova from my youth. It was so long ago... such a long, old story ago. I'm not being critical, my dear. It's just that I know you must have been called Anna when you were young. You were Antonia before you came here. Am I correct?"

In that moment, I felt a naked holiness, as though I were going to be given the key to a great mystery. "Yes, I was Antonia, and yes,"—why this little pin prick of fear?—"yes... I suppose the fact I had been called Anna led me in some small way to the name Osanna. But—how did you know, Sister Catherine?"

"From the beginning of your coming here, I have seen similarities between us. We are both drawn to specific saints. And I listened early and found you to be very musical." The sweetest smile passed over the radiant countenance of the dying One. "I knew your Uncle Orlando, Osanna, a very long time ago. And I remember knowing you were to be born. Your mother was the musical parent. She and I enjoyed each other's company."

"My Uncle Orlando? How could you ever have known him?" I leaned toward Sister Catherine as her coughing took hold. Stay with me, Sister Catherine. You cannot leave me now. I held her up, soothing her until she could manage to drink some water. "Did you grow up with my father and his family?"

"No, my dear, I come by way of Venice. I tried to live in Siena; but it would seem God did not want me in this region. God and I have struggled over the meaning of home for a long time. Your Uncle Orlando—is he happy with his family? Does he ever come back from Rome to visit with your mother and father?" Sister Catherine's voice trailed off, and she drifted with her thoughts. Her grasp on my hand loosened and let go.

Time stopped. I was stunned, disbelieving. Dear Lord, help Thou my unbelief. Sister Catherine, stay! Help thou my unbelief. Tell me you are the one we have all grieved for. Tell me you are a part of me, a part of my soul. Sister Catherine! Speak! "Sister Catherine?" I took the thin hand once more, "Sister Catherine? Can you tell me more? Please? Please?"

The dying one looked at me again in silence. Finally, "Is your Uncle well, Osanna? Will you tell him that I died happily and with thoughts of him, please?"

"He disappeared years ago, Sister Catherine. I never knew him. He didn't go to Rome. From what I've gleaned in overhearing things I wasn't meant to hear, it seems he became a Francescan monk. I also remember hearing he avenged the death of my namesake, Antonia, before he disappeared completely."

Sister Catherine struggled forward, grasping my arm. I became alarmed. I could not lose her. Dear God, help her. Help me!

"What do you mean, Osanna? What do you mean he 'avenged' her death? Tell me—is he alive? How do you know he is in the Brotherhood?" A fierce, worldly change came over her. I was stunned. My hands shook. I wiped Sister Catherine's brow and directed her attention out the window.

"Sister Catherine, I've never doubted he's alive. In fact, my father once showed me on a map the area where my uncle studies alone. It is over in that direction, on the outskirts of San Gimignano—that way—just a few miles from here," the dying one—was I dying, too?— looked out toward the home of the monk and settled, lying back into her pillows. "My father let me see his own sadness briefly that day. He said my Uncle Orlando was a 'magnificent' brother. And then he never spoke of him again."

She smiled at me sweetly and looked again out the window, "So close... so very close... finally," she seemed to be whispering to someone only she could see. "Thank you, my dear. I am sorry to alarm you. Please continue. I am all right now. Has your uncle been in communication with your family?"

"No, he has never sent even a note to my parents or to my other uncles. But his memory continues as a strong presence in my family. My Grandmother, who pined for that other Antonia and who loved me more deeply because of her, carried her grief over Antonia's death within her for the remainder of her days. We were very close. She talked to me about Antonia—Anna Giraud—frequently. It was she who called me Anna," I took a corner of the blanket and wiped the Silent One's eyes. My own tears fell onto the blanket. "How can you know these things, Sister Catherine. Who are you?"

So we—the young woman and the dying woman—looked out over the fading landscape, carpeted in shades of purple. Our speech faded with the landscape and with the knowledge that we, upon finding each other, would lose each other. The faint silver of the moon advanced low upon the obscure horizon.

Sister Catherine reclaimed my hand, "I am Antonia, my dear. I am Anna Giraud. I did not die, although I have died many times." And so I knew I would now die and go on to live. I fell into the breast of my namesake. Sister Catherine wiped my tears with the same corner of the blanket and began to coo a plaintive melody. "Rest now, Antonia. You have come home to me, as a daughter. Mother Superior has music for you to keep and learn after I go. Breathe with me, my daughter, and let us rest."

Sister Catherine coughed and quietened while I wept and quietened. As though I had slipped into Paradise, I heard, "Come, Orlando, come Home." A violin whispered evocatively from some nether region.

Antonia became Antonia.

I slept in the infirm embrace of the dying one. And we dreamed a dream—a dream of waters and colours and basil and glass—until all became one. Sleep, muse, weep, fuse...

"Yes?" I muttered at the sense of intrusion, a voice wafting in from outside the dream. I will not shake off this bond; never will I...

"Sister Osanna, come now. Yes, come, my dear. It is over," Mother Superior put her arm around me and gently urged me to my feet. "She is gone now; come with me and pray." As the old Mother shepherded me out of the room, two Sisters drifted quietly in to assist the angels.

A holy sibilance hovered over the room in that moment—just long enough to allow the lily-of-the-valley time to breathe in and out on the evening breeze.

LXIII

There are times still when I am haunted by the solitary gondolier in the night mist. I want to unmask him. I need to see him. It's as though he holds the key to some secret, a secret I have a right to know. I know it has something to do with Orlando. [Antonia, 1747]

She was alone in a narrow alley, looking out toward a large, crowded Piazza. The sun spilled gold milk over the burnt orange and sepia buildings surrounding the marketplace. People cheered, bugles blasted, tambourines crackled and drums gave a wild pulse-beat to the chaos.

Propelled by a sense of great urgency, she struggled forward into the chaos and caught sight of four magnificent horsemen. Their proud, ornamented animals pranced regally. She needed to reach one of the horsemen. She must! A dark force tried to pull her back into the wildness of the crowd.

As she resisted with all of her strength, the external force let go, and she fell forward at the feet of one of the horses. The horse reared. Putting her hand up to protect her face, she looked up into the countenance of the Horseman she had been seeking. The most direct of brown eyes returned her gaze, while his ceremoniously gloved hand dropped a medallion into her upturned palm.

Still holding the reins short, the Horseman pulled his steed up and away from her, looked back and sped through the crowd and up into the bluest of skies past an astonishing, distorted Gothic bell tower.

"No," she screamed, finding that she could not fly to be with him. "Come back for me!"

Sobbing, she broke through the maniacal crowd and found her alleyway. Animal carvings and brilliantly coloured flags flew past her face, jeering at her. She could not hold the thick folds of her black skirt high enough. She fell into her skirt, cutting her hands on the cobblestone. Hearing commotion, she looked back, only to find the frenzied crowd following her and taunting in a strident musical unison, "You will always be alone, little orphan! Always alone! Orphan!" Breathless, she forced herself up and ran, bleeding onto her black habit and white cuffs.

Suddenly, a colossal cathedral appeared and leaned toward her. She ran into the Sanctuary door and over a floor inlaid with screaming infants reaching for her feet and out a secret door, known only by her.

She ran and ran, sobbing and bleeding until she fell again. "Oh, may I die, for I am dead without him," she pleaded to the God of her rosary.

As her tears fell on her bloody palms, she saw that she still had the medallion the beautiful Horseman had dropped into her hand. Two stars and a full moon gleamed from within a tiny glass globe. As she rubbed the perfect glass over her palms, the blood dried and disappeared.

And then she sensed the familiar, evocative aroma. Immediately stilled, she became alert to her surroundings.

She was lying in a field of brilliant green basil. Its aroma strengthened her. The sky was a blue Madonna's skirt. She luxuriated in the sacred sights, textures and aromas. And, then, a cosmic Horseman transformed the sky into searing light and shadows. The man she sought smiled steadily into her upturned face!

"Orlando!" the raptured soul invoked, arms stretched heavenward. "Orlando! Come home to me!"

LXIV

When I've found her, and I believe I have, I want her to under-
stand the need to end my repetition. I want her to reject the clois-
tered life. I want her to live—and love—freely and abundantly. I
want her to dare to be all of who she is. And I want her to know
that, in a sense, she is my lost child. Her parents would approve...
I know this for certain because Alessandra and I were pregnant
at the same time. And they called her Antonia. There was only
one reason for her to enter this convent. And that reason was the
need for us to find each other. [Antonia, 1746]

Brother Francesco awoke to the familiar cry. He had fallen asleep
in daylight, leaving himself prey to the dream he loved and hated.
The powerful vision bore a hole in his brain. His chest was being
crushed. In a diabolical repetition, Antonia was lying broken and
dead, red against white, blood against innocence. Dying over and
over and over. Would it ever stop?

"No!" he shouted, "Leave me alone! Leave her alone!" The curtain
moved tentatively on a gentle breeze. The monk sensed something
more than the familiarity of the breeze and aromas. Was there a
whisper in the breeze? For the first time in years, he felt drawn
to pick up the violin. "Dite, Oime," it whispered, "Orlando... come
Home." He reached out and touched a fragrance.

And then he remembered that there had been a difference in this
dream. Antonia had stood up and walked toward him... healed...
radiant... her arms outstretched... smiling as she had in her moments of greatest happiness.

"I must go to the garden." Spent, the aging priest got up from his
lonely bed and moved to the violin. Oh, the crushing, the crushing
pain. "No!" He ordered the instrument that had kept her close and
contained all these long years to keep silent. He must not let the

feeling take hold; it was not good to allow it to stay. He stepped slowly down the cold stone stairs of the tower and into the garden. The olives, black against the darkening sky, were beginning to take shape, tiny, indigo replicas of the silver sphere taking its place over the horizon. Old images and fragrances whirled wildly toward him, tuning his senses and focusing his mind, blasting him with the pressing pain of cascading memories, the pressing pain of lost beauty.

Dear God! Antonia—so long ago, so intensely loved. Breathless and overcome, the priest grasped the back of a roughly hewn bench under the hoary ancient oak. "No! No! Antonia!" His voice roared and echoed through the trees and into the blank heavens. "Antonia!" until his chest would explode with the loosening of all that had been contained for too long... daring the empty sky to answer... daring it to explain this moment... this moment of light and dark and no shadows... this moment of choice... this moment of extinction.

And then the heavens split, riven by a white light.

And in that split second afforded all souls in the ultimate choice, Orlando Sagredo reached for the light. Merging, disappearing with the celestial, he stepped into the abundance of Antonia's young and vibrant smile.

LXV

I will take this manuscript now to Mother Superior. She is eager to read it. When she has finished, she'll place it in a vault in the Duomo that only the Sagredos will have access to.

As I approached the end of my writing, I felt strangely sad. I realized I felt as though I were abandoning Antonia. But, no—she lives on in me. And in my family.

My husband strongly encouraged me in the work of this history. In fact, it was he who talked with the others about purchasing a vault in the Duomo. "I want our Antonia to know your Uncle and his Antonia," he told me. I was so touched that I cried. Some of the tears were Antonia's.

Now, as I reluctantly let go of this work, I look out over the gardens and see little Antonia with her nursemaid. They've gone under the old oak for shade on this sultry July day. Natalia is teaching Antonia to clap.

The jasmine is in bloom. I smell it.

Now I must wipe the ink from my pen and close my desk. It is time to let Antonia Vivaldi live on.

And we shall find one another
as we once were—
In sprays of pomegranate blossoms
and the purity of surplices.
[Antonia, 1750]

The brown leather diary my aunt placed in my care was meticulously kept. Its red ribbon is frayed now, worn with the love that opened it, wrote in it and tied it up again. Antonia's handwriting was truly musical, with its occasional embellishments like those in the music she often wrote on the pages... fragments of melodies she needed to capture and see... fragments of her memories. This is not to say that this diary is pretty. It is not. The handwriting is strong. Nothing is tentative. This is the diary – no, I will say "book" – of an exceptionally courageous and intellectual woman.

I suspect this book was her dearest friend.

Here follow the excerpts I chose to quote in this manuscript: from the book Antonia of Venice called...

CONTEMPLATIONS ON MY LIFE

Anna Antonia

21 January, 1739

Who created us? Was it Alaric the Goth? Was it Attila the Hun? Did we rise from the sea malformed? Surely it could not have been in God's plan to create us. Venetians are neither fish nor fowl, nor are we fully human. We have grown from marshes and water. We have driven posts into the lagoon bottom to give us legs. We have oars for gills, spires for feathers and Mother Mary for a soul. We cannot walk very far without having to cross the water and that water is full of salt, killing us if we drink it. Are we a joke, a Divine Comedy? Is a Venetian always a stranger in a strange land? If so, Moses, then, is my father. And like him, I am doomed never to see the Promised Land.

15 March, 1739

I have returned to this book of the blankness. I've returned because I had a dream last night... a different kind of dream, far more symbolic than detailed... moody... ethereal, if one word must be chosen. I stood on a tiny Venetian bridge. An indigo fog drifted around me and a small group of people talked at the end of the bridge. It was dark, and a gondola, with an eerie light in its prow, passed under the bridge. He was the gondolier. He looked at me, so I ran to the other side of the bridge to see him again. It seemed to take so long for him to emerge from under the bridge. When he did, he would not look at me. I was bereft. And then I noticed I had on a creamy, elaborate ball gown. And over my eyes was a mask with cat's eyes. Is life my Carnevale?

Good Friday, 1739

My friend, Antonio Canale, painted magnificent Venetian vistas. I would study them and wonder why he did not paint the true Venetians into his paintings. Why would he not paint Piazza San Marco with its hordes of noisy, untidy market vendors? Why would he not paint mess and bartering and poverty? "The wealthy, Anna, live in a city they have constructed in their minds. Venice is a myth. I am to paint their Venice. It's grand, immaculate, rational. That is why they created the Carnevale... so they can wear masks and once a year become myths themselves."

Easter Sunday, 1739

What I remember most vividly from my earliest years at the Pieta are the feel of water in the air, cloying, rancid, if water can indeed turn sour, and the sound of violins coming out of the walls and slithering under doors and through windows and out over the Bacino. And always, as continuo for this music of water and violins, was the taunting of the other orphans... cruel, biting, hideous. And I, as I am now, was alone....

Ascension Day, 1739

Every year on Ascension Day, the Doge and a throng of noblemen and musicians go out to sea so that Venice can marry the sea. Once out in the Adriatic, the Doge throws a ring into the waters and cries out, "We marry thee, O Sea, and this ring is the emblem of our perpetual dominion over you!" Is that what marriage is to Venetians?

10 June, 1739

Mothers threw their bastard newborns into the waters three hundred years ago. Wrapped in seaweed, the little bodies were caught with the fish. The Procuratori instituted a law against this and founded the Orphanage, filled with suckling infants and wet-nurses. And so I am alive because of the charity of the Procuratori. And I am silenced because of their brutality.

1 July, 1739

Except for the sounds of music and teaching, the Pieta was silent. We orphans may have been unique as females; but we were under our own form of captivity. The Pieta was a museum in daytime and a mausoleum at night. In the day, we were the artifacts of the museum. At night we became the corpses of the mausoleum. And the Lion of San Marco, guardian and director, oversaw it all—from his position, high and disdainful over the Bacino.

22 July, 1739

July tears at my heart. Everything was planned around the July Palio that first summer of my life with Orlando. Would I were in our family, the way it all should have been. Instead, my family is memories of what almost was. I had simply never known a family until I met Lorenzo's family. I had no idea of what it was like to talk in a group, to quarrel, to laugh, to solve problems… and to love and hate. Were the other orphans my sisters? No! Were the Prioress and the Maestro my parents? No! My only family was made up of the Invisibles of my childhood. I had to abandon them, of course.

August 16, 1739

The Doge of Venice was a puppet. There were two puppeteers— the Pope and the Envoy of the Procuratori. Many Doges fell out of favour with their puppeteers, their only recourse being a retreat into seclusion. Truly, they were set up to fail while making others successful. Venice, while contained in a serene body, has an avaricious underbelly. The serenity channels itself through devotion to the Virgin Mary. The hunger channels itself through the Lion of

San Marco. It would seem to me, because the Virgin Mother visited San Marco in a dream, that there is a Venetian Trinity of the Madonna, San Marco and the Lion... Mother, Son and Holy Ghost. Every night, the Lion descends his high post near the Doge's Palace and skulks along the canals, taking care of abominations. He sends the Refiner's Fire through the waters. Hissing, the fiery waters expel Evil's debris into the Lagoon. The Lagoon is exceedingly capable of extermination.

30 September, 1739

All I ever needed was Truth. Instead, I was given marvellous attention to a great gift... and lies. And so my gift tortured me. Inherent in it was a keen sensitivity to love. And a longing for love. After all, the gift was music. The torture was that love often came wrapped in lies... beautiful, musical lies. But, while my gift could torment me, it could also comfort me because I could intentionally use it as a delirious escape from this world. I had only to pick up my violin, stroke it with the bow, and I would have stroked my own soul. And then Inspiration would take over. That was truth for me—the delirium of being consumed.

4 December, 1739

One of the Lagoon Islands succumbed to the waters ages ago... when the Black Plague swept through Venice. San Marco in Boccalama. They buried La Piaga's victims there. By the boatload. I suppose the island sank beneath the weight and the grief of it all. The Lagoon can be like that... mysterious, secretive and deadly, swallowing its victims. It's a doorway to Purgatory, I think.

11 February, 1740

Is life walked along a straight line? Or is there a descent that happens once childhood is over? Where does the innocence of trust go?

Must it be lost? I suspect it must. I also suspect descent is inevitable. Hell does not like waiting in the wings.

15 March, 1740

San Paolo said we see through "a glass darkly." He was talking about spiritual things. In that, I agree with him. In the matter of my love, though, I see all too clearly... through an open window on a sunny day. And I am a prisoner—behind glass.

Good Friday, 1740

The Viennese, for all their sobriety, have a parallel life to Venetians... music, Pagan Roman roots, Holy Roman roots. They tell the story of Pope Silvester who drove the demons out of Austria in the fourth century. Constantine named Silvester Pope. I dislike history establishing Constantine as the bridge. The bridge between Pagan and Holy Rome was his mother, Saint Helena. Like the Venetians I know, Constantine was driven by power and control. It was Theodosius who truly made The Roman Empire Christian. There are many stories of misplaced credit becoming history.

Ascension Day, 1740

What was it the Maestro wanted when he completed "Orlando Furioso"? Revenge? Forgiveness? Or was it, as he said, that he'd begun the opera years before and needed to finish it? Why, then, did he write completely new music? Who was Angelica? Who was Ranaldo? It was his most complex opera. And its name tormented me.

July 22, 1740

Venetians are obsessed with the construction and maintenance of two wooden instruments of travel. The gondola travels on water. The violin travels on air. Both transport people, and so people who live in luxury desire—demand—perfection. Woods, tone, colour, varnishes, quality—the making of both instruments follows careful rules and requires the ultimate in craftsmanship. But the Soul is the greatest instrument of travel, for it takes us into the mind of God. Venetians have no obsession for the maintenance of the Soul.

4 December, 1740

I found some old notes today. I'd written them years ago when I had returned from Siena the first time. Somehow they came here in a corner of an old trunk. For some reason, today was the day for me to find these pieces of myself. What am I to make of these remnants now? How can they possibly relate to Vienna? I'll copy what I can decipher into this book before all becomes dust... or ashes. And perhaps... perhaps... I'll write more and discover who I am.

3 February, 1741

Less than fifty years before the Maestro was born, Venice was again visited by La Piaga. No marauder could torture and kill to the extent that the plague could. From 1630 to 1631, over 40,000 Venetians died... horribly, violently. An offspring of a wicked god, woven into the air, its spectre continues to haunt Venice. Venetians are prey to an offspring of that plague. It is an invisible plague, one of their own doing. It skulks around in the bowels of the city until it can attach itself to a grasping politician, a weak Doge, a power hungry Cardinal. People follow the politician, excuse the Doge and view the Cardinal as God's designate. They are then contaminated. My Maestro became contaminated. This plague destroyed Venetian music and broke Father Antonio's heart.

15 March, 1741

Venetian politics has long been famous for its reverence of secrets and for its cruelty. I was subject to and the subject of both.

Good Friday, 1741
I loved Orlando's Light. And I loved receiving it. It harnessed mine. Together, we shone—we were composers of our own "Gloria." Our shadows were minimal when we were together... because we shared the same soul.

Ascension Day, 1741
Perhaps for everyone, the first experience of Eros is bittersweet. For the Pieta orphan, though, there is the prior knowledge that the father who gave you life did not love you. You were his shame. I thought often about that while I was growing up. That essential abandonment, coupled with my adoration of Father Antonio, created a belief in me that love was based on exceeding the expectations of the one I loved. In addition to that, my cloistered upbringing gave me very few skills in relationships. And then I became the subject of a painting, the object of a painter's eye, the desire of his heart.

1 June, 1741
Once I had seen beyond Venice, I yearned to see more. It wasn't that I wanted to return to Mantova. It was that the earthy places I'd heard of because of the Maestro's perpetual travel—Florence, Rome, Vienna—began to fascinate me. Why could I not go along with him, I wondered. And so I asked him. "My dear Anna," he said, "I know how shy you are. You would not want to meet so many people."

22 July, 1741
The Maestro was the most spectacular musician. In performing, he and the violin became one. They soared... drifted... flew. They spun and plunged, only to soar again. And they took the audience with them... into the heavens—into the dark night of desolation and into the face of the sun. There were times when I thought his playing would consume him. I believe... I know... he touched God. And

then he would have to come back to earth. And to the constraints of humanity. He found being human difficult.

5 September, 1741

In a rather morbid way, the Island of San Michele in the Lagoon always fascinated me. It seemed somehow sinister with its wall of cypress trees, and there were stories of trapped spirits haunting it and crying. The Francescan Convent there interested me as well. I imagined taking refuge there during my most difficult experiences growing up. No one would have thought to look for me there, desolate and off in the Lagoon as it was. Now I flee to another convent.

30 September, 1741

Shadows... shadows... I've run from them and I've hidden in them. I've created them and I've neglected them. They are evidence both of Light and of Light being blocked... or stolen. Shadows cast by others may or may not be trustworthy. My shadow, though, is the shape of my invisible self. It proves I am more than my body or what can be seen. My shadow is my soul's impression... as light as a grace note. Taken over by the shadows of Darkness, my soul disappears. The soul is shy and beautiful and will not, cannot, dare not, fight the brutal powers of Darkness. That the person must do. I, I the person, have not been strong enough to step back into my own shadow.

20 November, 1741

Plato wrote that if we turn toward the Light, our eyes will be "dazzled." Job said that God brings the "deep darkness into Light." When I turn toward the Light, I see the light of Siena. Orlando is Siena's light... still.

4 December, 1741

My time in Mantova was a strange time. I remember little of it in detail. There was always the sense of having to... having to perform, having to disappear, having to please—and having to practise! Practise, practise, practise... until I forgot what perfection was supposed to sound like... until I saw only the bar of music and forgot the composition... until I found I was the composition itself. And then, of course, there was the loneliness. I dressed like a nun. I acted like a nun. I managed to go out to pray. And I saw, for the first time in my life, or shall I say, I felt, for the first time in my life, the danger of physical attraction. My chief delight—because the Prioress was often called upon to assist in the court functions and many times could not be my companion—my chief delight was that I began to compose. The music came to me in visions, visions of colours... attracting, rebounding, playing, singing, swirling. That, and only that, was my salvation. And it was Jacopo who opened my eyes.

15 March, 1742

The Maestro did have a very deep faith. It was carefully and exactly worked out in circularity to include his politics and music. He used politics to further music. And he used music to further his politics. His faith remained as the heart of it all for him. "People come to God through music, Anna," he told me in one of our invigorating discussions. I could not blindly accept his premise. "But what about painting? What about something like Bellini's Madonna or Titian's Assumption in the Frari?" I had been so affected by art after I'd met Jacopo. "No, no, my dear. Painting is static. It needs music to give it life!" He was so rational, so vocal. I was so reflective, so inward. I did not want to apply only my mind to my beliefs. They needed to be private and felt. The Maestro's feeling was quick and then acted upon. I wanted the slow unfolding mystery of the illogical, even peculiar. He was inspired by brilliant, hard-edged revelation, I by supple contemplation. In the end, I saw he was right. Music, more than painting, allows and encompasses all human differences and similarities within its wide-ranging borders. Perhaps, then, music, in its mathematical basis, is God, and other art forms are inspired by God.

Good Friday, 1742

The Prioress was my bridge to everything. Without her, I'd have become a recluse. She was a beautiful woman, powerful both physically and spiritually. She was my beacon. And she was the only person—the only person—who really understood Father Antonio. A touch here, a word there, and he was enabled to bring stunning, virtuosic music into the world. Sister Paolina was mid-wife to the music.

Ascension Day, 1742

It floated in through my window and under my door one night. I had wakened from a dream of a garden outside of Siena with an ancient, crumbling stone tower off to the side. It was a peaceful, still dream, all green except for the ripe red tomatoes growing amongst the herbs. I might say the dream was fragrant, as odd as that may seem. But, while it was peaceful, I was left with tremendous melancholy. And that was when I felt the music float into my room... soothing, as quietly sad as my dream... played on a lute. Was I still dreaming? No—it must be the Maestro! But so late at night? I threw a blanket around my shoulders and hurried to the music room. The door was open and a gust of Adriatic air sent the music into my soul. I wanted to cry. And there he was—Father Antonio, leaning into his lute, his white and red hair falling over the instrument, the offering exquisitely, painfully beautiful. "What is it, Anna?" How had he known I was there? "This is not your music, Father." On the end of an arpeggio, he spoke softly, "No, it is a Passacaglia by a man named Biber. Stay if you wish." He looked up briefly and I saw the tears in his eyes. "It brings Paolina back to this room." I stayed, my chest crushed with the pressure of a lost mother and my lover, my Orlando.

4 December, 1742

Suppose I were to return to Venice to find Saint Catherine's foot. Suppose I were to wander into the city—leave the turquoise Bacino, cross canals, fly over domes, swim under bridges, gasp in the putrefaction where sea water is trapped and sinks into torpidity, where no fish can live, where the Goliath is fed human creatures—would I find that foot? If I found it floating in the Lagoon, would it take me south by water? If I found it in a maze of bridges, would it take me to its body in Rome? If I found it in the Basilica, would it take me out of this world? Or would it have washed out to sea—finding its own salvation and uncaring for mine? Ah, but if I found it in the herb garden, would it take me to its head in Siena? Her feet took her to and from Siena and Rome and Venice. And mine cannot take me south—to her home... and mine. Only will they do it, if he is not there but gone.

15 March, 1743

"Pax Tibi Marce Evangelista Meus." So says the Book the Winged Lion holds open for the Doge above the Palace Door. Two Venetian merchants stole San Marco's body from Alexandria in 828 and brought it to Venice. The relics were interred in the Doge's Chapel, and the Basilica was built as their final resting place. The Venetians claimed that San Marco belonged to them because he evangelized Venice and prophesied the return of his bones to the city. The Alexandrians in Egypt claimed San Marco was theirs because he founded their church. Am I to believe that Truth can be manipulated? That Truth varies? That there is no Absolute? Ah, but I have seen the Winged Lion fly over the Bacino. And I have heard the

Winged Lion sing as he stalks the brooding Night Waters. I know the truth of no absolutes.

Good Friday, 1743

When I was very young, I would beg the Maestro to tell me "the story of your earthquake...please, please!" He would banter with me and tell me that he was too busy. But always, he would make a grand drama of relenting and tell me... "Ah, la mia principessa, the fascinating story of my birth!" And he would laugh and set me on his knee. "Well, on that very day, at the very moment of my birth in Venice, there was an earthquake! It was so frightening that the mid-wife baptized me immediately, so sure was she that all of Venice would be killed!" And we would go on, I with my questions and he finally finishing with, "Because that earthquake was not the portent of a new plague, my mother knew I had been born for something very special." And then he would kiss me on the forehead and call for the Prioress. "Always remember, my Antonia, you have been born to fulfill a destiny, too. Music! You and I were born for music, Antonia!" I wish I could believe that now. I wish he were here to tell me.

Ascension Day, 1743

It wasn't that the Maestro was always demanding and perfection-istic. I remember clearly the times when he would read to me or sit down to play backgammon with me. As fiercely competitive as he was, he was tremendously proud of me when I won. He would lean back in his chair, clap his hands and shout, "Domine, Antonia! You have beaten the Maestro! Soon you will be called the Maestra of backgammon. Perhaps one day Venetians will call you their Maes-tra of Music. Nothing would make me prouder!" And he would get up and come over to give me a big kiss on each cheek. "Paolina! Paolina! Bring us something chocolate!" And from the sitting room down the hall, the Prioress would laugh in her rich, contralto voice, and shout, "I'll be there in a moment!" How I wish I could bring her back for one of her moments.

22 July, 1743

I remember Father Antonio telling me the story of Juditha when I was twelve. He had just finished his opera about her. Giacomo Cassetti wrote the libretto, as he had done before for the Maestro. I was surprised he had chosen a heroine to celebrate Venice's victory at Corfu over the Ottoman Empire. "Anna," he said to me, "Anna, you can grow up to be a significant musician. This is not easy for a woman. But you can do it, my dear. You can—like Juditha!" He was passionate about that. I knew he loved me and wanted fame to prove my talent… and his, for having formed me. My grief was that he did not see me as a separate human being. He saw me as Juditha, as Anna and as extinguished Antonia.

15 March, 1744

Was my flight to Jacopo in Mantova an omen, a preparation for Siena and him? If there was a Divine hand in our love, it was a fist.

Good Friday, 1744

There's a madness inherent in invention. Great inventors use their madness to create something completely new. Father Antonio, the Red Priest, Maestro Vivaldi, was an inventor. He was not only a composer. He invented new music that took the violin to its furthest edges, that stretched the soul into the Heavens and taxed the voice. And when the Lustrous took over as in 'Alma Oppressa' or in the Concerto in A Minor, there was a danger the consummate performer might not be able to finish. Was his madness to see how far he could push the edges before God intervened? Was he attempting to meet God, to force His hand? Was the answer to his reluctant priesthood contained within that form of arrogance? Or did he know that God could not be contained by or within anything... not even music? Did that, in a sense, drive him mad at times?

Ascension Day, 1744

I think of Orlando in Rome often. And I wish I had visited the city. I wish I knew it. Would I find him viewing the structure of the Pantheon? Wandering through the art in San Pietro? Visiting someone near Santa Sabina on the Aventine? And would she be with him or waiting at home for him with their children? No! He has not married. For some reason, I cannot believe he is in Rome. He does not keep company with Hadrian and Vespasian. He is a Tuscan, not a Roman. I know this. I know this because I visit him at night in the purple fabric of dreams.

22 July, 1744

Lorenzo's comment that I reminded him of Caravaggio's Maddalena stunned me. He, like Jacopo, opened me up to who I was outside of music. I had never thought of myself—ever—as separate from music. Nor had I ever thought of Mary Magdalene as separate from Jesus.

3 September, 1744

The Maestro and the Prioress kept me cloistered as a child. They were particularly concerned that I never trust anyone with a mask. "The tradition is evil, Anna," they would remind me. "It was once prohibited because of dreadful crimes committed by those concealed in masks. Even in convents! It's too terrible to tell you what happened. Now the mask is important again. Particularly when people go out to gamble in the night. Never go near anyone with a mask." How could this happen? As they would never let me out of the Pieta unless we went to the Basilica or the Scuola to perform, I could never understand this! And then one evening, when I was pulling weeds in the garden, I felt I must see beyond the doors on my own. I slipped out through the "Pediatrico e Materno" door, along the alley and into the concourse. It was dusk and a pungent, spicy aroma floated in from the Bacino. From the shadows, a sharp male voice called to me, "What are you doing, Novice? Come talk to me!" I looked up. He was approaching. I'll never forget my fear! Over his eyes was a ghostly white mask and from it dropped a veil of white, covering his mouth. The mask turned his eyes into black holes. On his head, he wore a three-cornered black hat. He extended his gloved hand, and I ran. He laughed and followed me. I fled back through the door and locked it. I can still hear his laugh and his strident knocking at the door. I never ventured out alone again. And I never told anyone.

4 December, 1744

I pray for Lorenzo's soul every day. I loved him dearly. And he loved me, I know. He laid down his life for me. The Romans gave votive offerings to the gods three times for a departed soul. Is praying for departed souls just as Pagan? I think not... if I remember it is for my need.

15 March, 1745

Inspiration has to do with love. Composition has to do with inspiration. And so, there must be love active somehow, somewhere, in composition. Love is not always happy. In fact, it may not often be happy. Love has the capacity to be painful, sad, very lonely and joyous. Therefore, composition must embrace all of love's capacities. Love herself attaches us passionately, deeply, painfully to another object. Whether that object is God or another human being does not really matter. Except, I suppose, that God is constant and does not die or disappear. Composition replicates and unleashes the experience of love. Composition can tear the composer apart at times.

Good Friday, 1745
What marker have I left in Siena? Is there anything to prove that
I was reborn there? That I died there? That I was happiest there?
That, above all, he lived there and that we loved there? Romulus,
another orphan, left his Roman marker. His son, Senus, founded a
city—Siena! No one can find my mark on the orange city. Ah... I
speak as a Pagan again!

Ascension Day, 1745
Saint Catherine knew persecution. She knew austerities. She implored God to reform the clergy. I suppose it was God's direction
to her to take her pleas to Pope Gregory in Avignon. She helped
change the river of history. I feel I have known persecution and
austerities, too. But, other than God, to whom was I to implore for
help? And where have I changed anything? As much as it grieves
me to do so, I question the spiritual life of penury and austerity. But
I know no other. And as I write this, I ask for forgiveness. I must go
to my garden... to the healing soil.

December 4, 1745
There came a time, while I was in Siena the first time, when I
felt Venice as a menacing shadow hovering over my life—Il Falcon,
ready to swoop. As life on land became more solid, Venice became
more amorphous. But the sense of Il Falcon's black, swooping wings
has never left me. Never.

15 March, 1746
Il Croco, the flower, established San Gimignano's early strength.
Even though the trade for saffron died a while ago, there is still
evidence of the Crocus Sativus in the valley. The phantoms of the
lost trade are there in the reds and purples and in the texture and
breath of the valley. What stories that breath could tell if we knew

how to listen. It would tell us of the colours of love and how loves transmutes into gold. I often walk into the valley and up the hill to the town. I visit the convent there. I pray. I wish for the power of saffron to heal me. And him. I feel very close to Orlando within the reach of the towers, as though he were the one of the towers.

22 July, 1746
I have sudden bursts of understanding my life. They disappear just as suddenly, but leave remnants of meaning. I gather the remnants. I spin them into yarn. I use that yarn as ink for my writing.

4 December, 1746
When I've found her, and I believe I have, I want her to understand the need to end my repetition. I want her to reject the cloistered life. I want her to live—and love—freely and abundantly. I want her to dare to be all of who she is. And I want her to know that, in a sense, she is my lost child. Her parents would approve... I know this for certain because Alessandra and I were pregnant at the same time. And they called her Antonia. There was only one reason for her to enter this convent. And that reason was the need for us to find each other.

15 March, 1747
There are times still when I am haunted by the solitary gondolier in the night mist. I want to unmask him. I need to see him. It's as though he holds the key to some secret, a secret I have a right to know. I know it has something to do with Orlando.

Good Friday, 1747
Had Siena not done away with its Pagan roots? Its celebration of the Palio seemed so profane in some ways; not in the idea of the races as such, but in all the other fuss and furor, as though the horses

allowed people to practise idolatry. I suppose it was more the frenzy I found disturbing, much as I had experienced in the Festa. And then one day, I began to laugh at myself. It was fear that kept me bound this way, that made me frightened to open up and celebrate with these people... fear that made me judge. I'd had a sudden realization that the whole of Roman Christendom had been built over—physically on top of—Roman idols! Saint Catherine's sarcophagus in Saint Maria sopra Minerva in Roma, I said to myself, is built upon the Pagan Temple of Minerva. I laughed aloud when the realization came upon me—and I found it very liberating.

4 December, 1947
My dream clings to me today. I am in a lush, green forest—everything is completely safe, the air dense and crackling. I stand before a river, a brilliant turquoise, gently undulating river. I am alone, calm, at one with everything. I reach into the river and pull out a beautiful feline animal, smaller than a lion. I hold it lovingly and it looks up at me knowingly. I embrace the animal in great love. Its hide is silver with large lavender spots. The water has given it an incredible sleekness. I know I am in the presence of supernatural beauty. I am comforted. And I do not know why. I feel Orlando close, as close as he was when he pulled his cloak around me and we rode off into the hills. I do not know why....

15 March, 1748

> Plant jasmine when I die,
> Against the towers in my dreams,
> Climb to its deepest greens;
> Upon the stones 'til blossoms cry.
> Spin steps of perfumed sighs,
> And in the billows where I rest;

I take you to my breast—
Soul-soaring One beyond the skies.

Good Friday, 1748

I think I did not know how to laugh until I met Orlando. Nor to play. He taught me to open up to joy and pleasure in the immediate moment—to touch, to feel, to listen, to see all that was happening in the world around me. I had no need to escape to my imagination when I was with Orlando. And so, I still touch and feel and hear and see him. He dwells in me.

4 December, 1748

There is nothing so elegant as the arcane purple of wisteria blooms against a buttery rock wall. Wisteria understands and drops its petals on the Istrian stone in love for the beholder. I was Orlando's beholder.

15 March, 1749

Why did the sun play a far more dominant role for me in Siena than it ever had in Venice? Was it love? The moon was my alchemist in Venice. And yet I hardly remember thinking about the moon during my two interludes in Siena. On my first two returns to Venice, I reconciled with La Luna, often taking my violin out on the balcony and playing to her. When I was most angry, I played the 'Adagio e spiccato' from the G Minor Concerto...pum-pum-pum-pum... 1-2-3-4... why-why-why-why... throwing my questions into the sky and letting them resolve into beseeching stars. At my angriest, I would launch into the 'Allegro,' my bowing furious... back and forth, back and forth, until I could contain it no longer. Until a neophyte melody emerged. This is how comets are born, the issue of creativity and anger.

Good Friday, 1749

Siena "dazzles" like Plato's Light. I am greatly comforted dwelling in the gentle hills in the Sienese countryside. In turn, the shadows cast by the sun and the light of Siena in the distance shelter the hills. My shelter these days comes to me from the Light Orlando left in Siena. And so, I can say he is still there. At times, I can believe it.

Ascension Day, 1749

Ah, gardens! What would I have done without gardens in my life, without the lushness of green herbs and the purity of white flowers? And the warmth of the soil, from which Orlando came... the warm, orange Sienese soil. I came from water, murky water. He taught me much about the earth and how to move about freely without fear of drowning in the narrow alleys of my mind. Most importantly, he taught me how to root myself in love. Because of him, I shall be able to make my final peace with the soil, in a sense to be with him. I have already made my final peace with water. I need Venice no longer. He waits for me always, not in any waters, but in the soil of gardens, and I am comforted. The Prioress and I were odd Venetians. We loved gardens and tended lovingly to our tiny garden at the orphanage. I suspect she will be one of the first to greet me after my body gives itself over to the soil—when I make a final peace with it... and when I make my final peace with God for having given me this life to live. I look forward to that reunion, when time no longer matters. I look forward to that final peace.

22 July, 1749

Sometimes it amazes me that I can remember so vividly, given all the years that have passed. I am very grateful for this, in spite of the pain that can be part of it. I am certain Orlando and I visit in a way that will be understood once this life is over. There are times when I can run my fingers through his hair, when I can see his eyes and his slightly crooked smile, and when I can feel his breath until we are breathing together. And in my dreams, we come together and I am fulfilled. [Antonia, 1749]

4 December, 1749

The longer I stayed in Siena, the more I craved land beneath my feet for the rest of my life. And the more I desired my Orlando in my bed for the rest of my life.

15 March, 1750

If I could paint, I would paint Siena! I would use only vibrant, brilliant, stunning colours. I would invent new colours… beyond orange… more pristine than blue… brighter than the most fiery yellow… holier than green. First I would spatter the canvas—a very large one—with yellow and orange. And then I would listen to the sounds of the colours and succumb to Inspiration, shaping saffron sunflowers and succulent grapes ready to burst into wine. The riotous flames of the sun would take over the centre of the canvas until the sun itself created Il Duce, clad in his armour and moving forward on his magnificent steed. And then I would open my arms wide to him… and step into the painting so that he could pick me up and we would finish our story together.

Easter Sunday, 1750

In Siena's Duomo, there is a marble floor inlaid with a mosaic. One of the subjects is "the slaughter of the innocents." When I first saw it and walked across it, I was certain that the little ones were reaching up to take hold of my ankles… to gain my attention… to plead with me to save them… to make this perpetual slaughter stop. I could hear them shrieking and see them bleeding. Were I to go back there now, it would be to look for one innocent, waiting for me to save her. I would pick her up in my arms and laugh and carry her out through the alleys into the fields and nurse her and play with her and teach her so many things. I would be Bellini's Madonna outside Siena. And she? Well, God would allow her to be His Holy Daughter.

4 May, 1750

The Tuscan hillside is often purple. I suppose the various greens and violets, the olives and the grapes, combine to produce the regal, deeply textured tapestry. And within that tapestry, in a small part of it, is my love story. Its sounds are muffled by the texture. That rich texture, created by the undulating breasts of Tuscany, keeps my story safe.

22 July, 1750

> Come with me, my love,
> And I shall fly you to the land of basil and glass
> That you may walk the old walk with me
> Of watery stones and mysterious melodies....

12 August, 1750

After I returned to these hills, I began to dream the same dream frequently. In the dream, I jump from my balcony at the Orphanage and run to the water. Lorenzo is there waiting for me in a gondola. He assists me into the vessel, and we leave for the mainland by the light of the full moon. As we come near the shore, I step out of the gondola and scoop seaweed into my arms. Lorenzo shouts, "No, Antonia. Leave it alone. Put it back where it belongs." I look down at myself and see that my dress has turned into murky turquoise seaweed with flashes of silver in it. I drop the seaweed from my arms... and wake up, wondering, confused. Until last night. In last night's dream, I disregard Lorenzo's fear. I sit down in the water in my dress of seaweed and gently open the seaweed in my arms. A beautiful infant looks up at me and smiles. And I understand the dream. And Orlando is with me.

undated, 1750

>Come with me, my love,
>and I shall fly you to the land of basil and glass
>that you may walk the old walk with me
>of watery stones and mysterious melodies
>
>And I shall heap sprigs of basil
>and clusters of dizzying lilies
>on the fat whiteness of our bed
>and compose a sonata of love
>
>And you shall see perfection
>before you touch and smell and taste it
>in the eloquence of olive oil
>and in the essence of wine
>
>Come with me, my love –
>Step into the spilt gold of the marketplace,
>Run through the misty hillsides,
>And capture our patterns in glass
>
>And we shall find one another
>as we once were –
>In sprays of pomegranate blossoms
>and the purity of surplices

Dear reader,

We hope you enjoyed reading *Antonia of Venice*. Please take a moment to leave a review in Amazon, even if it's a short one. Your opinion is important to us.

Discover more books by Ellyn Peirson at
https://www.nextchapter.pub/authors/ellyn-peirson

Want to know when one of our books is free or discounted for Kindle? Join the newsletter at http://eepurl.com/bqqB3H

Best regards,
Ellyn Peirson and the Next Chapter Team

You might also like:

Gilded Summers by Donna Russo Morin

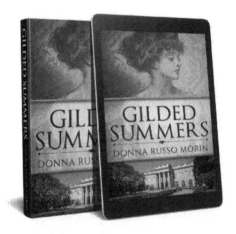

To read first chapter for free, head to:
https://www.nextchapter.pub/books/gilded-summers

ABOUT ELLYN

My whole childhood was spent in Regina, Saskatchewan, in the same house, about a block away from the intersection of the Canadian National and the Canadian Pacific Railways. I moved to "the east" as a rite of passage when I was eighteen. The bleak prairies live deep within me. They are most evident in the two completed short stories – Joey and Veronica.

Now that I've completed the my "career path" as a social worker and individual counsellor, I'm able to have writing, photography and photoart as my chief occupations. I perceive writing as the energetic combination of attention, eccentricity, music, perception and solitude. I love seclusion and thrive in an environment of music, Venetian glass, camera lenses, great writers living on my shelves and my family and very special friends. I happen to be Canadian with roots in England and France and a heart in Italy. I live in Guelph, Ontario, and at the family cottage on the northern shores of Lake Huron.

Having been raised by parents who were accomplished musicians, I tend to err on the side of believing my musical knowledge is not, shall we say, noteworthy. However, compared to many people's, it is extensive. I never heard my ex-concert-mistress-mother play her violin. I yearned to know her instrument. I yearned to hear her play; but she wouldn't. I think now it was some kind of perfection compulsion. Nevertheless, my younger sister and I grew up immersed in music. My mother's prodigious piano skills accompanied my father's beautiful tenor voice. And we talked as a family... in depth. Margaret and I benefited from the musical, intellectual and spiritual environment our parents, mainly our father, created.

One particularly quirky fascination I developed was that at age four, I fell in love with Venice. My eccentric and multi-talented mother introduced me to the strange city, so physically far from Regina, Saskatchewan. Somewhere along the line, my mother had learned that Vivaldi, whose music she had come to love as much as Bach's, had had an orchestra of female musicians. In the 1700's? Impossible! True. It was as though my mother had lived in the city.

As for who I now am, at least according to me, I've been shaped by my careers, roles, specific circumstances and my belief in the evolution of the mind and soul. I have been profoundly shaken by the loss to cancer of my fabulous son and my one and only sibling, my younger sister.

All that I have become along the way has driven the writings I have been prone to keep to myself. A number of factors came together when the time was ripe for serious writing: the effects of the life journey I had chosen, a passion for Venice, much reading, writing and training over the years, an obsession for period instruments, and, on one fine spring day, a poem about a "passionate soul" that wrote itself while I was gardening and began to turn itself into **Antonia of Venice**.

You can find Ellyn at ellyn@bell.com

PUBLISHED WORKS

- Short Story: JOEY, in The Danforth Review 2004

- Poem: ELEMENTARY, MY DEAR in Jones Av 2004

- Poem: THE RED PRIEST & THE WHITE ONE in red-priest.com 2003

- Co-Editor with Mary Peirson: I am Keats as you are by Glenn Peirson, ISBN 9780986741104; 2010

Printed in Great Britain
by Amazon